ALL OR NOTHING

ALL OR NOTHING

Elizabeth Adler

Hodder & Stoughton

First published in Great Britain in 1999
by Hodder and Stoughton
A division of Hodder Headline PLC

10 9 8 7 6 5 4 3 2 1

British Library Cataloguing in Publication Data
A CIP catalogue record for this title
is available from the British Library

ISBN 0 340 74836 2

Typeset by Palimpsest Book Production Limited,
Polmont, Stirlingshire

Printed and bound in Great Britain by
Caledonian International Book Manufacturing, Ltd.

Hodder and Stoughton
A division of Hodder Headline PLC
338 Euston Road
London NW1 3BH

ALL OR NOTHING

Chapter One

Al Giraud, Private Investigator, was sitting in the bar of the Ritz Carlton, Laguna Niguel, eating minature pretzels and drinking a Samuel Adams dark ale, contemplating life and the fact that he couldn't have a cigarette while waiting for the always-late woman in his life.

It had been nine months since he had last smoked. Enough time to give birth to a pack of Camels he thought, resignedly crunching down another pretzel. That was Marla for you. How come he'd let this woman have so much influence on his life? He glanced down at his old, faded jeans, short-sleeved plaid shirt, scuffed boots and the ancient snakeskin belt with the rearing mustang silver buckle, bought decades ago in his home town of New Orleans. Then he grinned. At least she hadn't yet managed to change his style.

Al had become a PI the hard way. The easier way would have been to become a criminal.

He was raised by his mother in one of the poorer parts of town, along with her five other boys. Somehow she managed to keep them out of trouble, though later he wondered how. It would have been easy for him to drift over to the other side into a criminal way of life. 'The *easy* life,' his friends called it temptingly. He'd had a few scrapes with the law, hung in there though and finished high school, got a job immediately to help with the family's finances. Then one of his brothers was killed in a drive-by shooting. Al's sorrow and rage was such he wanted to go right out and kill the guy who'd done it, he wanted revenge so bad it hurt. His mom talked him out of it. 'Two wrongs don't make anything right, son,' she had told him through her tears. 'Just get out there and try to do some good.'

The only way Al could figure out how to do good was either to become a minister or a cop. He was definitely more suited for the cop role. He was street-smart, athletic, ambitious and angry, with knee-jerk responses. He made his way up through the ranks to homicide detective, married, divorced.

The day came when Al had finally had enough of the cop's life; the hours, the harshness, constantly seeing the seedy side with its tragedies and traumas. He took early retirement, packed his meagre possessions in a small dufflebag, kissed his beloved mother goodbye, threw a raucous farewell party for his four remaining brothers and their wives and departed for LA. 'The land of opportunity'.

He had set himself up in a second-floor office on Sunset, with a glass door embossed with his name in gold and the words *Private Investigator* – with *All Work Confidential* in small print underneath. Purple bougainvillea trailed over the balcony, the busy traffic zoomed by on Sunset along with a constant parade of folk: smart businessmen; transients; hookers; record execs; dudes and gorgeous California girls. Enough to keep his mind off work, certainly.

He made contacts in the LAPD; in the District Attorney's Office; in a couple of the legal firms; and work began to trickle his way. Divorces; fraud; embezzlement. Women who wanted to know what their husbands were up to. And men who wanted to know if they were being followed, and who was trying to kill them. Then he hit the big time with the case of a prominent man accused of attempting to murder his wife. Al was able to prove that the timing was impossible and the guy got off. Suddenly, he found himself in demand.

The work was risky, often dangerous, but he was from the streets, he'd mingled with guys like this since he was a kid. Until his brother's murder he had called them his 'friends'. Now, he was definitely on the side of right.

Al worked hard for his clients. Some were guilty, some not: he just did his job and presented the evidence.

He lived alone in a small house in the Hollywood Hills – that is when he wasn't *in situ* at her Wilshire Boulevard apartment with his lady love, Marla Cwitowitz – blonde thirties, stylish, sexy, good-looking, and, although she looked like a movie actress, a professor of law at Pepperdine.

They had met at a grand Hollywood party given to celebrate the not-guilty verdict in the trial of a prominent actor accused of strangling his ex-girlfriend. Al had traced the actor's past as well as the girlfriend's. Just to be sure. Dogged as Sherlock Holmes, he had visited their home towns, gotten the scoop on them, found a stepfather accused of abusing the woman as a child. He had also found evidence that the stepfather was in LA the night of the killing – and witnesses who said that he was insanely jealous.

The defence took over from there and made mincemeat of the prosecution, casting full doubt on the stepfather. There was no way a jury could convict the actor with such testimony.

Al was by way of being the star of this party. For the occasion he wore a jacket along with his frayed jeans and plaid shirt, but he was uncomfortable in the marble halls of Hollywood filmdom.

He was standing by the window looking out at the floodlit fountains and elaborate terraced gardens, nursing his second good whisky and wondering how soon he could leave when a velvety voice from behind him said, 'Hello, Al Giraud.'

He turned and looked at one of the loveliest women he had ever seen.

'I've been waiting to be introduced, but no luck, so I'm introducing myself. Marla Cwitowitz. Professor of Law at Pepperdine, ex DA – and a great admirer of yours.'

She was wearing red. Short, strappy, low-cut and sexy – and if he wasn't mistaken, expensive. Her golden-blond hair tipped her shoulder blades, flipping up gently as she put her head on one side, looking at him with laughing grey-green eyes. And her mouth was amazing, full with a cushiony underlip.

'So? Do I pass muster?'

He realized he was staring. 'Excuse me, you took me by surprise.' He held out his hand and she took it in both of hers.

'As you did me,' she murmured.

They had gotten along famously from that moment – when they weren't fighting that is, and when she wasn't bugging him about becoming his partner. The idea of Marla as a detective was laughable. No one would ever take her seriously. She was too gorgeous – *and* from the other side of the tracks. A wealthy family, top schools, clever. Definitely not from the streets. Except she had been a DA for a couple of years, and you didn't do that in LA without seeing life at its rawest. Still, Al wanted to keep her away from all that.

'What the hell d'ya see in me? An uneducated bum, an ex cop, a two-bit PI? A lovely woman like you?' he had asked her, the first time he made love to her.

Marla sighed, looking thoughtfully at him. Al Giraud's face was all angles and planes; razor-sharp cheekbones, beetling black brows over deep-set, piercing, blue eyes, a pugnacious jaw. He looked like a cartoon detective. Put a fedora on him and a tie – he was Dick Tracy. In the plaid shirt and jeans, he should be propping up a cheap bar. In a suit, he could be running for office.

A chameleon of a man, Marla had thought, interested in the dichotomy. 'Excitement,' she whispered, kissing his ear. 'You're different. At the opposite extreme of what I do. My realm is clinical. Yours is hands-on. I like that contrast and I want to help you.'

'Help me? He was astonished.

'You know, to solve cases. I think I would be quite good at it.'

He'd stared suspiciously at her. 'Marla, you want a job, there are easier ways than sleeping with a guy.'

She smiled, 'Besides,' she whispered, nibbling at his mouth, 'you're such a good fuck . . .'

At that moment, as far as he was concerned, Marla could have had any job she wanted.

Chapter Two

In the Ritz bar at Laguna Niguel, Al looked with the keen eye of an ex-cop at the guy at the table opposite, reading the sports page of the *Los Angeles Times* and sipping a Bloody Mary. He envied him the celery stalk; his stomach was growling already and he was fed up with the pretzels. Why did Marla always have to be late, they had planned an early dinner.

The guy glanced toward the entrance then at his watch, then went back to reading the newspaper. Obviously he too was waiting for someone.

Al bet it was a woman. Who else would be this late? Taking a gulp of the Samuel Adams, he noted the conservative grey business suit, good white shirt, understated blue-silk tie. The shoes were well polished, crisp brown hair neatly combed, face recently-shaven. A nice-looking fella, waiting for whom? He wore a wedding band. But he didn't look like a man waiting for his wife ... he wasn't pissed-off enough. It had to be a girlfriend.

Passing the time, Al laid bets on what she would look like. Tall, dark, sexy? A petite California blonde, body-buffed and casual? A long-legged redhead? An Asian beauty?

He had just settled on the Asian beauty when he spotted Marla heading toward him. Every head in the bar turned as she walked past and he heaved a sigh of pleasure.

Marla too, could be any woman she wanted. 'A mistress

of disguise,' Giraud called her, with that sardonic grin that sometimes made her want to punch him.

From her immigrant parents, Marla had inherited the broad Slavic bones that cast elegant shadows on her cheeks and the heavy blonde hair that grew smoothly back from a widow's peak. Part Grace Kelly, part Madonna, she was a role-player *par excellence*: the prim law professor in a dark suit − skirt not too short, gold necklace, modest-heel pumps. The California girl in lycra and sneakers, working out. The society dame, elegant in a beaded lace gown; the party girl in the briefest Versace. And in the bedroom − she was anyone she chose to be. The only role Marla couldn't play was that of a nondescript person. No matter how she dressed down in sweats and sneakers, hair pulled back, no make-up, there was still something about Marla that turned heads.

'It's the way you walk,' Al told her resignedly. 'Somehow, you can never get that twitch out of your tail. Also, you can't resist flirting.'

It was true and Marla knew it. Flirting was a way of life, her favourite pastime, something she couldn't resist. It lightened her serious day, made her smile.

Al went to buss her cheek, but Marla was having none of it. She clasped her arms round his neck and brought her mouth up to his in a lingering kiss.

'Hi, darling,' she said, still only an inch from his lips. Her eyes were smiling and she had the look of a mischievous cat playing a game.

'You know how I hate a public spectacle.' He removed himself from her arms, waiting politely while she took a seat.

Marla heaved a gusty sigh that sent her bosom in the low-cut silk shirt atremble.

'No one would ever know you're such a glorious madman in bed.' She took a sip of his ale and picked daintily at a pretzel.

'It's not for anyone else to know.' He was laughing with her now.

'Good, I'm glad to hear it. Otherwise I might suspect you of having other women.'

He leaned closer, kissed her ear. 'Marla Cwitowitz, there are no other women. I wouldn't have the time for them, to say nothing of the stamina. Remember, I'm a forty-five-year-old guy ...'

'In your prime, Giraud,' she said firmly, but Al's gaze had travelled over her left shoulder. She swung round to see who he was looking at.

The young woman was tall with long straight blonde hair, a California tan, attractive in a cream silk skirt and jacket and high-heeled gold sandals. She was carrying a portfolio under her arm, and she was shaking hands with the man at the table opposite. She was not wearing a wedding band but a gold snake ring embossed with diamonds and with a large diamond eye coiled round the third finger of her right hand. It looked expensive and Al wondered briefly how she could afford it.

'Giraud, why do you always go for the blondes,' Marla complained. His eyes were still fixed on the couple.

'Just curious, that's all. I was laying bets on who he was waiting for; his wife, or a girlfriend.'

'So? Did you win?'

Al's dark-blue eyes moved back to her and he grinned. 'I hedged my bet.'

'Don't you always?'

He was laughing as he signalled the waiter and ordered a vodka martini for her.

'And bring some more of the pretzels, would you please?' Marla added, taking the last one from the silver dish. 'Did you also guess her profession?' She licked the crumbs off her lips.

'You shouldn't do that in public. It's obscene.'

She grinned at him, delighted. 'And to think I never knew. Anyhow, she's in real estate.'

'How did you deduce that, Miss PI?'

'The portfolio, the handshake – first time they've met, I'll bet. Plus the California estate-agent "look". Part casual, part business – the happy medium. I'll bet she's showing him pictures of houses right this minute.'

The martini came and she took a sip, rolling her magnificent grey-green eyes, shuddering with delight. 'You should bring me here more often, I like it.' She glanced round at the sumptous furnishings, the marble floors, the oriental rugs, the view of the ocean. 'I think I could live here.'

'I couldn't afford it.'

'With me as your partner, soon you'll be able to.'

'The businesswoman.' He snorted with laughter. Marla was still trying to persuade him to let her become a detective.

'Don't knock it 'til you've tried it, Giraud. I'm taking over the business end. Your fees are going up, plus from now on you're asking for a percentage.'

'A percentage of what exactly?'

She grinned and took another sip of the martini. 'Of anything I can get. Stick with me and you too will be driving a Mercedes.'

'Over my dead body.'

'Oh, I sincerely hope not.' She leaned across the table, took his hand in hers. 'I'm crazy about you, Al Giraud,' she whispered. Her eyes were luminous as twin stars as they looked deep into his. 'Take me to dinner. Then take me to bed. We'll talk over our business deal there.' She cocked her head to one side, not taking her eyes off him.

Giraud took a deep breath to steady his racing pulse. 'Finish the martini and let's go.'

On their way out they glanced curiously at the couple at the next table. The blonde was talking animatedly, waving her arms around, while the man studied the sheets with pictures and details of homes for sale spread across the table.

'Hideous ring,' Marla commented. 'But did I guess right?'

She held up her hand and Al gave her five. 'Right on, baby. 'Now, first things first. Let's eat.'

Steve Mallard must have been the only man in the bar who didn't turn to look as Marla made her exit. He was too busy looking at pictures of prospective houses and listening to Laurie Martin's spiel as she extolled the virtues of each one of them.

Steve was depressed. He was thirty-nine-years-old and had worked for a Southern California electronics company for seven years. Now they had relocated him from LA to San Diego. He was staying in a hotel and missing Vickie, his wife, and his two young daughters who were remaining at their home in the suburban San Fernando Valley until school was out – and until he found a suitable house. A task at which he wasn't having much success.

Laurie Martin was his latest hope. He had seen her ad in a local newspaper with a picture of a house that looked a possibility, in the right price range, with a distant view of the sea, and a few miles away from San Diego in the little seaside town of Laguna. He liked it there. He liked the oceanfront walk, the crashing surf on the rocks, the clean beaches, the tree-lined trees and small-town air of refinement. It would be a good place for his girls. He ran his hands through his brownish hair wearily. If he could only find somewhere, that is. Money was an important consideration and Laguna had expensive real estate.

Laurie Martin studied her weary client from behind her rose-tinted sunglasses. He was attractive, nice brown eyes, not too tall, and thin. She couldn't stand men with paunches and love-handles. She pushed a drift of pale blonde hair from her eyes and smiled at him, the kind of smile that lit up her triangular little cat face.

Transforming her, Steve thought, suddenly realising he was looking at a pretty woman. 'I'm sorry,' he said repentently, 'I'm so busy worrying about houses, I forgot to ask if you would like a drink.'

She pushed the rose-coloured glasses up into her hair, fluffing out her blonde spiky fringe with her French-manicured fingertips. 'Well, it has been a long – and tiresome – day.' She glanced at her watch, 'If you're sure you have time . . . ?'

'Oh, I'm sure. As I told you, I'm here all alone.'

'Well then, a martini would be nice.' As he signalled the waiter, Laurie thought that this would be an easy sale. A piece of cake, and she might just have the right house . . . the only trouble was the price . . .

Chapter Three

A week later, Marla was driving back from a brief sojourn at Rancho La Puerta, a spa in Tecate, Mexico, that she visited every now and again 'to regain her inner balance', she told Al.

Actually, what she did was hike to the top of Mount Kuchumaa in the early morning before the Baja heat struck its blow. There she would sit, in the lotus position, eyes open to the beauty of the sunlit chaparral, her head cleared of all extraneous thoughts, breathing deeply of the clean air and the peace. After an hour, she would hike back down again, jog through the grounds and dive into one of the swimming pools.

That was it. Her activities for the day were over. Not for her the aerobics dance class, aquacise, circuit training, super cross training or water volleyball. A salad of greens with herbs picked fresh from the garden for lunch. A nap. A laze in a hammock with a book, perhaps late-afternoon yoga. Then – her special treat – a full body massage that left her feeling limp as a sleepy kitten, ready only for supper and bed – perchance to dream of Al Giraud.

Anyhow, after three days she was up and rarin' to go. Ready to take on Al and whatever he might offer.

She grinned as she swung the big silver Mercedes S500 through the border crossing near Tijuana. They were to meet at the Hotel La Valencia, in La Jolla, where they would spend the night. She couldn't wait to see him.

This time, though, it was Al who was late. Marla checked

in, unpacked, took a shower and paced out onto the balcony. She was just wondering where the hell he could be when the phone rang.

'Where are you, you louse?' she asked, without bothering to greet him.

'It's like this, Marla. I'm here at the track at Del Mar with some of the guys. Had a couple of winners, you know how it is, we just had to catch the last race . . .'

'Hmmm.' Her foot in its red suede slingback tapped a staccato rhythm of annoyance. 'So you stood me up for a horse, Giraud.'

'Never. Anyhow, it was a mare, a grey and she came in at ten to one.'

'Good thing she did because this is gonna cost you.'

'Sweetheart, name your price. I'll be there in half an hour.'

'I'll be out on the terrace, having a drink.'

Damn it, *she* had driven all the way from Tecate and gotten there on time. But Al was a man who loved the ponies. She sighed, she guessed you took the good along with the bad. *But an hour and a half late?* She'd kill him when she got her hands on him.

She was sitting on the terrace sipping a vodka martini when she saw the guy and the blonde real estate agent again. They were sitting a couple of tables away, just like before, only this time it was obvious they knew each other better.

Marla sipped the icy cold martini, taking them in over the top of the glass. The blonde had no taste but her outfit was expensive, a different league from her office suit of last time. Bright blue lace, skirt too short and showing a lot of – quite good – leg. A little too tight, a touch too obvious. But the guy seemed to like it all right, he hadn't taken his eyes off her. And she'd bet they weren't talking business. No pictures of houses on the table this time, just a couple of flutes of champagne. She wondered whether he had bought a house from her and this was the celebration. If so, he didn't look a happy camper. Probably thinking about the size of his new mortgage.

She smiled as she saw Al striding toward her. 'Loping' was a better description. He had this shambling cowboy kind-of walk, sexy as hell. It was the first thing she had noticed about him at that party. That and his lean, hard body and his total indifference to the Hollywood glitz scene going on around him. 'Ah,' she had thought, 'a man of integrity. Here in Babylon. How intriguing.' She went weak at the knees now, just looking at him.

Marla was wearing white to set off her newly-acquired Tecate tan: an ankle-length silk jersey skirt slit to the thigh, and a tiny white chiffon top embroidered with pale green butterflies. It clung to her narrow waist and nestled on her round breasts, delicate as a breeze. Al thought she looked sensational and he regretted being late. Except he would enjoy getting her going . . . he liked to see her eyes flash when she was angry. Like now.

'Bastard,' she said by way of greeting.

He lifted a shoulder, grinning at her. 'Got it in one, sweetheart.' Though my mother wouldn't thank you for that description.'

She raised her face to be kissed. 'I've not met your mother.'

'A pleasure yet to come.'

She glanced curiously at him. 'Are you joking? Or did you really mean that.'

'I meant it. My mom is one of a kind. Brought up six boys singlehanded, and somehow instilled moral values into us all – though I admit, with me it was chancy.'

'A guy who loves his mom.' She squeezed his hand affectionately. 'No wonder I love you.'

'Love? I thought it was just sex between us?' She lifted his hand to her mouth and bit hard. He laughed. 'Owch. OK, OK, I didn't mean it.'

'So tell me, Mr Private Eye, is it sex or just plain business between our real estate tycoon and the poor sap who looks as though he's just realising he's paid too much for a house?'

Al glanced at the couple at the nearby table. 'Are they following us?' he asked, surprised.

'They're probably wondering the same thing about us. Perhaps we should say hello. I feel as though I already know them.'

Al stared thoughtfully at them. They were oblivious to anyone else, lost in their own conversation. Or rather *her* conversation. The woman was animated as all get out, smiling, arms waving, crossing and recrossing her excellent legs. 'Nah. She's putting on quite a show for him. Doesn't need us.'

'Think he's interested?'

'I wouldn't bet on it. The guy looks as though he's just swallowed a dose of castor oil instead of a mouthful of champagne.'

'Castor oil?' She looked mystified and he laughed.

'One of Mom's old-fashioned remedies for all that ails you. She used it frequently on us when we were kids.'

'I don't even want to think about it,' Marla shuddered. 'More importantly, where are you taking me for dinner? And before you answer, remember, I told you that tonight would cost you.'

Al took a wad of winner's greenbacks from his pocket, flicking through them with his thumb. 'Only the best for my girl tonight.'

'The best is a full partnership.'

'Are you kidding?' He was laughing as they wandered back down the terrace, leaving the real estate couple to mull over the too-expensive house they felt sure he had just bought.

They were both wrong. Steve Mallard had not bought a house. Laurie had shown him a dozen but none of them had worked out. He'd had a business meeting that afternoon that had run late and had decided the drive home to LA through the weekend traffic just wasn't worth it. On the spur of the moment he'd called Laurie and asked her to have dinner with him. It wasn't the first time they had dined together. He always looked at houses in the evenings after work and somehow falling into a café for a meal was better with company that without. Besides, she was an attractive woman.

He had shown her photos of his children and Laurie had said how pretty they were. And she had showed him a picture of her dog – a little black mutt wearing a red bandanna, one ear up, one ear drooping.

'His name is Clyde.' She smiled fondly at the picture. 'And he's a true rascal. I just love him to pieces.'

'What a nice couple we make. We both love kids and dogs.'

She was quick to laugh with him. She hadn't yet nailed this sale but she would. And maybe the guy as well. Her blue eyes smiled into his as she lifted the champagne flute. 'To the wonderful house I just know I'm going to find for you.' She clinked her glass to his. 'And to more evenings like this.' She smiled slyly at his surprise. 'I just meant it's so nice to have a rapport with a client. It's rare, I can assure you. And I can also tell you I don't have dinner with everyone I show a house to.'

He laughed too. 'Then thanks, Laurie, for saving me from yet another lonesome evening.'

'It's my pleasure.'

She put her elbows on the table, leaning close to him. Steve couldn't help noticing the curve of her breasts where the blue lace fell so seductively away. He thought Laurie Martin was an intriguing combination: sometimes so demure and professional, and sometimes so downright sexy it gave him a jolt. Her eyes burned with a kind of restless energy when she looked at him.

'Better luck next time,' he said hopefully.

'Trust me, Steve. I won't let you down.'

She stared meaningfully at him and Steve felt himself grow hot. He thought of his wife, probably dining with the kids at Burger King right this minute. Somehow, Vickie seemed a long way away.

Chapter Four

Two weeks later, Marla was reclining in the bathtub, up to her little pointed ears in Robert Isabell's Calla bubbles with a matching fragrance candle permeating the steam for good measure. Her blonde hair was in huge pink velcro rollers and a green pore-cleansing mask tightened her face in a vice-like grip. She surely hoped it was firming everything up because otherwise it wasn't worth the agony.

It was her night to 'wash her hair'. Meaning the one night each week she insisted on keeping for herself to catch up on all the little maintenance tasks a woman needed if she were to keep in tip-top shape. It was also a night when she liked to slop around in her white terry robe and the old bunny slippers that she'd had since she was fourteen and with which she would never part. They kind of went with the hair rollers and the eyebrow tweezing and reminded her of slumber parties and girlish gossip. Which was the other thing she did, on the phone while sipping a healthy glass of milk instead of a vodka martini, and munching on Snackwells in place of the childhood Oreos.

It made for a very satisfying evening and also served to increase Al Giraud's eagerness to see her. He had already called several times to say: a) that he was missing her; b) to tell her he was having a drink with a client at the Chateau Marmont; c) to say he was thinking of dining at Mr Chow's and was she sure she couldn't join him, and d) to say he had changed his mind. He hadn't fancied Chow's alone and was at La Scala on Cañon

Drive in Beverly Hills — a place her parents used to frequent years ago — if she changed her mind and wanted to join him.

Unlike Al, who always had music blasting in his car or at home, Marla was a TV news addict. She had a TV set in every room, including the bathroom, because she hated to miss anything. Not that anything much happened, just the usual shootings, earthquakes, floods, fires, rockslides and freeway mayhem, with the occasional celebrity wedding, movie premiere or gossip to leaven the dross. Now, her eyes fixed on the photograph of a woman that flashed on the screen.

'Missing from her home in Laguna Beach,' the newscaster said, 'real estate agent, Laurie Martin has not been seen since last Friday. When she failed to show up for work and could not be contacted at her home, her boss called the police. Her car, a metallic gold Lexus 400 is also missing. Police are asking if you have seen this woman, or her Lexus, licence plate LAURIE M, to contact them at the following number.

'The last time Laurie Martin was seen was when she left the office on Friday afternoon to keep an appointment to show a house. Apparently when the police went to check, the door to the house was open. Miss Martin was the only person with the keys so she had obviously arrived there. The police are now questioning the client to whom she was supposed to show that house.'

Bubbles floated onto the taupe marble floor as Marla shot bolt upright. She leapt from of the tub, flung a towel round her still bubbling body and grabbed the phone.

Al was munching his way through a veal *piccata* with a side of spaghetti bolognese — good old-fashioned Italian food that hit the spot when a guy was dining alone — when his cellphone rang. Annoyed eyes glared his way as he answered guiltily. 'Yeah, Al Giraud.'

'Al Giraud.' Marla's voice was muffled, she had forgotten the green facemask and her mouth was practically cemented together. 'Listen, it's her. On the TV ... she's disappeared. It must be him ...'

Al could tell she was excited, but she certainly wasn't making any sense. 'Calm down, Marla and talk rationally.

What's wrong with you anyway, you sound as though you've got lockjaw?'

'And I darn well nearly have. Listen, bum, it's on the TV. The real estate woman from the Ritz and La Jolla, remember? Yeah, well, she's disappeared. The police are looking for her, and they are questioning the man she had her last appointment with before she disappeared. What do you bet it's him?'

Al smacked a hand to his head, groaning. Marla, the detective was on the case again. 'Marla, I'm in the middle of dinner. What're you talking about?' Exasperated, he wound spaghetti round his fork, the phone glued to his ear.

'Didn't I just *tell* you? It's the real estate woman we saw in Laguna. *She's disappeared.*'

He swallowed the spaghetti. 'Skipped off with the client, you mean.' Marla's exasperated sigh buzzed in his ear.

'And you call yourself a private eye. No, you dope. *She* is missing, so is her car. Police are interviewing the last client. She was supposed to show him the house.'

'Interesting.' He cut the veal *piccata* carefully, took a bite. 'What d'you want me to do, Marla?'

'Oh.' She had thought he would know. He was the PI. 'Well – shouldn't we go to the police, or something. Tell them what we know . . . ?'

'And what exactly do we know, sweetheart?'

She thought about it, nonplussed. 'Just that we saw them together, their first meeting. That we saw them again a couple of weeks later – and they were definitely not looking at pictures of houses. It was a date.'

'The poor sap probably has nothing at all to do with it. You want me to get him into trouble with the cops?'

'Al! The woman is missing. She's been abducted, possibly murdered,' her voice quivered a little on the word. 'I think we have to say something.'

He guessed maybe she was right. 'Tell you what, I know a detective down in Laguna. I'll give him a call, find out exactly what the scene is, decide what to do.'

'Al?'

'Yeah? He gulped ice cold Peroni, his favourite Italian beer.

'You'll call me right back, won't you? Within the next ten minutes.'

He sighed. Marla was a determined woman. 'I'll do that, sweetheart.'

'Al.'

'Yeah?'

'Why is it I don't trust you when you call me sweetheart?'

He grinned. 'Probably something to do with instinct, honey. You like "honey" better?' He was laughing as she rang off and he dialled the number of Detective Lionel Bulworth of the San Diego Police Department.

Detective Bulworth was a large man, six eight and built, appropriately, like a bull. He wore size 17 shoes, a size 50 shirt and his hair combed over the bald part. He had twenty years experience on the job, was bright and affable – except when he confronted the guilty. Then he was the meanest man on the planet.

He took Al's call. 'How're y'doing, Al?' His huge feet were planted on his desk, and he leaned back in his chair, swaying gently, a balancing trick he had perfected over the years.

'Good, Lionel. How's the wife and kids?' Al had joined the Bulworth's backyard barbecues several weekends and was considered a friend of the family.

'Pretty good. Zack's flunking his grades, Jill's into nose rings, and Tod's – well Tod's too young – yet. Apart from that, all is well. And you? Still with the sassy Marla?'

'Yup, still with her. I don't think she's letting me off the hook that fast, y'know what I mean. Trouble is, I'm not sure if it's my body she's after, or my job.'

Al grimaced painfully, as Bulworth's big laugh bellowed down the line. 'Still intent on becoming a detective, huh?'

'She's hanging in there. And listen, this is her latest thing. She just saw a report on the local news about the missing Laguna woman. Laurie Martin. The thing is, we kind-of know her . . .

not exactly *know*, but we've seen her around a couple of times. And both times with the same guy.'

Bulworth knew about Laurie Martin. Everyone did. Not too many women went missing in high-priced, refined Laguna. It wasn't exactly the playground of the young and dangerous. Retired and staid was more like it.

He made a few notes as Al explained their encounters with the estate agent and her client. 'What's the guy look like?'

'Medium height, five tenish, light brown hair, brown eyes, probably late thirties. Thin build. Kind of tired-looking, I thought. Or maybe "weary" is a better word.'

'Giraud, you've just described our prime suspect.'

'Well I'll be darned, then Marla was right. Maybe I should give her that job after all.'

'Maybe you should. The client, Steve Mallard called us. His story is that Laurie Martin was looking for a house for him. She called Friday afternoon, said she had found the perfect house. She told him it was urgent, said someone else was interested and they would have to move fast. He arranged to meet her there, at five-thirty after work.

'When he got there she wasn't around. No sign of her car, a metallic gold Lexus. He waited half an hour then he tried the door. Found it was open. He took a look around, liked the house and tried to call her on his carphone. All he got was her answer machine. He called her pager, but again no luck. And that, my friend, is Steve Mallard's story.'

'And foul play is suspected.'

'You got it, buddy. And Steve Mallard is our prime suspect.'

Chapter Five

Vickie Mallard was a petite five two in her platform sneakers. 'A little bit of a thing,' her husband Steve called her affectionately. Her dark hair was cut short with spiky bangs, and her dedication to the local gym showed in her well-muscled arms and trim body. She was wearing grey sweats and wire-rimmed glasses, dishing out Pollo Loco chicken and mashed potatoes for supper. The girls were upstairs in their rooms, finishing their homework she hoped, and she had rented Disney's *Mulan* from Blockbuster as a treat after supper. The TV was blasting the local news.

'Laurie Martin, the Laguna real estate agent is still missing. It's been five days since she was last seen in her office, and police helicopters have been searching nearby canyons. Sniffer dogs have tried but failed to catch any scent. Miss Martin's metallic gold Lexus, licence plate LAURIE M is also missing, but police tell us there is no sign of a forced entry or a robbery at her apartment, which we show you here. We understand a man, a client of Miss Martin's is being questioned about her disappearance. Apparently, Steve Mallard, an electronics company executive, had an apointment with her to view a house the evening she disappeared.'

The foil tray of mashed potatoes splattered all over the immaculate white tiled kitchen floor. Normally a neatness freak, Vickie didn't even notice the mess.

'*Steve?*' she said out loud. 'Are they talking about *my* Steve?'

'*Mom*, you're talking to yourself. And there's mashed potato all over the floor.'

Her ten-year-old daughter, Taylor, stared accusingly at her.

'It's your father, on the TV,' Vickie said, still stunned.

'Oh, cool. Dad's on TV.' Taylor swung onto a stool, and gazed eagerly at the set on the kitchen counter.

'No, he's not on the TV. They were just talking about him. Could it be *our* Steve Mallard. An electronics executive, they said . . . they were asking him about some missing woman.'

'Asking Dad about a missing woman? Oh, cool.' Taylor repeated, and Vickie wished impatiently she would at least learn another adjective.

The phone rang and Taylor grabbed it. 'Hi,' she said brightly. 'Oh, hi, Dad. Mom said you were just on TV. Yeah, OK, I'll put her on. Cool, Dad . . .'

Vickie grabbed the phone. 'Steve, what's this all about?' Her face was anxious.

She took off the glasses and rubbed her eyes, suddenly frightened as Steve told her the tale.

'But of course you never saw her that evening?' Her voice rose at the end.

'Vickie, was that a *question?* Of *course* I didn't see her. That's exactly what I told the cops. And it's the truth.'

'Of course you told the truth,' she said hastily. 'I just wondered. I mean, what could have happened to her? Where has she gone?'

'How the hell should I know? But what I do know, Vickie, is I need a lawyer.'

He said goodbye and that he would call back later when he'd spoken with the family's attorney, and that she wasn't to worry and not to tell the kids. Vickie put down the phone. Automatically, she reached for paper towels, got down on her knees and began scooping up the mashed potatoes. A niggling little tremor of doubt churned her stomach. The Pollo Loco chicken suddenly didn't look so good.

She fed the girls the chicken, replaced the potatoes with toasted bagels, poured herelf a glass of chardonnay and sat by the phone in the kitchen, watching every newscast and waiting for Steve to call back.

Chapter Six

The Monza red 1970 Corvette roadster crawled uphill in the double line of nose-to-tail traffic on La Cienega Boulevard, growling impatiently, like its owner at the red stoplight. It edged into the right lane cutting out a pushy BMW, swung a sharp right and gunned down Sunset outpacing lesser vehicles, beat its way into the left lane then up Queens Road into the Hollywood Hills.

Al grinned as he negotiated the curving road. Smooth as fuckin' silk, he congratulated himself – or rather the car. He had found the Corvette – a wreck and obviously rolled over – in a scrap dealer's yard ten years ago and was instantly in love. He'd bought it for only five hundred, cash, because most of its workable parts had already been stripped and had had it towed home where he had looked after it as carefully as an invalid, nursing it back to glossy health. Over the years, it had probably cost him ten times its original 1970 selling price of almost five thousand dollars, but this was his baby, his Frankenstein, lovingly recreated in its makers' original image until not a scar remained unsmoothed, not a toggle switch out of place, not a spoke unchromed.

The 'Vette had a souped-up engine that Giraud had rebuilt himself, spending hours in his oil-stained garage, fiddling with it, tuning it, polishing it, patting it – loving it. Its 4-speed heavy-duty manual transmission was still the best; the tilt telescopic steering column was one of the first of its kind, and it – and the redesigned seats – allowed room for his six-foot-four-inch frame. Add the beautiful saddle-leather upholstery – all redone to the original specs and the refurbished walnut trim and this was one special automobile.

Al's childhood dream, fostered at the movies, had been to own a Corvette. Red, naturally. And hot. And now nothing – not Marla's expensive silver Mercedes S500, not a new Porsche Carerra, not even, he bet himself, a Ferrari or Lamborghini should he ever be in a position to afford one, which was debatable – would ever wean him from his first love.

'Loyal to a fault, that's me,' he'd told Marla, grinning when she had complained about the low bucket seats and the roar of the exhaust. 'Once I'm in love, that's it. I'm in love for ever.'

She had thrown him one of those wanna-bet looks, but there had been a trace of hope in her beautiful long-lashed grey-green eyes. Maybe he really meant it. And not just about cars.

Al's home was of an even earlier Hollywood vintage than the car: a 1930s Spanish stucco cottage with tall arched windows, hardwood floors, beamed ceilings and fancy iron grillwork over the doors and windows which, considering its proximity to the Sunset Strip, came in useful as an added safety feature in these more risky times. A terracotta-tiled courtyard fronted the house and also led into the separate garage at the left. A row of tall needle-like cedars ranged down the right side – a bone of contention between Al and his neighbours who wanted them topped, while Al wanted to keep them and maintain his privacy. And a pretty patio with an old Spanish-tiled fountain was out back.

Al's finger was already on the remote button as he swung into the side street off Queens and slid into the courtyard. The garage door opened smoothly. He sat for a moment in the cool darkness listening to the hum of the engine, almost as precious and real to him as the beat of his own heart. He patted the saddle-leather seat lovingly, brushing off a speck of dust from the console. He almost hated to get out of the car.

It was pleasant he thought, to achieve at least one of your ambitions in life. That Monza red Corvette had been so far out of reach for the poor New Orleans kid from the wrong side of the tracks, dreaming in the darkness of the movie house all those years ago. Now it was his and he enjoyed every moment of it.

His cellphone rang and he picked it up. 'Yeah?'

'I'll bet you fifty bucks you're sitting in that darn Corvette congratulating yourself on how far you've come since you were just a poor kid dreaming at the movies.'

He sighed. 'Marla, what is it about you and my Corvette? You act like I'm with another woman.'

'And that's just the way you act with that car, like it's a woman.'

'Aw come on, Marla, give a guy a break can't you ...'

'I know, I know, it's your pride and joy. I know where I stand in your affections, Giraud. A very definite second.'

Al's deep laugh boomed down the line. 'Don't they say everybody seeks their own level in life?'

'And I've found mine you mean?'

Marla's sigh was gusty and he imagined her, the phone propped between her shoulder and her ear, lying on a chaise in a negligee painting her nails Corvette red – though in fact it was more likely to be mulberry or skyblue sparkle depending on her mood of the day.

'Actually, I'm at work,' Marla said briskly, smoothing a wrinkle out of her grey flannel skirt and buttoning the jacket discreetly over the white T-shirt she wore underneath. Her hair was pulled severely back in a tortoiseshell clip and she wore little round tortoiseshell Armani glasses – not because she needed them but because today she was playing the role of the Intellectual Lady Professor. 'I have a lecture in two minutes ... So, what did Bulworth say?'

Al grinned. So much for the negligee and painting her nails – Marla was into her private eye role. 'Just as we thought. There's no doubt Laurie Martin was abducted – and very likely killed. And Steve Mallard was probably the last man to see her – though he claims she never showed. *And* he's Prime Suspect Number One.'

'He's either Prime Suspect *or* Number One Suspect, Giraud.'

Marla was a stickler for semantics when she was practising law.

'Yeah, well this guy is both. He's hot – too hot to touch yet. There's no body, no evidence and therefore no arrest. He's still at his job in San Diego. Meanwhile his wife and kids are at the family home in Encino.'

Marla frowned, thinking about it. 'I didn't get bad vibes from him, though, I mean the couple of times we saw him, he looked like a regular guy . . .'

'Don't they all?' Al was wise to the ways of abusers and wife-beaters, child-support dodgers and conmen. And killers. 'Meanwhile, it sure looks as though he was cheating on his wife – and with Laurie.'

'Mmm, absence doesn't appear to make the heart grow fonder – at least in this case,' Marla admitted. 'But surely he should have the benefit of the doubt.'

Al shook his head. That was Marla the attorney talking. 'He's getting that benefit right now. Until they find a body, that is.'

'Or until they find Laurie Martin alive and well and just taking a break in some Mexican resort.'

Al gave up. 'Have it your way, honey.'

'Meanwhile, what are we gonna do about that poor woman?'

'Which woman, hon?' Al glanced at his watch. He had an apointment with a client in ten minutes back at his office on Sunset.

'Vickie Mallard. The wife.'

'Beats me . . . listen, I've got to go. There's a client waiting. I'll talk to you later, Marla, OK?'

'OK.' Marla checked her own watch. Jeez, she was late too – and those darn kids would never let her forget it. She hurried down the shiny corridor to her class, unaware of the turned heads and admiring grins. Not even tailored grey flannel and glasses could diminish Marla's sex appeal.

Nevertheless, her mind was not truly on her class. The unknown Vickie Mallard lingered at the back of her mind like a bump on a log – she just couldn't stop wondering about her and her children. Was Steve Mallard a philanderer? Maybe. Was he a murderer? Perhaps. But Marla didn't think so.

As soon as class was dismissed, she was on the phone to the San Diego Police Department and Detective Bulworth. After a few minutes of schmoozing, she had the number of Steve Mallard's attorney and she lost no time in getting him on the phone.

'Mr Zuckerman is on a call, ma'am, Can he call you back?' The secretary gave her the high-pitched, sing-song reply she must give to everyone except important clients Marla thought, irritated.

'No, he can't call me back,' she snapped, 'and the name is Cwitowitz. *Ms* Marla Cwitowitz. Attorney. Tell Zuckerman I'm calling about Steve Mallard.'

There was stunned silence for a couple of seconds then a series of clicks and then Joe Zuckerman got on the line.

'Ms Cwitowitz? You want to talk to me about Steve Mallard?'

'Yeah, it's about your client. The fact is, Mr Zuckerman, I saw him. A couple of times. With Laurie Martin.' She heard Zuckerman's indrawn breath, pictured him as an older guy, grey-haired, an estate lawyer not a criminal one. Probably a friend of the family who had dealt with their affairs for years.

'The fact is Mr Zuckerman, that not only am I an attorney but I'm also a private detective.' She crossed her fingers, rolling her eyes heavenwards as she lied. After all, it was almost true. Or it would be before the day was out. 'My partner, Al Giraud and I happened to be in the bar at the Ritz Carlton in Laguna Niguel at what appeared to be your client's first meeting with Laurie Martin . . .'

She described the meeting, and their later sighting of the couple drinking champagne at the Hotel La Valencia in La Jolla.

'I just wanted to tell you, as Mr Mallard's attorney, that despite the champagne it seemed to me a business relationship. I mean, there was no touching, no holding hands, no eyes linked across the table . . .'

'I get it,' Zuckerman said patiently. 'But how does this help my client, Ms Cwitowitz?'

'It might not help him much but it might very well help his wife,' Marla said abruptly. 'It was her I was thinking about.'

She left her home phone number and Al's office number in case Zuckerman needed to get in touch and said goodbye, wondering doubtfully whether she had done the right thing and if Vickie Mallard would give a damn at this point who had seen her husband with Laurie Martin. Probably half the world had claimed to have seen them together by now.

Shrugging, she packed up her black leather Prada tote and drove slowly home. Vickie Mallard and her daughters were still very much on her mind.

She was in Brentwood, driving in the usual mass of traffic past the infamous Bundy Drive, scene of the OJ murders, when it occured to her. What if she were wrong? What if Steve Mallard was guilty after all?

Chapter Seven

One week later there was still no trace of Laurie Martin and the case was driving Detective Lionel Bulworth crazy.

'Gosh darn it,' he said – or words to that effect – pacing the white carpet in Laurie Martin's condo for the hundredth time and leaving a flattened trail of size 17 footprints in the thick pile. 'The evidence against Steve Mallard is piling up. We have everything except the body.'

His assistant, detective Pamela Power – known affectionately as Pammie to her friends, and as 'Pow!' complete with the exclamation mark, to her co-workers at the San Diego PD because of her powerhouse pushy ways, frowned.

'You mean another abuser is gonna get away with it?' Her lip curled scornfuly. 'Not if I have anything to do with it. *Sir*,' she added, as a token to the fact that Bulworth was her senior. She shoved her red hair firmly under her cap, squaring her broad shoulders. 'The fucker's guilty as hell.'

Bulworth eyed her speculatively. Sometimes Pammie's feminist dictates got in the way of her clear thinking. 'You've been reading too many mystery novels, Powers,' he said curtly. 'And there is the small matter of a body?'

'We'll find that, you can bet on it. He'll make a mistake, lead us to it. That guy's as nervous as a cornered rattler. Trust me ... Sir.'

Bulworth sighed. His team had gone through Laurie's apartment with a fine-toothed comb, every hair, every fibre, every fingerprint. Nothing. Except what belonged to Laurie Martin herself. Presumably the woman never entertained at home. Certainly not Steve Mallard, anyways. But Bulworth had wanted to check himself, just one more time. Frustration did that to you. He just couldn't believe they hadn't come up with anything. That there wasn't something there, perhaps so blatantly obvious that the searching eye skimmed over it. But no such luck.

Laurie Martin lived a quiet life. She went to work; apparently did a good job; attended a local church on Sundays.

But Bulworth already had a sizable dossier on Laurie and Steve Mallard. Witnesses had come forward claiming to have seen them together having drinks; and dining in restaurants, or riding in her Lexus. There were messages from Steve on Laurie's home answering machine, which was the old-fashioned tape kind and which she never seemed to wipe off. In fact Laurie seemed to have no private life – the only messages were those from Steve Mallard. Innocuous messages like: '*I'll see you tomorrow at six.*' And, '*I'm getting impatient, please get back to me.*' And, '*I'll be there at seven, better let me take you out this time.*'

But they were mesages that could be interpreted two different ways. To Bulworth, they sounded threatening. There was a pretty good circumstantial case already against Steve. Of his pursuit of Laurie – and perhaps her rejection of him. Like his assistant, Bulworth believed Steve Mallard had killed Laurie Martin in a jealous rage.

But there was nothing he could do about it until they came up with a body.

Chapter Eight

One hundred and thirty miles away, in LA's San Fernando Valley, Steve Mallard was driving as slowly as he possibly could in the edgy traffic towards his Encino home. He was not eager to face his wife, Vicky. He did not have good news.

He had just come from another tense session at the San Diego PD. His jaw clenched remembering Detective Bulworth's implacable face and the gimlet-eyed stare of Deputy Powers. That woman looked as though she could pick him up with one hand and make mincemeat of him — and what's more she gave him the impression that was exactly what she would like to do.

Steve had seen enough movies, read enough Tough-Cop novels though to know what to expect. And he knew that he had to stick to his story. Not to waver from it one iota. Because give those bastards an inch and they would make a mile out of it in a minute. God, and he used to think the police were on his side. No more, though. No. Not any more.

The rented black Ford Taurus coughed in low gear as he crawled reluctantly home. He did not want to see his wife. He didn't want to face her with what he had to tell her. But he had no choice.

He reran the interrogation for the umpteenth time. He had admitted he was at the house when Laurie was supposed to be there. He had told them he had waited for her outside. The front door was unlocked, they said. He told them he knew that. He had even gone in, taken a look around while he was waiting for Laurie – he liked the house, he was hoping he could afford it.

Laurie had to have been there, they persisted. How else could the door have been unlocked. 'Perhaps somebody else had shown the house first,' he had said after thinking carefully about it. He had kept his wits about him, knew it was important to think carefully . . .

They had given him that fish-eyed look. 'But Laurie was the only one with the keys. And no one saw you after you left work that afternoon . . . You were at the house – Where did you go after that . . . ?'

'Back to my hotel room,' he had said. Which was the truth. 'I spent the night alone in my hotel room.'

'What proof do you have of that? What time did you get there? Who saw you . . . ?'

Again and again they had asked him. And again and again he had told them.

There is no proof that's what you did, they had insisted and he had felt himself wearing down, nerves grating, patience wearing thin.

They had let him go finally, of course. They had to. They had no direct evidence, nothing linking him definitively to the disappearance of Laurie Martin. They still had not found her body.

But then had come the bombshell. And now he had to tell Vickie about it.

The pretty suburban development where he lived still had a look of newness about it. Neat front gardens, basketball hoops over garage doors, rollerblades in the driveway. He wished he had never left it.

He parked the rental car in the driveway and unlocked the front door.

Vickie was sitting on the denim-blue sectional in the family room. The TV was on and she was, as usual these days, watching the news. She jolted upright when she heard the front door open, clutching a hand anxiously to her pounding heart.

'Who is it?'

'It's only me.' Steve stood in the entrance to the family room and her heart gave another little jolt. He looked terrible. Shadowed eyes; unshaven; hair wild and windblown as though he'd driven all the way from San Diego on the freeway with the windows wide open. He looked so different from the man she had known for eighteen years, she was shocked. No, though, that wasn't true. She suddenly flashed back to the way he had looked when she'd first met him: wild, crazy, a live wire ready to ignite . . .

'What's happened? Why are you home?' He was supposed to be working . . .

He put down his briefcase, wearily peeled off his jacket. 'Where are the girls?'

'Over at Shauna Lyons' house, playing with her kids. Out of the way,' she added grimly, 'this is the first time the news hounds have left us alone. They'll be sorry to have missed you. All they've got so far is me in the Surburban heading for the supermarket or taking the kids to school.'

'Vickie.' He stood, arms dangling helplessly at his side. A wreck of a man, a man living a nightmare. 'The company suspended me pending the outcome of the investigation.'

Her sharp indrawn breath cut between them.

'They said it would be better for me if I took a leave of absence – until the whole thing blew over . . . They took back the car, my office, everything . . .'

Vickie's knees buckled. She slumped onto the sofa, her head in her hands. Her whole life was collapsing. Suddenly people were avoiding her, people she had called friends. And those that were loyal were advising her to watch out, to take care of herself and her girls . . . to leave him . . .

'I didn't kill her, Vickie.' Steve's voice was cold, lifeless, as though all emotion had been sucked out of him leaving only a vacuum, a space where feelings used to be. He stepped close to her, lifted her chin, forcing her to look at him. His dark-shadowed eyes burned into hers. 'Do you believe me?'

'Yes ...' Vickie replied, but her voice faltered.

'Don't worry, I wouldn't blame you if you didn't,' Steve said bitterly. 'After all, no one else does, why should you?'

He let her go, walked across the room, stared out at the turquoise swimming pool glittering in the sunlight, at the roses he had planted when they first moved in, at the striped beach towels flung carelessly across the white plastic loungers by his young daughters. Signs of a normal life. 'All I can tell you is that I did not kill Laurie Martin. I didn't even see her that night. I hardly knew her. The times we met were all business. She was a nice woman, pleasant, a hard worker. She wanted to find us that perfect home ...'

Vickie stared at her husband. She wanted so badly to believe him. She *did* believe him. He was the man she had loved since college, the father of her children. She knew him better than anyone else in the world. But that same old question jangled at the back of her mind.

If Steve didn't do it, then who did?

Chapter Nine

Steve acted like the family man that evening. Hair brushed neatly back and wearing shorts and a T-shirt, he barbecued burgers and hot dogs for his kids. They all sat at the table on the patio overlooking the pool, making conversation.

'You look tired, Dad,' his ten-year-old daughter, Taylor, commented, chewing half-heartedly on her cheeseburger – normally her favourite food.

He pushed the salad bowl towards her. 'Gotta eat your greens too,' he said scooping some on her plate. 'What about you, Mellie?' His younger daughter, aged six and as petite and small-boned as her mother but with her father's brown eyes, looked doubtfully at him over the top of the hot dog.

'No thank you,' she said politely. 'But Taylor's right, Daddy, you do look kind of funny.'

Vickie poured herself another glass of chardonnay. She did not look at her husband, nor at her girls.

'It's about that missing woman isn't it?' Taylor went on. 'Everybody's talking about you, Dad. It's on TV all the time.'

'I know, I know it is.' His hand shook as he helped himself to salad he did not want.

'At first I thought it was kinda cool – you know, my dad on TV. But now ...' Tears brimmed in Taylor's eyes and she put down the burger, suddenly choked up.

'I'm sorry, Taylor. I'm really sorry about all this.' Steve's hands clenched into tight fists as he faced his little girl across the table. My God, oh my God, what have I done, he thought ... how could this have happened to me ... to us ...

'It's OK, Daddy.' Mellie slid from her chair and hurried to his side. Putting her skinny arms round him she hugged him as tightly as she could. 'I don't care what anybody says, we love you, Daddy.'

'And I love you too, baby.' He stroked her hair as Vickie's eyes met his across the table.

'I can't take this,' he said abruptly. 'I have to get out of here, be by myself, think things out ...'

'But where will you go?' Vickie didn't say it but he knew what she meant. That the police were keeping an eye on him, making sure he didn't skip out of the country, run off to Mexico ... maybe kill someone else ...

'I'll go up to the cabin at Lake Arrowhead. It's quiet up there in the mountains, I can get away from all this ... this pressure. And you needn't worry,' he added, knowing what she was thinking. 'I'll let Joe Zuckerman know where I am.'

'Arrowhead?' Taylor loved the lakeside cabin in the San Bernadino mountains. 'Can we come with you? Oh please, Daddy, just for a few days ... it would be such fun ...'

She ran over to him, clinging to him too, on the opposite side from her sister. Steve put his arms around their bony young shoulders, hugging them and willing himself not to cry.

'Everything that means anything to me is right here in our home,' he said quietly to Vickie. 'I want you to remember that.'

She stared at him, big-eyed, as he dropped a kiss on the little girls' soft hair then pushed them gently away. 'I'm sorry sweethearts,' he said faking jollity, 'but you can't come to Arrowhead. Maybe later, next month perhaps ... But this time Daddy's goin' fishin' all by himself.'

He lifted his head, startled by Vickie's sharp cry. She was staring over his shoulder. And then there was the tell-tale flash of a camera.

'Get out,' Vickie screamed. She was up and running the bottle of Evian clutched in her hand. She hurled it at the two men crouching in the bushes, 'Get out you bastards ... *out ... out of my house ...*'

The girls were screaming now too, terrified by the strange men and by their mother's rage ... 'Mommy, Mommy, what is it ... what's wrong ... who are they ...?' They clung pathetically to their father and Steve stood there, holding onto them. He turned his face heavenwards so they would not see the tortured grimace that changed him from a simple suburban guy barbecuing in his backyard on a pleasant summer evening, to a hunted man. A man in torment.

Vickie was still standing over by the bushes where the tabloid photographers had hidden, glaring at the pretty flowering shrubs as though they had been contaminated with poison. He walked over to her, took her arm.

'It's better if I go. Once the paparazzi know I'm not here they'll leave you alone. It's better for you. And for the girls.'

She nodded, still not looking at him. 'I'll help you pack.'

'I won't need much ...'

'Better take a jacket. It gets cool in the mountains at night.'

They kept their voices on a normal conversational level, both looking at their daughters. Taylor and Mellie held hands, sniffing back the tears, staring, still frightened, at their parents.

'What's going on, Mom? What's happening around here? Did Daddy kill that woman, is that what it is ...?' Taylor's cool was gone now and she was just a frightened little girl.

'I didn't kill anyone, baby.' Steve had his arms round her, whispering in her ear. 'You'll see, in a couple of weeks this will all have blown over. The cops will have found Laurie Martin and everything will be all right again.'

'You promise, Daddy?' Taylor's bottom lip quiviered, cutting to his very soul.

'I promise, honey. You'll see, everything will be back to normal again.'

Later that night, after her husband had driven away in the rented

Ford Taurus and her girls were in bed crying themselves to sleep, Vickie was on the phone with the family attorney, Joe Zuckerman.

'I don't think I know Steve any more,' she wailed, knowing that she could confide in this old friend of her father's without fear of him divulging her secrets. 'I look at him differently, see him with different eyes ... You know, like when he has his arms around my kids I find myself thinking, did he stab that woman? Did he strangle her? What's he done with the body ... ? And then I tell myself I'm crazy, I've loved him all these years, been married for twelve ... he's always been a decent man, a good husband, a good father ... how can I possibly question him ... ?'

'It's understandable, Vickie,' Zuckerman's voice was calm, soothing. He waited while she choked back a loud sob. 'Listen, girlie, I've known you since you were born. I've known Steve almost as long as you've known him and I never had any occasion to doubt his integrity.'

'Nor did I. Until now.'

He sighed, understanding. 'The media are putting on the pressure, honey, that's all it is.'

'But was he having an affair with Laurie Martin?' Vickie's heart seemed stuck somewhere in her throat as she asked the question she had not dared to voice earlier. 'I mean, why else would he have drinks with her? Take her out to dinner? Isn't that the usual prelude to an affair?'

Zuckerman had to admit that it was. Then he remembered Marla Cwitowitz. 'Listen, Vickie, a woman called me today. An attorney who works as a private detective. She called because she was concerned about you.'

'About me?' But I don't know her.'

'No, you don't. But Ms Cwitowitz told me she had seen Steve in the company of Laurie Martin a couple of times. Quite by chance, she said. The first time was at the Ritz in Laguna Niguel. They were having a drink at the bar and she told me it was obvious that this was their first meeting and that Laurie Martin was showing him pictures of houses. The second time was a couple of weeks later, at another hotel in La Jolla. They were on the terrace drinking champagne . . .' He held the phone from his ear at Vickie's strangled cry . . . 'No, wait, Vickie. She wanted to tell me – to tell *you* in fact – that in her view it was purely a business relationship. "No touching, no holding hands, no eyes linked across the table . . ." is exactly what she said.'

'And the champagne?' Vickie's tone was bitter.

'Everybody drinks champagne these days, girlie, not just at weddings. Anyhow, she wanted me to tell you this specifically. She said she hoped it might help you.'

'But who is Marla Cwitzowitz?'

'She teaches law at Pepperdine. Claims to be partners with this guy, Al Giraud. I checked him out. He's a legitimate private detective, he's done some good work. Well-known in his field.'

Vickie's mind was racing. 'Do you have Giraud's number, Joe? I'd like to call him.'

Marla negotiated the curving Queens Road in the big Mercedes. It was dark. In her left hand was a paper cup – a 'Vente Costa Rican' no milk, two sugars – which, translated from Starbucks language meant a big strong cup of coffee. A cellphone was clutched between her right ear and shoulder and two fingers of her right hand were actually on the wheel – unless of course, she took a moment out to adjust her lipgloss in the driver's mirror.

She was laughing at her girl friend's description of her relationship with Al Giraud as 'sex and no shopping'. She liked it that way.

She hung a left and the big car purred up Al's street and as if on automatic pilot, into his tiled courtyard. She said goodbye to her friend, switched off the ignition and was out of the car in a flash, purse tucked under her arm, coffee cup still clutched in her left hand.

Unlike Al, she had no love affair with her automobile. She had never been a poor kid dreaming in the movies of owning a powerful silver beast that would carry her into a different, better, more glamorous world. Marla had been born right here in Beverly Hills. She didn't know more glamorous worlds. Hollywood was the place everyone ran away to – not from.

Not so with Marla's parents, though. Max and Irina Cwitowitz had found Paradise in Beverly Hills, far from the Balkan war zones that had been the basis of life as they knew it. And far from the ragged remnants of family life with too many people dead in battles, or lost and never found in bombed buildings, or scattered over generations by constant wars. When Russia had taken over the Balkans in the division of countries after World War Two, they had both still been children. Homeless, penniless – and fatherless. Their mothers had become friends, shared a pitiful dwelling together in the basement of a bombed-out church. Both women had, when their children were old enough, urged them to escape to another, better life in a free country.

Max and Irina were married in a secret wedding ceremony, something that made both mothers happy. Then they had left on their dangerous escape route from behind the Iron Curtain, knowing they would never see them again. It had been a long hard road before America opened its welcoming doors to them and granted them citizenship, and before Max's entrepreneurial side came to the fore and made him within ten years, a real estate mogul.

Max Cwitowitz had sold half of Beverly Hills plus a good portion of Bel Air and Brentwood in the forty years he had been in business and in the process had made himself a tidy fortune. His hope had been that his only child, Marla, would take over the business from him. 'Cwitowitz and Daughter' had a nice ring to it. But right from being a babe in arms Marla had had a mind of her own. Most parents had to push their kids into law school – Marla had actually demanded to go there. *And* she had graduated magna from UCLA, then with a Masters in Law. And now, she was studying for her doctorate as well as teaching at Pepperdine.

And now – she also wanted to be a private eye.

Marla wanted it so bad, it hurt.

She opened Al's front door with her own key, called out, 'Hi honey, I'm home,' giggling as she took a sip of the coffee. Costa Rican did not taste too great cold and pulling a face, she wandered into the kitchen, left the paper cup on the counter and drifted off in search of her man.

Al's home was about as spare and masculine as it got. No cushions on the brown leather nail-head-studded chesterfield; no flowers on the glass-topped iron coffee table; no rugs on the shiny hardwood floor. It was clean, though, she had to concede that to him. Manuel Vargas's cleaning crew came in weekly and left the house looking as though no one lived there. Not a towel unrolled, not a pillow creased, not a dish in the sink. Windows gleamed, floors shone and the bedspread was unwrinkled.

Al was not home and Marla flung herself on that unwrinkled grey linen bedspread and stretched out, arms over her head, wondering where he was. She kicked off her shoes then sat up and removed her jacket, unzipped her skirt and stepped out of it. Peeling off her T-shirt, she walked into the chrome-and-black bathroom, took a quick cool shower and wrapped herself in Al's grey flannel bathrobe. She wished he didn't have this thing for grey – although it was kind of fashionable this year. Still, it didn't do much for a woman's complexion – especially after she had washed off her make-up. Sighing, she added a brushload of black mascara, dusted apricot blush over her slanting cheekbones and on her eyelids, then added a touch of Tenderheart gloss to her full lips. She spritzed herself with Hermès' 24 Faubourg, sniffing appreciatively, then drifted back to the kitchen, grabbed a bottle of Evian and a glass and walked back to the master bedroom. Actually, there were only two bedrooms and the other, smaller one, Al used as an office.

She clicked on the TV, surfing until she found KTLA, the local channel with the news from ten to eleven each night. Leaning comfortably against Al's grey pillows, she sipped the chilled Evian and waited for her man to come home.

It was almost eleven when she heard the growl of the Corvette over Roland Galvan describing tomorrow's weather

43

– basically more of the same, this was LA after all. Then the sound of the door opening and Al's light, quick footsteps on the wooden floor. Al always moved quickly, he was a man in perpetual motion. 'As though,' she had complained, 'you always think you might be missing something.'

He'd grinned at her, that Machiavellian grin that lifted the corner of his mouth and his left eyebrow in a way she found *sooo* sexy and said, 'Honey, life's too short to miss any of it. Especially when you're around.' And he had taken her in his – oh *sooo* strong arms and just like in a romance novel – had carried her to his bed, stripped off her clothing and made passionate love to her.

God, how she loved him. Now she gave him a radiant smile that lit up her whole face as well as her fabulous grey-green eyes that told him just that.

'Well, well, look who's sleeping in my bed, grandmama,' he said, leaning against the doorjamb with his hands stuffed in the pockets of his jeans and that grin on his face. He was wearing an old white Pepperdine T-shirt she had given him so long ago the logo had faded to a greyish blur. He liked it better that way.

'You're mixing Little Red Riding Hood with the Three Bears.' Her eyes swept him up and down. 'Whatever happened to private eyes who looked like Don Johnson? You know in pastel linen Armani suits with a holster under the armpit? The kind with the smooth line of talk who took a girl somewhere glamorous for dinner and a vodka martini before taking her to bed.'

Al shrugged, 'Beats me. I guess times have just changed is all.'

Marla's sigh fluttered the grey flannel robe and he walked over to the bed, kissed her firmly on the mouth then headed for the bathroom, peeling off his clothes as he went.

Marla heard the shower running. She flipped off the TV and put on a favorite CD – Sinatra and Jobim. She lay back, eyes closed, waiting.

She did not hear him approach, didn't know he was there until she caught a faint whiff of the Issey Miyake cologne she had given him, underscored with that familiar musky male smell of him.

She ran her hands down his smooth lean back, feeling muscles ripple under her finger. Her hands were in his dark hair, pulling his face to hers, his mouth was on hers . . .

And then the phone rang.

Al lifted his head, looked at the phone. Looked at her.

'Al Giraud, you're not going to answer that,' she said, shaking her head incredulously.

'You never know, I might be missing something,' he said, sliding off her and reaching for the phone.

'Yeah,' he said, watching Marla wrap the grey flannel robe haughtily around her shapely body. She lay there, arms folded angrily across her chest, staring up at the ceiling. Listening to his half of the conversation.

Her eyes swung his way, though, when he said, 'Oh, good evening Mrs Mallard. Yeah, you've reached the right guy. I'm Al Giraud. How can I help you?'

Marla's eyes were fastened on him now and they were open wide in astonishment.

Al sat, naked, on the edge of the bed. His face was serious as he listened to Vickie Mallard.

'Mr Giraud,' she said in a quavery voice and Al could tell she was close to breaking point. 'I would like you to investigate my husband – it's about this woman, Laurie Martin.'

'I know it.' Al turned his head, frowning at Marla. Vickie Mallard could only have gotten his phone number from her.

'Mr Giraud,' Vickie was saying, 'it's matter of life and death. I want you to hire you to prove my husband's innocence.'

'I understand, Mrs Mallard.'

Then she added in a voice like a death knell. 'Or his guilt.'

Marla's eyes were still fixed on him as he made arrangements to meet Vickie Mallard at her home the next day. When he put down the phone, she sat up and grabbed his arm.

'Tell me what she said,' she demanded urgently. 'Is she turning her husband in? Why are you going there . . . ?'

'She wants me to find out if her husband is innocent. Or guilty.'

Marla drew in a shocked breath. 'You mean she thinks he did it? Killed Laurie Martin?'

Al paced naked to the window. He pulled back the curtain, gazing at the fountain that the birds would persist in using as a birdbath so he was constantly cleaning off bird crap. 'I don't think she knows what to think. The media has gotten to her is my guess ... the pressure ... after all, its not easy when your husband is suspected of murder.'

Marla was out of bed now, standing next to him at the window. Opportunity was knocking and she was about to seize it. 'OK, I was the one who called the Mallard's lawyer and told him we had seen them together. I gave him your number. I was with you that night in the Ritz bar, Giraud. I know as much about this case as you do. Legally that qualifies me to be your partner.'

'Legally?' She was bluffing her way in and he knew it. 'Not even *you* could convince a judge of that.'

Marla's mouth was set in the stubborn line he knew only too well. 'Aw come on, Giraud. Give me a break, won't you? I can really help you on this. I'm good with women. Let me talk to Vickie Mallard, I'll bet she'll tell me things she'll never open up to you about.'

'No chance, Marla. I already told you I don't need a partner.'

She glared at him, mad as a green-eyed cat, then she flung away from him, stalked back over to the bed and dropped the grey flannel robe.

Al grinned, 'I told you before, you don't have to sleep with a guy to get the job.'

But Marla ignored him, climbing into her clothes with a speed and an economy of movement that stunned him. In minutes, she was fully dressed. She turned and looked contemptuously at him.

She was wearing a black skirt, white linen shirt and shiny black J P Tod loafers and now she knotted a black cashmere cardigan round her shoulders. Pulling her long blonde hair back with a black ribbon, she did not take her eyes off him. 'Chauvinist pig,' she said in a polite tone.

Al thought maybe she had a point. And Vickie Mallard might prefer to talk to a woman, especially when Marla looked like this ... kind of preppy, well-bred, neat.

'OK,' he said grudgingly. 'You're in.'

It was Marla's turn to grin. 'You don't have to sleep with a guy to get the job, Giraud,' she said triumphantly, already stepping out of her skirt. 'But it helps.'

Chapter Ten

When Vickie opened the door to Al Giraud the following morning her first thought was that he was like no one she knew. She had never met a man like this. Offbeat in jeans and a T-shirt, he looked more like an over-the-hill rock'n'roll star than the successful PI she had expected.

'Good morning, Mrs Mallard.' He held out his hand and she took it reluctantly. As though, Al thought hiding a smile, she thought he might contaminate her.

They sat in the family room, she on the denim-blue sectional, he on the big old rocker that was Steve's favourite chair, taking each other in.

Giraud was polite, soft-spoken, attractive even, but Vickie thought nervously there was an air of menace about him. Perhaps that was what you needed in a PI she tried to reassure herself.

'Coffee?' she suggested suddenly remembering her hostess manners. 'Or a cold drink? Coke? A beer?'

Al shook his head. 'Thank you, ma'am, but no thanks. What do you want to tell me about your husband?'

She took a deep breath. She had expected to ask *him* the questions, tell *him* what she wanted. After all, she was paying him. 'There's not much to tell,' she said grimly. 'Except what you already know.'

Al stroked his bluish bristled chin, looking at her. Marla had been right, she wasn't going to open up to him about her husband. 'So, tell me what you want from me, Mrs Mallard.'

'I don't know anything about the detective business,' she said nervously, 'I mean I don't know how it all works, what we need to do. I don't even know who you are,' she added earnestly, leaning forward, hands clasped tightly.

'OK, so why don't I tell you about myself?' Al was easy, relaxed, doing his best to put her at ease. He described his background, then his business, though he never named names.

'Confidentiality is a given in my business, Mrs Mallard,' he added, 'so you've no worries on that score. You are the one paying me, and you are the one I account to. No one else.' She heaved a relieved sigh and he said, 'I'm proud of the fact that my business boasts a ninety per cent success rate.'

Her eyes flashed suddenly into his. 'What happened to the other ten per cent?'

'They were guilty.'

Vickie wished she had never asked.

'OK, so Laurie Martin has disappeared – who knows where?' Al spread his arms wide to embrace the possibility that she might be anywhere in the world by now. 'Was she killed? We don't know that yet. Still, we have to admit the odds are she was. And if so, by whom?'

'That's exactly what I want you to find out,' Vickie said tersely. He was irritating the hell out of her now and she wished she had never started this. Why didn't he just get on with the investigation.

What Al wasn't telling her was that if her husband was guilty there would be no hiding the facts. He would find out the truth about Steve Mallard, the man. As well as about Laurie Martin. Right now he wanted to know about Steve's past. Marla would take care of the present.

'I need to talk to your husband,' he said. She had expected that and told him he was in Arrowhead to escape the media. 'As well as escape from himself,' she added grimly. 'Steve can't live with himself anymore, Mr Giraud.'

Al nodded sympathetically as he made a note of the address and she gave him directions. 'He's in a tough position right now. You can bet he can't wait for it to be over.' One way or the other, he thought, putting away his notebook. Killers were like that. Confession was a catharsis; he had even known it bring a smile back to a killer's face . . .

He discussed fees with her, then hitched up his jeans and offered his hand in farewell. Vickie shook it. It was surprisingly warm – and firm too. A strong handshake. Did that mean anything, she wondered hopefully.

Al said, 'My assistant, Marla Cwitowitz, will be calling on you. She'll want to ask you some questions. Of a more personal nature,' he added as he saw the surprise on her face.

'I've nothing to hide.'

Al read the panic in her eyes, she was teetering on the edge of a breakdown. He felt sorry for her, it was a hell of a position to be in, wondering if your husband was a killer. 'It's OK, honey' he said. 'Excuse me,' he corrected himself quickly. 'I mean, Mrs Mallard. I'm a southerner, I call everybody "hon", no disrespect intended.'

But Vickie had not even noticed. As she closed the door behind him she felt suddenly lost. As though all hope had been abandoned when Giraud left.

She sank onto the sectional and for the first time, began to cry.

Chapter Eleven

Marla had dressed in what she considered appropriate private detective attire for her meeting with Vickie Mallard. Black turtleneck, short black leather skirt, black suede ankle boots with four inch heels, an enormous and expensive steel watch that showed the time in three different continents and a large black Prada tote containing a yellow legal pad, a tiny hand-held tape recorder, the latest John Grisham and a packet of Junior Mints, to both of which she was addicted.

Her golden blonde hair was piled up and anchored with a black comb, her earrings were grey pearls and her lipstick dark and glossy. Driving her silver Mercedes, she looked, she thought triumphantly, the epitome of the successful PI. A pity that Giraud, with his plaid and jeans, his scuffed boots and Olympics-95 Swatch watch and in his ancient red Corvette did not convey the same impression. She hated that car, she knew only too well how many hours he spent working on it, tuning it to a high performance that really came through for him when he needed it. But she had to admit there were times when he had needed it. Dangerous times.

Marla preferred not to think about that. She knew Giraud's life was not a piece of cake. Her own work with him would be more cerebral, working out the convoluted stories his client told. Finding out the truth from the feminine angle. She worked on logic. Giraud worked on gut. That was the difference between them, right there.

The Mallard residence was in a new development of pretty three and four-bedroom homes on small lots. Each had its neatly tended patch of garden with a new baby tree planted in the middle of the rectangle of front lawn, and each had tall double doors and a Cal-Mediterranean façade. The Mallard's was no different from the others. Except for the pack of news hounds and paparazzi lounging around outside.

Marla parked the car down the street and walked to the house. She felt their faces swing her way, heard the click and whirr of cameras as she walked up the path to the front door and rang the bell.

'Who is it?' Vickie Mallard's voice was muffled.

'Marla Cwitowitz, Mrs Mallard. Giraud's partner.'

'Come through the side gate, please, round to the kitchen entrance. I don't want to open the front door.'

Marla glanced at the windows. All the shades were drawn, like a house in mourning. She took a short cut across the sliver of lawn and through the gate at the side, feeling the camera lenses breathing down her neck as she slammed it behind her. 'The poor woman,' she muttered. 'What the hell has she done to deserve all this?'

Vickie Mallard was wearing white pants and a red shirt that emphasised her pallor. She wore no make-up and her eyes were shadowed, lids pink and swollen.

'I'm sorry.' The peace offering came out of Marla's mouth involuntarily. Vickie just looked so bad, so beaten. A woman on the brink.

'Thank you.' Vickie glanced vaguely round the pretty living room. Marla saw she didn't even notice the long-dead flowers in the crystal vase.

'Please, sit down,' Vickie said. 'Can I offer you a cold drink? Or maybe some coffee?'

'Don't trouble yourself. I won't keep you long, I can see you're tired.'

'Tired? Vickie laughed, if that short sharp bark could be called laughter. 'I don't think I'll ever sleep again.'

She slumped onto a sofa opposite Marla, who sat, legs crossed demurely at the ankle. A puzzled look crossed Vickie's face as she took her in. 'You and Al Giraud – you're partners?'

Marla smiled at her astonishment. 'Opposites work well together,' she explained smoothly. 'I fill in the spaces where Al is reluctant to go. We're a good team.'

'Vickie nodded. 'What do you mean, where he is reluctant to go?'

'Believe it or not, Al is a gentleman.' Marla took the yellow legal pad from the black tote and a Uniball Deluxe Micro pen – the only kind that never let her down. 'He would never ask how things were between you and Steve – sexually.'

The hot blush stole up Vickie's face, making her look suddenly like an embarassed teenager. 'And why should he want to know that?' she asked stiffly.

'Because it's something the police have already asked Steve. It's something a prosecutor would ask him. It's something we need to know, Vickie. Was he a good fuck? Did he chase girls? Did he hang out with guys at bars. What exactly was your private life like?' Marla sat, pen poised over the legal pad. 'The truth now, Vickie. It's important for *you*, as well as Steve.'

Vickie thought she was going into meltdown she was so hot with embarrassment. It wasn't like she was talking to a shrink or her gynacologist ... she hardly knew this woman who anyway looked like a Hollywood B-movie version of a Raymond Chandler private eye.

'I resent these questions, Miss Citovitz.'

'*Cwitowitz*'. Marla corrected her. '*Svitovitz*' in plain English.'

'Miss Svitovitz.'

Ms ... if you don't mind.'

Vickie swept her short dark hair fiercely back from her forehead. 'What the hell have I gotten into now?' she demanded, getting up and pacing the floor. 'Who the hell are you? I thought I'd hired a private detective and all I get is a pair of meshuggeneh exiles from *LA Confidential*. This isn't a private eye novel – *Ms* Cwitowitz – this is *my life* you're dealing with.'

'Exactly. Now, tell me about him.

Vickie sank back onto the sofa. She had that beaten look again. 'It was good, OK, you know. The sex.' She was blushing again. 'He's nice, gentle, he wouldn't hurt anyone . . .'

'What's he like, Vickie? Really, I mean. Tell me where he's from, what he was like as a little boy – his family, how you met.'

'He's from Hoboken, New Jersey. I've never met his family, he kind of cut himself off from them, and from what I've heard it's no great loss. He got a scholarship to USC – that's where we met, but he was working all the time too, trying to make ends meet. We fell in love. And the rest is history.

'That is,' she added, 'after the major family battle over the fact that Steve wasn't Jewish and not good enough for the Saltzmans' daughter anyway. Time and patience resolved that, and not only have my parents embraced him as their son-in-law, Steve has embraced their faith and given them a pair of beautiful granddaughters. The only act left to prove his worth is to provide them with a grandson and a barmiztvah to look forward to.

'I'm a California girl,' she said earnestly. 'Born and bred in the San Fernando Valley. My dad's a dentist. I've always been close with my family. When I was pregnant with Taylor, I gave up work and concentrated on being a mother. I didn't want anybody else bringing up my kids, and nor did Steve. Then Mellie came along. I did all the usual things: car-pooled, went to the gym, met my girlfriends after for coffee and gossip. Visited with my mother, arranged birthday parties and sleepovers, Hallowe'en costumes and Hanukkah presents. We vacationed in Hawaii with my parents and my sisters and their husbands and children. We were a happy family.'

'Until the nightmare began,' Marla said softly.

Chapter Twelve

Detective Bulworth was at lunch at Jack's deli round the corner from the precinct house, a place that he favoured with his daily presence, eating his way through the weekly specials from meatloaf and mashed to brisket and dumplings without a thought of cholesterol or fat content. He was a big man and he was surely gonna stay that way.

Anyway, because he was at Jack's Deli, it was Pammie Pow! Powers who took the call. She was up to her eyes in a backlog of paperwork, battling with a balky computer and was definitely not pleased when the phone rang.

'What?' she demanded, clamping it to her ear and continuing to stare balefully at the computer screen. When were they gonna make these darn things as easy to use as they promised? It couldn't be just her. Everybody had problems with them. Maybe there was something to be said for good old-fashioned typewriters and fax machines instead of e-mail . . .

'What?' she said again. Only now she wasn't looking at the screen any more. She grabbed the phone as though it might get away from her, ballpoint clamped in one large hand. 'OK, where?' She wrote quickly. 'When, what time . . . ? OK, OK, yeah. We'll be there. sugar. You can bet on it.' She laughed at the reply. 'OK, so you're not my sugar. At least now I know the truth. Yeah, like if you're a sex-symbol I'm Cleopatra . . . More like Mark Antony huh. Well, to tell the truth, I always thought he was better looking than Cleo . . .'

She was grinning as she put down the phone. 'Bingo!' she yelled loud enough to lift heads from desks. 'I'm outta here.' She grabbed her hat and swung through the door. 'Bulworth and I have business to attend to.'

Bulworth saw her coming. Hat rammed over her red hair, elbows aloft, broad shoulders swinging ... you couldn't miss her. He shrank back into his black leatherette booth hoping she might not see him.

'Sir.'

No such luck. He glanced up from his chicken matzo-ball soup. Darn it, he hadn't even gotten to the main course yet. 'What is it, Powers?'

She slid next to him in the booth without even a by-your-leave. Powers really knew how to piss a guy off ... she was more one of the gosh-darn guys than he was ...

'They found the car,' she said breathlessly. 'Abandoned by the side of the road in a remote canyon. Helicopter reconnaissance spotted it a short while ago. I'll bet my boots it's hers.'

'So why would anybody want *your* boots, Powers,' Bulworth replied gloomily. 'And what car did they find anyways?'

'A metallic-gold car. And I'll bet it's a Lexus.'

Bulworth put down his spoon, looking regretfully at the chicken noodle and matzo-ball soup as he signalled the waitress. 'Cancel the brisket, sweetheart.' He lumbered to his feet. 'And put this on my tab will ya. We're in a hurry.'

By the time they reached the car he was already on the phone mustering up his 'boys': detectives; forensics; prints; photographer; coroner's wagon – though as yet they did not know if they had a body. He was willing to bet on it though. And on who had done it.

The police convoy trailed up into the hills winding round deserted roads to the place where the vehicle had been spotted by the helicopter crew. The road was narrow, the terrain steep and unsuitable for a chopper to land so it had backed off and was waiting a couple of miles away for instructions. They passed it on the way up and Bulworth got out to talk to the two cops. They told him the car was almost impossible to spot, hidden under overhanging trees and scrub. The sun glinting off the windshield had alerted them and they had gone down as close as they could, identified that it was a vehicle.

'Guess we've found Laurie Martin,' the chopper pilot said.

'Guess so.' Bulworth grinned as he slapped him on the shoulder. 'Good work, guys. I'll get back to you.'

He got that adrenaline rush up the spine as they swung round the curve. And there it was. Laurie Martin's metallic gold Lexus 400. All four doors hung open and in the deep canyon silence he could hear the buzzing of flies. He knew what that meant.

He scanned the dusty blacktop carefully but even as he looked, the gusty canyon wind lifted the dust, scattering it. Whatever tracks or footprints might have been left were long gone, he knew it. Nevertheless, his boys were already out there, down on their hands and knees, measuring, sifting, taking pictures.

Powers was pacing up and down but Bulworth waited quietly, leaning his bulk against the police Crown Victoria, puffing on a thin brown cigarillo. 'His one vice', he liked to call it though his wife said the stink of it made up for just about every other vice she could think of.

He took a look at the car. Not a scratch on it as far as he could see, though the layer of dirt covering it might be hiding anything. Later, wearing gloves, he carefully swung back the driver's door and looked inside. He did not find what he was expecting and he sighed as he drew his head out again.

'She's not in here,' he said regretfully. 'My best is she's been thrown over the edge into the canyon.'

'So why didn't the killer take the car?' Powers was breathing down his neck and he didn't like it.

'Probably driving his own car. They came up here together – I'd guess under the guise of a lovers' rendezvous. He couldn't very well drive two cars back down the mountain.'

'No, Sir.' Powers was half-way in and half-way out of the vehicle and her voice was muffled. 'Goddamn flies,' he heard her mutter. Then, 'Hah, that's blood that's drawing 'em. Look at this Detective Bulworth. Blood on the back seat.'

He looked. She was right of course but she might have waited, he would have found it in due time. *And* he was the senior detective. They sure didn't call her Pushy Powers for nothin' . . .

'The keys are still in the ignition,' he said, taking charge. 'And get your head out of there, Powers for God's sakes. Let forensics take a look.'

She backed out, red in the face with triumph. 'We've surely got the fucker now, Sir,' she said jubilantly.

He glanced sceptically at her, brows raised. 'Yeah, detective. Now all we need is Laurie Martin's body.'

Chapter Thirteen

Steve Mallard was expecting Al. Vickie had called, told him he was on his way. 'He's our only hope,' had been her words. But when Steve saw Giraud loping up the tree-lined path to the cabin, he hoped not. He thought Giraud looked like a loser. Still he was polite, shook hands, asked him in and if he wanted coffee, he had just brewed a pot.

Al declined. Standing by the picture window overlooking the tree-shadowed lake, he watched Steve pour coffee into a yellow mug with a frog on it, automatically noting that he took it black no sugar. Details, Al had found out the hard way, were what made the difference in catching a criminal. One small thing, just the way he walked or the fact that he was right or left handed or the way he took his coffee, might be the very thing that could put a man behind bars for life.

This man looked tired – or perhaps careworn was a better description, as though he carried the weight of the world on his shoulders. Or else the burden of guilt.

Still standing by the window, thumbs thrust in his jeans pockets as usual, Al said, 'Tell me about yourself, why don't you?'

Steve looked steadily at him. He took a sip of his coffee. 'Not much to tell,' he said with a dismissive lift of the shoulder. 'I'm just your regular hard-working suburban guy. One wife, two kids, a mortgage . . .' He laughed bitterly. 'Or at least that's who I used to be.'

'I'm interested in who you were before you became the suburban man. Like where you come from? Your family?'

Steve leaned an elbow on the stone mantel, staring into the empty firegrate. 'Didn't Vickie tell you all this?'

'I didn't ask her.'

His eyes swung toward Al. 'Why not?'

'I prefer to get my information right from the horse's mouth.'

'You a betting man?'

'It has been known.'

There was a long silence while they took each other's measure. Then finally Steve said, 'I'm from the east coast. Hoboken. My dad drove a truck. Long haul, anywhere and everywhere across the country. I didn't see much of him, even when he was home he was usually at the bar with his buddies. He ate dinner with them, hung out at the poolhall. He wasn't what you might call a family man.'

'Maybe that's why you chose that role – the suburban guy, the family guy.'

'Maybe.' Steve's look was guarded. He sipped the coffee, staring back into the empty firegrate again. 'My mom worked too. In the garment district in lower Manhattan. She left the house early, got back late. I was an only child, a kid with a latchkey round my neck since I was seven. To compensate, I guess, I worked hard at school, got straight As. I needn't have bothered, neither of them seemed to care.'

Al was leaning against the window, arms folded across his chest. His eyes were fixed on Steve.

'For financial reasons, by rights I should have gone to a local New Jersey college,' Steve said, 'but I wanted to get away. I wanted to be my own person.' He shrugged again. 'My parents certainly didn't care where I went, as long as they didn't have to pay. The west coast was as far away as I could get. I applied to several colleges. USC's was the first acceptance letter I received – and they offered a scholarship, full tuition, partial board. I was too scared they would take it away from me to wait for other offers. I took it. It was hard, but working summers and nights,

I managed to get through. I did well in class, graduated with a degree in electronics.

'By then I knew I could never go back east. Besides, there was nothing to go back for. I never heard from my mom, not once.' He thought for a minute then added softly, 'And boy did I love California. The way the sun shone for more than two hundred days at a time and the way a sprinkle of rain had folks looking for Mount Ararat and Noah. And for the first time in my life I had friends, guys I hung with and sweet, understanding girls who knew I was too broke to take them out anywhere much except the beach or a movie.' He heaved a sigh.

'And then you met Vickie Saltzman.'

'I met Vickie.' He paced back to the tiny galley kitchen, poured more coffee, taking his time.

Al wondered what he was avoiding telling him.

'And the rest is history,' Steve said with a note of finality. But for Al the interview was only just starting.

'So tell me about Laurie Martin.'

Steve turned his back, paced into the kitchen, fiddled with the coffeepot, paced back again. 'I've already told the police everything I know.'

Giraud nodded. 'And now you'll tell me.'

Temper flared in Steve's eyes and Al made a mental note that the man was on a real short fuse. Was this usual? Or were the circumstances just getting to him?

'Why the hell should I?'

'Because your wife hired me to help you. No other reason.' He unfolded his arms, shrugged. 'You don't want help, that's OK too.' He walked to the door wondering if Steve Mallard would let him just walk out of here, knowing he might be his last hope ...

'OK, OK, I'll tell you. You already know from Vickie I'd been relocated. I was looking for a house. We wanted a place with a sea view but I was having a tough time finding it. At the right price that is. There were plenty of more expensive houses that would have done just fine − but not on my salary. I saw Laurie Martin's picture and ad in the local newspaper, called her up, asked if she had anything I could see. We arranged to meet that evening.'

'At the Ritz in Laguna Niguel.'

Steve glanced sharply at him. 'You knew that?'

'I happened to be there that evening. Saw you waiting in the bar. Saw Laurie arrive, noticed she had good legs. You said you saw her photo in the ad. I wonder, did you call Laurie because she was just another real estate agent? Or because she was a looker?'

'Goddamn it!' Steve slammed his mug on the kitchen counter so hard the coffee slopped over the sides. 'What do you mean by that?'

Al took it in his stride. He had seen men get mad before. Often. 'Just what I said, buddy. Maybe you like blondes.' He lifted a shoulder. 'Lots of men do. And that includes married men.'

'Well it didn't fuckin' include me.' Steve slammed his fist on the counter, this time sending the mug flying. He was on the edge of that hairspring temper again, face reddening, eyes blazing, hands atremble. 'I thought you were supposed to be on my side. Aren't I paying you?'

'Your wife is paying. But don't get me wrong, I am on your side. And because of that I need to know the truth. So why don't you just tell me what happened. Straight from the shoulder. I'll take it from there.'

Steve began to pace the floor. His face was contorted with grief – or was it fear? Al knew he was cracking. This was confession time, all right. If the guy had anything to confess . . .

'Laurie was friendly, enthusiastic on the phone,' Steve said finally. 'She said she knew exactly what I needed and was sure she would find it. We arranged to meet after my workday, in the bar at the Ritz Carlton. I happened to have been out there for a meeting earlier that day and she had been to look at some properties in that area. She had taken care of business though and showed me particulars of a lot of houses. I picked out half a dozen and we arranged to meet the following evening to look at them.

'I was depressed by the houses we saw, none them were as good as their photos, none of them worked out. It had been a long day, I was tired ... I invited Laurie to join me for dinner at a nearby café. We talked ... you know how it is, two people geting to know each other. She knew I was married of course, and I showed her photos of my wife and my two daughters. She was very complimentary, said how pretty they were. And she showed me a picture of her dog – a little black mutt in a red bandanna she called Clyde.'

He paused and Al said, 'So how was it?'

'How was what?'

'The dinner, you know, how did you two get along?'

'It was pleasant. We got along OK, I guess. But I still didn't have a house. I remember when she was getting into her car I said to her, "Better luck next time." And she replied, "You bet, Steve. I won't let you down."'

'You saw her often after that,' Al said, picking up the story.

'We looked at a lot of houses.'

'And you also had dinner?'

'Sure we had dinner, drinks – part business, part pleasure. She was attractive, good company. Mostly we talked about California, the real estate game, possible houses ...'

'So Laurie had found you the perfect house?' Al paced the small cabin, he was dying for a cigarette, why had he ever let Marla talk him out of quitting ...

'At possibly the perfect price.' Steve was slumped in a chair by the empty firegrate. He looked exhausted.

'So were you two, like y'know ... an item?' Al was less direct that Marla.

Steve's eyes took his measure. 'You want to believe that, nothing I say will make any difference. Oh sure, maybe I shouldn't have asked her to dinner, lunch, whatever, but I was lonesome and she was there. But that's all there was to it.'

'No sex?'

'No sex.' His voice was firm. He had answered these questions a hundred times before.

'How about you and Vickie?'

Steve was on his feet, eyeball to eyeball with him, mad as hell. Al did not flinch. 'Y'gotta come clean, buddy,' he said softly. 'I'm working for you, remember? You don't tell me the truth, we don't get nowhere.'

Steve groaned, closing his eyes. 'Just leave me alone why don't you? I'm tired. And I'm sick of denying it.'

'Then maybe you don't have to any more.' The suggestion was in Giraud's soft southern drawl, the temptation, the relief – of the truth . . .

Their eyes locked.

'Go to hell, Giraud. I didn't do it!'

Violence flickered between them in the silence. Then Giraud turned away. He walked to the door, turned, stood watching him. 'And your wife Steve?' He repeated the earlier question.

'Vickie's great.' There was a break in Steve's voice as he turned away, retreated to the chair by the empty firegrate. He looked like a man beyond hope now. Or, perhaps Al thought, beyond redemption.

'Things were good between us. It wasn't the throes of first love – we've been married twelve years – but still good, you know. We suited each other.'

Al noticed his use of the past tense. On the surface Steve Mallard seemed a pleasant, easy-going, nice-looking guy. But as history had proven so were a lot of killers. Was he guilty? Al didn't have that crawling gut feeling that said yes – but only time would tell. One way or the other.

'Pity about the house,' he said casually. 'It sounded perfect.'

Steve shrugged. 'What the hell. We probably wouldn't have gotten it anyway. Laurie said someone else was interested and we'd have to act fast.'

Al's ears pricked up. 'Someone else? Like who?' He knew Marla would have made him say 'like whom' but he'd been brought up different.

Steve shook his head wearily. 'She didn't say. I thought it was just a real estate agent gimmick to keep the price up . . .'

The shrill ring of the phone split the silence. Steve Mallard leapt as though he had been shot then just stood there staring at it. On the fifth ring Al picked it up.

'Yeah. Oh hi, Mrs Mallard, it's Giraud. Yeah, your husband's right here. You wanna talk to him?' He was about to hand the phone to Steve when Vickie Mallard said something. He drew in a deep breath, still looking at Steve. 'Well, I'll certainly tell him that, Mrs M. You wanna talk to him yourself? No? OK, I'll pass on the message.'

He put down the phone. 'They found Laurie Martin's car on a remote canyon road. There's blood on the back seat. The police are pretty sure they'll find her body in the canyon, they've sent in the tracker dogs, got deputies combing the area.' He didn't take his eyes off Steve. If the man had looked terrible before, now he looked worse. Al noted the vein throbbing in his temple, the bulging eyes, the clenched fists. Steve was a man on the very brink . . . maybe on the brink of that remote canyon reliving the events that had created his hell. 'You sure you don't want to tell me about this,' he said softly. 'I'm on your side, buddy, remember?'

Steve slumped into the chair as though his legs would no longer support him. Tears brimmed and he put his face in his hands. 'There's nothing to tell,' he said between sobs. 'Nothing . . .'

Al walked over to him, stood silently watching. 'You'll need a different attorney,' he said finally. 'Zuckerman's not going to be able to deal with a murder case. I've got somebody I can recommend. Name of Lister. Ben Lister.' He wrote down the name and telephone number, tore off the sheet and placed it on the table next to Steve. 'I'll give your wife a call too, tell her about Lister. He's a good man. If anybody can help you, he can.'

Steve lifted his head. 'You're leaving?'

''Fraid so, buddy. Gotta get back to the real world. Don't worry though. I don't think you'll be alone for long. My guess is you can expect company within the next hour.'

'Company?' Steve's face was blank.

'The cops, buddy. Detective Bulworth and his men. No

doubt they are going to want to take you in for questioning at this point.'

'But they can't ... you can't leave me here alone ...'

He was panicked, frantic as a hooked fish. Giraud took pity on him, and besides he really didn't want him to do anything crazy like make a run for it. *Or kill himself ...*

'So I'll wait with you. It shouldn't be long. Maybe I'll have that cup of coffee now.' He wished he had a cigarette.

Bulworth didn't waste any time. He arrived at the cabin via helicopter and the local sheriff's squad car.

'Stephen Frederick Mallard, we are taking you in for questioning about the abduction and disappearance of Laurie Martin. You have a right to remain silent and the right to have a lawyer present at all times.'

Steve Mallard just stood there, his shoulders stooped and his arms hanging limply, as though he was already facing his executioner.

'I might have guessed I'd find you here,' Bulworth said to Giraud. 'And no, the body has not been found yet. But it will be. And soon.'

But Al was already on the phone to Ben Lister, explaining the situation and his own role in it. The attorney promised to meet them and Al promised that Steve would say nothing until he got there.

Al knew he would have to work in conjunction with Lister in order to gain access to any evidence. Lister's law office had a computer that would keep tabs on everything going down at the SDPD regarding Steve Mallard and Laurie. The attorney could also gain him access to Laurie's home and to her office where he needed to check Laurie's file on Steve, though he knew the cops had got there before him. Still, if he got lucky he might come across something they hadn't noticed.

As they took Steve Mallard away in cuffs, he wondered whether he had killed her.

Chapter Fourteen

Marla was waiting for Al when he got back from Arrowhead. 'You were there,' she said accusingly. 'I saw the whole thing on TV. Bulworth looking like a stuffed lobster, so pleased with himself that he'd caught his man ... Steve Mallard arrested ...'

'He's not arrested. He's being detained for questioning.'

'That means they don't have the body yet.'

Al grinned, 'And how are you too, honey ... thanks for asking ... it's been a rough day ...'

'Don't bullshit me, Giraud. Why didn't you call me, tell me you were going to Arrowhead? I wanted to come with you. I could have helped.'

Al took off his shirt, and flung it over the edge of the brown leather chesterfield. 'Not this one you couldn't.' He'd kicked off his sneakers and was already stepping out of his trousers.

Marla's eyes were fastened on him. Her cushiony lower lip caught in her teeth and a little sigh escaped her. 'Why don't you wear the Calvins I bought you?'

'I'm just an old-fashioned guy, Marla. A Jockey man from day one.'

'Perhaps you should try changing with the times.'

He grinned at her as he walked past and she hooked her fingers into the back of his shorts. 'Hold it, where d'you think you're going?'

His eyes were as innocent as his smile. 'What else would a man who's had a hard day do but take a shower?'

'Not yet ...' Her hands slid down inside his shorts. 'Oh God, Giraud,' she moaned, 'why must you have the butt of a teenager?'

'And what do you know about teenagers' butts?' He turned so she could get a better grip and so he could put his arms round her.

'I was a teenager once ...' She was kissing him now, nibbling hungrily on his mouth.

'A long time ago ...' He gripped her hair, pulling her face from his, laughing.

'Don't play the detective with me,' Marla said. 'Anyway it wasn't so long ago, not nearly as long as you.'

He sighed. 'You got me there, honey.' And then he kissed her. Forcefully. The way a man kissed a woman he was crazy for, Marla thought happily, already wriggling out of her short little blue slipdress.

'Jesus!' He looked at her stunned. 'I can't believe you're not wearing underwear.'

'I was coming to visit you. It's just quicker this way ...' She was in his arms, belly to belly, pointed breasts crushed against him, excitement rising. She gave his ear a little bite. 'Fancy a shower?' she murmured.

'Either that or a cold beer.'

'Bastard,' she yelled as he picked her up laughing and carried her into the bathroom.

The black tiled bathroom was a cool cave, the water gently warm and the halogen light directed at the shower definitely not conducive to romance.

'It's like starring in a porn movie,' Marla gasped, thrusting her long wet hair out of her eyes. 'Oh God, oh God, Giraud, do that again, yes, oh yes, do it again ...'

Her back was against the wall, her legs wrapped around his waist, her buttocks gripped in his hands as he thrust into her. 'Oh, Giraud, Giraud,' she sobbed, 'you're the best, the very best ...' And she was whirling over the edge into that other consciousness, that altered state of being that nothing could equal.

Al still gripped her to him, legs trembling, sweat mingling with the water from the shower. 'I'm getting too old for this.'

She snuggled her face against his shoulder. 'Not a chance, baby. You're still up there with the best of them. At least,' she added maliciously, 'in my experience.'

'Bitch.' He nuzzled her neck, dropping kisses on her throat. Then, muscles groaning, 'I can't go on like this, you gotta let me go.'

Marla laughed, sliding her long slim legs the length of his until she was upright, belly to belly with him again. 'I think I love you, you decrepit old man,' she whispered.

Al's booming laugh echoed from the black tiles. 'Yeah, honey. Wait 'til you see the porn movie, though. You'll look great.'

'I knew there was something about the angle of that halogen. And to think I put my trust in you.' She was soaping his back now, very busy with the sponge.

'Better watch out, you might get yourself in trouble again.'

'Wanna bet?' She was laughing as he took her in his arms again.

'Where are you going?' Marla sprawled contentedly on the grey linen bedspread that was, by now, severely wrinkled, eyeing Giraud who was stepping into a pair of clean shorts, hopping on one hairy muscular leg like an unbalanced stork. 'I thought maybe we'd send out for pizza. A Margarita with pepperoni on one half. *Your* half,' she added, smiling.

'Sorry, babe, but I'm on my way. I'll order in for you though.'

She shot up, eyes flashing again. 'What do you mean? You're on your way? To where?'

'San Diego, hon. Laguna to be exact. I have an appointment with Steve Mallard's destiny.'

She sank gloomily into the pillows. 'I might have known it. Kiss and run, that's you.'

'At least I don't kiss and tell. You want that pizza?'

'Of course I don't. I don't even like pizza. I only eat it to keep you company.'

He paused in buttoning his shirt to look at her. 'Hah, then who is it eats half my pizza whenever I order one? Must be some other woman in my bed.'

Oh all right,' she said sulkily, pushing her still damp blonde hair from those famously flashing orbs. 'But I only like it after sex.'

'With me, I assume?' He was laughing at her now. 'Sorry, hon, there's nothing I'd like more than pizza in bed with you. I'd even pour you a glass of Italian red to go with it. A nice little Chianti from Vons supermarket that I happen to have in my extensive wine cellar.'

'Your wine cellar is under the kitchen counter and I happen to know it contains two bottles of cheap Italian red, a good bottle of Californian chardonnay that someone must have given you because you certainly would never pay sixty bucks for a bottle of wine, and several large bottles of Asahi Japanese beer. Oh and a couple of Perriers, though why they're not in the refrigerator beats me.'

'OK, so I'm no wine connoisseur, I never took time out to learn all that stuff. Pour it by the glass and I'm happy.' He zipped up his jeans and thrust his bare feet into the sneakers. He bent to tie the laces. 'Wanna come with me?'

'What?' She was out of bed in a second, tugging the blue mini-dress over her head.

He looked up at her. 'I just changed my mind.'

'What d'you mean?' She pushed her feet into cream leather slides, tugged down her skirt and beamed at him. 'I'm set.'

'Do you really think I'm gonna let you out of here in that outfit? With no underwear?'

She tugged at the skirt again. 'Oh don't be such a prude, Giraud. I promise to keep my knees together.'

'Hah! No way, lady. No way are you going to the San

Diego PD dressed like that. Or *undressed* like that is more like it.'

'Ohh ...' She strode across the room, opened the drawer of the grey metal filing cabinet where Al kept his underwear. 'There, she said, pulling on a pair of his Jockeys. That should cover all that's necessary.'

They drooped around her slender thighs, hung off her butt. Despite himself, Al laughed. 'I've gotta hand it to you, Marla. You have an answer for everything.'

'It's the legal training. They don't let you out of law school without knowing all the answers.' She hitched up the Jockeys and said, 'And that's why you need me with you when Bulworth is interrogating your client. I'm the legal mind that will stop him tripping himself up. You're the one looking for loopholes in what he's telling them.'

'Y'got it, babe.' He had her by the elbow and they were in the garage and he was opening the door of the Corvette for her.

'Uhuh, can't we go in my car?' She stared beseechingly at him.

'Nah, but I'll tell you what I'll do for you. I'll put the top down – your hair'll dry on the freeway in minutes.

'Shit.' She climbed in gloomily and he slammed the door.

'Love me, love my car,' he laughed as they roared out of the garage, down into Queens Road and the Sunset Strip, heading for the 405 south. But his mind was already back on Steve Mallard and the mounting circumstantial case against him.

Chapter Fifteen

Bulworth wasn't talking to Giraud at this point. His broad beefy face had that closed look about it and he was into his hard-eyed mode, a cop with a man he knew was a killer and whom he wasn't about to let off the hook. He certainly wasn't allowing Giraud access to the suspect and to his interrogation. Only Mallard's lawyers could be present.

'That's OK,' Giraud said easily, 'Ms Cwitowitz is joining Mr Lister as Mallard's attorney.'

Bulworth flicked him a hard glance. 'You got your own Dream Team now Giraud?'

'Darn right, buddy. And Ms Cwitowitz has all the necessary qualifications.'

'I'll bet she does.' He looked at Marla. In that outfit with her hair pulled back and no make-up she looked about sixteen. 'She doesn't look old enough to order a drink in a bar never mind represent a suspected killer.'

'*Suspected* is the correct word, detective,' Marla said crisply. 'And I have my ID if you'd care to inspect it.'

Bulworth sighed, outflanked. 'No, I guess you're in.'

Marla buttoned her pale blue cashmere cardigan up to the neck, tugging down her skirt as she followed him into the interrogation room. She hoped the Jockeys didn't leave a visible panty-line under her dress.

Steve Mallard was already seated at a Formica-topped table that contained a single dirty ashtray and a glass of water. He was not smoking. On his left was Ben Lister, a small, rotund balding man whose deep-blue eyes were magnified by the thick lenses of his glasses, and whom Marla knew from legal fraternity encounters. She introduced herself, stated her position and took a seat on Steve's right.

She checked him out from the corner of her eye. He looked OK. Calm, though beaten down. Still, there was something about being unshaven that always made a man look guilty.

She placed her yellow legal pad on the table and settled in, ready to listen to what came next.

Giraud wasn't too surprised when the three of them emerged half an hour later, followed by a frustrated-looking Detective Bulworth and his cohort, Powers.

'So how'd it go?' He was sipping a diet Coke out of a can.

'Fine,' Bulworth retorted bitterly. 'Just fine. Your client is outta here, but he shouldn't count on for how long. I already told him that.'

'Great. Then we know just where we stand. Thanks detective.' He already had his hand on Steve's elbow, easing him out of there. The guy walked as though his legs were filled with lead. 'Remember me to the wife and kids, Bulworth. We'll have to do that barbecue again sometime.'

'Yeah,' Bulworth sighed. 'Soon, I hope.' He watched his suspect exit the station. 'Soon as I get this mess cleared up and that fucker in jail' was what he meant.

They were seated in a booth in a Denny's coffee shop right off the freeway exit just north of Laguna. Ben Lister had ordered a burger and fries, Giraud was having two-eggs over-easy with sausage and fries and Marla was eating a toasted sesame bagel. Steve was drinking a cup of coffee thirstily, his third in as many minutes. No wonder he was wired, Marla thought.

'You really should eat something,' she said, though the truth was she didn't really feel like coaxing Steve Mallard to eat.

He hadn't come off too well in that interrogation, clamping his mouth shut unless he was given permission by Lister to reply, and then those replies had been minimal, mostly just yeses or nos.

'Here, have some bagel.' She pushed the plate in front of him and for a second his eyes met hers. Nice brown eyes, she thought. Frightened eyes.

'Thanks. Thank you ...' He took the half bagel and, suddenly famished, wolfed it down.

Giraud called the waitress over. 'Another toasted bagel, and a couple of fried eggs for my friend, please, honey.'

The waitress, middle-aged and comfortably endowed and at the end of a long day, gave him a pointed glare and Marla grinned.

'Don't mind him, he's a southerner, he calls everyone "honey",' she said.

'Not the guys I hope,' the waitress snapped as she walked away.

'You should take lessons on how to make friends and influence people, Giraud,' Marla sighed. 'You never know when it might come in handy. And by the way, *legally* that's known as sexual harassment.'

'Is that so?' He raised a wicked eyebrow. 'And all this time I thought it was gentlemanly appreciation for a fine looking woman.'

Lister laughed and even Steve cracked a smile.

'OK, so the scene is this,' Lister said between bites of the burger. 'There is no body. But there are bloodstains in the car. On the rear seat. They're being tested for type – to see if there's a match for Steve's.'

'There isn't. I mean there can't be. I was never in her car,' Steve blurted.

'Never?' Giraud asked the question.

'Well, yes, a couple of times when we went to look at houses. Laurie drove because she knew the way. That's what real estate agents do. But not on that night I wasn't.'

'The night she disappeared,' Lister said gravely.

77

Steve hung his head miserably, just as the waitress arrived with his eggs and the toasted bagel.

'OK, without the body it's impossible to check DNA with the blood found in the Lexus,' Lister said. 'So, if that blood is *not* yours Steve, they still can't prove it's Laurie's. Meanwhile, as we speak, they have infra-red helicopters over that canyon, plus tracker dogs, the works. They're digging through local landfills and dumps. We should be prepared for the fact that, sooner or later, they're gonna find her.'

Steve stared at the eggs. He looked sick.

Marla helped herself to half his bagel. 'Kind of in trade,' she explained, biting into it hungrily, watching Steve as Lister spoke.

'They've already lifted Steve's prints from the Lexus, but as Steve just said, there's a logical explanation for that. They've also found other, as yet unidentified prints, probably other clients of Laurie's. Deputies are tracking them down even now.'

'*As we speak,*' Marla murmured mockingly, shooting a sly glance at Giraud. He glared back. '*Subversive,*' he mouthed, then looked away and she grinned, wondering if he was remembering the jockey shorts preserving her dignity under the blue dress. But no. Giraud was all business.

'They've checked Steve's Visa account, turned up every place he ever went with her, restaurants, hotel bars – and like that. Steve has already acknowledged that he was with her at those times. He has never made any secret of it.'

'And how many times was that?' Marla asked.

Lister looked enquiringly at Steve.

'Six, seven maybe. That's all.' He gulped the coffee not looking at them

'OK.' Lister took a last bite and washed it down with Coke. 'So there's no way they can hold Steve. Nothing to charge him with. We all have to wait now for Laurie Martin's body to surface.'

'And then the crap hits the fan,' Giraud said quietly.

'And then we shall take it from there, my friend.' Lister smiled at him. 'Steve, I suggest you go home to your wife. Take it easy. Trust me, I'll be working on this. Meanwhile get some rest, see your kids, that sort of stuff. OK?'

Steve nodded, frozen-faced. As if, Marla thought, he simply did not feel a thing.

'Here's my home number, and my car-phone,' Lister added. 'Feel free to call me any time, Steve. *Any time*. I mean that. OK?'

'OK,' Steve repeated like a man in a dream.

He left the untouched eggs on the table, along with a large tip from Al.

'Bye, *honey*,' the waitress called mockingly after Al as he exited.

He was grinning as they got in the car and headed back on the 405 to LA. Marla was not as happy to be relegated to what was laughingly known as a 'back seat' in the Corvette, but Steve was a big guy and besides she didn't fancy having a suspected murderer sitting behind her all the way to LA.

'We'll have you home in no time, Steve,' Al said easily. Only Steve wasn't at all sure he wanted to go home.

Chapter Sixteen

Not since Jon Benet Ramsey's murder had there been such an outcry. The name of Steve Mallard had become synonymous with killer. Polls were taken on his guilt – fifty-six per cent said he was guilty; twenty-three per cent not guilty. The rest didn't know. Rivera; Larry King; Matt Lauer ... Steve's possible guilt in the abduction and murder of Laurie Martin was discussed on TV every night; in the tabloids every day; on radio; in every magazine ... it was being talked about in England, in France, in Australia ... and the final outcome was always the same. 'Who knows where Laurie Martin is?'

The question was unanswerable; the implication clear.

Another week had passed and Laurie Martin's body had still not been found.

Vickie Mallard had stopped her daily workouts at the gym – she couldn't bear the turned heads, the whispered comments, the speculative glances. Everywhere she went she felt as though people were watching her, talking about her. She stopped marketing at her local Gelsons and took to driving long distances just to pick up groceries in a store where she might remain anonymous. And even then she was trailed by tabloid paparazzi, and followed as she drove out of the garage with the kids in the back of the Chevy Suburban on their way to school. Then she saw her daughters' pictures in a tabloid under the black banner headline 'A KILLER'S KIDS ...'

She drove straight home, slammed into the kitchen, dropped

the brown-paper sacks of groceries onto the counter and ran upstairs to confront her husband.

He was lying on the bed, as he always seemed to be these days. Their big California king bed with its patchwork quilt made by somebody's grandmother in Appalachia and bought on one of their vacations. The bed where their children had been concieved – the same children who were now being made outcasts. *Branded* . . .

'I can't take it any more.' Her voice had the high pitch of hysteria and Steve lifted his head wearily.

He looked at her for a long moment, 'I know.' He lay back, eyed closed again.

'*I'm going crazy.* Have you seen what they are saying about my children?' She flung the newspaper at him. It landed on his chest. 'Read it,' she screamed, 'just read it, goddamn it. They are calling them *A Killer's Kids.*' Tears choked her and she sank, sobbing onto the end of the bed. 'I can't take it, I just can't . . . I can't go on like this, not knowing . . . it's hell for them at school, too. Oh sure everyone's been told to act normal, but it's not the same. They are little outcasts. *I* am an outcast. What happened Steve? *What happened to our lives?*'

Steve got up and stood next to her. He put out a hand to touch her then drew back. Whenever he touched Vickie these days she just tensed up, as though he might be going to hurt her.

'I'm under siege in my own home,' she sobbed. 'I'm stalked by photographers when I do the marketing, the girls are trailed by men on motorcycles with cameras . . .'

But Steve had not missed that telling little phrase . . . 'I can't go on – *not knowing.*' He knew it was over. He had to make a move.

'It's better if I just leave you,' he said quietly. 'I'll go when it gets dark.'

She looked up at him with tear-stained eyes but did not protest. 'Where will you go?'

'Arrowhead, I guess.'

Vickie said nothing but she knew she couldn't stand him

being in the house any longer. He had to go. 'I'm sending the girls to stay with my sister,' she said more calmly. 'It's impossible for them here, it's just not fair.'

'But that means you'll be alone here.' Instinctively he reached out to her, put his hand on her shoulder and felt her stiffen. He stepped back, shoulders stooped wearily. 'I don't know what else to do, Vickie. What else to say.'

She didn't look at him. She was thinking of their rabbi who had been a tower of strength, helping her any way he could. And of her father who had loved Steve as his own son. 'God does not find a man guilty until it is proven that he *is* guilty,' her father had said, looking sadly at her, but there had been a furrow of doubt between his eyes.

It was that doubt that killed her. When she looked in the mirror, she saw it in her own eyes and she hated herself for it.

'I'll help you pack,' was all she said.

Chapter Seventeen

'You have to ask yourself why this woman – young, attractive, bright – was such a loner.'

It was the following Sunday morning. Al was sitting on Marla's squishy, down-cushioned, taupe, chenille sofa. His feet, in their scuffed boots, were propped on her expensive glass coffee table leaving smudges of dust on its pristine surface. He had on his jeans and a T-shirt – black today for a change, though so well worn it was tending towards grey, and he was surfing through the channels looking for the best football game while Marla, in a white terry robe and nothing else, lay with her head in his lap, scanning the *Los Angeles Times*, rising occasionally to take a sip of cold coffee.

It was their favourite time of the week and one they had vowed never to tarnish by discussing business.

'Perhaps she had something to hide?' Marla's logical brain sifted through the information at the same time as she was reading her horoscope. 'Stanley Omarr says I should beware of people wearing masks of falsehood. Whatever do you think he means?'

'What's mine say?' Al reached for her coffee, pausing en route to drop a kiss on her tousled blonde head.

'Scorpio's rising,' she snickered. 'Watch your back, true love may not be as true as it seems.'

'The man's lying.' He gulped the rest of her coffee and put the empty mug back on the table. 'Get your clothes on honey. We are going out.'

Marla groaned, looking at the rain trickling down the floor-to-ceiling bank of windows that were supposed to frame a bird's eye view of the Pacific Ocean.

Her apartment was as glamorous as Marla herself, a big – 3400 sq. ft. – ocean-view condo on the eleventh floor of a glossy white marble building in the Palisades. The floors were pale limestone, the kitchen black granite and steel, the bathrooms – three – blond marble and glass. The huge expanse of windows offered a view of Pacific Coast Highway immediately below, and across from that, the beach with the waves rolling in and – on most days – the surfers.

It was almost as sparingly furnished as Al's place, except Marla called this style 'Comfortable Minimalist'. Overstuffed taupe sofas; deep-jewel-toned oriental rugs; an aluminium console teetering on spindly legs in the hall; a single crystal vase three feet high holding a tall branch of pussywillow; white Phalaenopsis orchids in the bedroom and an antique Chinese bed in scarlet and gold lacquer that was like a small room with panels that closed around it like little doors, supposed originally to keep out the draughts of ancient China.

Al thought Marla's home was exactly like her, a place of many facets, many moods. What he didn't understand was how she could afford it.

He was never one to beat about the bush, when he wanted to know something he asked.

'Dad, of course,' she had replied. 'He bought it from the floor plan as an investment a couple of years ago. Sometimes it's useful him being in real estate.'

Which brought Al's thoughts right back to the missing Laurie Martin again.

'It's raining out,' Marla said. 'Besides, I thought this was *our* day. Our lazy let's-not-get-dressed-for-anyone-let's-not-see-anyone-let's-not-talk-to-anyone-about-business day!'

'Honey, are you or are you not my assistant? We've got a murder on our hands and our murderer is still out there. How can you spend a Sunday lazing on the couch, reading a newspaper and watching TV, knowing Vickie Mallard and her family are going through hell?'

Marla sat bolt upright, remembering her role as assistant PI. 'You hard-hearted bastard. Even cops get a day off. And I've already put in four days at my other job. Plus I have tests to prepare for tomorrow.' She was planning on giving her law students a surprise test; see how much they had actually learned in the last couple of weeks, trip them up, jolt the little bastards awake ... she was sure some of them slept through her classes.

'No, you've gotta ask youself this, Marla. Here's Laurie Martin, a single woman living alone in a nice condo she bought two years ago. She drives a Lexus 400 – leased from a local car dealership. Her payments are prompt, her credit cards are current, as are her accounts at a couple of department stores, and she has no bank loans. We know she was quiet socially. No real friends, more like business acquaintances. She attended a local Baptist church regularly. No family members have come forward. She has never been married. Laurie was, in every respect, a loner.

'And that's something else that puzzles me. Laurie was quite a looker, in that bouffant blonde kinda way. So how come there was no boyfriend? No parties? Not even nights out with the girls at the office?'

'Beats me,' Marla thought about it, frowning. 'You think she had something to hide?'

Al beamed at her. 'That's exactly what I think, honey. Now all *I* have to do is find out what that was.'

'We,' she corrected him. He lifted a puzzled eyebrow. 'What *we* have to find out. Remember me? Your assistant.'

He grinned. 'How could I forget.'

Laurie Martin's condo was in Laguna Beach, a cute little town – part artistic, part tourist, filled with galleries, gimmick stores and gift boutiques. The good hotels and the Pacific beaches brought in the tourists as well as the surfers, and houses and apartment buildings were scattered throughout the neighbouring hills.

This was the first time Giraud had been allowed access

to Laurie's home and it had taken the combined efforts of Lister and Marla as Steve's attorneys, to get Bulworth to agree to it now.

'Thanks for getting me out in the rain on a Sunday afternoon,' the detective who met them at the condo yawned. 'I was enjoying a rare peaceful afternoon at the precinct until you came along.'

The apartment was light and compact rather than spacious. 'Around sixteen hundred square feet,' Marla the real estate developer's daughter assessed. 'Plenty for one person.'

'Unless they're like you,' Al said, 'then they need twice as much.' He stared at the pastel decor: white, pink, turquoise. 'Kind of tropical-looking. I thought she came from Texas.'

'Looks more like Florida to me.' Marla was looking at the framed photo on the mantel. It was of a dog, a black mutt wearing a red bandanna round its neck. 'Cute,' she murmured, ever soft-hearted. 'I wonder what happened to him.'

Al checked the kitchen and the bedroom. No dog basket; no dog bowls; no dog paraphernalia. 'Who's taking care of the dog?' he asked the detective.

'There is no dog. Never was one. They're not allowed in this building.'

The detective stepped out onto the balcony for a smoke and Al looked thoughtfully at Marla. 'Steve said that when he showed Laurie the pictures of his kids, she showed him a picture of Clyde. She talked about the dog as though she really had it living here with her. Like Steve had his kids. Y'know what I mean? And you notice there are no pictures of people here?'

'Perhaps she only loved her little dog.' Marla took the dog photo from the shelf and slipped it out of the frame, looking for information on the back, but there was nothing.

Al was scanning the shelves of books. He stared at the bottom shelf then glanced over his shoulder at the detective out on the balcony. 'Marla, go make nice with the detective,' he whispered. 'Keep him busy.'

'Oh. But how?'

He threw her a withering look. 'What kind of PI are you?

You're asking *me* how a woman keeps a man interested in her conversation?'

'Oh. OK . . .' Marla drifted across the room to the balcony.

'Got another cigarette, detective?' Al heard her say in her velvetiest voice. She didn't even smoke. He knew he would pay for this later.

He reached down, took the leather-bound volume from the bottom shelf. As he had thought, it was a photograph album. He riffled quickly through the pages. Most of the pictures were of houses that Laurie must have sold and of various holiday landscapes. Then he came across a page of pictures of the little black mutt. In one, it was perched on the hood of a car. Al couldn't make-out the licence plate – it was too blurred, but it didn't look like a California plate to him. Quickly, he slipped the photo into his pocket and replaced the album on the shelf.

He could hear Marla coughing out on the balcony and he called her back in. 'I'm glad I never was tempted to smoke,' she grumbled, 'my mouth tastes like a garbage can.'

'All in a day's work. Every detective I know smokes.'

'Except you. Now I've trained you better. No more garbage mouth . . .'

He heaved a regretful sigh. 'You have no idea how good that garbage tasted sometimes.'

They were standing in the bedroom now. 'Girly,' Marla commented, taking in the thick pile white carpet; the queensize white-and-gilt, Louis-style bed loaded with ruffled pillows; the round tables with ruffled turquoise silk skirts and glass tops; the pink velvet chaise with a collection of dolls; the bedside lamps with beaded pink shades. 'So this is what our woman is really like.'

'Take a look in the closet, why don't ya honey. Check out her clothes. With your know-how you should be able to get a fix on her.'

The good-sized, walk-in closet was jammed with stuff, and to Marla mostly it looked like work outfits. Little silky suits and dresses, skirts and jackets. Decent quality but not expensive. 'About what a young woman in her position could afford,' she told Al. 'Except, wow! Just take a look at these.'

She took out half a dozen dresses and held them up for him to see.

'Mmmm, what my mother would have called "house-dresses",' Al said, inspecting the frumpy floral prints, the long sleeves and the little white collars. 'Now why would a woman like Laurie buy outfits like that. Unless she was living two different lives.'

'Three!' Marla said, delving into the back and emerging with a batch of lace and silk; short skirts, bustier tops, a strapless black sheath and that bright-blue lace number she had noticed Laurie wearing the night she had spotted her with Steve on the terrace at the Hotel La Valencia. She didn't have to look at the labels to know what they had cost.

'Where would she get the money for these?' She fingered a supple suede designer jacket from a Rodeo Drive store.

'And while we're at it, where did she get the money to buy this condo?' Al looked round at the well-designed apartment with its wall-to-wall white carpet and granite-and-marble fixtures. *And* she drove an expensive car. Our Laurie must have come into money a couple of years ago.'

'She inherited it,' Marla guessed. 'Her mother died, she got the family jewels.'

'No chance. I'm willing to bet there were no jewels in the household she grew up in. Wherever that was.' he added, frowning. He stared gloomily out of the window at the rain, running his hands through his hair, worrying about Laurie Martin. Who the hell was she? As well as *where* the hell was she? Dying for a cigarette, he picked up a handful of jellybeans from a glass dish on the coffee table.

'That's evidence you're tampering with, buddy.' The police detective was grinning at him. 'Heard you'd given up smoking. Starting to put on a few pounds now, huh bud?'

'He could use it. Unlike some people I know.' Marla glanced pointedly at the detective's beer belly.'

He grinned as he shook a cigarette out of a pack and made a big show of lighting it up. 'You folks finished? I'm about ready for a coffee and a doughnut.'

Chapter Eighteen

Al was checking with Laurie's co-workers at the real estate office, trying to find out what kind of a person she was. Friendly? Flirty? Flighty? Or lonely? Solitary? Aloof? Meanwhile, Marla had been delegated to visit the Baptist Church Laurie attended in Laguna Beach.

The Reverend Bones Johnson suited his nickname perfectly, a skeletal young man whose white dog-collar bagged around his scrawny neck and whose mild blue eyes had a faraway expression.

As though he was already in another world, Marla thought, exasperated. She had already asked him twice what he knew about Laurie Martin and both times he had begun to answer and then wandered off the subject into his feelings about the ministry and his congregation.

'Yes, Reverend, but about Miss Martin,' she brought him back to the point again, keeping the impatience out of her voice with a mighty effort. This was getting her exactly nowhere. Trust Giraud to have given himself the plum job talking to the co-workers and left her to pick up the pieces with this whacko minister. 'Did she attend church regularly?'

'Laurie Martin?' His eyes widened, as though surprised they were talking about her. 'Ah yes, poor young woman. Yes she came here often. Pretty much every Sunday. Except when she was working. She was a real estate agent, you know . . .'

Marla raised her eyes to heaven. 'Yeah, I know.'

'Sometimes on Sundays she had open house or took care of special clients, but she hated to miss a service.'

'I can understand that.' Marla tried a smile but the Reverend's eyes were fixed on some point in the middle distance.

'She seemed like a nice, quiet, shy young woman. Took part in church activities, communal suppers and helping with the old folks, things like that. She was always willing to lend a hand,' he said finally.

'I know this is probably confidential, but I'm sure you'll understand my asking . . . did Laurie ever talk to you about herself? About where she came from? Her family? Men problems?'

He lifted his shoulders in a shrug, shaking his head. 'No, she never did. I don't think any of us knew her that well. Except maybe John MacIver. You should talk to him about Laurie.'

The road leading to MacIver's house led up a hill on the outskirts of the little town. Kind of isolated, Marla thought, as well as impressive. The house must have been built in the fifties in a grandiose mock-Tudor style, all blackened beams and diamond-paned windows and huge, curlicued, iron gates topped with little spear points.

She sat in the car eyeing the hefty German Shepherd barking at her from behind those gates, wondering how she was going to get in. Between the gates and the dog, the place was a fortress.

Then she saw the old man hobbling down the gravel driveway. 'Ah, saved by the bell,' she murmured, glaring back at the dog which bared its teeth at her in a nasty snarl.

'Shut up, Gestapo, why don't you. You'll have the neighbours complaining again.'

Marla stared at him, startled. *Gestapo?* What kind of a name was that for a dog? Even if it was a German Shepherd. She glanced round. And as far as she could see there were no neighbours. Certainly none near enough to complain about a dog barking. He must be a little dotty, she thought taking mental PI notes as he approached. *White hair, must be in his eighties, walks with the aid of a stick. Must be the caretaker.*

But no, he was a little too well dressed for that role. Probably John MacIver's father.

'Good afternoon,' she called, giving him the benefit of her most winning smile. 'My name is Marla Cwitowitz. I've come to speak with Mr John MacIver.'

He peered at her through the gates, the dog still snarling at his side. 'I said shut up, Gestapo,' he said again in a quavery voice. 'Sit.'

To Marla's astonishment the dog did as it was told. 'He's not home,' he said curtly.'

'But it's about Laurie Martin. Tell him I'm trying to help find her. I'm trying to help her.'

His face lit up. 'You're going to find Laurie. Well why didn't you say so. Come in, come in . . .' He pressed a buzzer, the electronic gates swung open and the dog charged out.

Quickly Marla put up the car window. She couldn't hear for the growling but the old boy must have given another command because the dog dropped away reluctantly. She flinched as she heard its claws scraping down the side of the Mercedes, imagining what it had just done to her silver-grey paintwork. Giraud would pay for this, she fumed, stepping cautiously out of the car.

The old boy had Gestapo on a heavy chain now, though it was no contest as to who weighed more and who was stronger. Marla stiffened her upper lip. She was taking her life in her hands for Laurie Martin as she walked up the gravel driveway with the old boy. The dog walked on his opposite side, still snarling softly.

'I call him Gestapo because he always acts this way, has since he was a pup. Won't let anybody near the place. Not until he knows them that is. Now Laurie, he liked her, she could come anytime she liked. And always brought him something good, a new food she had discovered or a nice fresh bone. Told me she went specially to the butcher at the supermarket, asked them to save a good beefbone for her. She liked dogs . . .' He sighed feelingly.

They were at the front door now. It stood ajar and he

pushed it wider with his cane. 'Come in, come in ... what did you say your name was again?'

He was obviously hard of hearing and Marla leaned closer to him. 'Marla Cwitowitz,' she said into his ear, 'but you can call me Marla.'

'Marla huh? Nice name.'

He led her through a spacious black and white marble-tiled hall into a room that was obviously a den. More like a lair, Marla thought, taking a look around. Floor-to-ceiling mahogany shelves lined with books; heavy plum-coloured velvet drapes smelling of dust and shutting out the sunlight; a small television set atop an antique walnut chest; a cracked, green leather sofa; club chairs in old flowered slipcovers; an ancient Turkish carpet. And an ivory grand piano looking as out of place in this room as a sequinned Las Vegas chorus-girl in a church. Over the massive, intricately carved, Jacobean mantel hung a portrait of a haughty-looking blonde woman in a satin evening gown and diamonds, holding a single lily in her hand.

She was quite something, Marla thought, staring at the portrait. And was she wrong, or was there a slight resemblance to Laurie Martin? Something about the eyes, perhaps ...

'That's my wife,' the old boy said, slumping backwards onto the sofa as though his legs had just given out on him. 'Imogen. Died ten years ago.'

'A lovely woman,' Marla replied politely, though personally she thought she looked a hard-faced bitch. That contemptuous curl of the lips, the hint of impatience in her eyes. 'The artist captured her perfectly,' she added with an insincere smile.

'Eh?' He put a hand to his ear, then seemed to realise what she'd said. 'That's why I liked Laurie, she looked like her,' he said. 'Sit down, Miss Marla, sit down, sit down ...' he waved a frail hand.

'And I understand your son attended church with her. The Reverend Johnson said he knew her well.'

'Bones Johnson said I had a son? What's gotten into him, of course I don't have a son. No, it was I who attended church with Miss Martin. I was her friend.'

Well, well, well, Marla thought, pausing to catch her breath. So this was John MacIver! And it seemed Laurie had a friend after all . . .

'It's terrible, terrible, what that man has done to her.' His voice was even more quavery now and a tear trickled down his sunken cheek. 'Where is she? *Where is she?*' He clasped his arms across his chest, rocking back and forth in his pain and Marla got the impression that this was not the first time he had broken down like this about Laurie. He obviously cared deeply about her.

'I'm sorry, Mr MacIver.' She went and sat next to him on the cracked green leather sofa. 'I understand how you must feel. She must have been a very special lady.'

'A lady is exactly what she was. In the old-fashioned sense of the word. Gentle, kind, caring. And lovely, quite lovely.' His faded eyes focussed on Marla's face, close to his. MacIver's glasses magnified even bigger than Ben Lister's, and she bet he had cataracts and was having trouble seeing clearly, even with those thick lenses.

'Did you know Laurie?' MacIver asked.

'Ahh, well, not exactly. Not personally.'

'Then you don't know what you were missing.' Struggling to his feet, he hobbled across to the fireplace and took a photograph from an antique Italian table. 'This is her.'

Marla was looking at a different Laurie Martin from the glitzy California blonde in the Ritz bar. But it was her all right, no doubt about that. Laurie in one of the floral-print house-dresses with the long sleeves and long skirt. She clutched a large white handbag and wore low-heeled white pumps. Her hair was pulled tightly back into a knot and she smiled timidly into the camera. It was obviously her Sunday, church-going image.

'She certainly is a lovely woman,' Marla said reverently. 'I can see what you mean, she has that nice . . .' she struggled for a word '. . . old-fashioned appearance.'

'That's why I liked her.' His voice cracked and he bent his head as the tears came, faster now. 'I loved her,' he admitted brokenly, 'I'd asked her to marry me. And she said yes. But not right away, she said first she wanted me to be sure I knew what I was doing. And she didn't want people talking about us, about her . . .'

Marla's astonished eyes swept round the room again; the old boy had money, no doubt about it, and Laurie had obviously known that. 'I can see what she meant.'

MacIver took off his glasses and mopped his eyes. 'You have a nice face, Miss Marla, gentle, like her. I've not told anyone about Laurie, not even the Reverend Johnson. Laurie said it was our secret. But she allowed me to buy her an engagement ring. She told me that would be nice, sort of special between us,'

'The coiled snake with its tail in its mouth and the diamond eye,' Marla remembered suddenly. So that's where Laurie had got such an expensive ring. 'An unusual choice, for an engagement ring,' she said.

'That was Laurie, she always surprised you. But then, Laurie was an unusual woman.'

'I hope you won't mind me asking, but didn't Laurie care about the age difference? I mean she was . . . what?'

'Laurie was in her thirties and I'm eighty-four. But you don't understand, Laurie was a very spiritual woman, the age difference meant nothing to her. She said we were on the same plane, that our minds were alike, that we had been together in previous lives. And now chance had brought us together again, though she preferred to call it Destiny.' MacIver threw Marla a sharp glance though she wasn't sure his clouded blue eyes were seeing her without the thick glasses. 'And it was physical too, of course,' he said proudly, 'I'm still active, there's still life in me . . .'

Well whoopee for Viagra, Marla thought but she said smoothly, 'And of course Laurie was a woman who appreciated the finer things in life.'

'And I could give her that, provide for her,' he said eagerly. Though don't get me wrong, she wasn't after my money. Oh no sir. She wouldn't let me give her anything much.'

'So what exactly did you give her, besides the ring?'

'She never took a penny. Not for herself. Never. Though

I did help her out once, when she needed money to pay for her sister's child to have an operation. And for a special charity she was involved in, to help children at Christmas time.' Tears stood in his eyes again. 'Laurie was a good woman. A very good woman. And I know she loved me.'

'How do you know that?' Marla was curious. He was no oil painting after all and he was a bit doddery and getting on in years.

'She told me so,' MacIver said simply. 'Said she had never loved any man since her husband died ten years ago. I was the first. And you know why? Because she felt she could trust me. She was scared out there in that big ugly world, a gentle woman like her, vulnerable, alone. Men hit on her all the time in her line of work, she told me that too.'

Marla sat back in the green leather sofa, stunned. As far as anyone knew, Laurie Martin had no sister. Nor had she ever had a husband. Nor, as far as she knew, was she involved in any children's charity.

She patted MacIver's hand gently. It felt like bird bones, the thin flesh transparent, purple veins pulsing beneath. 'I'm sorry I upset you, Mr MacIver,' she said sincerely. 'And I want to thank you for confiding in me. I'm sure it's going to help in our search for Laurie. Meanwhile, another thing that would be of enormous help is her photograph. I understand that it's precious to you, but may I borrow it just for one day? I'll have several copies made and I'll give you some too. It will be of such help in our search.'

MacIver looked at her suddenly panicked. 'You told me you weren't the police,' he said. 'If I'd known it was the police, I wouldn't have said anything, Laurie wouldn't have liked that.'

'Oh?' Marla's ears pricked up. 'And why wouldn't Laurie have liked you talking to the police Mr MacIver? You can tell me,' she smiled, gently patting his hand. 'I'm definitely *not* the police.'

He sighed with relief. 'I didn't think you were. No, Laurie didn't like the police, didn't trust them. Said they harassed her once or twice, over some minor car things. She said if they weren't on your side, forget it.'

Marla nodded, 'I understand. And thank you again Mr MacIver. I'll have the photograph back to you tomorrow without fail.'

She got to her feet and so did the dog, growling softly at the back of its throat, showing the whites of its eyes and its fangs.

'Forgive me for not accompanying you,' MacIver said, 'but I'm quite exhausted. I'll buzz you out of the gate. Gestapo, sit.' The dog slumped to the floor and Marla's spine crawled as she stepped gingerly past it, waiting for those fangs to sink into her ankle. But the dog did not move.

'Well, well, well,' she thought hurrying down the drive to the safety of the Mercedes still parked in the road. 'Just look what I've come up with. The mother lode.' She grinned wondering how successful Giraud had been with Laurie's co-workers. Not as good as her, she'd bet. Wow, did she have a lot to tell him.

Chapter Nineteen

Al hitched himself onto a stool at the horseshoe-shaped counter at the Apple Pan on Pico, one block east of Westwood. The place had barely changed since it opened in the forties and was his favourite eatery. He had been waiting ten minutes already and the line still curved both sides of the screen door. Behind the counter four guys worked the grills, shovelling fries onto paper plates and burgers into buns, piling toasted rye a mile high with tuna salad or egg salad. And slicing great slabs of possibly the best apple pie in LA. At least in Al's opinion. And, judging by the line, a great many others.

'How're y'doin' Al? The usual?'

He had been coming here for fifteen years and the guy behind the counter had been here even longer. 'Ya have to ask?'

'Never know when you might change your mind – go for the tuna instead.' He slid a can of Coke across the counter along with a little paper cone in a plastic holder in case Al wanted to be lady-like, and in less than a minute had a burger with the works and a paper plate of fries and another paper plate with two slurps of ketchup in front of Al.

He had just taken the first bite when he felt a draught behind him. Like a whirlwind he thought, turning to look. Marla was elbowing her way to the counter. She was dressed, if you could call it that, in workout-gear. White lycra shorts, a brief white sports bra, sneakers and a Lakers cap.

'Excuse me, pardon me, excuse me ...' Marla was already at the front of the line, sliding onto the just-vacated stool next to him. 'I'm with him,' she explained over her shoulder to the irate customers still waiting behind her.

'Marla, how could you do that,' Al hissed. 'That poor guy has been waiting for ten minutes. There is a line, in case you hadn't noticed.'

'I knew I'd find you here. And yes I had noticed, but this is important.' She grinned at him.

'You'll get us thrown out of here.'

'I've been thrown out of better places – as they say.'

'Waddya want, lady?' The server was getting impatient, she was holding up his smooth-running schedule ... around fifteen minutes from sitting down to out-the-door was what he generally worked on. But not with women like this one.

'Mmm, now let me see ...' Marla studied the menu card on the counter. Hamburger, cheeseburger, tuna salad, egg salad, fries, pie. She cocked her head to one side smiling, 'What I really wanted was lox and cream cheese on a toasted sesame bagel.'

'Al and the server both glared at her. 'Lady, you'll find Junior's Deli right around the corner. We got burgers and fries. Now, whaddya want?'

'Egg salad, no fries, please,' she said meekly.

'You might have the grace to blush,' Al said, dunking a French fry in his ketchup.

'Women don't blush these days. We've given it up.'

'So what d'you do instead?'

'Apologise,' she said with a mischievous grin. She turned to the guy still waiting behind her. 'I'm so sorry.' She smiled engagingly at him and he smiled back. 'I'm sorry,' she said to the server who was just slamming a paper plate with the egg salad sandwich onto the counter. 'Oh my, this is big enough for four. I may need a doggy bag.' Al rolled his eyes and she added quickly, 'I'm sorry.'

'OK, so now you've apologised to everybody just eat the darn sandwhich and lets get out of here.'

'But I've got so much to tell you ...'

She had been here five minutes and hadn't even taken a bite yet. The Apple Pan's schedule was shot to hell. 'You've gotta understand, this is not the Ritz, Marla,' Al hissed at her. 'These guys work on numbers, turnover is their mantra.'

She picked up the paper plate and the can of Coke and slid off the red stool. 'OK, so I'm not holding anyone up any longer. I'll eat it in the car ... damn it, I didn't want it anyway.'

Al had already finished his burger and paid for both of them. He left the fries, grabbed the coke and her arm, elbowing his way out of there.

'I've been coming to this place for fifteen years and now I'm not sure I can ever show my face again.'

'Whyever not?'

She was genuinely astonished and he heaved a gigantic sigh. 'Never mind, Marla. And what's so important anyway?'

They were in her Mercedes now, at an expired meter on Pico. Al got out again and put a quarter in the meter. He climbed back in, slammed the door shut and took a long and necessary slug of the ice-cold Coke.

Marla licked the top of the egg salad. 'Mmm, yummy,' she said appreciatively.

'Best in town,' Al said as proud as if he owned the joint himself.

'I guess from your lousy demeanour you didn't have much success with Laurie's co-workers?'

Al finished his own Coke and sequestered hers. 'Marla you know what, you can be a real pain in the neck?'

'Who? Me?'

She batted her long eyelashes innocently at him and he shook his head. 'Honey, don't do that to me. This is business, remember? And I'm the boss.'

'Yes, sir.' She sat up smartly and the paper plate slid off her knee and landed, egg-salad-side down on Al's boots.'

She stared doubtfully at it. 'Look at it this way, the mayo will give your boots a nice shine, and it's better than on my black carpet.'

He took a deep breath. 'In case you haven't noticed, Marla,

I am now speaking through gritted teeth.' He scraped the egg salad off his boots with the paper plate and attempted to rub off the rest with the tiny shiny little diner napkin.

'Here,' Marla thrust a box of Kleenex at him. 'I'm learning,' she said mournfully. 'I've already apologised three times in the last fifteen minutes. OK, so here I go again. I'm sorry, Al.' And she leaned over and grabbed his face between her two rather eggy hands and planted a great kiss on his lips.

Their lips lingered and Al felt his heart do a couple of little leaps and bounds. Like a teenager on a first date, he thought happily, kissing her some more.

'So, what was so important anyways?' he said when she released him finally. Her green eyes had darkened and her lips looked bruised. God but she was beautiful – and sexy – he had to keep himself under control.

'I found Laurie's boyfriend.'

'And?' He leaned against the comfortable black leather pretending indifference, staring deliberately casual out of the window.

She slammed a fist into his arm.

'*Ouch*. Watch what you're doing, you could hurt a guy.' He was laughing at her and she knew it.

'OK, *Boss*, this is the scoop. Laurie Martin met a Mr John MacIver at the local Baptist church. She was wearing one of her house-dresses and he was wearing silver hair and Mr Magoo glasses and a walking cane. He's eighty-four and well off and she's in her thirties and playing some kind of game. Remember the serpent ring? Well, that's her engagement ring. He paid for it, she chose it.'

Al's low whistle expressed his astonishment. 'Then why wasn't she wearing it on the proper finger?'

'She didn't want anybody else to know, not yet. It was to be their secret. She wanted him to be sure he knew what he was doing. Besides, she didn't want people to talk about her. She's just a poor simple woman, alone and vulnerable in a big wide world.'

Al whistled again.

'Did I do good?' she asked, beaming.

'Honey, you did great.'

'Not only that, according to MacIver, Laurie's just about ready for sainthood, a good woman in the old-fashioned sense of the word was what he said. Reminded him of his dead wife, Imogen — and from Imogen's portrait I thought she looked like a real tough cookie. Hard as nails would be the way I would describe her.'

'What about him?'

'MacIver?' She thought for a minute. 'He's not a gentle sort of man, I don't know that I liked him much. But he was definitely the vulnerable one, old, alone, kind of doddery. He can hardly see and his hearing's bad. But both he and Gestapo loved her.'

'Gestapo?'

'A German Shepherd that was ready to rip me apart if I made one false move, but who apparently adored Laurie. Of course when she visited she was smart enough to bring him a juicey beef-bone to munch on, instead of on her leg. She also tapped MacIver for a few bucks — several thousands I imagine — for a so-called sister whose kid was in need of an operation, and for a children's charity she was supposedly active in at Christmas time.'

'Surprise, surprise.' Al leaned back with his eyes closed.

Marla stared at him, ready for the *coup de grâce*. 'She also told MacIver that he was the first man she had loved since her husband died, ten years ago.'

Al's eyes popped open and she grinned with satisfaction. 'Gotcha at last, Giraud,'

'A husband huh? And a sister with a kid? Life is getting more interesting, honey.'

'And *this* is Laurie Martin herself.' Triumphantly, she flourished the photograph of Laurie in the house-dress.

'Laurie's Life Number Two,' Al said examining it interestedly. 'And now I think I've also got an angle on Life Number Three.' He handed her a brown manilla envelope.

Marla opened it and looked at the photo of the little black mutt, Clyde, sitting on the bonnet of a car.'

'I had it enlarged,' Al said. 'Notice anything interesting.'

She shook her head. 'Nice dog, though, Cute in the red bandanna,'

'Cute Clyde is sitting on the hood of a Buick Regal vintage 1980. As an observant PI you might have noticed that it also has a Florida plate and the licence number is now quite clear.'

'Florida!' Marla remembered Laurie's condo with its pastel pink and turquoise Florida decor.

'So, guess where we begin our investigation, honey.'

'I always wanted to see South Beach,' she said.

Chapter Twenty

Al stared at the passing panorama outside his office window. Sleek California girls on roller blades, long blonde hair flying, long suntanned legs gliding rhythmically, earphones clamped over their heads, the latest in music destroying their eardrums 'even as we speak . . .' he remembered Ben Lister's use of that phrase and Marla's pick-up on it. The woman was a subversive no doubt about it, but she made him laugh.

A bearded guy on a red Ducati 916 – the fastest bike on the planet – throbbed at the stoplight waiting while an older woman in a flowing white dress adorned with baby-pink ribbons and a huge hat covered in matching pink roses tottered slowly on white stilettos across the road. A couple of expensive blonde women – were all Beverly Hills women blonde he wondered – smart in designer suits and lavish designer breasts, toting designer-labelled packages stepped into a waiting chauffered black limo. And at the café across the street a motley crew of young folk sipped iced mochaccinos and double lattes idly taking the world apart and putting it back together again more to their liking. Either that or they were gossiping about 'friends' who were not there. Gossip made the world go round, especially here in Hollywood. There would be a lot of people out of work if it were not for gossip.

And the traffic on Sunset just rolled on and on. A hooker twitching along in thigh-high red boots; hip-hop kids with shaven heads and baggy pants six sizes too large and so long they concertinaed over their sneakers the way Charlie Chaplin's used to; workers carrying lunchtime takeaways back to the office; teenagers heading for 'life' at Tower Records; and a never ending snaking parade of ordinary folk heading – who knows where?

Al turned from the window and looked again at the information he had just received on the car with the Florida licence plate. It had had several owners in Florida whose names meant nothing to him, and one in Texas whose name was also unfamiliar.

The Texas owner was definitely out. The car Al was interested in had a Florida plate. He smiled as he imagined Marla accompanying him there. Panama City was not exactly Miami and South Beach.

The phone rang and he grabbed it.

'Ben Lister, here. I just had a call from your friend, Detective Bulworth.'

'We're only friends when we're not working on the same case. Right now, he doesn't share any information with me.'

'Well he does with me. And the blood found in the car was not Steve's.'

Al whistled. A pleased grin spread over his blue-stubbled face – he had no shaving gear at Marla's place which is where he had ended up after a glamorous and horrifyingly expensive dinner at the Bel Air Hotel, watching swans float by and eating delectable food that he figured cost about ten bucks a bite. Marla had said he owed her for her good work on the John MacIver boyfriend situation. He'd given in easily enough. Sometimes you just had to pamper your woman, make her feel good . . . and boy had she looked good, and had she enjoyed it. And afterwards, they had enjoyed each other in an even more deliciously carnal way.

But he was digressing. 'Any idea whose blood it was then?'

'None. And they can't match it with Laurie's because there's no body. Yet.' Lister always added 'yet' because he firmly believed the body would turn up any minute now. 'They're still out there looking, as we speak,' he added.

Al laughed. 'Meanwhile, the cops don't seem able to come up with any concrete evidence against our client. It's purely circumstantial.'

'But there are no other suspects.'

'True. I guess I'll just have to find some for them.'

Lister said, 'You do that – buddy. Let me know how you get on.'

'Will do. And thanks for the good news, Lister. I appreciate it.'

Al glanced at his black Olympics-95 Swatch-watch – the one Marla despised, along with the Corvette – then dialled her carphone. She answered at once and he heard the rumble of traffic as she said loudly, 'Hello?'

'Hi, honey.' He knew she was on the speaker.

'I'm in traffic,' she yelled, 'you have to speak up.'

'Put the windows up Marla. And pick up the phone.'

'What?'

He ran a hand exasperatedly through his thick dark hair. 'Honey, I said put your windows up. Then you'll be able to hear me. I mean they make those Mercs practically soundproof, don't they?'

'Better than old Corvettes anyway.' She had put up the windows and was on the phone and coming through loud and clear now. 'What's up, *honey?*'

'The blood found in the Lexus is not Steve's.'

'Whoopeee . . . then he's off the hook?'

'Not exactly. It's probably Laurie's blood but they're unable to do any tests.'

'Because they have none of her blood to compare it with.'

'Marla, sometimes you're so smart I just don't believe you.'

'Listen, you bastard, I'm only a *trainee* private eye, remember? And you have been in business for fifteen years. Give me a break, why don't you?'

'OK, so here's the deal. I'm on my way to Florida.' He flinched as he heard the screech of brakes.

'You're what?'

'I'm on a one-thirty flight via Atlanta.'

'What happened to Miami?'

'This auto didn't come from Miami babe, it's from Panama City.'

'Mmm, doesn't sound like my kind of town,' she said doubtfully.

He grinned, 'Of course, if you'd care to come along . . . ?'

'No . . . no, I think I'll let you take care of this one. *Boss*. Sure you can manage without me?'

'Honey, I'll do my darndest.'

Her voice dropped to a purr. 'I'll miss you tonight, though, Giraud. I'll be lying in my big lonely bed, thinking of you . . . remembering last night . . .'

'Hold on to that memory, honey. I'll be back in your bed real soon.'

'Promise?'

'Well now, I'm not a promising kinda guy, but I am a betting man and the odds are ten to one.'

'I'll take 'em, she said laughing. And take care, Giraud. Don't get into any trouble without me.'

He said he would try not to then put down the phone, picked up his bag, locked up his office with the glass door that said who he was and *Private Investigator All Work Confidential* – just like in a forties movie. Then he strolled across Sunset and joined the young folks drinking lattes in the café, except he ordered a double espresso. A guy had to do something to combat lack-of-cigarette fatigue.

Panama City was a little seaside town with that flat-fronted, low-rise prefabricated Florida look about it. The sun blazed in a cloudless hard-blue sky, grilling through Al's T-shirt until he felt like a kebab approaching medium rare. It was definitely not his kinda town, let alone Marla's.

He'd spent the night in the kind of cheerless motel he wished he had only read about, and was driving a rental car he could have lived without. It was a conspicuous and particularly hideous shade of electric blue, the steering was loose and the brakes slow and his heart ached for the red Corvette.

Plus the motel had been the kind with holes in the screens that let in droves of mosquitoes. It had doors that rattled and flapped in the hot wind, and a neon sign that flickered green and red all night through his flimsy window shade. Humphrey Bogart never had it this bad.

But the folks were nice in Panama City and it didn't take him long to find the information he wanted. A Buick Regal with that licence plate had belonged to a marine based in Pensacola. Marine James H. Victor. Only trouble was, Jimmy Victor was dead. Died in a tragic fire in his trailer about six years ago. It was in all the newspapers at the time.

The local Pensacola newspaper had carried it in a couple of editions and Giraud read them both, ensconced in the archives, sneezing with the dust of ages flying off the pages along with the story.

Apparently the propane tank had exploded, leading to a conflagration. Jimmy's wife, the former Bonnie Hoyt of Gainesville, Florida, had been out walking the dog at the time. She had come runing back but the trailer was already engulfed. They said how brave she was, she had tried to drag him out of there and had gotten quite a few burns herself in the process. Jimmy's body was found half-in and half-out the door.

He had been buried in Pensacola and when Al found the cemetery only a plain headstone with his name and the dates of his birth and death marked the spot. There were no flowers, no grass, no shade trees. Only the relentless Florida sun to burn Jimmy all over again.

From experience, Giraud knew that the place to find any information – especially in a naval town – was the nearest bar. This one was dark and secretive. Half a dozen pool tables took up the back of the large room with shaded lights hung low over the green baize and a few guys lounging around waiting to take their shot. The long scarred wooden bar had a shiny layer of acrylic varnish that failed to obliterate decades of stains. Peanuts and pretzels were definitely not served along with the Budweiser at this establishment. You were lucky if you got a paper coaster.

Al slid onto a stool and ordered a draught Bud from the tough-looking woman behind the bar. Her hair was what had once been known as strawberry-blonde, a kind of reddish-gold fluffed to immense heights then falling in a cascade of curls down to her shoulder blades. Her ice-blue eyes were rimmed in black pencil and her lipstick was a shiny pink, generously applied. She had the look of a sixties teenager grown middle-aged without ever changing her style.

Al leaned an elbow on the bar, swivelling on his stool, checking out the action. It was late afternoon. Not the busiest time. He hoped he wouldn't have to hang around here too long, drinking Bud and possibly wasting his life. Meanwhile, there were few customers at the bar.

He turned back to the barkeeper. 'You worked here long, honey?'

She favoured him with a glossy pink smile. Apparently she was not bothered about sexual harassment. Al guessed it came with the job.

'Sure have, mister. Around ten years now. Once my kids were grown I got myself out of that house and out of that marriage and into this job. Best move I ever made.'

'Sounds good.' He sipped the beer.

'I ain't seen you here before?'

'I'm just passin' through, as you might say. I was hoping you might know about a friend of mine. A guy called Jimmy Victor. Knew him a long time ago, when he was a kid. Heard he'd become a marine and then he was killed in a fire in his trailer . . .'

'Sure I remember that. A few years back it was, though. It was in all the papers – and on TV.'

Al took a good slug of the beer. 'He have many friends out here?'

'Sure. He was a popular kinda guy, y'know what I mean? Good-lookin', all the girls were after him.'

'I thought he was a married man.'

She gave him another pink smile and a broad wink. 'Isn't everybody?'

'I guess you're right there,' Al laughed with her. He resisted glancing at his watch and thinking about the next flight out. 'You know where I could get in touch with some of his friends. I'd kinda like to hear about him, you know, for old time's sake.

She frowned with the effort of thinking, patting her lacquer-stiff golden-red curls gently. 'Well now, they don't come in here so much. I think you might find a couple of them, though, over at the Fishin' Shak, a few blocks down the street. Marty Knudsen used to hang out there with Jimmy, I know. And Frankie Alford.'

'Thanks, hon. I'll be sure to give that a try.'

He paid for his drink with a ten, told her to keep the change and found himself on the receiving end of another glossy pink smile.

The Fishin' Shak was much the same only without the pool tables. This was strictly a drinking joint despite the phony fishing nets and dusty lobster pots cluttering up the wood-plank walls. The whole place, including the makeshift bar looked as though it had been cobbled together from four-by-twos and felt as though the powerful air-conditioning might just pick it up and blow it away like a hurricane.

The barkeeper this time was a guy, older and wiser and a bruiser. His broken nose and pudgy fists pegged him as an ex-boxer and his shaven head as a man who followed trends. Either that or he belonged to a white supremacist skinhead group.

Again Al ordered a beer, asked if he knew Frankie Alford or Marty Knudson.

'Who's askin'?'

Al remembered Marla's technique and tried a winning smile. It got him nowhere. 'A friend.'

'So how come you're so friendly if I ain't never seen you here before?'

'I'm a friend of a friend. An old buddy of Jimmy Victor's. We palled around together there for a while. Before he was killed in the fire. I was in town and remembered he was stationed here. Just kinda wanted to hear about him. How it happened. Where he's laid to rest, so I can pay my respects. That kinda thing.'

The barkeeper stared at him for a long time, head lowered like a bull about to charge and Al was glad of the width of the bar counter between them. Then he lifted his head, flicked his eyes over Al's shoulder and called out, 'Hey, Frankie, here's a guy says he knew Jimmy Victor real well.'

'Oh yeah?'

Frankie was tall, beefy and about thirty-five years old, with a cropped marine haircut and a face red from too much sun and a great deal of booze.

Al offered his hand. 'How're ya doin? Name's Al Giraud. I knew Jimmy way back when, before he even got into the marines. Knew his family too. Kinda lost touch later, though. Our lives took different paths so to speak. I was just passing through town and I remembered this was where he had died. Wanted to pay him a visit, at the cemetery y'know. Pay my final respects.'

'Oh. Oh, sure. I understand.' The marine squeezed the hell out of Al's hand and let it drop. 'Good guy, Jimmy. Terrible, what happened to him. Jesus, I can only imagine the hell he went through . . .'

'You went to the funeral?'

'Sure. His wife and a couple of us buddies were the only mourners. As far as I knew he had no family. Oh and the little black mutt – Clyde, she called him – was there. Always wore a red bandanna. Bonnie took him everywhere.'

Al ordered up a couple more beers. 'What was the wife like?'

'Bonnie?' He shrugged. 'Dark hair, dark eyes. Kinda strange if you want the truth. Something about the way she looked at you. But a good body, nice legs. Jimmy cheated on her all the time y'know. Couldn't keep his hands off any woman. He was a good-lookin' guy. Anyhow, Jimmy heard Bonnie had taken up with someone else. They were always arguing, him and her. Never saw her again though, after the funeral.'

Al asked for directions to the cemetery. He had already seen Jimmy's grave but he asked just to keep up the charade. He bought another round for the barkeeper and Frankie Alford, wished them goodbye and was on his way.

Well, well, well he thought with a big grin on his face as he drove hell for leather – or as fast as the electric-blue rental car would push it, to the airport at Pensacola, hoping to make it in time to catch the six o'clock flight to Atlanta. *Bonnie and Clyde.* Did he have a lot to tell Marla.

Chapter Twenty-one

Sometimes, Marla thought impatiently, being a private eye was just plain boring. Like now, for instance. Al had delegated her to search out every blood bank in the San Diego area to see whether Laurie Martin had ever given blood. Armed with her credentials as Steve Mallard's attorney, Marla had spent two days doing just that. She needn't have bothered, the police had been there before her and with the same negative result.

She burned rubber on her way back to LA, bitching mentally about being sent on a fool's errand. Sometimes she wondered if Giraud really knew what he was doing.

Her car phone beeped and she snatched it up.

'Hi, honey, how're y'doin'?'

Al's voice had a breezy tone that she knew meant he had something up his sleeve. 'Thanks to you I've had a terrific day, hanging out in hospitals and watching people donating blood. How could you ask me to do this Al, you know I can't stand the sight of blood.'

'Put you off your lunch, did it, honey? Well, never mind, I'll treat you to dinner tonight.'

'Well thanks a lot!' Then, 'Where?' she asked, suddenly interested.

'Typhoon? Meet you there about seven-thirty?'

'You'd better be on time,' she said suspiciously.

He laughed. 'Sure I will. If *you* will.' He was still laughing as she slammed down the phone.

Typhoon was an interesting little place built into the second floor of an old aircraft hanger overlooking the runway at Santa Monica Airport. Entertainment was provided by the cute little incoming Cessnas and the lavish private jets decanting rock stars and businessmen and sometimes movie actors, as well as by the sun setting in a blaze of gold and red over the not too distant Pacific Ocean. The martinis were good and the food an eclectic mix of California-Pacific Rim including Thai spring rolls and curries, whole crispy-fried catfish in an Oriental sauce, Singapore spicy noodles and All-American tiny spareribs. Plus an interesting section of the menu labelled 'Insects,' though Giraud had never yet seen anybody partake of a locust or a grasshopper.

Marla was deliberately late. He'd known she would be and he propped up yet another bar, drinking an icy cold Asahi beer – his favourite after Samuel Adams and quite different – dry and crisp as opposed to syrupy and smooth.

Heads turned as they always did when Marla strode into the restaurant. Her blonde hair was pulled back Spanish-flamenco-dancer-style in a knot at the nape of her slender neck. Delicate tendrils drifted round her oval face and she had on the small round Armani tortoiseshell glasses – only they were sunglasses this time. Marla always complained that the angle of the sun at Typhoon bothered her – until it had set that is. She wore a long black skirt and a soft white linen shirt rolled at the sleeves and shiny black JP Tod flats. Tonight she looked, Al thought, like a very tall ballerina.

As always, she threw her arms round him and kissed him soundly. 'Missed you,' she murmured gazing into his eyes through her darkened lenses.

'Missed you too, hon.' He unwound her arms from his neck, aware of the grins of the other people at the bar.

When they were seated at a table near the window he ordered her a vodka martini and himself another Asahi. She stared out the window at the sleek little Eagle jet streaking by. 'When are we going to make enough money to afford one of those, instead of having to take flights via Atlanta?'

'I guess maybe when *you* get to be as good as *I* am at my job.'

She heaved a genuine sigh. 'I hated today. I got exactly nowhere.'

'I think maybe I can tell you why you got nowhere.'

Her eyes popped open in surprise that changed to a glare. 'You mean you sent me on a wild goose chase? You *knew* I would find nothing. And here I was hanging out in hospital corridors all day. I still smell of Lysol even after a shower . . .'

'Marla, Marla, let me tell you what happened.' She sipped the martini while Al filled her in on the Jimmy and Bonnie Victor situation. And the little dog named Clyde.'

'Bonnie and Clyde.' she said, astonished.

'You got it, honey. The bad girl and boy of the thirties.'

'You think Bonnie is Laurie Martin?'

He nodded. 'That's just what I think.'

'So why did she change her name? I mean, she didn't kill her husband. They said she tried to save him, dragged him out of the burning trailer . . .'

'I don't know why she changed her name but I'm willing to bet it's because she had something to hide.'

'But her papers, social security, drivers licence, credit . . . it's all in the name of Laurie Martin.'

'Unfortunately, honey, these days that's not too difficult to arrange. All you have to do is go downtown, drive along Alvarado Street and you'll be offered anything you want. From phony green cards to phony drivers licences and phony social security. All it costs is money – and not too much of that.'

'Al,' she frowned as she thought about it, 'what if they never find her body?'

'Then Steve Mallard gets away with it. But I have a hunch that a woman like Laurie, aka Bonnie, was by nature a devious soul, one who always covered her tracks even when there was no apparent danger. It was just second nature to her. Why don't you check those blood banks again tomorrow, Marla? See if anyone named Bonnie Victor donated blood. It's a wild card but you never know.'

'Why would she risk donating blood though? I mean, why bother?'

Al shrugged. 'Perhaps seeing her husband die like that made her aware of the need for blood in emergency situations. Maybe *her own* emergency situation one day. Why does anyone give blood?'

'Same reason,' Marla agreed.

They nibbled on the miniature ribs and fried calamari, picked at the sweet-flesh catfish and devoured delicious greenbeans in some kind of sauce, while Al told Marla about the motel outside Panama City and the bars. 'You wouldn't have liked it, hon,' he concluded.

'You know me so well,' she mocked, getting up and heading for the ladies room.

While he waited for her, Al watched the aircraft gliding gracefully onto the runway. He thought maybe Marla had a point. When was he gonna make enough to afford one of those things?

Chapter Twenty-two

The call from Lister came just before six a.m. Marla groaned sleepily, covering her ears with her hands and wrapping her long legs around Al to prevent him from moving.

'Let it ring,' she moaned, 'it's too early.'

'Honey, nobody's getting out of bed to call me at this time in the morning unless he's got something to say.' He wrestled away from her and picked up the phone.'

'Giraud, they've found the body.'

He recognized Ben Lister's voice. 'Where?'

'Cadaver dogs sniffed it out. Near the bottom of a canyon, further away from where they were originally searching. The terrain's difficult, it'll take a while to get her up. Plus after all this time – and the rain, who knows what state she's in.'

'I'm on my way. I'll check with Bulworth en route and get back to you.'

Giraud was already throwing on his clothes. Marla leapt out of bed and grabbed ahold of him. 'Wait, wait, what's happened?'

'They've found the body in a canyon. I have to get over there right away.'

'I'm coming with you.' She stepped into her underwear, dragged on the black skirt from last night and pulled his grey Russell Athletic sweatshirt over her head. She heard the rain drumming on the roof and groaned. A remote canyon in the pouring rain. Great.

In no time they were back at Santa Monica airport, only now they were climbing into the chartered four-seater Cessna Al had arranged over the car phone, looking back at Typhoon as they soared into the sky on their way to San Diego and Laguna. There was, Al said, no time to lose.

The rain was coming down in a solid sheet giving the fire rescue services a blurred ghostly image, like deep-sea divers in their helmets and boots. It had been several weeks since Laurie's disappearance and the body was by now badly decomposed, adding to their difficulties.

'It'll take the guys forever to scrape up the pieces.' Bulworth muttered, pacing the rim of the canyon like a sergeant major directing manoeuvres.

Marla, in a shiny licorice-black slicker, and a matching fisherman's sou'wester, gulped, trying not to think about what he had just said. The cadaver dogs had done their duty and were warm and dry in the back of the K-9 Division wagon, and she only wished she could join them.

'They're coming up,' Bulworth yelled, and the guy from the Coroner's office started up his wagon and edged closer, ready to take away the remains for autopsy, and the PD photographers switched on their lights and focused their videos and still-cameras. Laurie Martin was about to star in her own version of a Hollywood B-movie.

Even in a bodybag the smell of decomposing human flesh saturated the air as the rescue squad finally hauled it over the edge. Marla's stomach did an about-turn and she gritted her teeth, willing herself not to throw up.

You'll never live it down she warned herself, you'll shame yourself as well as Giraud and in front of Bulworth and that toughie Pow! Powers and all those brave guys out there with nerves and stomachs of steel. Giraud will never let you work with him again ...

Al was standing near the coroner's wagon, speaking to Bulworth. He stalked back to her through the mud, looking at her through the sheet of rain.

She raised her eyebrows. 'What now?' she asked in a voice that trembled.

'I vote for a cup of coffee,' he said grimly, leading the way back to the rented Explorer.

Hot strong coffee in a steamy-windowed Starbucks put Marla's stomach back on normal and she breathed a huge sigh of relief.

'You did great, honey.' Al reached out and patted her hand gently. 'That was definitely not pleasant. I shouldn't have allowed you to come with me.'

'What? And miss that plane ride?' She managed a wobbly grin. Was it our girl, Giraud?'

'The body was too far gone to be sure who it was. They'll do an autopsy later today. They'll have to go on dental records, check the DNA with the blood in the car.'

'Meanwhile ...' He fished the cellphone from his jeans pocket, took out Marla's list of blood banks and dialled the first number.

She sipped the coffee, burning her throat and listening to Al's conversation.

Finally, he clicked the 'End' button. His eyes met hers. 'Got it in one,' he said quietly. 'Bonnie Victor donated blood two months ago.'

'Then we can check it right away,' she said eagerly.

'Not so fast, hon. That batch of plasma is on an oil tanker bound for Hawaii.'

Her eyes opened even wider. 'Then is anyone trying to get the darned stuff back?'

'You betcha,' Al said, already calling Bulworth. *'Even as we speak,* baby.'

They spent the night at the Ritz in Laguna Niguel, the same place where they had first seen Laurie Martin with Steve Mallard.

Only now, Marla thought, uneasily, Laurie was just a mass of rotted flesh – and Steve Mallard was hiding out from his wife and family – and the police – up in Arrow-head.

The rain still poured, lashing the windows in an early tropical storm recently downgraded from Hurricane Dora but still giving Baja and the southern California coast a touch of its fury. White-caps dotted the surging tide and it was definitely the kind of night for a cosy fire, a good bottle of red and some comfort food. The Ritz provided all that – and then some.

Snug in their suite, wrapped in the hotel's white terry robes, Marla and Al sipped Mondavi Cabernet Reserve in front of the fire, feasting on char-grilled steak and garlic mashed potatoes, waiting for the phone to ring. That is, Al feasted on the steak. Unfortunately, Marla's thoughts were still on Laurie/Bonnie in the bodybag and she picked at the mashed potatoes wondering if she would now have to become a vegerarian.

Meanwhile, in San Diego, Bulworth was pacing the shiny grey corridor outside the Coroner's Department, gulping bad coffee from a styrofoam cup, waiting for the results of the autopsy taking place behind closed doors. He was permitted inside the room but he didn't have the stomach the pathologist had. A body was one thing. Remains were quite another.

Not so, Pow! Powers. She was in there, doing her duty and enjoying every minute of it because every minute brought her closer to arresting Steve Mallard. Homicide was Pow's game and she never got over the thrill of pinning the right crime on the right person. It was, she felt, something she had been born to do and she watched fascinated as stomach contents were extracted, weighed and evaluated; and fragments of rotted flesh – sliding from the bones – were examined and numbered; and jaws inspected and photos taken of the teeth and dental work.

But still she wasn't prepared for the end result.

It was two in the morning when the call finally came from Bulworth.

Marla was sleeping on the sofa, her head in Giraud's lap and she stirred uneasily. They had been up since six the previous day and even Giraud was beginning to experience what felt like jet lag.

'Giraud,' he answered softly so as not to disturb her.

'OK, so prepare yourself for this one,' Bulworth said grimly. 'The body is not that of Laurie Martin.'

'And how do we know that without checking the blood, the DNA?'

'Because, my friend, this body is a guy. A male Caucasian, aged around forty.'

'Al whistled, disappointed and Marla came suddenly to life. 'Like a pet dog answering his master's whistle,' she thought, instantly awake. 'What's up? she added as Al put down the phone.

Al told her.

She stared blankly at him. 'So what happens now?'

'I guess we just have to keep on looking. Meanwhile, they are going to have to check out the dead man's DNA, his hair, blood, body fluids, skin, prints — if there are any left, to try to identify the guy. As well as check the missing persons records.' He frowned impatiently. 'It'll all take time. And meanwhile, we are no further along.'

'There's still Laurie/Bonnie's plasma on the tanker heading for Hawaii,' she said helpfully.

Al had temporarily forgotten that and now he smiled, lifting an eyebrow the way she loved, deep blue eyes gazing into hers. 'You're right, Marla Cwitowitz, Assistant PI,' he agreed, kissing her. 'And there's also the fact that Bonnie Victor took off immediately after her husband's funeral. And the next place the Buick Regal surfaced was in Falcon City, Texas.

'Which is where you're going next,' she said resignedly. 'I might have known it.'

Chapter Twenty-three

The deep silence of night settled over Vickie Mallard's little house. She strained her ears, listening. Even the usual annoying roar of the freeway would be welcome, but tonight it was only a distant whisper. Suburban San Fernando Valley was sleeping. All except her.

She switched on the TV. Not that there was anything she wanted to watch, even if she could concentrate on a programme — which these days she couldn't because her own gigantic problems crowded into her mind eclipsing anything and everything else. Still, it provided background noise. She couldn't stand the silence. Just couldn't take one more lonely night.

She took another shower, her third that evening, put on a clean T-shirt, a pair of flannel boxers and the terry bathrobe with the pink hearts on it that Steve had bought her last Valentine's Day, tying the sash with a vicious tug as she remembered him.

Since she had got the court restraining order the news hounds had been forced to keep their distance, and now at least the neighbours had stopped complaining. Her girls were still with her sister. They were getting along OK, hanging out with their cousins and attending school. But they were heartbreakingly different children, subdued, all joy gone, keeping close to the house and rarely venturing out after classes. Vickie saw them every day of course, but boy, how she missed them. Missed knowing they were tucked up in bed in their rooms at the other end of the hall; missed their squabbles; missed Taylor's 'what is there to eat in this house anyway?'; missed Mellie's whining about wanting the next Beanie Baby, or whatever ...'

Steve's new lawyer, Ben Lister was tough. And so was Al Giraud, though personally she would rather deal with Ms Marla Cwitowitz. She still didn't trust Giraud somehow. She didn't know about men like him. It was Marla who kept her informed, Marla who had told her that tempers and frustration were simmering at the SDPD. And that Lister wouldn't let the cops talk to Steve any more. 'If they had any concrete evidence against Steve,' Marla had said, 'they would have arrested him by now.'

Vickie supposed they did not. She wished she could be as sure as Marla seemed to be, though.

God, but she was lonely. She paced downstairs, flicked on the over-the-counter lights, staring round her pretty kitchen. They had bought the house because of this kitchen with its attached family room. She had fallen in love with the big fireplace and the sliding windows opening onto the pool area with its barbecue, and with the pale-blond wood cabinets and deep-blue tile counters. She had thought it looked kind of Mediterranean, reminding her of constantly blue-skies and sunshine and happiness. Which, she thought sadly, just goes to show you.

She opened the refrigerator. Closed it again. Opened cupboards, tidied a few shelves. Her brain was working overtime, worrying about Steve. Did he? Or didn't he? God, she couldn't stand not knowing, couldn't take Steve's silence. He never called her any more, though she knew he was still in Arrowhead because Marla had told her so. She couldn't take this empty house, her now-empty life. She needed to talk to someone ... anyone ...

Snatching up the phone, she dialled Marla's number. *Oh be home, please, please be home*, she prayed, as it rang endlessly ...

'Giraud, what are you doing up this late in Falcon City?' Marla answered.

'Marla, it's Vickie Mallard.'

Surprised, Marla glanced at her watch. It was late, twelve-fifteen. She was just about to turn out the lights. 'What is it, Vickie?'

'Marla I can't stand it, I can't take the loneliness, not knowing ...'

Marla recognised the familiar note of hysteria in Vickie's voice. It was there every time she spoke with her.

'I need to talk, Marla ... do you think you could come round ... there's stuff I just have to tell you, about Steve ...'

'Put up the coffee, Vickie. I'll be right there.'

This was what a PI's life was all about, Marla thought, throwing on a pair of jeans, a black sweatshirt, sneakers. Midnight assignations, secrets discussed until dawn ... Vickie must have something new to tell her.

On her way out she picked up a bottle of wine. It might be a better idea than the coffee ... loosen Vickie up a bit.

Suddenly hungry, Vickie fixed herself a bagel with lox and cream cheese and put up the coffee. The TV mumbled in the background and she clicked through the channels looking for a newscast, which was all she watched these days.

Her ears pricked up. Was that the door? Could Marla be here already? She pressed the TV mute button and swung round, listening. There it was again.

'Marla?' she called. The silence was different now, so dense she seemed to breathe it like a texture in the air. Her heart thundered and her mouth was suddenly dry as the desert. Panicked, she turned, reached for the phone.

The hissing came from behind her, like a wildcat, then strong hands clamped around her throat ... *she wanted to scream, she wanted to scream so bad* ... A gloved hand smacked over her mouth.

Hot panic flashed with adrenaline up her spine ... she was bursting for air, the top of her head was going to blow off ... She was choking now, her tongue stuck from her gaping mouth and she could taste her own blood ...

This can't be happening to me, it can't ... his hands are choking the life out of me ... I'm losing the battle ... Oh God help me ...

An image of Taylor suddenly flashed to the front of her mind, and Mellie too, so clear it was as though they were there ... *she had to fight, she had to see her babies again ...* With new strength,

125

she kicked backwards, jammed her elbows into his stomach, felt the grip on her throat slacken. Again she punched back ... heard a gasp like a punctured balloon. Gulping air, she swung round ...

And oh God, oh God ... now he had a knife ... a fury in a black ski mask, mad eyes burning with hate into hers ... stabbing at her, hissing with the effort of each blow ... arm raised again ... and again ... and again ...

From a long way away she heard herself whimpering ... it was the last sound she heard ...

Marla parked in the Mallard's short driveway. She glanced round the quiet street. A couple of cars were parked in the road and, PI-style she made a mental note of them: a black Explorer and a blue Accura. Most of the lights were out in the houses and she thought with a smile of kids in bed, of getting up early for the school drive, of juggling work and babysitters. Oh the joys of young married life where work never ends.

A lamp was on somewhere in the back of the Mallard house, she could see the glow through the curtains. Standing on the front step, she rang the bell. No reply. She rang again, peering at the curtained window. Vickie was expecting her – so where was she?

She tried the door. It was locked. Frustrated, she opened the side-gate and walked to the back of the house. The light was coming from the kitchen. She rang the bell, still no reply. She frowned. That was odd. Perhaps Vickie had gone to the bathroom, maybe she was on the phone ... maybe with Steve. She peered through the side window but could see nothing.

To her surprise, the back door was open. She peered down the dark hallway.

'Vickie,' she called loudly, 'it's me, Marla.'

She couldn't say exactly why she walked on tiptoe except the house was so darned silent it made the back of her neck bristle. She was glad when she got to the softly-lighted kitchen. 'Vickie?' she called again, tentatively this time, putting the bottle of wine on the counter.

And then she saw the bagel and lox on the floor – and something else – a discarded ragdoll, arms outflung. Only this was no doll. It was Vickie. *Lying in a great pool of red . . . Blood was pulsing from her neck, her chest, her arms . . .*

The scream erupted from somewhere deep inside. Marla hadn't known she could ever make a sound like this . . . fear, anguish, horror . . .

Was it a faint indrawn breath she heard or pure instinct that sent her whirling round – and right into the arms of the masked figure standing behind her . . . a tall, thin man . . .

Fear was hot – not cold as she had always imagined, flashing up her spine like a flame.

She screamed again and he slammed a hand over her mouth, snapping her head backwards. Her teeth sank into her lower lip and she tasted fresh blood . . . and then he hit her again, rocking her head back once more . . .

The fight-or-flee adrenaline surged through her veins, her heart thundered and she jolted upright, mad as hell. He was reaching for her, his right arm raised, she caught a glimpse of the bloody knife . . . *The same knife with which he had killed Vickie.*

Fury blinded her, she didn't know what she was doing, only that it was him or her and she wasn't ready to die yet. She smacked her knee viciously into his groin, dodged the downsweep of the knife, shrieked with rage as she jammed her fingers into his eyes. She heard his howl of pain . . . a howl that matched her own as she fought for her life . . . the way she knew Giraud would have expected her to . . .

She jerked away from him, dodged round the kitchen counter, with him right behind her. She was on top of the counter already sliding over the other side. He grabbed the back of her sweatshirt and she was dangling over the counter's edge throttled by her own shirt. Then she felt the knife slash down her arm and the warm silkiness of rushing blood. Oh God she hated blood, hated the sight of it, the slick feel of it, the iron smell of it . . . nausea swept over her, she was going to faint.

Dazed, she lifted her head. And looked straight into her

attacker's eyes, dark coals flickering with hate. And she knew she was looking into evil.

Crazed with pain and fear, somehow she slid out of the sweatshirt and fell, half-naked, to the floor on the opposite side of the counter. He was quick though, and agile. Before she could get to her feet he had straddled her ... again she jammed her thumbs into his eyes, heard his hiss of pain. He grabbed the wine bottle from the kitchen counter. She saw it coming at her as if in slow motion ... then faster and faster ...

Chapter Twenty-four

Falcon City near Laredo, Texas was hot and dry enough to scare up a thirst in a dead man. It shimmered in the midday heat looking like a scene from a western as Giraud, in a Jeep Wrangler this time – they went in for the more sporty-type vehicle in San Antonio where he had rented it – bowled down the highway that went right through the middle of town and out the other end. It was gone before he had even realised it was there. He stared back over his shoulder, saw a single palm tree and a glint of water. Maybe it was just a mirage. The traditional oasis-in-the-desert type.

He checked the highway. Nothin'. Swung the Jeep round and chugged back into town.

Main Street, Falcon City was lined with typical store-front establishments, anchored at one end by a supermarket and a drugstore and at the other by a mini-mall. In between were Blick's Hardware; Toys'n'More; King Ho's Chinese Restaurant and Take-Out; a Burger Boy; Lucille's Fabrics and Sewing; Corky's Chilli Parlour – and like that. Plus, a car dealership, Marston's Autos and Body Shop. Giraud's eyes swivelled left as he drove by, checking it out. He wondered whether Bonnie had traded in the Buick there. But first he needed to talk to the woman who now owned the car.

Miss Gwynneth Arden lived in a small brown-shingled ranch house overhung by a giant eucalyptus tree whose peeling bark revealed a trail of black widow spiders skittering rapidly upwards. Standing on the rickety front-porch ringing the doorbell, Giraud wondered if Ms Arden knew about them. He didn't know any woman who was fond of spiders and Black Widows were not exactly the kind with which any household wanted to be infested.

As he wiped the sweat off the back of his neck he now understood why all those cowboys wore bandannas. It wasn't just a sartorial trend, it kept the sweat from running down the back of their shirts.

Behind the dusty screen, the front door stood open but all he could see was a blank wall about four feet away, which in his experience made it the smallest front hall ever. An old-fashioned sepia picture of Jesus in a crown of thorns and a blazing heart – hand-tinted in living-colour – hung on the wall to greet Miss Arden's visitors. She certainly let you know what to expect, he thought, ringing the bell again.

'Hello?' He pushed open the screen door, stuck his head inside. A smell of must and church incense tickled his nostrils, making him sneeze, and a small black cat rustled quickly past him and out the door.

'Come on in, come in,' a woman's deep voice commanded. 'If that's you again, Jackson Miller, you can put the groceries on the kitchen counter and tell your ma I'll see her at the bingo hall this evenin'. OK?'

Even though he wasn't Jackson Miller, Giraud stepped inside. To the left of the four-foot-square hallway was a kitchen. A sink spilling over with dirty dishes, countertops piled with empty cartons, cat bowls, Coke-cans and clutter of all kinds. A cat litter box desperately in need of cleaning, and a linoleum floor that had been there for a couple of decades and was now worn to an indistinguishable mottled brown.

To the right was a living room. Miss Arden was parked on an ancient green velvet Barcalounger in front of the TV set blasting what must be a riveting episode of *Days Of Our Lives*, because she didn't even turn to see if Jackson Miller had put the groceries in the kitchen, or who the hell it was standing in her front hall. Another large Jesus picture hung over the brick fireplace and half a dozen candles burned in front of a prie-dieu with a small shrine dedicated to the Madonna. The smell of incense and cats was staggering but Giraud guessed you got used to anything after a while.

All he could see was the back of Miss Arden's head. 'Excuse me, ma'am, Miss Arden,' he said loudly over the TV, 'I'd like to talk to you about something.'

'What?' Her gaze never wavered from the screen and he stepped further into the room, came round in front so she could see him.

'Excuse, me Miss Arden, I've come about your car.'

She was immensely fat in an orange and blue muu-muu and with a home-dye-job that had left her hair blacker than any crow. She wore a blue bow in her hair, fluffy blue slippers on her fat feet and pale plastic eyeglasses propped on the end of her tiny nose. Her rosebud mouth was coloured orange to match her outfit – though Giraud guessed with Miss Arden's taste, it could just as easily have been blue.

'Wait a minute,' she waved her little banana-fingered hand impatiently. 'Can't you see I'm watching this?'

Al waited, trying not to breathe too deeply. Between the litter box and the incense and the heat it was enough to choke even the strongest stomach. Five minutes passed then the final credits rolled.

Gwynneth Arden sat up in her Barcalounger and peered over her shoulder at him. 'Who're you and waddya want?' she snapped, her gimlet-eyes taking him in from behind the glasses.

Al didn't blame her for snapping; after all a stranger was standing right there in her living room. It occurred to him that he was in frontierland and she might very well have a shotgun next to her in that Barcalounger. He explained himself quickly. 'Sorry to disturb you, ma'am, but I wanted to talk to you about your car. A 1986 Buick Regal ...'

'I know what my automobile is. And why're you askin' anyhow?'

'We're trying to trace the previous owner of that vehicle, Miss Arden. Could you tell me who you purchased it from?'

'*Who?* It weren't no "*who*". I got it from Harmons, the car dealers, six or seven years ago now.' She was already clicking through the channels to her next programme but Giraud knew to be patient. After all, she wasn't obliged to answer any of his questions if she didn't want to.

'The car dealership on Main Street? I thought that was Marston's.'

Her tiny eyes flicked over him for a second before she turned back to the television. 'Not from round here, are ya?'

'No, ma'am, I'm not . . .'

'Else you woulda known Harmons went outta business a few years back.'

Shit, Giraud thought. That took care of that – there was no way to check the records of a now-defunct auto dealership. And Miss Arden obviously had nothing more to say. Her antennae were already tuned in to the next episode of *General Hospital*. He said thank you and goodbye but doubted she even heard him.

Outside, he took a few deep breaths and dusted himself off, feeling as though the smells of the house had adhered to him. He noticed the black widow spiders, four or five of them, not moving as he walked past. His skin crawled, he could almost feel the poisonous little bastards' eyes, watching him.

Now what, he thought in the Jeep driving slowly along the backroads into town. He had reached a dead end; there was no flight out of San Antonio until tomorrow and he was out here in the boondocks in a hundred and ten degrees with no bar in sight. Soon he would be hallucinating a bottle of Samuel Adams, frosted-droplets dripping down its icy sides. Meanwhile, he would have to make do with a Coke from the machine at the Chevron station.

He drank it down, bought another and a packet of barbecue potato chips. Lunch Texas-style, he thought gloomily, eating them in the hot Jeep, wondering what to do next. He needed a shower and some sleep, then maybe his brain would come in from the heat and begin to function again.

Of course the motel was named 'The Bluebird', and of course it looked pretty much like Miss Arden's ranch house only bigger,

132

and the smells here were of must and Pinesol instead of cats. An electronic fly-zapper in the stuffy reception room buzzed incessantly and this time the TV was tuned into a racetrack. He watched interestedly for a minute or two while a sway-backed chestnut bolted from the back of the herd and headed like a homing missile for the finishing line.

'Good mover, that mare,' he said approvingly.

'Yeah, owned by a local family, the Harmons. She looks like hell but she sure can run. Just made myself a few bucks on her. Y'can trust her to make it over three furlongs, no more than that though.'

'Thanks for the tip,' Giraud paid his thirty-five bucks and took the key to room number six. 'I'll remember her name if I ever see her at Del Mar.' He wasn't strictly a betting man; he liked to see his horses in the flesh, racing their brave little hearts out, steaming and blowing and sweating with the effort. A racehorse was a thing of beauty not just a machine to make money from. Though that was a nice incidental.

One day, when he was rich, he would own a couple of them just for the fun of it. He grinned at the thought as he opened the door to number six. He had about as much chance of owning racehorses as he did of owning one of those sleek little private jets Marla coveted. But she was right. A detective with his own plane would have been out of here, instead of stuck in unlovely room six with its brown carpet worn black in spots, its fake-wood nightstand and dresser, it's printed 'patchwork' quilt and cigarette-blistered Formica bathroom sink. At least the shower, though its chrome was rusty, gave out a plentiful supply of cold water. He stood under it for ten minutes, towelled off and stepped out feeling human again.

He threw back the bedspread and the top sheet. Thank God the sheets were clean and he lay there, naked, thinking about things. *Harmon*. That name had cropped up twice now. The ex-owner of a car dealership and now a racehorse-owner. Must've made a bit of money to be able to make that kind of a switch.

He opened the nightstand drawer and took out the telephone book. H . . . H . . . H . . . Harold, Harley, Harper, Harley
. . . no Harmon. Shit.

He lay back against the pillows, hands behind his head,
frowning. The Buick was here. Bonnie had to have been here.
The goddamn answer was *here* . . . somewhere.

He sat up and flicked through the Hs again, checking to
see if he could have missed it . . . but no. He thought of Bonnie
Victor/Laurie Martin. On a hunch, he checked both names.
There was no Bonnie Victor, but there was an L. Martin. At
122 Linden Drive.

He was into his clothes and out the door before you could
say Gwynneth Arden, asking the heavy-better behind the counter
for directions to Linden Drive.

Number 122 was as traditional as it got: white clapboard,
a lumpy burnt-brown lawn with a pepper tree shedding like
crazy all over it and a front porch with a rocker and an old
Sears refrigerator. A woman was sitting in the rocker and she
glanced up as Giraud parked in front of her lawn.

She was in her fifties, neat in a crisp red-and-white spotted
cotton shirtwaist dress, with short wavy grey hair pushed back
behind her ears. She wore a string of pearls and little pearl
studs and a gold v-shaped wedding band set, with a small-carat
diamond. She looked what she was, a nice lady.

'Sorry to disturb you, ma'am,' Giraud called as he stepped
from the car. 'But could I have a word with you?'

She sighed, shaking her head. 'Now, young man, if you're
selling somethin', I just don't want to buy. I can't afford it.'

He laughed and she laughed along with him. 'Well ma'am,
that's nice and upfront,' he said, 'but actually, I wanted to talk
to you about a missing person. I've been assigned by the family
to try to trace her and we know she spent some time here. I
have a photograph, and I wondered if you might know her?'

'Why me?'

She was certainly not stupid, he thought. 'It's like this,
ma'am, your name was found amongst her things, in her
apartment . . . we're checking everyone she knew.'

She nodded, and held out her hand. 'Let me see that photograph.' He handed her John MacIver's photo of Laurie, and waited patiently on the porch while she found her glasses, put them on then studied the photograph.

'Why I surely do remember her,' she exclaimed. 'That's Bonnie Harmon. Though I almost didn't recognise her. You see, she had red hair then. And I remember, she had this cute little black dog. Clyde she called it. It wore a little red bandanna and I could see how she adored it.'

Bingo, Giraud thought, remembering Miss Arden. 'What did you say her name was then, Mrs Martin?'

'Her name was Bonnie Harmon. At least it was later. When I first met her she was Bonnie something else though I'm darned if I can remember what. Anyways, I'm sorry to hear she's missing, though maybe I'm not surprised,' she added thoughtfully.

'So, how'dya meet Bonnie, Mrs Martin?'

'Oh, my, I'm forgeting my manners,' she waved him to a chair. 'Please have a seat Mr . . .'

'Giraud. Al Giraud. And thank you.'

He took a seat on a white wicker chair opposite her.

'There's a cold drink in that refrigerator if you want one,' she added hospitably. 'Coke, Gatorade, just help yourself.'

'Thank you ma'am, I surely will. It's hot out today.'

She laughed, a small tinkling sound in keeping with her petite bird-boned appearance. 'You think this is hot, Mr Giraud, you should be here when we get the hot winds blowing. Temperature goes up another twenty degrees and you can fry your breakfast on the hood of your car. This is just pleasant-to-middling temperature.'

He laughed with her, then asked again where she had met Bonnie.

'I'd been eating lunch at the diner by the gas station near Lummond, a few miles down the highway headin' west. It's still there,' she added, 'and I want to tell you they do the best peach pie in this country, as well as darn good chicken-fried steak. Still eat there regularly.'

'Anyways, I'd lunched at the diner that day and before I left

I visited the restroom, then went on my way. Ten minutes later I was half way back to Falcon City when I remembered – I'd left my handbag there. So of course I turned round and went right back again, hoping to retrieve it. Though you never know, it's a busy place, lots of people in and out all the time . . .

'Anyways, as I came through the door a young woman was just handing it to the waitress.'

'Well thank you, young lady, I said, and I surely was grateful. I'd been to the bank, had close on seventy dollars in there and my checkbook and ATM card.

'"You're very welcome, ma'am," she said. "It was the only Christian thing to do."

'And you know what, Mr Giraud? That simple statement touched my heart. You see so few acts of good faith these days.

'Anyways, we got to chatting and she asked if I knew where she could sell her car. An old Buick she had parked outside. I told her the name of the local dealership I used myself and went there with her to make sure she got a good price. Then she asked if I could drop her off at a motel. Next thing she's asking where the nearest Baptist church is. Now I'm Episcopalian myself, but I didn't hold that against her. I just drove her there first. She introduced herself to the pastor, said she was staying in town and wanted to join his congregation.

'She was a good girl all right, I could tell that. Kind of old-fashioned, y'know. With all that red hair tied back and no make-up, not even lipstick. Not a bad-lookin' woman for all that, though.

'Anyways, after that I drove her to the nearest motel, told her if she needed any help just to call me. But I could see she was an independent sort. I wished her luck and went on my way.

'You can bet I was surprised a few months later when I read in the newspaper about the nuptials between her and old Boss Harmon, who was ninety if he was a day and rich with it. His family boycotted the marriage – it caused quite a scandal round here. And when Boss died a couple of months later in a fire – I believe she said he'd been smoking in bed — there was a lot of talk about it.'

'She inherit Boss Harmon's money?'

'Well now, that I don't know. And she must have left town shortly after, because I've never seen her around.'

'Is that right?' Al nodded thoughtfully.

'So you can see why I was surprised when you showed me Bonnie's picture. She's blonde now though, but still you can see it's Bonnie.'

Giraud put away the photograph, thanked Mrs Martin for her time and her help, and for the Coke, and asked where he could find the Harmon family.

'Oh, the son and his wife moved on, after the fire. Sold the car dealership to Marston, sold up their home and the old man's property, and went to live in San Antonio. I believe he has a couple more dealerships now, and that he owns racehorses.' She shook her head, 'Boss Harmon must be turning in his grave. The old man never missed a Sunday at church and he was set against gambling and drinking and all those kind of vices.'

'Except smoking.' Giraud said.

Her brows lifted in surprise. 'Except smoking,' she agreed.

Chapter Twenty-five

San Antonio, population almost one million, and site of the Alamo, was a pleasant city, Spanish in feeling with shady plazas and waterways. Beau Harmon lived on the outskirts in a palatial colonial-style mansion that Giraud thought bore more than a passing resemblance to Tara. Crunching up the wide sweep of gravel drive in the dusty rented Jeep, he figured that after all Bonnie couldn't have gotten away with too much of Boss Harmon's loot. All she'd had to show for it was a nice condo and a leased Lexus while son Beau was living like a king.

He parked the Jeep in the shade of a towering live oak that was still planted in the giant wooden crate it had been shipped in – probably from some real plantation house where it had grown for more than half a century, he guessed. In fact the whole of Beau Harmon's estate had that raw look of newness about it. You could still see the seams in the turf on the vast lawn and practically smell the paint drying.

The wide front steps were marble and he walked up them and rang the bell. Somewhere inside he could hear it playing 'Yellow Rose Of Texas'. As he waited under the two-storey colonnaded portico he lay bets with himself on what Beau Harmon would look like. J. R. Ewing? Lyndon Johnson? Barry Goldwater? Or John Wayne playing any one of the three?

He looked up interestedly as the door swung open, but it was a silver-haired man in a white coat and striped grey pants.'

'Sir?' he said with a distinct British twang, taking in Giraud's usual attire at a glance and lifting a supercilious eyebrow.

A butler! Giraud was impressed, he hadn't realised car dealerships made this kind of money.

'Al Giraud for Mr Harmon,' he said. 'He's expecting me. He had taken the precaution of telephoning Harmon from Falcon City. He had no wish to be evicted from anybody's marble front doorstep, and knew that the magic word that would gain him entry was Bonnie Harmon. Beau had jumped like a shot man, he could sense it over the phone – his gasp and the long silence. He asked no questions, just told him to get there that afternoon at two.

'Please come in, sir.' The butler looked at him as though wishing he had a coat or hat, or at least a scarf he might relieve him of the way no doubt he used to in the ancestral castles he had worked in in England. Al was glad he had at least put on a clean T-shirt.

Inside was like a refrigerator and Al could almost feel his sweat glands closing up in protest. Another couple of degrees and you could have hung meat in here.

'Wait here, sir, I'll tell Mr Harmon you are here.'

The butler disappeared down the polished marble hall and Al took a look around. An enormous crystal chandelier burned brightly over his head though it was still only early afternoon, with enough wattage he felt sure to light most of Falcon City. A double staircase carpeted in several acres of lavender triple-velvet carpeting anchored on each riser by a gilded rod with gold swan finials, ascended to lofty heights, with a glimpse of yet another large hallway at the top. Several thick double doors at least twelve feet in height led into sumptuously furnished rooms done out in shades of rose and lavender, or peach and green, and one immediately opposite, was in pure startling white. All were furnished with Louis-the-something and plenty of gold trim.

He whistled, trying to assess what this whole thing might have cost. More than a man could make on a couple of car dealerships, he was sure of that. Either Boss Harmon had inherited family money and left that to his son, or else Beau had married it. His bet was on the latter.

'And *who* are *you?*'

Al lifted his head and met the eyes of a tall slender brunette standing near the top of the curving staircase. Her dress matched almost perfectly the lavender of the carpet and he had no doubt who had the upper hand in decorating the place. Mrs Harmon's taste was stamped on her person and on her home.

She was in her late fifties, he guessed, but moulded by the surgeon's scalpel from nose to thighs. Not a line on her face, not a crease in her dress, not a hair out of place. She was as sanitised as an operating theatre, as cold as the air conditioning and as unsexy as a china doll. For a second he wondered about a possible relationship between Beau Harmon and Bonnie, but no – she had married his old man.

She came slowly down the stairs, walking carefully in strappy kitten-heel sandals that also matched her dress. 'Who are you?' she asked again, a faint frown of irritation between her brows as though she wasn't used to seeing men like him in their white T-shirts and jeans and scuffed boots messing up her elegant front hall.

'Excuse me, ma'am – Mrs Harmon. My name is Giraud. I have an appointment with your husband.'

She came towards him on a waft of perfume but he knew under its façade she would be odourless with no feminine scent to entice a man. Sterile as a steel scalpel, he thought.

'And what do you wish to talk to my husband about?' She stood at a distance as though afraid of contamination, inspecting him with hard blue eyes.

'Hum . . . it's kind of a personal matter, ma'am. To do with his father,' he added seeing from her quick frown she wasn't going to take that for an answer.

'Boss Harmon's been dead these five years,' she said briskly. 'And good riddance it was too.' And with that she stalked past Giraud into the all-white room and closed the door carefully behind her.

Shutting out the unpleasant sight, Giraud thought.

At least she didn't slam, and that showed some iron self-control. The woman was an iceberg. He'd bet it was she who kept the air-conditioning down to meat-hanging numbers.

'This way, please, Mr Giraud.' The butler was back and Giraud loped after him, boots clattering on the marble.

Beau Harmon was sitting behind a grandiose desk, the kind Giraud figured Napoleon would have owned, carved and gilded and immense. And like Napoleon, Beau was a diminutive figure, stocky as a peasant in contrast with his string-bean iceberg of a wife. He was a deal younger than her too, blond hair, ruddy skin, bleached blue eyes and the mottled nose of a man who partook of good bourbon rather more often than he should. Giraud knew his guess had been right and that Beau had married money. Why else would he have taken her on?

Beau did not get up. 'Take a seat, Giraud,' he said coldly. 'And then explain to me exactly why you are here.' He glanced pointedly at his large expensive gold watch, the kind commodores of yachts might have worn to sail the high seas. Al had no doubt it told the time on three continents and hoped Beau could also tell the time right here in Texas. With the kind of two-inch brow Beau had, he wouldn't bet on his intellectual capabilities.

He sat in the shiny red leather chair on the opposite side of the big desk from Beau. 'I'm here, sir, to discuss your father's wife. Bonnie Harmon.'

'Ex-wife.' Beau said rudely.

'Excuse me, sir. In fact *widow* would be the correct appellation.' Giraud could get fancy with words when he wanted to.

Beau grunted, sitting back in his own red leather chair – except his was twice the size of Giraud's and had the effect of making him look like a little boy in his father's office. Which was, in fact, Giraud thought, probably what Beau had been for most of his life. Until he married Miss Moneybags.

'Mrs Harmon is missing, sir, and I have been employed to find her. She disappeared four weeks ago in California, where she was working as a real estate agent.'

'Hah! Bonnie? An estate agent? That little tramp couldn't do more than sling hash at Benboy's Steak House. You sure we're talking about the same person?'

'Oh yes, I'm sure.'

'Well, I'll be darned. Can't say I'm sorry she's gone missing, and I can't say I wouldn't be sorry to see her come to a bad end. That woman almost ruined my life, Mr Giraud. *And* took off with a great deal of my Pa's money.'

'She was married to your father, right?'

'Right. She lit into town with her red hair and high heels. Met him at Benboy's Steak House where she waitressed – he went there a couple of times a week. She must have schmoozed him, come on to him y'know – and him, an old man for Christ's sakes. Anyhow, before you knew it, she had him under her spell. And the old fool wanted her, I guess she made him believe he could still do it, y'know.'

'There's no fool like an old fool,' Giraud said helpfully.

'Before we knew it he was planning on marrying her. Loretta swore he had shamed her family – my wife's family goes back fifty or so years,' he added proudly. 'Larson's oil, you may have heard of it.'

Giraud had and he nodded. 'Anyway, she had him in her coils and nothing we could do could stop the old fool. Loretta had an intervention, tried to get Pa committed to a very nice little institution out near Austin that she knew about. There had been some little . . . unhappiness . . . in her own family once so she knew from experience it was a fine place.' He ran his hands through his sparse blond hair, bleached blue eyes squinting across at Giraud. 'A man like you will understand these things,' he added and Giraud nodded that yes he did.

'But Bonnie wasn't having any of that. She must have gotten wind of it somehow and had her own team of medicos and psychiatrists and the like there to meet us, with papers already stating that Pa was *compos mentis* in all respects. Except in regard to her, of course,' he added bitterly.

'To cut a long story short, the silly old bastard married her and four months later he was in his coffin. Or what was left of him was, after the fire in bed.'

'Was old Mr Harmon a heavy smoker then?'

'Sure he was. God knows how he didn't get lung cancer, must have been the bourbon kept it at bay. A bottle of ninety-proof will combat any disease in my opinion.'

'And then there was the question of your father's will.'

'Hah!' Beau levered himself out of the massive chair. He stalked to the window, put his hands behind his back and stood gazing out at the new landscaping looking for all the world like a picture of the exiled Napoleon in Elba gazing out across the sea to France, the land of his dreams.

'He left her everything: the business, the house, his Cadillac and all his money.'

'Naturally you contested that.'

'You bet your ass I did. Loretta's attorneys came down on that woman like a ton of bricks. Told her they were going to instigate a further investigation into Pa's death – and into her past if she didn't play ball. Scared the shit out of her, I guess. Anyway they came to terms and paid her off. Got rid of the bitch.'

Giraud cleared his throat before he asked the delicate question. 'And exactly how much was Mrs Harmon paid, sir?'

Beau swung round from the window. There was a bitter smile on his florid face as he said, 'Two hundred thousand bucks.' He threw back his head and laughed. 'Take it or leave it, baby, they told her. So she took it. Was out of town the next morning, cash in hand. Wouldn't take a cheque. Not even a cashier's. Her sort never does.'

Al knew he was right. 'And you never heard from her since? She never came back asking for more cash?'

Beau shook his head. 'Nope. Nothin' – until you showed up askin' questions. And I'm not even going to ask you what you think has happened to her. I just plain don't want to know. I don't want my family name dragged through the mire again.'

Al knew he couldn't promise Beau that but he thanked him for his time and said his goodbyes.

The door to the white room stood open slightly as he followed the butler back down the hall and he caught a glimpse of Loretta Harmon's mask-like face turned his way.

As the front door closed solidly behind him he breathed a great sigh of relif. In his opinion Beau and Loretta Harmon deserved each other.

Chapter Twenty-six

Marla knew she was a long way away – submerged in a bad dream that kept replaying itself over and over in her head . . . her poor aching head . . .

In the dream she could see a bagel lying on Vickie Mallard's kitchen floor so she knew that she must be in the land of the living. Unless they had Western Bagels in heaven, that is.

Her blurred gaze slowly focused on the man in the black sweater kneeling over Vickie. She shook her head, puzzled. She must be hallucinating. Her spine crawled with fear. She just didn't want to believe this. She lay perfectly still, afraid to breathe.

Suddenly two burly cops slammed through the door, guns raised. In seconds they had Steve Mallard on his face on the floor in all that blood and gore, guns at his neck as they handcuffed him.

In her dream, tears trickled down her bruised face. Tears of what? Relief? Pain? Sorrow?

A cop with a kind face loomed over her. 'Hang on sweetheart,' he said, 'the ambulance is coming, we'll have you at the hospital in minutes. *Just hang in there.*'

Then the paramedics rushed in, hovering over Vickie. The way the angels carrying Vickie's spirit to heaven would, Marla thought wearily. They had Vickie on a stretcher, now. Blood still oozed from her, dripping onto the floor as they lifted her.

And then the dream disappeared into blackness.

When Marla came out of her dream, she was in a hospital bed and Giraud was holding her hand. There was a look of such tender anxiety on his face it was almost worth getting nearly killed for. She managed a painful smile.

'Well, hi there, honey,' she croaked in a voice that certainly didn't sound like her own. That's what happened when you were almost strangled she guessed. The shock of the terrible memory widened her eyes, making her gasp and clutch tightly to Giraud's hand. She never wanted him to let go.

'Hi, there to you, honey.' He stroked tendrils of soft blonde hair back from her battered face. His gaze lingered on the bruised throat and blackened eyes, on the gauze covering the knife wounds on her arms; on her battered head. By some miracle Marla had flung herself to one side, deflecting the blow from the wine bottle. Otherwise she would not be here today.

Giraud felt the same way he had when his brother was shot. Murder was in his own heart as he looked at her. The need for revenge boiled hot inside him.

'A neighbour heard screams,' he told her. 'She called the cops.' *And only just in time, or Marla would be dead*, he thought, his throat tightening with emotion.

'I should never have let you get involved. I should have known better.'

She took his hand in both hers, squeezed it tightly. 'Didn't I do good, though?' she said in that new husky whisper. 'Marla Cwitowitz PI? I caught Steve. *In the act.*'

Al nodded, still churning inside. He had almost lost her. If he had not allowed her to help him on this case, it would have been *him* Vickie Mallard called, *he* who would have gone there to talk to her.

'You did good, Marla. I'm promoting you to equal partner. And I'm also not letting you out the door alone again.'

She gave him a lopsided grin that changed to a look of anguish. 'Oh my God. What about Vickie,' she whispered. 'Is she . . . ?' She couldn't bring herself to say the word dead.

'She's in a coma. She was strangled, as well as stabbed. The knife punctured an artery and also her lung. The doctor tells me it missed her heart by a fraction of an inch.'

Marla breathed again. 'Lucky,' she murmured.

Giraud wasn't so sure. With her terrible wounds, nobody could say for sure what Vickie Mallard would be like when she came out of that coma. *If* she ever did.

The medication was taking Marla down again and he held her hand for a long while as she dozed. He wanted to pick her up in his arms, kiss her all over, hold her close and never let anyone near her again. He would kill anyone who even looked the wrong way at her. He took a deep unsteady breath. He knew this was not the right way to feel. Revenge achieved nothing. Marla was alive. She would survive, with maybe a couple of scars but nothing a good plastic surgeon couldn't take care of.

But no one could fix the anger that burned him as he looked at her.

Eventually he left her to sleep and wandered out into the shiny hospital hallways in search of a coffee machine. He slotted his coins in and held the paper cup while the boiling brown liquid euphemistically termed 'espresso' splashed into it, thinking about Steve Mallard and the way things had turned out.

As he sipped the coffee, he wondered why Steve had done it. Had Vickie found out the truth about him and Laurie after all? Had she found out Steve had killed Laurie?

The puzzle was not yet complete.

Chapter Twenty-seven

Steve Mallard was being held at the Twin Towers jail, an ultra-modern fortress right in the heart of downtown LA – presumably, Giraud figured, so those incarcerated would be able to gaze longingly from the slit-like windows at more fortunate people going about their daily business in the busy streets below.

It had always seemed an odd location for a prison to Giraud, but never more so than when he accompanied Ben Lister on a visit to his client. Outside, you could be in McDonalds in a minute; at the fancy Music Center for a show in five; Chinatown and the terrific seafood at Mon Kee – especially the huge scallops – in less than ten. He guessed it added an extra gut twist to a criminal's sentence, knowing all that was available – so close and yet so far – as they say.

Steve had been arrested by the LAPD for the attempted homicide of his wife. He had, as Marla had pointed out, been caught in the act. Now he was brought in handcuffs into a private room for the meeting with his attorney.

Giraud slipped his conscious-mind deliberately into neutral as he took a quick assessing glance at the man who had almost killed Marla. He had to be neutral, that was his business. If Marla were not involved, he would not have felt this way. Now he had to force himself to revert to that impartial mode, that way of thinking. Of course his subconscious still boiled, but for now he was a man with ice water in his veins.

Steve was clean shaven but in bad need of a haircut. His face was so pale it was almost translucent and his eyes had dulled to a glazed stare. He looked, Giraud thought, like a man who hadn't seen daylight in years. A cave-dweller – which come to think of it, was pretty much what this prison was like.

'How're y'doin', Steve?' Lister shook his hand, Giraud did not.

Steve nodded, slumping into the straight-backed wooden chair on the opposite side of the table. 'OK,' he said in a clipped tone. His lips were set in a tight line and he did not look either of them in the eye.

With attorney/client privilege at least they were not required to sit at opposite sides of a thick bullet-proof glass panel and communicate through telephones. Giraud hated this whole jail thing. It got him nervous, thinking about his own past and his youthful misdemeanours. *There but for the grace of a good mother, go I,* he misquoted to himself. He wished he had a cigarette. He wondered if the cuffs were really necessary.

'They treating you all right?' Lister asked, taking out a digital recording machine. He wanted Steve's actual words on record for later assessment.

'OK,' Steve said again, staring down at the grey plastic tabletop.

'You wanna tell us your story, Steve?' Giraud suggested.

'Why?' For the first time Steve lifted his head and looked at him. 'You already know it. I've told Lister – and the police a hundred times already.'

'So why not do me a favour and tell us again.'

Steve's mouth was set in a hard line now. His eyes had that blank look again.

'You'd better tell me, buddy,' Giraud said softly. 'If you ever want to get out of this mess.'

'There is no way out. Don't you think I realise that? I was caught kneeling over my wife. In her blood. The knife was right there . . .'

'There were no prints on that knife.'

'No. But I'm sure you already know that the attacker wore

gloves. And that the knife is one of a set we keep at the Arrowhead cabin.'

'I didn't know that.' Giraud glanced at Lister, surprised.

'Sorry, Al, must have forgotten to tell you,' he said.

Giraud raised an amazed eyebrow; apparently Lister was so sure of his client's guilt he didn't think the knife mattered that much.

Steve leaned his cuffed hands on the table, shoulders stooped, head bowed. 'I was at the cabin in Lake Arrowhead. There was a telephone call. Someone – a man, I didn't know his voice. He told me my wife was in danger, that I should get back home before it was too late. I didn't think twice. I just got in the car and drove back home. I used my key to open the front door. It was dark – there was no light on in the hall. I heard a noise and I called out to Vickie that it was me – I didn't want to alarm her. And then I walked into the kitchen. I saw Vickie covered in blood . . . I ran to her. My only thought was to help her, she was . . . oh God, she was just covered in blood, it was jetting out of the artery in her neck . . . I realised she must still be alive because she was still bleeding . . . I jammed my finger into the hole in her neck to stop it spurting . . .' His head sank even lower and there was a lengthy silence.

'And then the cops had me face down on the floor in all that blood with guns pointed at my head.' A sigh rattled his thin frame and Giraud suddenly became aware of how much weight the man had lost. He guessed homicide did not enhance the appetite.

'So what time would you say you got the anonymous telephone call?' Giraud was putting the questions this time around. Lister had already been there.

'Around ten-thirty, I guess.'

'You were over a hundred miles away, up in the mountains and someone said your wife, back in LA was in danger. So why didn't you call the LA police?'

'You might remember I wasn't exactly on good terms with the cops. They were after my head – and I was about to call and report anonymous threats to my wife? They would have had me behind bars before I could blink.' His bitterness was like a bad taste in the mouth.

'It might have been better to take that risk,' Giraud said quietly, thinking of the consequences.

Steve's dark eyes flickered anger and Giraud thought, pleased, at least he had touched a nerve, got some kind of human reaction out of him.

'I thought it was just someone playing a bad joke. There are people who do things like that, crazies who've read about us, about what's happened ...'

'A long shot.' Giraud commented icily, not letting him off the hook. 'So what did you do next?'

'I got in the car and drove back to LA.'

'The rented Ford Taurus, wasn't it?'

'Yes. The company took back my car when they suspended me.'

'You make good time in a car like that? On those mountain roads?'

'I'm a good driver. I managed. I got there at twelve-fifty-eight.' Giraud raised his eyebrows and Steve added, 'I noted the time on my watch. It was late, all the lights were out in the houses down the street. I didn't want to disturb the neighbours slamming the car door ...'

'Notice any other cars parked on the street?'

'I didn't even look. Besides, I told you it was pretty dark.'

'No street lights?'

A couple, it's a cul-de-sac ... our house is kind of in between the lights.'

'And you didn't see anyone when you opened the front door?'

'No one. But again, it was dark.'

'And the back door was also found open,' Lister interrupted.

Giraud nodded. 'OK, so you're in the house, you see your wife ... what did you do next?'

'I told you, I ran to her, I knelt beside her, stuck my fingers in the wound to try to stop the bleeding ...'

'In fact you saved her life, according to the paramedics. The artery was punctured and only that kind of pressure could have stopped it. Tell me, Steve, did you save Vickie before – or *after* the cops arrived. Did you do it to invent an instant alibi? The dedicated husband scenario?'

'Goddamn it.' Steve slammed his cuffed fists angrily on the plastic table.

'And while you were doing it, did you by any chance hear anything? Footsteps, for instance. Or sense another presence in the house? Y'know what I mean, the kind of sixth sense that grips like icy fingers at the back of your neck?'

'I wasn't even thinking about that.'

'You didn't even think about the fact that a killer might still be in the house? That you were in danger?'

'I did not.' Steve's reply was stiff, his face a mask again, all traces of anger and human emotion gone.

'So tell me, what *did* you hear? There had to be something, some kind of sound. The killer must have left the house by the back door when you came in the front ... he would need a getaway vehicle ...'

Steve was frowning, thinking now. 'Somewhere,' he said hesitantly, 'somewhere ... in the background ... I might have heard a car starting up ... but I was too concerned about Vickie, all I wanted to do was save my wife.'

There was, Al figured, not much more to be said. Lister packed up his recording machine and they said their goodbyes, waiting while Steve was escorted out of the room and back to his cell by a uniformed prison guard.

'So how about that?' Lister asked as they walked back down the bleak hallway and out into the free world. 'You think he's lying? Or is he the only killer who ever tried to save his victim in the hope of saving his own neck?'

Al grinned. 'Hey, you're his defence attorney. You're supposed to believe in his innocence.'

'Don't bet on it,' Lister retorted. Then he added 'buddy' and a broad wink as he got into his car and drove away.

Leaving Al pretty much up in the air. Had Steve tried to kill

Vickie and Marla? He thought it possible. He guessed Vickie must have found out the truth about Laurie and been going to turn him in.

Except, he wondered as he slid the Corvette silkily out of the parking lot and into the traffic. What the fuck *was* the truth about Laurie Martin?

That afternoon when Giraud got to the hospital, Marla was sitting in a chair by the window, sipping orange juice through a straw and looking a hundred per cent better than she had the day before. That didn't mean she was a hundred per cent yet, he thought, examining her critically from the doorway. Black eyes; bruised throat; a lump on her head with fifteen stitches in it; more stitches along her arm . . . but she was alive and she was smiling at him and that was all that counted.

She was wearing a long white cotton T-shirt and a red silk robe and with her blonde hair scraped back and no make-up she looked like a little girl playing dress-up in her mother's clothes.

Her bottom lip was ragged where her teeth had bitten into it when Steve had slammed his hand over her mouth to stop her screaming, so instead he kissed her left cheek, the one without the stitches. 'This is getting tricky,' he smiled at her. 'There's almost no place left to kiss.'

'Wanna bet?' She smiled sexily back at him – or as sexily as a woman with a split lip and two black eyes could manage. 'Like some orange juice?'

'No thanks. I'd like you out of here though, back home where you belong.'

'Safe and sound,' she teased.

'I'll bet that's what your father said.'

She took a slurp of the juice. 'You just missed him – and my mother. You're not exactly their favourite boy right now.'

'Or ever,' he bet gloomily, making her laugh.

'So what's with Steve Mallard?'

'He claims he didn't do it, that he got an anonymous phone

154

call warning him his wife was in danger. When he got there she was lying on the floor bleeding to death. He put pressure on the artery – the medics say he saved her life.'

She frowned, puzzled. 'You mean he tried to kill her – then when he heard the cops coming pretended he was attempting to save her life?'

'That's the way it looks.'

She shook her head, 'It was him, Al. I *saw* him . . .'

'You saw him with the knife in his hand?'

'Damn it, Giraud, where do you think I got these cuts. I looked right into his eyes.'

He sighed. 'You're right, of course.'

'Vickie is still in intensive care,' Marla said. 'Still in a coma.'

'I know.' He had telephoned that morning to find out how Vickie was, as well as Marla.

'So? How was Falcon City, Texas?'

Al filled her in on the interview with Miss Gwynneth Arden, then he told her about meeting the real Laurie Martin. And about his talk with Boss Harmon's son.

'So, honey,' he said finally. 'Ms Bonnie Hoyt/Victor/Harmon took her no doubt ill-gotten inheritance. I believe she killed Jimmy Victor and got the car, then she killed old Boss Harmon and got his money. Plus she stole the real Laurie Martin's social security number from the handbag left in the restroom that afternoon. Then with Boss dead and a couple of hundred thou in her pocket, she turned up in LA with a new car, a new wardrobe and a new blonde hairdo, as well as a new identity . . . Laurie Martin.'

'And presumably a new ambition by the name of John MacIver,' Marla said thoughtfully. 'Quite a girl our Laurie. Do you think someone caught on to her game, realised what she was up to?'

'You mean like Steve?' Giraud shook his head, frowning. 'It just doesn't fit.'

'You know what I think?' Marla said. 'I think we need to find out more about the first Bonnie – Bonnie Hoyt. Who she is, where she came from, what her past was — before she got into killing men for their assets.'

'You're right, honey. And that's where I'm off next. Gainesville, Florida. I have a flight at four p.m.'

'You mean you're not going to wait until I can get out of here?' Marla's eyes flashed outrage.

'You mean, "after all you've done for me"? Sorry, hon, but I'm taking the opportunity to go while the going is good and while I know exactly where you are.'

'Safe and sound,' she added bitterly.

'Got it in one,' he said, kissing her wherever there was no bruise.

Chapter Twenty-eight

Gainesville was a college town, not quite as big as San Antonio, but close. Giraud read the population count as he drove into town from the airport – almost 85,000, which he guessed must swell some each September when school started. Situated between the Gulf of Mexico and the Atlantic, it was another hot spot – and humid with it.

There were no Hoyts listed in the Gainesville phone book but State records gave their address. As Al drove there in a rented Lincoln Town Car – he had been upgraded by Hertz as a frequent customer – he looked around, getting a fix on where Bonnie/Laurie had come from.

This was no trashy trailer park, it was respectable, a modest, low-income area of plain stucco homes with single-car garages and a lot of oldish vehicles parked on the street. Tidy lawns sloped to the sidewalk uninterrupted by any fences and a few overgrown pines that were obviously not indigenous to the area threw patches of welcome shade as well as scattering needles and a few withered cones.

Number 977 Windward Road was a house just like the others, dusty white stucco, paper blinds on the picture window shutting out the heat, wire hurricane fencing separating it from its neighbours on each side. Except this was the only house with a baby stroller parked outside the door and a playpen under the overhang in the side yard.

Al checked the address in his notebook, wondering if he'd

got it right. The Hoyts were too old for babies – unless of course Bonnie had provided a few and stuck the grandparents with raising them.

The door was opened quickly to his ring and a young woman, not more than her early twenties he guessed, smiled enquiringly at him. Even from here the house smelled of babies. He thought at least that was better than cats.

'Excuse me,' he said politely, 'but I'm looking for Mr and Mrs Hoyt. Bernard and Barbara Hoyt, that is. I understood they lived here.'

'Yeah, they used to, I guess.' The young woman shifted the two-year-old from one hip to the other and pushed back her limp dark hair. 'We've lived here five years or so now, though.' She grinned a shining white grin. 'My five-year-old was born right here, so she's a native of Alachua County all right, and so are the rest of my kids. All four of 'em,' she added, laughing.

'So by any chance do you know where Mr and Mrs Hoyt moved?'

'Nope. The house had been empty for a long time when we bought it. Not a lot of folks want to move to the old neighbourhoods like this, but it was all we could afford, with five kids and all. And it's nice, y'know? The neighbours are all older folk, they're good babysitters and they don't charge much and you can bet they're more reliable than some high school kid.' She laughed again, 'I can remember when I was in high school, no sense of responsibility at all.'

'Is that right?' Al said companionably. She was a chatterer and in his experience good information could come out of chatter.

'Like the Kramers, next door for instance. They've lived here for ever, since these houses were first built. I remember they said they paid around two thousand for it way back then. Can you imagine?'

'So the Kramers would have known the Hoyts pretty well then.'

She looked surprised. 'Yeah, I guess so. Maybe you should

ask them where they've gone. They're real sweet, they'll tell you anything.'

Giraud thanked her and walked ten paces down the narrow cracked cement sidewalk and another five to the Kramer's front door. No baby strollers this time. Just a well-polished brass doorknocker, shiny clean windows and pristine white venetian blinds. Mrs Kramer kept a nice house. There was just room for him and the large tub of red geraniums on the front step as he rang the bell. He was beginning to feel like a door-to-door salesman – he wondered how many of those there were left in these days when people were afraid to open their doors to strangers. But not old Mr Kramer. He heard him struggling with locks and bolts and guessed they normally used the kitchen door.

'Sorry to put you to so much trouble,' he said to the little old man looking surprised at him. 'I was looking for Mr and Mrs Hoyt ... Bernard and Barbara Hoyt. I know they used to live next door ...'

'That's right, sure they did.' Mr Kramer adjusted his large spectacles and smoothed back his sparse hair that was standing on end in the breeze, looking like white cotton candy. 'You knew Bernie then?'

'Actually, no. I only know of him. The fact of the matter is, Mr Kramer, it's their daughter I'm interested in.' Al took out Laurie's picture and showed it to him. 'She's gone missing and I've been employed to help find her.'

'Missing, you said? Huh, I can't say I'm surprised.' He examined the picture, holding it so close to his face Giraud figured his breath must be condensing on it and making it sticky.

'Sure, that's Bonnie. Been a long time since I saw her looking like that though.' He glanced sharply at Giraud, assessing whether it was safe to ask him in. He must have approved because he said, 'Come on in, sir, why don't ya, it's kinda hot out here on the step. My wife was friends with Barbie Hoyt, though Barbie's daughter was younger than ours. Thank God,' he added as he turned and led the way into the shiny little house.

Mrs Kramer was surely a good duster, Giraud thought casting a glance around the immaculate little room with its dark oak furniture and middling-sized TV set – turned off, for once. There was not a speck of dust anywhere and Mrs Kramer was sitting in a chair near the empty fireplace, where a large bunch of plastic daffodils hid the empty grate. She was as tiny as her husband and despite the fact that it must have been close to 90 degrees in the house, a multi-coloured crocheted blanket covered her knees. She was reading but she put the book aside when she saw they had a visitor.

'This gentleman is asking after the Hoyts, Mimi,' Kramer said. 'Seems Bonnie's gone missing and he's been sent to look for her.'

If ever a woman was not meant to have the name Mimi it was Mrs Kramer, Al thought. She was so plain as to be what his mother would have kindly called, 'homely', with long teeth and a long face and grey hair. She bore more than a passing resemblance to a horse – a nice horse though – and none at all to the glamorous stripper-types called Mimi who worked the clubs in places like downtown Vegas. Mimi's mother had obviously been an optimist.

'The name's Giraud, Mrs Kramer. Al Giraud, and I'm a private detective.'

Her rheumy eyes lit up. 'Oh, my, a real private eye. And here I was just reading the latest Elmore Leonard. Harry gets me them from the public library, y'know. I'm such a fan, I write to Mr Leonard all the time, tell him where I think the plot fell down. I feel sure he must appreciate a little helpful criticism.' She smiled, showing those long white teeth – false no doubt – and a considerable amount of gum, but strangely the smile lit up her whole face and she suddenly looked a decade younger.

Mimi Kramer was OK, Giraud was thinking as he shook her hand and said it was a pleasure to meet her. Harry Kramer offered him a seat on the flowered sofa and Mimi asked if he would care for a cold drink, she believed they had some lemonade in the refrigerator. He said no thank you and got down to business. At least it only smelled of Lemon Pledge in here.

He explained about Bonnie living in California and the fact that she had disappeared, but he didn't worry the Kramers with the gruesome fact that she had probably been murdered.

'I needed to find out where Bonnie came from, kind of who she was, y'know, like that,' he added, knowing from Mimi's eager look she was anxious to tell all.

'Well, you've come to the right person. There's no one knows more about the Hoyts than us. We were their neighbours for goin' on forty years. And that Bonnie was always a wild child, her folks just couldn't keep up with her. She was daring, kind of a show-off even when she was little. She was caught shoplifting a couple of times, the police warned her and her father surely gave her hell for it. Took the strap to her, so I heard. But Bonnie didn't give a hoot. She just drove those poor folks crazy. Skippin' school, smokin', drinkin', doin' drugs.'

'How old was she when she started drinking and doing drugs, Mrs Kramer?' Giraud was all ears, Finally he was getting to know the real Bonnie/Laurie Martin.

'Why, since before she even started high school, I believe. Barbie Kramer was sick about it, couldn't understand how a child of hers could behave that way. They were God-fearing folks, Mr Giraud. Never missed a Sunday at the Ebeneezer Baptist Chapel, always collecting for church charities, always ready to help a neighbour, or folks poorer than themselves. And let me tell you the Hoyts had a lot less than most of their neighbours. Bernie told us he'd paid off his home on a ten-year mortage by scrimping and saving and doing without. There was nothing more important to them than to own their own home. Nothing. That way he said nobody could take it away from them and nobody could turn them out, the way they did rentals in those days if you had little kids, or animals.' She shook her head, bewildered by the iniquity of her fellow men.

'Then, when she was seventeen, Bonnie told them she was leavin', going off to Pensacola to live with a marine she'd met. She just packed her bags, took what money her mom had in her purse and skipped on out of there. Of course they tried to stop her. They set off after her but they didn't get far. They were killed in an auto crash out on the highway.'

Tears sprang to her eyes and instinctively Giraud reached out and patted her frail hand. 'It's hard to lose good friends – especially so violently,' he said quietly.

'Now, Mimi, no need to get upset all over again,' Harry Kramer told his wife. He looked at Giraud, frowning. 'The police said it was the brakes and that surprised me. Bernie Hoyt was fanatical about his automobile, looked after it like a baby. It wasn't new but from the paintwork and the gleaming engine under the hood, you surely would have thought it was.'

Mimi sighed deeply, patting her eyes with a Kleenex taken from a seashell-studded box. 'Bonnie inherited what bit of money they had, plus the house, which she sold right off. Next thing we heard her husband died in that trailer fire. Seems like tragedy stalked that girl.' She breathed another soft sigh as her sad eyed met Giraud's. 'After that she took off. Who knows where?'

Al thanked them for their trouble, apologised for upsetting Mimi and waved goodbye to them as they stood in the front door. There was no doubt Bonnie Hoyt the teenage hellraiser was both Bonnie Victor and Bonnie Harmon – as well as Laurie Martin. But he wasn't ready to share that information with Detective Bulworth just yet.

Chapter Twenty-nine

When Al got back, there was a message on his e-mail.

> *Help! Have been kidnapped from the hospital. Am being held prisoner in my old home. Have been forbidden to see you again. Mother says Marla why don't you get a nice boyfriend, a doctor, an orthodontist? I said Mom I'm not sixteen any more. Mother says No, you are thirty-two and almost dead, forget the jerk. Meet me at the Ivory Tower at midnight ...*
> signed, *Marla Cwitowitz, Asstnt PI.*

Al laughed. He assumed the Ivory Tower was Marla's marble apartment building in the Palisades. He checked his watch. Eleven-fifteen, still time to hit Greenblatts on Sunset for the best take-away roast chicken with perhaps a little fresh asparagus on the side. Marla liked asparagus. He picked up a bottle of chilled champagne while he was at it, then headed for the Palisades.

Marla flung herself dramatically into his arms. 'I knew you would come and rescue me,' she murmured, kissing every available part of him, totally into the role of the ravished maiden.

'Take it easy, hon,' he said mildly, rescuing the bag with the chicken from between them where it was in danger of becoming crushed. He looked at her. Instead of blue-black her eyes were now a sickly greenish-yellow and so were the fingermarks on her throat. The staples had been removed from her head and so had the stiches in her arm where the long scar loomed a vivid purplish-red.

'*Take it easy?* Is that all you can say when I was *kidnapped* from the hospital. Huh, some lover you turned out to be, Mr Tough Guy Private Eye. And here I was expecting you to rescue me.' She stalked into the living room and hurled herself onto the taupe chenille sofa, pouting prettily.

'Honey, there's no way I would ever rescue you from your parents. They're are all yours, baby. Anyhow, it seems like you took care of them all by yourself. Besides, your Dad is tougher than I am.'

He put the packages in the kitchen then took another look at her. She was wearing a glamorous white satin nightdress he had never seen before – Marla usually slept naked or in a T-shirt, sometimes with sweat-socks – she always had cold feet at night. Her blonde hair was brushed carefully over the scar on her head and she had on red lipstick and a lot of eye stuff. 'So who are we tonight? Jean Harlow?' he asked with a grin. 'By the way, I like the comb-over.'

'Beast!' She threw a cushion at him and he caught it neatly.

'And red lipstick is particularly fetching with yellow eyes,' he added, dodging as another cushion followed the first.

'I was meant to look like the poor wounded woman in a thirties movie, like in those Ginger Rogers things,' she added vaguely.

'Honey, to my knowledge Ginger never played the poor wounded woman, she just danced her toes off with Fred Astaire.'

'So dance with me.'

She was in his arms in a fragrant cloud of something spicy and floral and he knew that, unlike Loretta Harmon, there was a real woman under that perfume, full of delicious scents of her own. The mere thought of it made him hot and he picked her up and carried her back to the sofa.

'Champagne before I ravish you?' he asked. 'Chicken and asparagus pre ... or post?'

She was laughing as she snuggled into him, fitting her body to his, wrapping her legs around him, hands already tugging the T-shirt from his pants.

'Oh, *post*, you fool,' she said,

And then his cellphone rang.

She lifted her head and their eyes met. 'I'll kill you if you answer that,' she said evenly and he believed her.

'You win,' he said, giving up without a fight. And he was glad he did. Her skin was satin under his hands, her pointed breasts cushions of delight that made his loins zing, and he could swear her nipples tasted of roses and sweet wine. He stretched out on her huge downy bed, letting her have her way with him ... she was doing things to him, reaching parts of him he hadn't known he had ... God the woman was a genius ... He grabbed ahold of her before it was too late, lifted her onto him, felt her swoop down on him, over and over until his heart was bursting and his head was swimming and he groaned out loud, feeling her shudder with him.

And then his cellphone rang again.

Their eyes met. 'Don't you dare,' she said softly over the rings.

He stuffed the phone under the pillows, eased her off him and lay her beside him on the bed. 'You didn't really think I would, did you?' he said. And then his head was buried in the soft golden mound and he was tasting her, teasing the very essence that was Marla from her, giving her as much pleasure as she had just given him, loving her. And from her final little yelps of delight, he knew he had succeeded.

He kissed her all the way up to her wounded mouth where he lingered lovingly, dropping tiny butterfly-wing kisses on her still-swollen lips. 'Wonderful, beautiful. You're my dream girl Marla ...'

His hand was already under the pillow reaching for the phone and she jammed her elbow on it. Hard.

'Can't you at least have the decency to wait a few minutes before you find out who called? I'll bet you were think-ing about who it was all the time we were doing it.' She was furious.

'No I was not.' He was indignant. 'It's just that I'm on a job — and I might remind you, so are you. At your *own request*, Miss Cwitowitz, *Assistant PI* as you sign yourself these days.'

'Ohhh . . . fuck you.'

He was laughing at the aptness of her turn of phrase as he dialled his office number, hoping that whoever it was had left a message there.

There was no message – at least none of any recent vintage and he sighed, exasperated as he pushed the endcall button. It was one-thirty a.m. Fuck, it had to have been important.

He heard the pop of a champagne cork and walked into the living room.

Marla was putting a large tray containing the Greenblatt's chicken, the asparagus and the champagne onto the huge glass coffee-table. She glanced up at him. 'Looking your best, I see,' she said mischievously.

He had forgotten he was naked. He did an about-turn and came back a minute later wrapped in the black terry robe she had bought specially for him. Or at least he hoped she had bought it for him and it hadn't been a lover's 'prop' here for the convience of the man of the moment. He sighed, you never knew with Marla. But Marla was definitely a one-man woman now and he was glad that man was him.

Marla was back in her Harlow cream satin but most of the red lipstick was gone and her eyeshadow had smudged leaving silvery traces over the yellowed bruises. There was a pretty flush to her cheeks and a sparkle in her green eyes.

'You look adorable,' he said, snatching her to him.

'And you still have the phone in your hand,' she said, moving pointedly away. 'Champagne?'

'Why not?' He accepted the glass and went to sit beside her on the sofa.

'Fascinating, what happened in Gainesville,' he said.

Her eyes widened, 'I'd forgotten all about Gainesville.'

'Well with your life being so exciting and all, the kidnapping I mean and a mom who wants you to marry an orthodontist. I can't say I'm surprised.'

She rolled her eyes, 'OK so what happened in Gainesville?'

'Seems little Bonnie Hoyt was a hellion, into everything, drink, drugs ...

'Sex and rock'n'roll' she finished for him.

'You got it.'

While they ate the chicken he told her about young Bonnie's problematic youth and how she had run away at seventeen to go live with a marine in Pensacola.

'Jimmy Victor,' she said, chewing on a chicken wing then wiping her fingers delicately on a sheet of paper towel pulled from the large roll she had brought in from the kitchen.

'Yeah, Jimmy I guess. And then her parents – decent God-fearing folks who never missed a Sunday at the Baptist chapel and who had scrimped and saved to pay off a short-term mortgage because the most important thing to them was to own their own home – tried to stop her. They took off after her – got themselves killed in an auto crash on the highway en route to Pensacola.'

Marla stopped chewing. 'No kidding.'

'Darling Bonnie inherited the little house and sold it right away. Just took that money and ran.'

'Oh ... my ... God ...' Marla put down the chicken, suddenly sickened. She took a gulp of the champagne looking at Al over the rim of the glass. 'You don't think ...?'

'What d'*you* think?'

'*I think she killed her parents,*' Marla took another good slurp of the cold champagne.

'Quite a gal, huh?'

'It's odd, how she profited everytime somebody close to her died ... she got the house – or the money from it from her parents; the Buick from Jimmy; and she got ninety-year-old Boss Harmon's money too, or a good part of it. Next thing she was planning on marrying MacIver. She'd already taken him for quite a bit, judging by the Rodeo Drive clothes and the flashy diamond ring.'

'Plus whatever MacIver gave her to help out her mythical "sister" with the "sick kid", as well as the nonexistent "children's Christmas charity".'

Marla's eyes bugged as she stared at Giraud, looking he thought interestedly, like a couple of poached eggs in her Harlow-face.

'Our Laurie/Bonnie is a serial killer,' Marla said solemnly. 'And she kills for gain.'

He grinned at her, that sarcastic little grin that lifted one corner of his mouth and his left eyebrow and usually irritated the hell out of her, but now she was pleased.

'You finally got it, honey. Laurie Martin aka Bonnie-Hoyt-Victor-Harmon is one bad lady.'

Chapter Thirty

The phone rang. Both pairs of eyes swivelled to the table where it lay, trembling with noise. Then Al's met Marla's enquiringly.

'Answer it, Mr PI,' she said.

'It's two-thirty a.m. Marla,' he said lazily. 'Who do you think could be calling?'

'So answer it and find out, why don't you?' she said as though it had never been a problem between them. She poured more champagne, hearing Al's exasperated sigh.

'Nah ... it can wait 'til morning ... office hours, y'know what I mean?'

By now she was burning with curiosity. 'Damn it, Giraud, answer, it's driving me crazy.'

He shook his head, drumming his fingers nonchalantly on the arm of his chair.

'Oohhh!' She snatched up the phone. 'Hello?' Oh! Hi, I'm fine thanks, how are you? You're looking for Al? I'm not sure he's available right now Detective Bulworth, a private eye like him has to get his beauty sleep, you know what I mean ...?'

She was laughing as Giraud grabbed the phone from her. 'Ignore all that, Bulworth,' he said. 'It's just a woman scorned kinda thing, y'know what I mean?' He glared balefully at Marla and she flounced to the window, showing, he noticed quite a lot of gorgeous leg where the Harlow satin was slit to the thigh.

'Yeah, I told her it had to be important if you were calling at two-thirty a.m. – which means it had better be,

Bulworth my friend, because if not then I'm in a hell of a lot of trouble.'

He listened for a long time, saying nothing. 'It didn't, huh?' was his first comment, and Marla swung round, all ears.

'No shit,' he said again, thoughtfully, and she stalked back towards him. She stood close, her ear practically glued to his, trying to catch the other part of the conversation.

'Well, thanks, Bulworth, for the info. Sure. I'll get back to you.' Al clicked off the phone and lay back against the cushions, staring thoughtfully up at the ceiling – coved and twelve feet high – Marla's father was not a real estate mogul for nothing.

'*What?*' she demanded, looming over him. '*What* did Bulworth say?'

'Oh, you know, nothing important – not at two-thirty in the morning.' She punched him hard in the gut and with an *ouff*, he bent double. 'Jesus, Marla what did y'do that for?' he gasped when he'd finally caught his breath.

'Because you deserved it, you jerk,' she said calmly. 'So now tell me what Bulworth said.'

He gave in.

'Bulworth got Bonnie/Laurie's blood back from the oil tanker in Hawaii. It did not match the blood in the Lexus.'

It was not what she had expected to hear and she stared blankly at him. 'Then who's was it?'

'Jimmy Victor's. *He* was the guy found in the canyon. He'd been shot with a bullet from a .40 Smith & Wesson handgun.'

'*Oh . . . my . . . God . . .*' She sank onto the sofa, stunned. 'But Jimmy died ten years ago in the Florida trailer.'

'Seems he didn't.' Al searched in the pockets of his robe for the pack of Camels before he remembered he didn't smoke any more.

'Then who did?'

He stared at her, irritated. 'Marla why do you have this annoying habit of asking the obvious?'

'If it's so obvious why didn't *you* ask?' She glared back at him.

'Because I already have the answer.'

She got up then, stepped closer to him. Her eyes were wide with astonishment. 'You *do*? Then *who*, dammit?'

'Someone else,' he said, dodging her next blow and laughing.

'No, seriously Giraud, *who* died in the trailer fire?' Marla still didn't get it.

Nor did Al. 'Some poor unfortunate. The guy was burned beyond recognition. My guess is Bonnie thought it was her husband. Turned out she was wrong and ten years later Jimmy shows up to haunt her. Blackmail her more likely.'

Al was up and pacing, stringing the story together as he went. 'Steve said she told him she had another appointment to show the house that same afternoon. That could have been Jimmy.'

'Oh my God!' Marla brought her hands up to her face in horror as she realised what had happened. 'Laurie killed him. She killed Jimmy at the house because he was blackmailing her. And she knew Steve Mallard was coming at five-thirty to take a look at the same house. *She framed Steve.*'

'Damn it, Marla, give me a cigarette won't you.' Al drummed his fingers impatiently on the tabletop.

She ignored his request. 'So what happened next?' She was like a kid with a bedtime story.

Sticking his hands in the pockets of his robe, Al started pacing again. 'My guess is she shot him in the car, then drove him to the canyon and dumped him. Then staged her own disappearance, knowing Steve Mallard would be implicated.'

'And that of course the police would believe he'd killed her. The blood on the seat, keys still in the ignition, car doors open . . . her condo abandoned . . . it all pointed to an abduction and possible murder.' Marla was excited. Then she stopped suddenly in her tracks. She stared blankly at Al.

'But then why did Steve try to kill Vickie?'

'He didn't. Someone else was at the house that night. Marla, don't you remember anything at all about your attacker? Come on, hon, I know it's difficult but just search your mind. How tall? How strong? His build . . . His – *or hers* . . .'

Marla stared at the floor, casting her mind back through the fog of concussion and fear to that terrible night. She bit her lip, flinching as she remembered it was still sore, thinking hard.

'A little taller than I am. Thin, I would say, but strong. And the eyes,' she paused. 'I remember the eyes clearly. I've *dreamed* of those eyes . . . Dark, filled with hate . . . crazy . . .' She shivered, not wanting to remember. 'I felt he was evil.'

She dragged herself back from that fearful night then looked at him, astonished. 'What do you mean? Him – or *her?*'

'Think about it, Marla. It could have been a woman, couldn't it?'

'You mean . . . *it was Laurie?*'

'That's exactly what I mean. When Jimmy's body was found in the canyon, Laurie feared the police would be onto her – so she decided to kill Vickie and frame Steve Mallard – a second time. It was Laurie who called Steve in Arrowhead and left the anonymous message that his wife was in danger, knowing he would come running. Only she didn't count on you showing up too, Marla, to spoil her plans.'

'*Oh! My! God!*' Marla leapt in the air then did a kind of wiggly, joyous war dance round the room. 'This means Steve Mallard gets out of jail.' She danced back to Al and threw her arms round his neck in a fierce hug that involved most of her body.

Much as he liked it Al realised he was getting the hug under false pretences. 'Hold it, Marla.' He removed her arms from around his neck. 'Steve is going nowhere. He stays right where he is.'

'*In jail?* Accused of the attempted homicide of his wife and a suspect in the murder of Laurie Martin?' Marla gave an indignant snort. 'You forget I'm a lawyer, Giraud. I could get him out in a minute on this evidence.'

'Sure you could. But you won't. Not yet.' Her brows rose over angry grey-green eyes. Al thought you might safely say she was smouldering. 'Not until we find Laurie Martin.'

She thought about it, biting on her wounded lower lip as she always did when she was thinking hard, flinching again when it hurt. She felt for Steve Mallard, and for Vickie, still in a coma.

She thought of their two daughters living with Vickie's sister, of them believing their father was a murderer, of what they all were going through. It was cruel not to put them out of their misery and tell what had happened, but she saw Giraud's point. Unless they proved Laurie Martin was alive there was still a case against Steve.

She said solemnly, 'We have to find Laurie Martin. Bring her in. Dead or alive.'

Al was forced to laugh. She was like a B-movie detective.

Marla ignored the laugh. 'So how do you suggest we go about proving Laurie is not dead?' She poured more champagne into their glasses, tasted it, it was warm and she made a face, took a couple of ice cubes from the icebucket and plopped them into the champagne. It fizzed wildly in protest. She took another sip. 'That's better,' she muttered, sinking into the cushiony sofa.

'Laurie Martin has the ability to change her looks as well as her identity, her whole persona.' Al was thinking it out as he talked, frowning, concentrating. 'One thing that bugs me about leaving the car in that remote canyon, is how did she get away from there?'

'In Jimmy Victor's car,' Marla said brightly.

'You mean Jimmy was murdered, then drove his own car to the dump site? OK, Miss Logic-Lawyer, think again.'

Marla did think, and quickly. 'Obviously Jimmy had a vehicle to get to the show house. I know,' her eyes lit with excitement. 'Jimmy was driving a sport utility, or a truck, an RV, or whatever ...'

'And Laurie hitched the Lexus to that, towed it to the canyon ...'

'Dumped him ...'

'Then split in the RV ...'

Giraud laughed. 'Marla did I ever tell you, you have a brilliant logical legal mind that sorts out every angle, and that you are amazingly beautiful, And that I love you madly, even though you drive me to distraction and won't let me have a cigarette ...'

She was in his arms now, 'Just think of all the other things

I let you have, baby,' she said, running her tongue lightly over his eyelids, over his mouth, over his ear . . .

'So,' Al said, thoughtfully. 'The first thing to do is find out if Jimmy Victor owned an RV, or if he had rented one.'

'You think Laurie Martin is still driving it?'

'If she has any sense, she will have dumped it by now. But not all killers are sensible. She may just think she's gotten away with it.'

Chapter Thirty-one

Laurie Martin was in the process of acquiring a new identity.

The Firebird Motel in San Francisco was the sixth – or maybe the seventh she had stayed in since she left Laguna – using a different name at each one, and she wasn't happy about moving from cheap motel to cheap motel. The fact was she couldn't do anything about it until she got herself that new identity – and that's why she was taking the train to LA this morning.

With it she could rent an apartment, nothing fancy like her beautiful condo though, because she didn't have the money. Then she could start to have a life again. Of course it was possible to pick up a new identity right here in San Francisco, but since this was where she planned to live it was a little too close to home.

The Bart line deposited her at the Oakland Amtrak station in the Jack London Square building, and she climbed aboard and took a seat by the window, though she wasn't looking at the scenery as the big silver Stratoliner snaked its way down the coast. Anger boiled in her just thinking of the luxurious metallic-gold Lexus, and of her beautiful apartment and her lovely clothes all of which she had been forced to leave behind to make her own 'murder' seem believable.

Experience had made her a cautious woman though, and she had kept a stash of money – fifty thousand of Boss Harmon's 'legacy' to be exact, in the freezer compartment of the refrigerator, buried inside packets of frozen lasagne. In her position she couldn't afford to be complacent, you never knew when you might have to pick up and run.

She had planned on moving on anyway, after marrying John MacIver. That wouldn't have lasted long, a couple of weeks and he would have been found dead in bed. Shit, it would have been so easy, the stupid old fart didn't know from nothin'. He would have trusted her to the ends of the earth. He had already handed over twenty thou – *and* she had seen his bank statements and his securities portfolio. Under the guise of maybe wanting to move somewhere smaller and easier to maintain, after they were married, an apartment, say, close to the ocean, she had got him to have the big Tudor-style house appraised – at the very satisfactory sum of $1.2 million, and was already half way to having his name replaced on the title deed with her own. MacIver would have been way more lucrative than Boss Harmon.

Her dark eyes slitted and her hands clenched into tight fists. If it were not for Jimmy Victor, by now it all would have been hers. She would be the millionaire she had always aimed to be. Now she had to start all over again.

The train journey was long and boring. She had no interest in the beautiful coastal scenery passing outside the window, no interest in the fact that the sun was shining and the sky and the sea were a matching blue. And no interest at all in her fellow passengers, most of whom were hidden behind newspapers or books or coping with their restless kids. Dogs were less trouble. She couldn't exactly have left a kid with the cleaning woman at the motel. A kid would have cost her a fortune, money she would rather spend on herself. The fifty thou was her nest egg, money she now had to build on in order to move to the next level. Her 'operating level' she liked to call it.

By the time the train finally clanked its way into LA's Union Station, Laurie was out of her seat and waiting for the doors to open, and she already had several ideas buzzing in her head. Meanwhile, it was time to take care of business.

She picked up copies of local newspapers from the station newstand then went into the coffee shop. She ordered an iced cappuccino, sipping it through a green straw while she perused each newspaper, searching for the obituaries column. She read each obituary carefully, then wrote down two names, finished her drink and took a taxi to the Public Records Office at City Hall where she knew that death certificates were available for public inspection.

From experience, Laurie also knew that death certificates often included the deceased's social security number. Without such a number she could not open a bank account; rent an apartment; get a driver's licence; a telephone; or a job.

She got lucky. Maria Joseph, aged forty, of Glendale, had died five days ago. And right there on the death certificate was her social security number.

Laurie wrote it down carefully then walked calmly from the Records Office. No one turned to look at her, a nondescript woman with black hair falling in a spiky fringe over her forehead, cut brutally short in the back as though she wanted to make herself look even plainer and more masculine. The heavy-framed eyeglasses didn't help either. And the dark suit she wore looked cheap and dowdy.

Laurie's metamorphosis was complete. There was no vestige of the attractive California blonde she had been just weeks ago. It gave her a buzz just walking past police headquarters knowing that she was the woman the entire state was looking for, past cops on duty who didn't even spare her a glance.

So much for their smarts, she thought, elated. She was smarter than all of them combined. Except maybe for Al Giraud and that glamour-girl professor friend of his. *And speak of the devil . . .*

Marla, in her legal persona of strict black suit, white silk shirt, black hose and medium heels was just going into City Hall. She had a meeting there about one of her students whom she was recommending for a job. For once the last thing on her mind was Giraud, or her second job as Assistant PI – or Laurie Martin.

She strode up the steps, frowning with concentration as she

thought of what she was going to say about her star pupil, who she just knew had a brilliant future as a criminal attorney. He just had that kind of mind: sharp; seeing round every corner; seeing six points of view and verbalising them; he'd be straight-arrow as a prosecutor and devious as they come for the defence. She didn't like him much but she knew he was good.

She barely-noticed the dark-haired woman on the step. *Except wasn't there something vaguely familiar about her?* Puzzled, she turned to look.

Laurie turned at the same time. Their eyes met. Behind the black-framed glases, Laurie's were dark, burning. Then she turned and hurried into the crowd.

Marla put a hand to her leaping heart. She was going crazy, imagining things. With an effort, she pulled herself together, shrugging it away as one of those eerie things; a ghost walking over her grave. The killer's eyes were burned into her brain, that's all. And that poor woman must have wondered what she was staring at.

Pity she hadn't finished her off that night, Laurie thought furiously, but Steve had turned up earlier than she'd expected. Pity she hadn't finished Vickie off, too, but Marla had interrupted her. She had set it up so perfectly. Now things were messy and she hated mess. She knew from experience it only led to trouble. Look what had happened with Jimmy. She had known one day Jimmy would come after her, but when it happened she was taken by surprise.

Chapter Thirty-two

The first big shock of Laurie's life had been six years ago when she had stood outside that torched trailer in Florida, thinking of Jimmy burning to a crisp inside. She had thought by now he must look just like his favourite food – Peking Duck – and she had laughed out loud. Then Clyde had barked and she'd swung round – and looked straight into Jimmy's eyes. God, but it had given her a nasty jolt, like a flash of lightning through her body. Her first thought had been who the hell is it anyway, burning up in the trailer right this minute? Her second was that now Jimmy knew she had tried to kill him.

Then she heard the scream, a sound of such agony it sent a true thrill into her heart. She swung round and saw a man framed in the burning doorway. His clothes, his hair, even his skin was on fire. He was melting before her eyes.

His screams rent the moist Florida night as she stood there, watching him die. It was her lover. He must have stopped by to see her earlier, the door was always open. He had probably been drinking, fallen asleep. Too bad, she thought, as he held out his burning arms pitifully to her.

She turned to look for Jimmy but he had disappeared into the night at the first sound of approaching fire engines and squad cars. She felt the pain in her own blistered hands and arms, scorched when she had put the flame to the trailer and the propane tank exploded. By now, her lover had dwindled into a messy heap near the burning steps. She thought quickly about what to do, then she ran towards him.

The Sheriff found her there, kneeling beside him, her hair and arms blackened from the flames, calling out his name . . . 'Jimmy, Jimmy . . .'

She looked tearfully at the Sheriff as he helped her up, threw a blanket over her shoulders, led her towards the paramedics.

'I tried to help, I tried to save my husband,' she said in a weak little voice, holding out her scorched hands for him to see. 'It was just too hot, too much, I couldn't.' She was still sobbing when they placed her in the ambulance. The little black dog jumped in after her. They made to push him out but she grabbed him fiercely to her.

'Clyde goes with me,' she yelled in a voice so newly strong it startled them. Seeing the surprise in their eyes she lowered her tone again to tearful despair.

'Clyde is all I have left now,' she murmured, burying her face in his soft black fur.

They let her keep the dog.

Turned out she had done Jimmy a favour. He was facing a potential court martial after being accused by a local girl of raping her. And the marine doctor said Jimmy's hands were too badly scorched for prints, but his wife's testimony proved it was Jimmy Victor. Now he was officially 'dead', the rape charges were dropped. And Jimmy had vanished like snow in a spring thaw.

But she knew Jimmy. He was mean, vindictive. She hadn't seen the last of him. One day he would find her. And this time he would kill her.

That's when she got the idea of changing identities; changing her whole look, her entire persona. Starting out again somewhere new, thousands of miles away.

Even at the funeral as she stood over 'Jimmy's' grave with Clyde by her side, along with a few of his marine buddies, she was already planning her next move. As a new woman with a new life, and perhaps a rich new husband. She thought an older man would be best, more malleable, and surely less trouble than a young stud. First though, she had to get the hell out of there.

She had nothing much to pack, just what few new things she was able to buy with the insurance money. And Clyde of course. She was in that Buick and on the road the very next morning, bright and early. She sang as she drove along, pausing now and then to pat little Clyde who gazed adoringly back at her. She liked dogs, they were no problem. Not like people. She had cried buckets when her first little terrier had died, but she hadn't shed a tear when her mom and dad went.

And that was another story.

Chapter Thirty-three

How she had hated growing up as Bonnie Hoyt, in that too-small, jerry-built, frame house, with the termites gnawing their way through the beams and the Florida sun grilling mercilessly down, unfazed by the sole window-unit air-conditioner, bought from Sears in a half-price sale, and the whirring ceiling fans installed by her pa. She would lie naked on her bed at night with the humidity sending streaks of sweat down her neck, down her whole body, watching the twelve-inch, black-and-white TV with the volume turned up loud so as to annoy her parents, cursing them for not being rich, for living *here*. The first Clyde sprawled on the tile floor next to the bed, limp as a rag-doll from the heat; it was too hot even to wear his usual red bandanna.

She had seen the movie *Bonnie and Clyde* and, filled with envy and admiration for the daring and beautiful and vicious Bonnie, she had changed the terrier's name to Clyde. He wore a red bandanna just like the real Clyde, and she imagined him as her partner in crime, robbing banks, slaying FBI men . . .

Her fantasies were wild and violent, far different from the serene face she put on when she was dragged off to the Ebenezer Baptist Church every Sunday morning. Her mother and father were regular churchgoers and she'd had religion thrust down her throat since she was just a baby. She was sick of it. She had learned all she wanted to learn about the Lord and his doings. Somehow she had always felt more comfortable with the idea of Satan. Sounded like at least he might let you have a bit of fun.

A single event had been the highpoint of her young life. Something so scary, so powerful she had never told anyone about it. Not even Jimmy.

She and Jennifer Vanderhoven were sitting together in their school lunch break. Jennifer had big blue eyes and thick blonde hair in a long braid down to her waist and she always wore nice clothes. She hated Jennifer, but Jennifer was goofy, soft and malleable, and she, Bonnie Hoyt, was strong. Jennifer sucked up to her power and she bossed her around unmercifully.

It was winter and cold. The heat had been turned on in the school that week and the janitor was kept busy stoking the old iron furnace. 'Let's go take a look at the furnace room,' she had suggested idly to Jennifer. She had always been attracted to fire.

Jennifer was reluctant, she hated to get her clothes dirty, but Bonnie had linked her arm in hers and practically dragged her there. She knew the janitor would be out having his lunch.

It was hot down there, dusty and smoky. Taking the big iron tongs she pulled open the iron doors and a great heat whooshed out. It wasn't burning exactly, just kind of glowing. Excitement rose in her as she coaxed Jennifer to come stand next to her to feel the warmth. And then, when they were close together, without even thinking she just shoved Jennifer right into that glowing oven and slammed the door. Then she ran out of there as fast as she could.

Ten minutes later when her heart had stoped thudding, she had wandered round the yard asking if anyone had seen Jennifer. And when Jennifer didn't show up in class that afternoon, people got worried and started looking for her. Later that afternoon the police were called in, there were detectives all over the place.

When they found Jennifer's remains in the furnace, the black janitor was arrested and charged with murder.

Bonnie was a witness at the trial and she enjoyed every minute of the limelight, testifying that she and Jennifer had lunch together then they walked around for a bit. Bonnie had left her to go to the bathroom. She never saw Jennifer again. At this point she broke into loud sobs and was hustled gently from the courtroom as other eyes filled with tears of sympathy.

The janitor got a guilty verdict and a death sentence. He went to the electric chair five years later, after all appeals failed.

Bonnie followed every word of the news reports on that case on the twelve-inch, black-and-white TV, and when he was found guilty she laughed out loud. The cops were all such fools, they never looked beyond their noses. Make it obvious and they went for it. It was a philosophy she still used today. Hence the expert disappearing act of Laurie Martin and the obvious implication that Steve Mallard had killed her.

She never thought of herself as evil. She just didn't care. The knowledge that she had killed Jennifer gave her a feeling of strength, of confidence, of superiority. She was stronger than the others. And killing gave her a thrill that was almost sexual, a feeling of tremendous power. She was her own woman, as she had told her dumb parents when she left home, aged seventeen, to join Jimmy Victor in Panama City, adding, 'And there's nothing you can do to keep me here.'

Chapter Thirty-four

Jimmy was different from the teenage boys she knew. Older, sexy, he knew his way around. She found him irresistible. Unfortunately, as she found out later, so did plenty of other women.

Her father had tried to stop her leaving. She had known he would and laid her plans beforehand. She needed money, Lord knows Jimmy didn't have any. And she needed to get rid of her family. She'd already figured out how to fix the brakes. The crash was a spectacular one shown on all the news reports. The car hit the median and flipped over several times. It was totalled, crushed almost flat — as were her mother and father.

At her parents' funeral, the church was packed with the congregation who had known them all their lives, their neighbours, their friends. Bonnie could feel their animosity, their sheathed anger like heat on the back of her neck as she stood at the graveside. She shrugged it off easily, inherited their modest legacy — the little tract house which she promptly sold, plus a couple of thousand dollars in the bank.

She and Jimmy had gone to the Bahamas for a couple of weeks, bought new clothes, gambled in the casinos, had the time of their lives. She never went back to Gainesville.

Jimmy rented the trailer for them near the base, but he was rarely there. He always seemed to be on duty and she complained he worked too hard. They didn't live in a regular trailer park, but off on their own in a little clearing in the woods just off the main road.

Bonnie didn't like it, she was lonely, even with Clyde for company. And she was bored. She would show up at the local market driving the Buick with the little black mutt in its red bandanna, her constant companion. People stopped to stay hello to the cute little dog, pass the time of day, but she had no friends except Jimmy, and Jimmy was not proving to be a good husband.

She found out the truth when she stopped by a bar and grill in Pensacola, and got chatting to the bar-person – a young woman about her own age named Verena Noble.

'I know everybody in this area, how come I haven't seen you before?' Verena asked, serving her a frosty-cold Millers.

'I'm new to the area.' Bonnie eyed the other woman warily: she was attractive with a good body, sexy in a low-cut black dress that fit her like a second skin.

'D'you know a guy called Jimmy Victor?' she asked after a few pleasantries had been exchanged.

Verena rolled her eyes heavenwards. 'I should say. He's in here almost every night, *and* with a different woman every week. That's one guy who surely likes the ladies.'

Bonnie's eyes bugged and her breath came out in an explosive hiss.

'Hey, I didn't speak out of turn, did I?' Verena said, shocked. 'I mean, he's not your fella, is he?'

But Bonnie had ignored her. She had gone right out of that bar, bought herself a black dress, cut low like Verena's, and gone dancing. She spent the night with a guy she picked up, and found she liked it. As with everything, once you knew the ropes it grew easier, she told herself. And it had been easy finding lovers – men were all the same, only too eager, sniffing after her like dogs in heat.

Now, sitting in the train, heading north, back to San Francisco, Laurie laughed to herself at the apt synonym. Her lover had been like a dog in heat – and he had died like that.

*   *   *

After 'Jimmy's' funeral she drove the Buick as far west out of Florida as she could get before running out of gas. She ended up in a small town somewhere in Carolina, drove to a drugstore and bought herself a packet of Coppernob Hair Color, then stopped off at a McDonalds where she ordered a Big Mac for herself and a plain one for Clyde. They ate them sitting in the front seat of the car, then checked into a motel. She emerged the next morning a coppery red-head and continued to drive aimlessly west, always heading vaguely for California.

Chapter Thirty-five

When she hit Falcon City, Texas, she found the real Laurie Martin's purse in the restroom of the diner. Looking through it, she saw her social security card. She had resisted the temptation to take the seventy dollars in cash – this was a small town and it was too risky. Besides the social security number would be more useful to her later, and she wrote it down carefully before handing in the bag.

She sold the Buick because she knew that Jimmy would be able to find her by tracing the car, then made the smart move of joining the local church where she quickly singled out the members of the congregation who had a bit of money behind them.

She found it amusing that the church was the best place in town to find a catch. The Lord had provided her with easy pickings. But she thought Satan would have enjoyed the joke.

Boss Harmon was in a wheelchair and he hadn't been named 'Boss' for nothing. In his time, he had founded a successful car dealership, the same one to which she had just sold the Buick and which was now run by his son. Sexy, in a tight black dress like Verena's and heels, she had got a job as a waitress in the local steak house Boss patronised on a regular basis, and gradually, through Church meetings and Sundays services, where she dressed more demurely, she had wormed her way into Boss Harmon's life.

She made a fuss of him, talked to him, let him ramble on to

her. She patted his withered hand lovingly, smoothed his sparse white hair, lit his cigarettes and never complained, as his son and his wife did, about his terrible cough. She even dabbed his lips with a napkin when he drooled disgustingly over supper.

Boss had said humbly, he couldn't live without her, and she had laughed and said well they had better get married, then he wouldn't have to. 'Otherwise,' she added, 'I might just have to set off on my travels again.'

They were married three weeks after that with her in a white silk dress and matching white stilettos bought on an expensive spending spree in San Antonio. She had always wanted a white wedding. Under the long veil her red hair looked even redder, tumbling around her naked shoulders, and she carried a bouquet of roses in an almost-matching shade of coppery-red. It was *her* day, even though there were no guests and the groom showed up in an ancient tux that hung off his now-scrawny body and had to be pushed down the aisle by a male nurse — Frankie Moreno — whom she dismissed soon after the honeymoon.

The Honeymoon. What a farce that was. Her and Boss and Frankie Moreno in New Orleans at Mardi Gras. Boss didn't want to do much except watch TV in their fabulous suite at the Windsor Court Hotel — she could have lived there permanently, she loved the luxury and pampering, and the 'good morning Madame' and 'Can we be of assistance, madame', stuff so much. So in the daytime she went out and spent Boss's money on an entire new wardrobe. And at night, when she had fed the old boy his sloppy-style supper (his teeth were no longer up to steaks), and she had pleasured him orally or manually, which was as much as he could manage — and about as much as she could manage too, it almost made her lose her cookies right there but she figured at least he'd got something out of the bargain. She wasn't all bad — and it was his fault he couldn't climax, Lord knows she tried.

Anyhow, after that Frankie bathed him and put him to bed, then she and he hit the town. You might say they painted it red. Red as her hair, Frankie had said, laughing when he found out later in bed that she wasn't a true redhead.

Of course, after that little episode he'd had to go. She didn't want any gossip back in Falcon City. She had enough trouble with Loretta and Beau and she wasn't about to give them any more ammunition. So she told everyone she intended to take care of her husband herself.

'That's what the Lord would expect a good wife to do,' she explained solemnly to the pastor at the Sunday morning service.

She kept her waitressing job too. 'So you can't complain I married him for his money,' she told Beau and Loretta, but the truth was she already planned to use it as an alibi. Meanwhile, she had a new name and a new identity. She was safe from Jimmy. He would never find her now.

It had been easy to drop the lit cigarette onto the bedcovers while the old man slept. She had driven immediately to the restaurant in his old Cadillac with the gold radiator grill and its 'BOSS I' numberplate.

She was nervous, pacing like a cat, hoping that her scheme would work, worried that she hadn't been able to stay to take care of things. She poured herself a cup of coffee. It was so hot it burned her throat, but she was grateful for the heat. It seemed to melt the numbness in her chest, in her stomach, in her heart. The waiting was terrible. Her vital organs seemed to have calcified.

After Boss's funeral, where she wore a black veil and placed copper-red roses on his coffin, she said with a sorrowful smile to the attorney in charge of the estate, 'It's all over bar the shouting.' Meaning the angry statements about murder being put around town by Boss's son and his wife, who were contesting the will that left her fifty per cent of Boss Harmon's money plus the house to live in for the rest of her life if she so wished. If not, it went to his son. It was not as much as Bonnie had expected and she was angry. She had paid her dues with that dirty old man. He should have taken better care of her.

Then that bitch, the hoity-toity Loretta, brought in the heavyweights with their threats of investigating Boss's death, and also her past. Remembering the trailer fire and the other dead 'husband', Bonnie knew she couldn't allow that. And so they had won. She cut her losses, took the two hundred thousand and the Cadillac and split.

She was all packed, suitcases stashed in the Caddi along with as many little valuables as she had been able to hide from the eagle-eyed Loretta, and she called for Clyde to come on and hurry up into it baby because they were on their way.

There was no response and none either to her piercing whistle that usually brought him bounding to her side. Puzzled, she searched the house. Then the garden, the pool.

Filled with foreboding, she ran down the long gravel driveway, saw him lying near the gate. He was so still she knew immediately he was dead.

She sank to her knees and stared at his bloody mangled body for a long moment. Then she began to scream. Those screams ripped out of her like a hobgoblin in hell.

Sobbing, she picked Clyde up, wrapped him in her five-hundred-dollar cashmere sweater and placed him gently on the back seat of the car.

Heartbroken, she wept buckets for him. Cursing Beau, who she knew in her gut had done it to get back at her, she drove like a wild woman over to his place, ready to kill both him and his wife.

'An eye for an eye,' Beau said smugly, when screaming, she accused him of killing her dog. But her eyes burned with hate and he stepped quickly back.

Bonnie saw his fear and could have killed him right there and then. But then she would have lost everything and Beau would have won.

So, with the two hundred thou in her pocket, she turned up in California with a new blonde hairdo, a new wardrobe, and, thanks to the real Laurie Martin's social security number, a new identity. She couldn't risk being identified as Mrs Boss Harmon when the time came for her next victim to die from smoking in bed.

Chapter Thirty-six

First thing, she bought a brand new condo, everything pristine, clean, shiny. She furnished it in the tropical Florida colours she had always admired in magazines when she was a poor kid: white carpets, white sofas, pink drapes, turquoise and pink rugs. And a huge colour TV set. It was her fantasy home and she loved it.

She sold the Cadillac and leased the Lexus. She was as happy as a clam. She was smart, attractive, tanned from sessions at the local tanning salon. Her nails were manicured, her hair glossy. She checked out the local churches, joined the one with the richest congregation.

She hated dressing the frump when she attended church but knew it was in her best interests. To combat the effect it had on her, she always wore sexy lingerie underneath to remind herself of who she really was and what she had to offer. This time, she was going for the big one though. This time, she wanted to be a millionaire. And John MacIver was just the ticket.

Meanwhile, she went legit and got a real estate certificate and a job. She was Laurie Martin the businesswoman now, with her own home, her beautiful car, her nice clothes. And John MacIver was eating out of her hand.

She got the second biggest shock of her life when Jimmy showed up and ruined it all.

Jimmy Victor was living down the coast in Pacific Beach, an area of surfers and beachbums, which is what he had become. He drank too much, partied too much, and worked as little as possible. He had found Laurie/Bonnie by accident. An accident that promised him some badly needed cash.

He told her he was browsing through the newspaper when, he saw her photograph in the Homes section, over a half-page of listings. His eyes travelled over it at first without registering. Then something about the blonde woman's smile triggered a memory. He studied the face, examined every feature. It was Bonnie all right. He grinned, delighted. His ship had finally come in. And its name was Laurie Martin.

Laurie jumped when he called her on the phone and said, 'Hello Bonnie, remember me?' She knew he heard it in the indrawn gasp, the long outward sigh, the faint tremor in her voice as she said, 'Who is this? You must have the wrong number.'

'Want me to come over there and check you out?' he had suggested, grinning.

There was a small silence, then she said, 'Meet me tonight, eight o'clock, in Von's parking lot on North Shore Drive.' She gave him directions to the supermarket, then asked, 'What are you driving?'

'A vintage Winnebago,' he said. 'You can't miss it, it has an orange stripe down the side.'

She hadn't missed it. It sat like an eyesore in the middle of the smart suburban Mercedeses and Fords. Rage simmered in her breast as she strode towards it.

'You've improved, Bonnie,' Jimmy said, opening the door to let her in. 'Being a blonde suits you.'

'Cut the crap, Jimmy, what d'you want?' Her voice had an ugly edge; she knew what was coming and she had the Smith & Wesson .40 handgun in her purse. She wanted to kill him now, be done with him ... but she couldn't. But, she didn't know what Jimmy might try and she needed to be prepared.

'What d'ya think I want? From the woman who tried to *murder* me? The woman who killed her lover instead? Then buried him – *in my grave?*'

His voice had a steely edge that she recognised. She knew

what he wanted and had already thought about what to say. 'How much?'

'What say we start with fifty thou?' He smiled at her.

'Fifty? Are you crazy? Where d'ya think I can get that kinda money?'

'You wanna play hardball? OK. A hundred then.' He grinned maliciously at her again. 'That's my last offer. Take it, or leave it.'

He didn't need to say what would happen if she 'left it'. Fury was a tight knot in her stomach now. 'You always were a bastard, Jimmy,' she said, forcing herself to speak calmly. 'I can't lay my hands on that much money right away, but I'll tell you what I'll do. I'll get what I can, and give it to you tomorrow. Think of it as a first payment. I'll have to sell off some things, stocks, jewellery, to raise the rest. It will leave me broke,' she warned, 'so don't even think about coming back for more.'

He laughed as she said it. Blackmail was an ever-open door and they both knew it.

She climbed out of the RV. 'Meet me tomorrow, four o'clock at 1203 Cielo Drive in Laguna. You'll find it on the street map. I'll be waiting for you.'

And waiting she was, with a gun in her hand. She had left exactly an hour and a half to take care of Jimmy and get out of there before Steve showed up. She had set Steve up perfectly. The police would believe he had abducted her. She would have to change her name and her identity once again and she resented it like hell, hated losing her condo, her savings. But she knew that at some point, maybe months, maybe years from now, Jimmy's body would be found and identified through DNA, and the trail would start to unravel and end up at her. She couldn't allow that to happen.

So she shot Jimmy in the back seat of the Lexus when he was counting the fifty thousand she had always kept hidden in the frozen lasagne. He just kind of looked down, surprised, at the blood spurting from his chest, then at her. *'Bitch!'* he spat as the death blood gurgled from his mouth.

She put the money back in her purse along with the Smith & Wesson, wrapped his body in a blanket and pushed him out of sight onto the floor of the car. Then she hitched the Lexus to the RV and drove it to the remote canyon.

It was hell getting rid of the body.

First, she changed into a black sweat suit and hiking boots. Then she wrapped a rope around the body and dragged it to the edge of the ravine. She couldn't be sure it would go far enough down if she just pushed it over the edge, so she started on the long haul down, pulling it, dragging it, pushing it over rocks, stumbling, cursing, until she finally came to an escarpment with a sheer drop.

She waited a minute until she caught her breath, then heaved the body upright and gave it a shove.

Jimmy Victor barelled down that steep slope bouncing from every rock until he disappeared into a gully. Finally, she was free of him.

The climb back up had taxed her strength, and because she didn't want to leave the car with the body, she'd had to drive, several miles along the winding canyon roads, then struggle to unhitch her Lexus from the RV. She was sweating by the time she'd arranged the Lexus to her liking, doors gaping wide, keys in the ignition. She'd wiped up the blood as best she could but there were still stains and that bothered her. She hoped the police would assume it was hers though with all this new scientific stuff she wasn't sure.

Then she drove the RV back onto the freeway and headed for San Francisco. Later, she dumped it on a street in a bad area with the keys still in it. She knew it would soon be stolen.

Chapter Thirty-seven

Then Laurie Martin was back in the cheap motels again. She had almost forgotten what they felt like, the way they smelled of air-freshener and stale sweat and old Chinese takeaway. She had forgotten the thin mattresses and the slippery polyester sheets and the insalubrious dark little bathrooms, and she hated Jimmy even more for bringing her down to this.

She dyed her hair black, and stood in front of the chipped bathroom mirror, hacking it off with a pair of nail scissors. Tears ran down her face, as salty as her bitterness.

'Just look what I've come to,' she whispered, regarding her new ugly self in that cruel mirror. 'And I used to be so beautiful, so successful. I almost had it all.'

The wait for Steve Mallard to be arrested had seemed interminable and she wondered what was wrong. She worried endlessly about it, and she began to lose weight. She just couldn't face real food somehow, her stomach was too fluttery, but a bottle of tequila slid down well, accompanied by potato chips and pretzels while she scoured the TV news programmes, just the way Vickie Mallard was doing, for progress reports.

Al Giraud and his glamorous sidekick were investigating the case, she saw them on TV, read about them in the tabloids. Giraud was too clever, she was getting nervous. The confidence that she was always right, always stronger, was taking a beating. That's when she came up with the plan to kill Vickie Mallard and frame Steve. Then the police would be forced to arrest him for homicide and then she felt sure they would assume he had also killed Laurie Martin. She was desperate, it looked like her last chance.

She made her plans carefully, including obtaining a phoney driver's licence, which was so easy it made her wonder how many of the populace bothered to get real ones. Then she had bought a fourth-hand 1989 Accura and driven to Arrowhead. Disguised as a hiker, she waited on the trail near the Mallard's cabin until she saw Steve depart, driving a Ford Taurus in the direction of the village.

He hadn't even bothered to lock the door, many people didn't up here in the boondocks, and it was a breeze to find a suitable kitchen knife, short and sharp-bladed, in the wooden stand on the kitchen counter.

She must have been half way back to LA before Steve returned. She timed that journey carefully so she would know exactly the right moment to call him disguising her voice as a man's, so he would come running home and find his wife dead. And then right after, the cops would show up – she would make sure of that.

Vickie had been easy – in fact she had enjoyed it – enjoyed the stark terror in her eyes, the gurgling sounds she made as her hands pressured the life out of her, the smell of her blood.

Then Marla had shown up just when she was in the middle of it and it was like being interrupted in the middle of great sex. Even now she could remember how furious she had been, that overwhelming anger that made her crazy. And how the bitch had fought her, until she had – she thought – finally finished her with the wine bottle.

And then she had heard the front door opening – and she was out of there in a flash, hidden by the darkness, driving out of the cul-de-sac heading north on the 101, careful not to go too fast and get stopped.

That lost confidence came right back afterwards when she saw the TV news report of Steve Mallard's arrest on attempted homicide of his wife, and that he was also a suspect in the homicide of Laurie Martin. *She had won again.*

Chapter Thirty-eight

Al and Marla were sitting in a window-booth at James Beach, a restaurant in Venice – California that is, not Italy, Marla thought wistfully. She would have liked that. It would have gotten her away from the endless conundrum that was Laurie Martin. She waved hello to the bartender, John Henry, and he sent her her usual vodka martini without having to ask. She was a regular here and they knew her well.

'Am I such a creature of habit?' she asked Al suddenly. 'I used to be this free person, the first to catch onto something before it even became a trend. Now look at me? They know what I drink, what I eat, probably what I'll be wearing.'

'Never that,' Al said, studying her. 'They'll just think you're in your underwear,' he added, because to him that's exactly what her outfit looked like. Tonight she was wearing an ankle-length seafoam-green silk slipdress overlaid with some gauzy fabric in a paler green. With it she wore towering silver mules trimmed with a blob of maribou (Dolce & Gabanna and they cost a fortune she had told him when he had complained about them) and long dangling antique earrings with green stones that he hoped were not emeralds because they would probably have cost more than he earned in a year, and a huge matching ring. Bizarrely, he thought, she had on a huge steel watch which looked like the kind of timepiece a railroad worker might have used to time steam locomotives in the old days, and also green nail polish.

Marla heaved a gigantic sigh. 'What do you know Mr

Fashion Plate?' She swept a withering glance over his white T-shirt and khakis. Then she smiled. He looked so darned good, so lean and lithe and downright sexy she could have eaten him up – in the nicest possible way of course. 'Only you could look sexy in that outfit,' she added. Generously she thought.

He grinned back at her, his left eyebrow lifted mockingly. 'Seen the Gap ads lately? Plenty of sexy guys wearing exactly what I'm wearing.'

She sipped her martini. 'I think I need to introduce you to Armani.'

'You already did. You bought me the shirt, remember?'

'Yeah, I remember I've never seen you wear it.'

He laughed and took her hand across the table. 'I'm making you a solemn promise,' he said, one hand on his heart. 'One day I will wear that Armani shirt you bought me.'

But Marla wasn't satisfied with this 'one day' nonsense, she knew him too well. '*Which* day?' she demanded, gripping his hand hard so he couldn't wriggle away. 'I need to know so I can plan my own outfit accordingly.'

'OK, the day we capture Laurie Martin. What d'you say to that?'

'I say great, fine, let's hope it's soon.' She stared moodily into the martini glass, shoving the olive around with one finger. Her striped amber/gold hair hid her face but Al could sense something was wrong.

'What's up, hon?' he asked softly. 'Something's bothering you, I can tell.'

She lifted a shoulder, 'Ohh, nothing I guess. Except it's just that I saw someone this morning who reminded me . . .' her voice trailed off and she frowned, studying the olive in the martini glass as though she was about to dissect it.

'*Who* did you see?' He was surprised, Marla didn't usually act like this, sort of . . . fey . . . and distracted.

'Just some woman. Walking down the steps at City Hall.' She shivered remembering the look in the woman's eyes.

The waiter stopped by and they ordered a Caesar salad to

share, then the special striped bass for her and the New York strip for him, medium rare – with fries.

'So what spooked you about the woman?'

'Looking into her eyes, it reminded me of that night . . .'

'At Vickie's?'

She nodded and took another sip of the martini. Her hair slid over her face again but Al could see she was upset.

'Hey, hon, what was it about her eyes? You know it couldn't have been Laurie.'

'Hardly likely, coming out of City Hall with the LAPD right around the corner. No, it wasn't Laurie. This woman was dark, thinner, dowdy – kind of clumsy-looking. But something made me turn to look at her. And you know what, she turned and looked at me too. Must have felt my eyes on her I guess. You know that feeling you get when somebody's watching you.'

'So *how* did she look at you then?'

Marla thought about it. 'I've seen that look before,' she said slowly. 'Like she wanted to kill me.'

Al whistled. He gripped her hand across the table. 'Hey listen, hon, you've got to get over this. I know it was a terrible trauma and maybe I should have done something about it earlier. But now I think you ought to get some help, see a psychiatrist, y'know, that kind of thing.'

She looked at him. 'I wasn't imagining it,' she said evenly. 'This woman hated me. I could feel her hate, like prickles up my spine. I don't need a psychiatrist for that, Giraud.'

He was stumped. 'Then who the hell was she that she hated you so bad?'

Marla shrugged as the Caesar salad was placed in front of her. She thanked the waiter then said, 'It was just some nut I suppose. And just my bad luck to have to see that kind of thing twice.'

'Never again, honey, I promise you.'

Her smile was tremulous and Al thought worriedly he had never seen her like this. Marla was his golden girl; the superwoman. She was bossy; in charge; feisty as they come and perky as hell. He didn't like what was happening to her – and all because some crazy bat gave her the evil eye on the steps of City Hall.

'OK, so I'm snapping out of it,' Marla said determinedly, 'but Al, let's just find this Laurie Martin. I don't like the idea of her running around out there, getting ready to strike again.'

'One thing's for sure, Laurie won't be striking you or Vickie again. She's already got Steve Mallard taking the rap for that. It would ruin things if somebody else had another go at you. Nope, you are safe, Marla. Besides,' he grinned at her, 'I'm not letting anybody near you ever again.'

She laughed. 'Even another woman?'

'Especially another woman.'

She perked up and he thanked God. It took a lot to get Marla down but now she seemed over it. They ate their Caesar salad, enjoyed the striped bass and the steak and she ate half his fries. They were onto the chocolate soufflé which came in a huge French coffee cup and was to die for, like hot molten gold sliding down your throat, when she brought up the subject again.

'When are you going to tell Bulworth what you know about Laurie?' she asked suddenly.

'I hadn't planned on telling him any time soon. Why?'

'Because don't you think he ought to know? After all, he's investigating the case.'

'I'm not employed by Bulworth. I'm employed by Vickie Mallard and her attorneys. I have no obligation to report my findings to the police. Yet,' he added.

She shook her head, frustrated. 'But they may be able to find Laurie quicker if we tell them what we know.'

'You forget, Marla, that these are the same police who have put Vickie's husband in jail charged with her attempted homicide. They found him bending over her body, the knife by his side, and you half conscious on the kitchen floor. The police *believe* Steve did it. And we have only *a theory* that Laurie Martin is alive and is the killer. You tell me, Marla, how we go about proving that to the cops because I'm not sure I can.'

'You're right, I guess,' she admitted reluctantly, but Al knew that in her heart she was afraid and wanted Laurie Martin behind bars and out of her bad dreams.

'Come on, hon, I'll make you some coffee at home,' he promised, scribbling in the air to the waiter for the bill. 'And then I'll tuck you up in bed and sing you a lullaby.'

That got her attention at least. 'Thanks, Giraud,' she said drily as they waved goodbye to the waiter and to John Henry at the bar. 'But I'll take my coffee straight – with no lullabies. As a singer you sound like a hog being butchered.'

'And what do you know about hogs being butchered,' he demanded. And then he wished he hadn't.

By the time they got back it was after midnight, and what was known in California as a 'marine layer', but which personally he still called plain old fog, enveloped the Hollywood Hills. As he swung the Corvette into his courtyard a small black dog skittered from under the wheels. Marla swung round, staring at it and he knew what she was thinking.

'It's not wearing a red bandanna,' he said. 'It's just a stray, or a neighbour's dog attending to his duty before he gets put to bed in a nice warm doggy basket.'

But he could tell Marla was still spooked and it worried him.

Chapter Thirty-nine

Detective Bulworth was not exactly sitting around on his butt, he informed Giraud irately over the phone. And then he added 'But I guess you and the famous Assistant PI/legal eagle are because I haven't heard one gosh-darn word from you in a couple of weeks. Surely by now you have something to tell me? Or is your investigation now closed.'

'Like yours is, Bulworth,' Giraud grinned, imagining the big man with his size 17s propped on the battle-scarred desk and Pow! Powers bringing him yet another cup of the evil drink he called coffee. He guessed you could get used to anything, including bad coffee and Pow!

'Y'mean you've nothin' to tell me, Giraud? I can't believe that.'

'So what d'ya wanna know? That Vickie Mallard is still in a coma? That you have Steve locked up and that, unlike you, Lister is working his butt off preparing his defence? That you still haven't found Laurie Martin's body after weeks of looking. You *are* still looking I assume?' He asked the question knowing perfectly well that by now the Laurie Martin search had been scaled down.

'Still no sign of her, as you are well aware, Giraud. Don't give me this bullshit, just fill me in on what you are up to – because I *know* you and I *know* you must have something up your sleeve.'

Al stuck the ballpoint into his mouth pretending it was a

cigarette and blew an imaginary smoke ring. He was laughing as he said, 'And how d'know that, friend? You psychic now as well as one smart cop?'

'You're just too quiet. You're keeping out of my way and I know if you didn't have something you would be bugging the hell out of me and my department.'

'But Bulworth, why should I bug you? You have your man safely locked up in jail. What more can I ask of you?'

'Bullshit!' Bulworth snarled again. 'You're holding out on me and I know it.'

'You're in fantasyland, detective. Come on now, you're my friend, would I hold out on you? No, we're in just the same boat, wondering who killed Jimmy Victor as well as what happened to Laurie Martin. Quite a few unsolved crimes you've got around there, buddy. Better get back to your desk.'

He laughed as he heard Bulworth's snort of annoyance and then the phone was slammed down. That would give the cop something to think about, though in truth Bulworth was a clever detective – he had known he was holding something back.

'Not yet, Detective Bulworth, my friend. I'm not telling just yet,' he said, as he locked his office door and headed in the Corvette for the Apple Pan and a lunch of a piled-high tuna sandwich and fries. Marla would kill him about the fries, but what the hell, a guy was only young once.

Marla parked in the hospital lot then walked through the steel-grey reception and took the elevator up to the third floor – and another world.

This was a silent floor, devoid of the usual human bustle and camaraderie. Nurses in scrub-green hurried along the shiny grey corridors, peeking into rooms whose doors were left open for constant vigilance. Inside those rooms patients in intensive care were hooked to monitors and drips, ventilators and catheters, their lives now totally dependent on others. Vickie Mallard was out of intensive care but not out of the coma she had fallen into almost four weeks ago.

Marla said hello to the nurses on duty who smiled at her as she went by. They knew her by now, she was there almost every day, though she always chose a time when she knew the family would not be around. She didn't want to bump into Vickie's sister – and especially her daughters – because they knew she had also been attacked and that she had seen Steve, bending over their mother's bloody body. It would not have been a happy meeting for any of them.

Vickie was petite but now she looked shrunken in the hospital bed. She was hooked to the monitor but they had, at last, been able to take her off the ventilator and she was breathing on her own. A tube fed a yellowish liquid into a vein in her wrist and a catheter supplied essential nutrients.

Marla lifted Vickie's limp hand, it felt cool, cold almost and instinctively she covered it with her own warm one. *It could have been me lying there*, she thought, remembering that awful night. *Me being fed by tubes, being kept alive while my brain, my soul, the real me is* . . . who knows where?

Who knows where Vickie Mallard is right now? Is she dreaming about her pretty little daughters? Is she worrying about them? Is she going over and over in her lost mind what Laurie Martin did to her? Does she even *know* it was Laurie?

She sat by Vickie's bed, stroking her hand, talking quietly to her, telling her things only she and Giraud knew. She just didn't want Vickie to die believing her husband had tried to kill her. Vickie, at least should know the truth.

'It wasn't Steve, Vickie. I promise you it wasn't him, *I know the truth.* Laurie Martin is alive, she is the killer,' she whispered into her ear. 'Steve didn't do it, Vickie, believe me. Soon he'll be here with you, I promise you that. And your life will be back to normal. Just trust me on this Vickie, trust me with your life . . .'

But there was no answering squeeze of the hand, no flicker behind those closed eyelids, not even a sigh from Vickie Mallard.

Instead, it was Marla who sighed as she arranged the pink-and-green parrot tulips in a vase and set them where Vickie might see them when she woke up. *If she woke up.*

She dropped a kiss on Vickie's colourless face, heard the faint rasp of her breath and thanked God that now she was breathing unaided. At least it was progress and made her less frightening to her children. And at least now she looked human. Her wounds had healed, though the scars still looked raw, and in the event she returned to this world she would need extensive reconstructive surgery on her face. But she looked like Vickie and not like Frankenstein and that helped.

On her way out Marla was surprised to meet Ben Lister hurrying down the shiny antiseptic corridor.

'What are you doing here?' she asked astonished. Attorneys' lives were ruled by time – and their time cost money. A hospital visit was surely not in his brief.

'Steve asked me to come and speak to Vickie, since he can't do it himself.'

She nodded. Of course Steve couldn't, he was still locked up in the Twin Towers. She turned and walked back with Lister, matching his hurried pace. 'What does he want you to talk to her about?'

His myopic glance flicked her way. 'What d'you think?'

'To say he's sorry he tried to kill her?' She knew of course that he hadn't but she wanted to see what Lister would say.

His reply was a deep sigh as they stood at Vickie's doorway. 'He might as well, but he's still insisting he's not guilty. Beats me though, how the hell we're gonna prove that.'

Marla could have told him but for once she kept her mouth shut. Instead, she stood next to him as he looked down at Vickie Mallard in her tightly-sheeted, neat white hospital bed. Lister looked deeply uncomfortable.

'Er, Vickie,' he began ... 'my dear, I've come from Steve to tell you this. I was with him just a half hour ago, and he asked me to come here to tell you that he loves you.'

He glanced desperately up at Marla, 'It's like talking to a corpse,' he muttered, agonised. 'I'm sure she can't hear.'

'Maybe she can,' Marla urged him on.

'Er, Vickie, my dear,' he began again. 'Steve says to tell you the truth, that he did not do this to you. He is innocent, Vickie.

Innocent, he says. And he also says to tell you that we will find whoever did this terrible thing and they will pay the ultimate price. Trust him, he said, Vickie. Just trust him. And get well. He so badly wants you to get well. He wants you back again Vickie, in the land of the living.'

'And not the half-dead,' he whispered to Marla, backing away from the immobile figure on the pristine white bed.

Marla patted Vickie's hand again before she left, 'Trust him, Vickie,' she whispered. 'Trust Steve and everything will be all right.'

But she wasn't sure it would be all right for Vickie, ever again. Still, somehow she felt better that perhaps Vickie now knew the truth.

Chapter Forty

Laurie liked her new name, Maria Joseph. It was kind of a word play on the biblical names of Mary and Joseph and that made her laugh.

She decided that the sprawling suburb of Oakland, home to Berkeley University and its thousands of students, was a better place for a person to lose herself. Maria Joseph could slip by unnoticed among the masses. Besides, it was cheaper than San Francisco and there were plenty of places to rent.

The small apartment she finally found was close by the University, on a wide street with busy traffic. Her two rooms though, were in the back, facing a small ragged garden. The place was old with a thirties art-deco green-and-black-tiled bathroom with a cracked washbasin and a tub-shower with a shower curtain stiff with age. The kitchen had an ancient Kenmore stove, and a Formica breakfast bar separated it from the ten-by-twelve-foot living room, containing an ancient red vinyl sofa with a matching club chair and a chipped glass and chrome coffee-table. The other end of the ten-by-twelve accommodated an ugly yellow oak table with two odd chairs, and the bedroom, of approximately the same size, had twin beds with cheap but new mattresses and a yellow oak dresser with a mirror over it.

It was the new mattresses that decided her; most of the other places she had seen were real flea-bags. This was a building used by students and she guessed she had just gotten lucky, that the old mattresses must have been in such bad shape the property management had been forced to buy new ones.

She sighed as she took stock of her new domain. The pang in her heart as she remembered her beautiful pristine condo was like the turn of a knife. Somebody had to pay for bringing her down to this, she thought vengefully. And somebody would.

She paid a visit to the nearest J. C. Penney where she bought towels, sheets and blankets, and a couple of white coverlets that she hoped would make the bedroom look more elegant but somehow only served to show up its shabbiness. She found a couple of cheap lamps as well as a few necessary dishes and cutlery and she stocked the refrigerator with bottles of tequila and wine, plus several frozen lasagne into which she placed the remainder of her fifty thou – less the considerable amounts she had spent on living in the past few weeks.

She refused to buy a cheap TV set though. Never again for Bonnie Hoyt/Victor/Harmon was there going to be a twelve-inch, black-and-white. Circuit City had a good bargain on a thirty-two-inch Panasonic colour set that they installed the same day, and she spent that evening lying on the red vinyl sofa in front of it, watching every newscast for word of any progress in the case againt Steve Mallard, hoping a trial date might have been set. And also checking anxiously to see if Jimmy's body had yet been found in the canyon.

Nothing on either front. Bad news and good news came in pairs. Sighing, she downed the tequila and glanced round her dark, empty, new home. She was lonesome.

The next morning, early, she combed every dog pound in Oakland and the surrounding areas looking for a mutt to replace Clyde. It had to be small, black and fluffy. It had to be *exactly* like the old Clydes. She was obsessed by it.

Finally, after a week of searching, she found a one-year-old dog who looked sufficiently like the original. He was smart. He came when she called, sniffing her hands eagerly and giving her face an enthusiastic lick when she bent to pat him. She bought him an expensive collar and lead, a red bandanna and a McDonald's burger (plain). Bonnie and Clyde were reunited.

After that, she began her search for a church, one with a suitably older congregation that was also wealthy enough for her purpose. As always she was thorough in her research, first finding the names of churches, researching the demographics of each neighbourhood, then going personally to inspect them. She drove round half of Oakland and its outlying areas before she pinpointed two churches, then made a point of attending a couple of Sunday sevices at each before making a decision. When she did, she knew it was the right one.

She wore a curly blonde wig and a nice pink-flowered dress that first Sunday morning, with a wide-brimmed straw hat, white sandals and a white handbag. During the service she kept a discreet watch on the worshippers, discarding mentally those men who though old were more vigorous, as well as several old women who had they only been male would have been perfect targets. Statistics were against her in her quest: they said men died at a younger age than women.

After the service, she introduced herself to the Reverend Isaiah Light as Miss Maria Joseph.

'I'm new to the area, Reverend,' she said, giving him her shy smile, 'I'm from Florida originally and my family have always been devout Baptists. Now I plan on becoming a regular member of your flock.'

The Reverend Light had fat jowls and grey hair and he beamed a welcome. 'Always glad to see a new face, and especially such a ...' for a second or two the Reverend was lost for the right word ... 'such a *charming* one,' he finished gamely.

She gave him that shy smile again and he said, 'Why don't I introduce you to some of our members, they'll be glad to welcome you too, and to offer any help you might need. I know relocating is always difficult, unless of course you have lots of old friends here?'

'Actually, no, I don't have friends,' she admitted, sounding as wistful as she knew how. 'I'm all on my own. That's why I came to you. I knew that church would be a good place to meet people and start my new life.'

'So, here's Ethel and Murray Levitch.' The Reverend grabbed

hold of a passing couple. 'Say hello to our newest church member, Ethel. Miss Maria Joseph recently moved here from Florida, and knows no one.'

Murray and Ethel were in their seventies, nicely turned out in golf clubbish attire, kind-eyed and smiling. They bid her welcome and mentioned she would have to make a point of attending the monthly church suppers, held regularly on the last Tuesday of the month. That way she would meet all the church members and was sure to make friends real soon.

'Next Tuesday is all planned,' the Reverend added jovially. 'Why not come along and meet some more of our members? I'm certain they'll give you a hearty welcome.'

It was that easy.

She was there on Tuesday all right for the church supper, wearing black this time, with just a touch of pink lipstick and the string of cultured pearls Boss Harmon had given her, as well as the snake ring from John MacIver that she never took off. It had become part of her personality. The coiled snake with its tail in its mouth symbolised her cleverness at wriggling out of danger, her ability to become someone else, and to keep a secret.

That Tuesday night she retained her shy demeanour and her smile, not pushing herself forward, and waiting to be introduced. But she made sure she met everyone, especially all the men. There were one or two who looked likely prospects. She felt that old buzz of excitement. Things were definitely looking up. And this time she would make sure she became a millionaire.

Meanwhile, money was dwindling fast. She had paid cash for the old Accura. Then there was the security deposit and two months' rent on the apartment and the cost of equipping it. Plus a whole new wardrobe. To say nothing of motel and living expenses for the past couple of months. She needed a job.

It was too risky to attempt to go back into real estate yet. Maybe next time – but then she wouldn't need to work next time would she? She was going to be rich. Still, you never knew, she might want to keep her hand in, might want to become even richer. After all, she enjoyed what she did.

In the meantime, she took a job as a waitress at the Mansion Bar & Grill in Oakland. She hated it but it paid the rent and expenses, and she got free food – plus she always made sure to take a bit of steak or a burger for Clyde, who waited patiently in the car in the parking lot until she had finished her shift.

Of course, she looked quite different when she was working. Then she was the Maria Joseph with the short dark hair and the heavy glasses and she didn't smile much at the customers. Didn't see the need for it really, most of them left a tip anyway they were just so used to doing it. Waitressing was tough enough without having to be pleasant with it.

She was biding her time, starting to feel safe again and things were going her way. Old Morgan Davies, aged eighty-five, was already raising his hand and smiling eagerly at her when he saw her in church on, Sundays.

Morgan was a widower – he had told her his wife of fifty years had died two years ago and that he had missed her every single day since.

'Of course you have,' she said patting his hand comfortingly. 'Why, I've missed my mother and father like that ever since they were killed in the auto accident down there in Florida. And that was years ago now.

Morgan held his hand to his ear, concentrating on the movements of her lips and she know that, like a lot of men his age who were losing their hearing, Morgan hated wearing his hearing aid. That was OK, it made her job even easier. Bad eyesight was good too, in fact the more decrepit the better.

She laughed out loud, thinking about it and old Morgan, bewildered, laughed along with her. Hadn't they been talking about her parents being killed in an auto accident? Then why was she laughing. He must have missed something, darn it.

'An auto accident?' he asked.

'She nodded and a sad look came into her eyes. 'It was terrible. Of course I was very young, only seventeen. Their car hit the median on Highway 95. It flipped over and they were both crushed. I ... I was the one who had to identify them ...' her voice dropped to a low sigh and instinctively Morgan reached out and took her hand.

'Poor girl, poor little girl,' he said comfortingly.

Morgan's hand felt like sparrowbones in hers, dry and hot and very definitely old. A fierce yearning hit her suddenly, and she wanted to be holding the hand of a young man, a virile young stud who would crush her to him and fuck her brains out. Instead, she would have to manipulate this one to some sort of Viagra-driven ecstasy. Her stomach revolted at the thought, but then she remembered the money and everything slotted into place again.

She had her mark and was all set.

Chapter Forty-one

Giraud was stumped. If he had expected Laurie/Bonnie to surface, she wasn't doing it. Nor was she leaving any clues around, either in LA or in her own old neighbourhood of Laguna. Bulworth was still out looking for her body and now Giraud was starting to doubt himself. Maybe he was wrong? Maybe Laurie *was* dead? Maybe Steve did kill her after all and the Jimmy Victor thing was just a coincidence?

Some coincidence! He chewed on the ballpoint pen wishing deep in his heart it was a Camel unfiltered. Of course he wasn't wrong. Laurie was clever, that's how she had gotten this far. By now he would bet she had a new identity, a new persona, a new look, just the way she had done it before. But finding her was going to be like looking for the proverbial needle in the haystack. Meanwhile, the case against Steve was progressing and trial dates were expected to be set. He couldn't let this charade go on much longer, but he knew that Bulworth would dismiss his theory as bullshit – though the Jimmy Victor corpse might give him pause for thought.

It was a dilemma and not the sort Giraud was used to facing. He had promised Vickie Mallard he would find out if her husband was guilty or not. Now he was sure he was not, but he couldn't prove it. Not until he found Laurie Martin.

He had come full circle again in his thoughts and he sighed, drumming his fingers on his desk. Vickie Mallard was still very much on his mind and on an impulse he left his office, picked up some roses from the florist on Sunset and drove to the hospital.

Marla was rollerblading with the other habituees of the Venice Beach boardwalk. It was more fun than the gym, which she hated and it kept her in shape. Besides, she could admire the muscle boys on the beach while getting full aerobic benefit and where else could you do that?

Today she was wearing black lycra biker's shorts, a white plastic sun visor and a T-shirt that said, '*I don't do Perky.*' Along with, of course, the requisite gloves, elbow and knee guards. Not that she ever fell, she was far too expert for that. She could practically do ballet on those in-line skates. All she needed was the obligatory little dog in a red bandanna running alongside like most of the others on the boardwalk. The red bandanna made her think of Bonnie and Clyde, aka Laurie, and she too heaved a deep sigh.

When was Giraud going to come up with something? It seemed they had been standing still for over a week now – a week that she knew must feel like eternity to Steve Mallard. There was still no word of a stolen or abandoned RV, though Giraud had his contacts in all the right places and would surely have known if anything had turned up.

And as his assistant, she should have been thinking, getting onto it, investigating things. But what things? They had it all figured out – and nowhere to go with it.

She zoomed along, expertly dodging pedestrians, children and dogs, oblivious to the roar of the ocean, the heat of the sun, the smells of hot dogs and cotton candy. She passed the stall selling miniature baseball caps for dogs, with matching bandannas – as modelled by a bored dachshund and a yappie Yorkie who didn't seem to take too kindly to his outfit, and it brought her – full circle – again to Bonnie and Clyde.

Bonnie/Laurie couldn't know, of course, that Giraud had sifted through her past and now knew who she was as well as what she was. And Bulworth certainly didn't know – yet –

though he had found out that Jimmy Victor had supposedly already died in a fire in Florida several years ago. The remains in 'Jimmy's' grave had already been exhumed and DNA and dental tests were being done to try to identify the true victim of that fire. Marla was wondering who it could be too, when she was hailed loudly.

'Hey, miss, ma'am, stop right there please.'

She heard a bike racing behind her and swung round in a perfect curve, skating backwards. 'You mean me?'

'I sure do.' The bicycle cop propped his machine against some convenient railings and took out his book. He was young, blond, suntanned and muscular in black biker's shorts like hers and a white poloshirt with POLICE written across the back in dark blue. And he wasn't cracking a smile, though Marla gave him her best.

He also had ice-green eyes and Marla bet when he smiled he had a perfect set of all-American-super-straight-California-white teeth. He was, in short, to die for.

'So? What's up?' she asked conversationally.

'You are aware that there is a speed limit on the boardwalk for bladers. And you ma'am, were exceeding that speed limit.' He indicated with his pen the sign that said, plainly, '*Bladers 5 m.p.h. Violaters will be fined $50.*'

'Aw, come on,' Marla said jokingly, as he began to write busily in his book, 'you can't be going to give me a ticket for roller-blading!'

'That's the law, ma'am.' He was solemn as the Pope and as unhumorous as Kenneth Starr.

'There's no way you could have known how fast I was going,' Marla fumed. 'And anyhow, how could I go faster than five when there are all these pedestrians?'

'Exactly. It's the pedestrians I'm concerned about, ma'am.' He handed her the ticket. 'Maybe next time you'll keep within the law.'

Marla snatched the ticket and inspected it. 'I'm going to fight this in court,' she said angrily.

'I wouldn't advise it, ma'am. I have a record of your speed

right here, and I was riding behind you and clocked fifteen miles per hour on my odometer.

He adjusted his silver helmet and was already climbing back on his bike. 'Take care, ma'am.'

She stared after him as he cycled away. His fine-tuned muscles moved rythmically and a small patch of sweat stained the white shirt between his shoulder blades.

Quite a hunk, she thought with a sigh.

Her cellphone rang. 'Hello?' she said, skating moodily back in the direction of Santa Monica where her car was parked.

'Oh, it's you Mom. And no, I wasn't expecting anyone else. Well, actually, yes I was. No, not a boyfriend, Mom, business.' She wiped the sweat off the back of her neck with a small hand-towel she carried. 'You've met *who*?' She groaned loudly as she heard the answer. She might have known it.

'Mom, I don't care *how* eligible he is, I'm not interested. And yes, I am still going out with that lout – I happen to like him. A lot.' She laughed at her mother's next remark. 'I don't know who I inherited my bad taste from. I hate to think. And no, *Mom*, I am not available for dinner at the Ivy tomorrow night. Or any other night with *Mr Right*. OK?'

'Good try, Mom,' she grinned as she pushed the end-call button. The phone rang again immediately and she sighed, thinking it was her mother again. But it was Al.

'Marla?' he said.

'Of course it's Marla, who do you think would be answering my cellphone?'

'I'll bet fifty bucks you've just been talking to your mother,' he said.

'How did you know?'

'Because when I rang a couple of minutes ago your phone was busy, and you always sound snippy when you've been talking to your mother. She trying to set you up again?'

'Of course she was.' Marla sighed again.

'Ever think maybe you should take her up on it? Go out and meet one of these eligible Mr Rights?'

'What? So I can compare them with Al Giraud, famous

ex-redneck and notorious Private Investigator you mean. Nah, you wouldn't stand a chance and I couldn't bear to do that to you.'

'Thank God,' he said, 'because I don't think I could take it.'

Marla was laughing now. 'You mean there's a sentimental streak in that flinty heart, Giraud?'

'You bet. And it's had me in tears already this afternoon. Marla, there's been a miracle — a minor miracle but still a miracle. I'm at the hospital. I came over here just by chance because I hadn't seen Vickie in a while and, after all, the lady is my employer.'

'You mean you have a conscience too?' she said laughing. Then it hit her. 'What miracle? *Giraud … oh, you don't mean …?*'

'No, she's not out of the coma — but she opened her eyes. I yelled for the nurses and they came running, and the neuro specialists too. They are testing her now, checking whether she sees anything or whether it was an involuntary reaction.'

'I'm on my way.' Marla was already speeding back down the boardwalk. 'I'm in Venice, I'll be there in half an hour, wait for me, Giraud. By the way, what was it you were you saying to her when she opened her eyes?'

'I was holding her hand. I said, "Vickie, this is Al Giraud. Trust me. Steve is innocent. And I will prove it."'

'And then her eyes popped open, just like that?'

'Just like that.'

From behind her, Marla heard the bike cop shouting at her again. She spun round the corner, dodged down an alley, snaking her way through the little streets until she came to Main where her car was parked. The to-die-for cop wasn't going to give her another ticket. No way. This was an emergency.

In minutes, she was in the Merc, tugging off the skates. Without even taking the time to put on her shoes, she was pulling barefoot into the Saturday afternoon traffic, heading for the 101 freeway and the hospital. And quite possibly a speeding ticket.

Chapter Forty-two

There were so many things whirling around in Vickie's head she didn't know where to begin to sort them out, and that frightened her. She was college-educated, had a logical mind, she always knew exactly what she was doing. So why not now?

Her eyes refused to move to the right or left and therefore all she could see was a rectangle of white ceiling. And those strange faces that from time to time loomed over her. They waved their hands over her eyes but she didn't even blink. She couldn't blink. *Why the hell couldn't she blink?*

It had something to do with Steve, she knew that. *Steve* ... what was it they said about him? Someone had said something. It was important, she knew, but now she couldn't sort it out from the rest of the jumble that was her brain. It felt as though the wires had gotten crossed and all the connections were coming out wrong. Tears filmed her vision, she felt them snaking down her cheeks, felt their heat against her chilly flesh, tasted their salt on her dry lips.

'*Oh my God,*' Marla put her hands to her own eyes as she felt her own tears coming, 'Al, she's crying. *She's actually crying.*'

But he was already bending over Vickie, mopping up her tears, talking to her slowly and so tenderly it made Marla cry even harder.

'It's OK, Vickie. You had a bad accident. Now you're going to be just fine. Take it easy. And remember this, Steve loves you. OK? He asked me to say that specially. *He loves you.* And he is *innocent*, Vickie. So don't worry about a thing except getting well again.'

Vickie wanted to thank him for clarifying the hurly burly of thoughts, the scraps of information, the snippets of conversations in her head and moulding them into a whole thought. But she could not. *Steve loved her.* Steve was *innocent.* She would cling to those words, hold on to them like precious jewels until she fought her way out of this stifling fog ... *oh my God, the girls ...*

'And your daughters are well, they come every day to see you, you know that?' Marla was sitting by the bed now, stroking her hand. 'The doctor has called them and they are on their way to see you ...'

'Even as we speak,' Al muttered and Marla laughed.

Vickie liked the sound of that laugh, it made her smile too even through her tears.

'*Oh my God, she's smiling. She understands us,*' she heard the woman say with a whoop of triumph that brought other people running to peer at her again, to take her pulse, her blood pressure, to wave things in front of her eyes and more.

And this time she blinked. 'Oh my God', was right, Vickie thought, and she had Him to thank for the fact that she was alive, that she could blink and smile and see – at least a little bit.

And for the fact that she was out of that deep dark pit of despair where her brain had roiled around like heat in her head, burning her, stabbing her ... but she didn't want to think about that. Not now. She wanted to see her babies, her little girls, whose names were ...? Oh now she couldn't even remember their names. The tears started again but this time she welcomed them. This time she knew they meant she was alive.

Chapter Forty-three

Marla's car was in the courtyard blocking his garage entry. Giraud smiled as he parked the Corvette next to her Merc, giving his own automobile a proud little pat before he unlocked his front door.

Music drifted through the house. Now, Al's tastes ran toward big bands or smoky nightclub jazz, while Marla was strictly *au courant* with whatever was going down music-wise at the moment. But this was Barry White, rolling out those songs from somewhere deep in his gut and his nerve ends, sensual as sex. Firelight glinted off the table set with flowers and crystal and candles – and champagne waited in a frosted silver bucket.

Light streamed from the kitchen as Marla appeared, silhouetted in the doorway. She was wearing a very short black dress with ruffled white petticoats peeking from beneath, a white organdie apron, fishnets and stilettos. Oh, and a little white halo of a cap perched on her golden blonde hair. She was Marla's version of a French maid.

'Ah, Monsieur is home!' She strode toward him, hips swinging, 'Welcome, m'sieur. Your bath is ready, sir.'

Taking him by the arm, she hurried him to the bedroom, pushed him onto the bed then knelt and began to unlace his sneakers. 'Ah such poor tired feet,' she murmured throwing the sneakers over her shoulder and bending to kiss his toes.

He watched, amazed. 'Any woman who can kiss a guy's feet straight out of sneakers, it must be true love,' he said.

But she was already unbuttoning his shirt, unbuckling his belt. She threw that over her shoulder too, with a contemptuous Gallic '*Pouf*'. Marla had always been jealous of that rearing-silver-mustang belt, she suspected it of being a gift from some previous paramour.

She was leading him into the bathroom now. The black tub was filled to the brim with pink bubbles and smelled, he said, like a New Orleans cat house.

'And what do you know about New Orleans cat houses?' Marla demanded suspiciously, slipping out of her role as the French Maid.

'Scuse me, mamzelle, it was purely a figure of speech.'

'Monsieur will get in the bath and soak and his little French maid will bring him a nice cold glass of champagne,' she said, pouting prettily. He protested he was a shower man at heart and that he hated bubbles, but she gave him a helpful little shove until he was partly submerged.

'Monsieur will do as he is told,' she said firmly.

'Wrong role,' he called after her. 'Isn't that the Governess/Dominatrix?'

'Ohh ... *pouf*,' she said again, on her way to get the champagne.

She was back minutes later bearing a round silver tray with a single crystal flute. Kneeling by the side of the tub, she offered it to him.

'Mmm,' he took a sip, 'not bad for box-wine.'

'Philistine,' she muttered, snatching it back from him and tasting it. 'Delicious,' she added, closing her eyes dreamily. Nothing but the best for my poor m'sieur. And now I must go prepare *le diner*.'

He groaned. 'Marla, don't tell me you're cooking? I'm not sure I'm up for this.'

'You'd better be,' she said saucily, peeking her head back round the bathroom door. 'I'm not going to all this work for nothing.' His laughter followed her to the kitchen.

He lay in the bubbles, sipping champagne, thinking about Marla in that short skirt and the fishnet stockings. There was a smile on his face. Life wasn't too bad, after all, he decided.

'Ready, m'sieur?' Five minutes later and Marla was back again, holding out a fluffy white bathsheet, helping him from the tub. She patted him dry, taking care over his more personal parts then led him by the hand into the bedroom.

'What? Before dinner?' he asked, raising his eyebrows

She gave a very French little snort. '*Mais non, M'sieur*. For the French, food always comes first.' And she held out a dark-blue velvet robe with satin lapels for him to slip on.

He groaned, putting his arms into the sleeves then peering bewildered at himself, 'I feel like an ad for Victoria's Secret.'

'You look like a Frenchman,' she corrected, kissing him, but she was laughing.

Al closed his eyes, making the most of it. He would have liked more of the kisses, but she was too busy.

'Come, m'sieur.' She had him by the hand again, leading him to the table.

'Beautiful, delightful,' he said, eying the white orchids, the damask napery, the Christofle and the Baccarat. 'But where the hell did you get all this?'

'Borrowed it, from my mother,' she retorted.

'*Borrowed? Your mother?* You mean she *lent* you this?'

'I told her I was giving a little dinner party for a thirty-six-year-old unmarried orthodontist.'

He was laughing as he she held the chair for him. 'There's something wrong here. The table is set for only one person.'

'But of course. A French maid never eats with her m'sieur. She is only here to serve him.'

He nodded. 'Is that so? Then tell me something, mamzelle, when exactly do the French maid and the m'sieur get together? Y'know what I mean?' He wiggled his eyebrows suggestively and she giggled and slapped his hand.

'Oh, M'sieur is *soooo* naughty.' And she whisked away with a deliberate little flip of her minute skirt that gave him a distinctly pleasing rear view.

She was back in a flash carrying a tray, a little lopsidedly – he heard dishes clanging together as she tottered on her stilettos and a muttered 'shit' as she corrected her balance and the sliding tray. 'I'm not great at this waitress bit,' she announced, plonking the tray thankfully onto the table.

Al looked interestedly at what it contained. Caviare in an iced crystal bowl; fresh asparagus with a lemon Hollandaise; poached salmon exquisitely decorated with wafers of cucumber and sprigs of dill, a salad of snow peas and other green growing things. There were even tiny blinis for the caviare.

He looked her in the eye. 'Marla, where d'you get all this?'

'I slaved in the kitchen all day for my m'sieur,' she fluttered her eyelashes prettily. Then, 'Actually it's from Gelsons in the Palisades,' she confessed.

'You gonna join me, hon? Or are we keeping up the French maid and m'sieur thing all night?'

'Oh, but I wanted to surprise you, to play a little game with my m'sieur ...'

He dunked an asparaus tip in the caviare and held it to her mouth. 'Taste,' he commanded.

She groaned, regarding the caviared asparagus and shaking her head disgustedly. 'Philistine,' she murmured again, taking it in her mouth.

'I love it when you curse,' he said, kissing her when her mouth was full. He licked the caviare off her lips. 'Do you think anyone ever ate caviare like this before? Who needs blinis when they have a French maid?'

'Oh, *pouf*,' she giggled flipping her little French skirt at him. And then she was sitting on his knee, feeding him spoonsful of caviare in between kisses. And in no time at all they were on the rug in front of the fire, glasses of Cristal to hand; Isaac Hayes outdoing himself in smooch on the stereo; Gelson's poached salmon and jade salad forgotten as they kissed lingeringly.

His hands slid under her little French maid skirt and she was naked under those stockings, just as he had known she would be. 'Why do you have to have the butt of a teenager?' he mocked, gripping her rounded rump lovingly.

'Because I am — almost — still a teenager,' she murmured back, licking the curve of his ear and sending delightful little chills through his entire body. 'Oh yes, baby, oh yes,' she sighed as his hands slid inside the stockings. And then she was wriggling out of them and he guessed you could almost see the little electric zigzags of passion flashing like lightning between them.

Marla's vocal repertoire when he made love to her was a wonder to hear: demands; ecstatic cries; soft little yelps . . .

'I always did like a yelper,' he said a long time later, when it was over and they were sipping flat champagne contentedly in the fire's afterglow.

'*Oui, m'sieur*, a French maid always aims to please,' she said in that sexy whisper.

'And you can betcha this French maid succeeded,' he added, laughing.

In fact he hadn't given Bonnie/Laurie a thought in almost two hours.

Chapter Forty-four

Having the new Clyde triggered thoughts of the old Clyde for Laurie. Especially around two in the morning after half a bottle of tequila when all outside was silent and she had only her thoughts and memories to crowd her mind.

She had found the first Clyde when she was just a kid, a scrounging rascal she had picked up at the roadside, abandoned and with bleeding paws from whatever long trek he had endured before he ended up in her arms and sleeping on her bed, despite her parents' very vocal protests about fleas and rabies and stray dogs in general.

'If Clyde goes, I go,' she had raged at them and something about the look in her eyes had stunned them into acceptance. Clyde had stayed until he died ten years later, of old age she guessed. One morning he just didn't wake up and she had sobbed her heart out as she buried him tenderly in a little plot she dug in the meagre backyard. She guessed Clyde the First's bones were there to this day because nobody in that area ever bothered to do much gardening.

Clyde the second had been her trusty companion though, found at the pound in Jacksonville, Florida, after a long search, just the same as Clyde the Third in Oakland. And he had turned out to be the perfect Clyde to her Bonnie. Smart, game for anything, up to tricks she didn't even know dogs could do – like growling at people she saw in the street and didn't like; or knowing when she was depressed and he would come and lick her hand and face and climb up next to her, leaning his weight and warmth against her so she no longer felt lonely; or just staying quiet when she needed him to. Clyde never had to be told – he was just on the same wavelength as her. They were truly Bonnie and Clyde in a way that this new dog, who was sitting at her feet while she lay on the red vinyl sofa watching *The Silence of the Lambs* on cable and moodily knocking back the neat tequila, could never be.

She had no time for Margarita mixes any more. She wasn't into that sophisticated cocktail drink stuff. She liked the smooth burn of the hard liquor down her throat, the tingle in her chest as it slid down to her stomach, the warmth of it inside her. And unlike other people she never got drunk. None of that falling down in a stupor shit for her, Jimmy had always said she had a cast-iron stomach.

Jimmy! That bastard! He was the cause of all her problems.

She took another slug of the tequila, thinking of what she would do to Jimmy Victor if he were here now, something that had a close connection to what Hannibal Lecter was supposed to have done to his victims in the movie she was watching. Then she remembered, she had already taken care of Jimmy. But now they had found his body and the bastard might come back to haunt her again. Or at least to haunt Laurie Martin.

There was no way the cops could trace Bonnie Hoyt/Victor after all these years, she was certain of that. And once she had become Bonnie Harmon she had left her past behind in another state, another world. And as far as anybody knew, Laurie Martin's disappearance had nothing to do with Jimmy Victor being killed. No, she, *Maria Joseph* was safe.

Of course, too, none of this would have happened if it had not been for Beau Harmon. She would have had Boss's money and there would have been no need for her to go to work as an estate agent. No way Jimmy would have found her. No need for all *this*. She could just have continued having the good life, a nice condo, expensive clothes, diamond rings, cruises . . . and no need to stroke any old man's ego along with his private parts in order to get what she wanted.

Beau Harmon was the cause of her downfall. Beau Harmon and that bitch Loretta had brought her to this. *Beau Harmon had murdered Clyde.*

The pain that shot through her heart as she remembered Clyde's mangled little body lying on the gravel driveway in the Texas heat with the flies already buzzing round him made her howl again and the new Clyde jumped to his feet, barking and pawing anxiously at her.

A bullet in the heart would not have hurt as much as this. And this new Clyde only made her long for her old Clyde more. This dog looked pretty much the same but he was a bit sappy. Too unaggressive, too goddamn friendly, he ran up to strangers on the street, sniffed them, licked their hands. The first Clyde would never have done that. He belonged to her, she to him, that was the unspoken pact between them.

Jimmy Victor had paid the price for threatening her. Now she vowed it was Beau Harmon's turn to fuckin' suffer, just the way she had done ever since she lost Clyde.

She contemplated driving down to Texas, confronting him with a shotgun, taking him 'out' — *and* that embalmed wife of his. The haughty Loretta wouldn't look too immaculate any more with a nice big red stain spreading across the bosom of her lavender silk dress and probably spilling onto the white sofas and the velvety white carpet in that all-white room that was like some goddamn shrine to virginity. Maybe Loretta was still a virgin? Didn't look like any man had ever placed a hand on one of those plastic tits, never mind stuck it in her.

Laurie laughed at the thought as she opened the second bottle of tequila. No José Cuervo Gold for her, the cheap stuff was just as potent, just as satisfying, and she liked what it did to her head.

She watched fascinated, as the murderer circled the pit where the terrified victim was imprisoned. Was her skin going to be removed while she was still alive? Was it going to be cured and tanned and made into a skin jacket? Jeez, this guy was really nuts ...

Clyde settled down again. He rested his head on her knees,

gazing soulfully at her. She fondled his head absently, thinking of the other Clyde. And of Beau and Loretta. She had promised herself revenge on them one day. Now their time had come.

There were two other people who needed to be taken care of as well. They were already on her list. But Beau came first.

How though? That was the riddle she set herself that night. How to kill Beau and Loretta?

A rattler in Loretta's bed? She laughed out loud at the thought of Loretta finding a snake in her bed – of Loretta finding anything in her bed other than herself. That would send the old bitch screaming and fainting. Loretta moved slow as an oil slick on water, the snake would be sure to strike her before she had even moved her ass.

There was only one problem with that, though. No, two problems. The first was to obtain a rattler. The second was to gain entry to the Harmon mansion and put it in Loretta's bed.

Frowning, she downed more tequila, watching the end of *The Silence of the Lambs*. She liked it that he got away, the clever ones like him and her always did.

The Unabomber! The thought flashed into her mind, sharp as an arrow. *A letter bomb*, that was the answer. It was easy, it was anonymous – and since everybody opened their mail without even thinking about it, it was almost always successful. All she had to do now was to find out how to make the bomb.

She was smiling as she switched off the TV, shunted Clyde off her lap and walked – slowly and carefully but without staggering, which considering she had downed a bottle and a half of tequila was quite a feat – into the bedroom. Once again, the glaring white of the new bedcovers made her realise the shoddiness of the rest of her surroundings and tears sprang to her eyes.

She would get even with those bastards, if it was the last thing she did.

Chapter Forty-five

There was no problem making a letter bomb, Laurie found. In fact, it was easier than first-year science class. The problem was to conceal her identity when she purchased the necessary items: the Jiffy bags of a specific size, the mechanical assembly and the detonator and plastic explosive, even the sheets of cardboard that would be packed around it. The envelope had to fit tightly because its pressure kept the bomb from detonating, but once the envelope was opened and the pressure removed – you were looking death in the face.

And death was almost too good an option for Beau Harmon.

She was confident there was no way anyone could link the letter bomb to Maria Joseph, or to Bonnie Harmon, but nevertheless she took all possible precautions, purchasing the necessary components in places miles away from Oakland and buying each piece in a different place.

She was sweating as she put them all together though, wearing surgical gloves in case of fingerprints and handling the plastic explosive like a newborn. Christ, this was tough, you surely needed nerves of steel, but then she had always prided herself on just that. Except she had never been threatened before and it would be too ironic if she blew herself up at this point.

She was laughing as she sat at the scratched yellow-oak table in her apartment, with Clyde on the chair opposite interestedly sniffing the pungent almond-like odour of the plastic explosive as she packed it around the mechanical device, then inserted the detonator and placed the whole between the two sheets of thick cardboard.

Next, she printed Beau's name and address on the thick brown envelope and affixed a Neiman Marcus sticker to allay any suspicions he might have about the package. Not that she expected him to have any, after all he wasn't in the habit of receiving letter bombs, but just in case.

Finally, she slid the device into the envelope, made sure it did not move and felt rigid under her probing fingers, then she sealed it and stuck a layer of Sellotape over the seal.

She drove to a post office in San Francisco, far from her home, to have it weighed. The postal clerk commented that it was quite heavy for its size as she franked the big brown envelope.

Laurie was smiling as she hurried out of the post office. Death was that easy.

Chapter Forty-six

The Texas sun broiled down but inside the Harmon mansion the temperature was glacial. That was the way Loretta liked it and as Beau knew from long experience, whatever Loretta wanted she got. Well, if she thought she was going to freeze him out, she was mistaken.

He climbed the shallow lavender-carpeted stairs passing Loretta's suite, a poem in lavender, peach and apple-green Colefax and Fowler English chintz.

'Don't y'ever stop to think we live in Texas for Christ's sakes?' Beau had said when he had seen it for the first time.

'Don't worry, you don't have to share it. Your room is down the hall,' Loretta had retorted briskly.

And it was, immediately on the left of the spacious upper hallway with, naturally, a private sitting room and bath.

The decor here was more masculine, more in keeping with the way Beau saw himself than the way Loretta wanted him to be. Deep red walls glazed with many coats to a high shine; a heavy and genuine Jacobean four-poster, carved-oak bed with red damask curtains; black-lacquered furnishings and a cocktail bar hidden in a chinoiserie armoire. A big-screen TV popped electronically from a faux cabinet at the foot of the bed and Beau would have had mirrors on the ceiling if Loretta had permitted it, but she considered it vulgar. Besides, Loretta didn't like to fuck. And that was at the root of his problems with her.

Loretta was as frigid as her house. He figured she had

some internal kind of air-conditioning system that left her in a permafrost. Untouched and untouchable. Oh, he had 'touched' her of course, but there wasn't much joy in it, nor much relief, and he had been forced to find that elsewhere, with women like Bonnie.

Actually, Bonnie had been quite a luscious little piece of ass when she had upped and married his Pa. He had been thinking about putting the make on her himself, over a couple of bourbons at the steakhouse, especially when she flounced around in that short skirt that showed a lot of thigh and very good legs. He'd bet anything she knew he was watching her, checking her out – staking her out in the steakhouse. He grinned at his own joke. Then goddam if the little bitch hadn't pulled a fast one on him and snuggled up to the old man.

He walked into his closet that, had he known it, was three times as big as Bonnie's current bedroom, pulled on a red cashmere sweater then went back into the sitting room, pressed the button that opened up the cocktail cabinet and stared at the glinting mirrored array of crystal glasses inside. Ignoring them, he plucked a bottle of Famous Grouse from the back and drank deeply from it. He shuddered as it went down. God, that was better, this place was enough to freeze a fuckin' brass monkey. Come to think of it that was probably part of Loretta's plan for him.

'Women with their own money are a problem,' Boss had said when Beau told him he was planning on marrying Loretta Larson. 'You'll never rule your own roost,' he had added. But then Beau had never ruled any roost, Boss had made sure of that. He had always been kept on a tight financial rein, always been made to feel inferior, always been beholden to Boss for every cent he got, even though he worked hard at the car dealerships. Why, he'd practically run the place those last few years.

But Boss had been right of course. Marriage to Loretta meant a marriage to Loretta's oil money and she was as tight with him as she was indulgent with herself, spending a fortune building and furnishing this house, and on her clothes and jewellery, and on the butler and the stables with the expensive horses, though she never rode. Like everything else with Loretta, it was all for show.

It had been a good day though, when her attorneys had come to his aid and stopped little Mrs Bonnie Harmon from getting away with all of Boss's money. A couple of hundred grand was worth it to see her off. Now he had finally found some kind of independence – but not the kind that could ever give him courage enough to leave Loretta and go off with the nineteen-year-old blonde in Dallas whom he had met at the line-dance palace, and who claimed she loved him and who, whenever they were together, which was as often as he could slip away 'on business', certainly acted as though she did.

Beau stood at the window slugging bourbon from the bottle, looking at Loretta's sleek horses grazing in Loretta's lush green paddocks. At Loretta's lavish gardens and enormous koi ponds where the fish glinted gold and orange in the sun. At her gardeners toiling in the heat. At her English butler walking down the front steps to greet the mailman, taking the bundle from him to be placed on a silver salver in the front hall – that was the way the English aristocracy did it, Loretta had informed him. Beau guessed whatever was good enough for Brit aristocrats was good enough for Loretta though back home in Falcon City he and his mom and Boss had usually sorted the mail on the kitchen table.

The mailman also handed Pearson, the butler, a parcel which he tucked under his arm. Loretta had probably bought something from one of those QVC TV shows, Beau thought. You would never expect it of a woman like that, but she did all her Christmas shopping that way. Saved all the hassle – as well as a lot of money, she said. Loretta was mean as well as cold. Beau definitely did not like Loretta, and most folks roundabouts knew it.

But they still showed up for the Saturday dinner parties, the Sunday brunches, the late-summer Texas hayrides in the stables and meadows which Loretta organised in her role as doyenne of local society, with Loretta in pink gingham and her hair in artful beribboned pigtails that had taken her hairdresser all morning to fix. Nobody was turning down Loretta Larson

Harmon's hospitality. They came in droves to the Christmas carol party around the giant tree – pre-trimmed by party planners with giant gold-gauze bows and gilded silk roses, though there were no childish stockings hanging on their mantel, Loretta couldn't abide kids, she said they would mess up her beautiful home. So, after the Christmas carol party was over, they each went to their separate rooms, Beau to drown his Christmas spirit in Famous Grouse, Loretta no doubt to embalm herself in night creams and Neiman's most expensive silk shroud. Only she called it a peignoir.

Here she came now, speeding up the driveway in a spurt of gravel that cost a fortune to buy and even more to maintain – the gardeners knew to sweep it regularly every hour on the hour – in her custom lavender Range Rover which she thought gave her the proper sporty English-lady-of-the-manor appeal. Hah, as if any decent Englishwoman would ever drive a lavender Range Rover.

He took another slug of the bourbon as he heard Pearson open the front door and greet milady with his 'Good afternoon, madame. I trust you had a pleasant day'.

'I sure did, Pearson,' Beau heard Loretta say. 'But now I'm exhausted. Would you please have tea sent up to my room? And the newspapers – ironed of course.' She couldn't abide creases and newsprint that came off on her fingers.

'Of course, madame, right away. The Earl Grey tea I assume, Madame?'

'You assume correctly,' she said already on her way up the stairs.

Beau stood behind his door, listening until he heard her go into her own room and the door close. He breathed again.

So Madame was exhausted from lunching with the ladies was she? Well then he might have to plan a little exhaustion himself, say tomorrow, in Dallas. Yes, a little visit to Dallas was definitely on the cards. He took another swig of the bourbon as he dialled the blonde's number and arranged an assignation.

That would be Pearson on the stairs, taking Madame's tea

tray and the newspapers. He listened for the tap on the door, heard her tell him to come in, heard him leave.

Then, 'Oh, Pearson,' she called in that loud twang Boss had always claimed belonged on a Texas hillbilly, 'has the mail arrived yet?'

Pearson informed her that it had and she instructed him to bring it up to her room.

Beau had no interest in the mail. All it would be was bills and more bills that Loretta, anyway, would take care of. She did have her uses, but since she was the one spending all the money it was only right she paid them. If she ever found out about the blonde she would take him to the cleaners. He would be finished. But unlike other prominent men, he knew how to keep his mouth shut and so did the blonde. No hiding behind office doors for him, just a nice discreet little apartment, a monthly stipend, and some fun sex between consenting adults. Now, who could object to that?

Beau sighed as he slumped into the cushions of the red damask sofa which were so downy they billowed up on either side of him. He took another gulp of the bourbon, staring moodily out the window. He couldn't wait to get to Dallas, he would catch the early morning flight and would be gone before Loretta even knew it.

He had just settled into a doze when a sound like a rocket blastoff ripped through the house, jolting him yelping from the sofa. '*Jesus Christ, what happened?*' he screamed, running for the door.

Smoke billowed from the place where the tall double doors leading to Loretta's room used to be. Pearson came pounding up the stairs, a look of alarm on his usually impassive face.

It took a fuckin' explosion to get the old goat to unfreeze his face, Beau thought as he stepped over the heavy double doors that now lay in the hall and stood in the entrance to Loretta's wrecked room.

He could see her lying on the peach floral chaise surrounded by the shattered remnants of the Spode tea service and other expensive broken bric-a-brac. One arm dangled like a puppet's at an odd angle, dripping blood onto the floor. The thing was, though, there was no hand on the end of that arm.

Beau turned and vomited neatly into the Chinese export vase on the console, while Pearson backed away and dialed 911 from the upstairs phone.

Whatever had happened, Loretta Larson Harmon certainly never knew it.

Chapter Forty-seven

Al and Marla were dining *à deux* at Tra da Noi, a cosy little Italian bistro in Malibu, tucked away in a corner where Marla felt they could smooch unobserved and where Al, with the ex-cop's instincts, felt more secure with his back against the wall. Not that he was expecting anything to happen, it was just the way he was. Besides, this was law-abiding Malibu where they said the cops were so bored the only high they got was issuing traffic citations and keeping a watchful eye on the paparazzi who stalked the local movie stars.

The decor was Malibu funky, like any little place in Tuscany might be, the staff friendly and the food good and plentiful. Marla's favourite was the spaghetti bolognese and she sucked in a strand now, cheeks hollowed, slurping happily while Al tucked into a massive veal chop.

'You've got to taste this,' he said appreciatively, cutting a piece and holding the fork to her mouth. Even biting into a forkful of veal Marla looked sexy, especially in the skinny white tank top and tight blue jeans she wore tonight, and with her multi-blonde hair tumbling around her face in wispy curls in a new style she had adopted. The tank top said *Naughty* on it. He alone knew how naughty she was and it made him grin just thinking about her.

'Know what? You look beautiful tonight,' he said, polishing off the last of the veal.

'Mmm,' her mouth was still full but she leaned across and

kissed him anyway. 'So do you,' she mumbled. 'Notice anything about me tonight?'

He inspected her up and down. 'New hairdo? I like it.'

'Well, yes, and thank you kindly for the compliment and for noticing — even though I did have to point it out to you. But I meant something else.'

'OK, I give up.'

'You mean you didn't notice that tonight I'm dressed exactly the way you are? Jeans and a T-shirt. Proper PI attire.'

'First of all, I don't wear anything with spaghetti straps and the word "Naughty" written across my chest, and my jeans are not as tight as yours.'

She stroked her lean hips, grinning. 'You wish,' she murmured. 'Anyhow, I thought private investigators wore shiny suits and loud neckties and snap-brim hats tilted rakishly to one side.'

Al grinned, 'Hon, I'm about forty years too young for that kind of gear. You've mistaken me for Frank.'

'Frank who?'

He sighed as he took his cellphone from his jeans pocket and dialled his number for his messages. Sometimes he forgot how much younger she was. 'Marla, there is only one Frank.'

She ordered tiramisu with two forks while he listened to the litany of calls. When he got to the last one, his face changed. He glanced at his watch, frowning.

'That's strange,' he said, 'I got a call from Beau Harmon. About an hour ago. He sounded weird.'

'Weird?' She looked expectantly at him, then down at the luscious mound of creamy tiramisu. It was hell for the figure but it surely tasted good.

'Yeah, y'know . . . scared.'

Now she was alert. 'Why is Beau Harmon calling you anyway? I got the impression he was glad to see the back of you as well as of Bonnie.'

'He was. And so was his wife. That's what makes it all the weirder. Unless of course, Bonnie has reared her evil little head again.'

'In San Antonio, Texas?' Marla was suddenly excited. 'With the time difference, it must be after midnight there. Why is he calling so late?'

'Something's up. Finish the tiramisu, Marla.' He waved to Luigi for the bill. 'I need to get back to my office.'

They were in Marla's Mercedes and she was driving – or at least approximating what was normally called driving, as she sipped at the cup of coffee she had insisted on picking up from Starbucks en route and at the same time punched in her own phone number with her spare hand.

'Marla,' Al said as they sped down Pacfic Coast Highway, 'you have no hands on the wheel.'

She listened to her messages and took another sip, steering now with a couple of fingers of her left hand. 'Sure I do. Don't tell me you're nervous, Giraud?'

'Yeah, I'm nervous. The thing is, Marla, when you're driving you're supposed to concentrate. You seem to think it's an excuse to do three other things as well.

'Trust me, I could do four,' she said, giving his thigh an intimate little squeeze.

'Trust me,' he replied, 'in this instance, I'd rather you just drove.'

She flung him a look of triumph as she swung left onto Sunset and foot to the floor, zoomed up the hill. 'Coward,' she murmured, to which he agreed that – in this instance – yes he was.

She had to slow down though, when the road began its series of serpentine curves through the Palisades, past the Bel Air gates, through Beverly Hills and into Sunset Strip. She swung into the parking lot in the rear of Al's offices and jolted to a sudden stop. 'How's that for record time?' she demanded breathlessly, applying fresh lipgloss in the driver's mirror.

'Great.' He was already out of the car and walking up the slope from the lot to the Strip.

'Hey, wait for me . . .' She ran after him, linking her arm in his, her long legs keeping up easily with his loping stride. 'Trouble is, you're more interested in Beau Harmon than you are in me,' she sighed. 'I mean what kind of man goes to his office at midnight on a Friday?'

'A PI with an urgent phone call. Get used to it Marla,' he said as he unlocked the door.

'Oh, bullshit' she grumbled, picking up the letter parcel that was waiting outside his office door and carrying it in with her. She set it down on his desk then perched next to it, one leg swinging, waiting while he got Beau Harmon on the phone.'

'Harmon?' Beau had answered the phone himself and Giraud wondered fleetingly what had happened to the butler. He would have thought Loretta would have had him working all hours. 'Yeah, it's Giraud here. You asked me to call as soon as I could, regardless of the time. I hope I didn't wake you.'

'Nothing could wake me,' Beau said, so loudly that even Marla could hear. 'I don't think I'll ever be able to sleep again.'

'OK, so calm down fella, I can hear you, no need to shout. Now, what's your problem?'

Al paced up and down with the phone glued to his ear, listening intently.

Unable to hear any of Beau's conversation, Marla checked out the parcel. There was a Neiman Marcus sticker on the packet. Mmmmm, now who could be sending Al gifts from Neiman's? The famous San Antonio couple, Loretta and Beau? From what she had heard, they didn't sound the sort to be free with gifts. Then who? Could Giraud have a secret admirer? Or maybe she wasn't so secret ... She peered at the handwriting. There was no return address and Al's name and address were printed in block capitals. She hefted it again, scowling, jealousy gnawing at her. It was heavy for its size. She knew for a fact that Al never shopped at Neiman Marcus. The Gap was lucky to get his patronage.

'So what woman is sending you stuff from Neiman's?' she said loudly, already inching the Sellotape from the top, glaring at him as she ripped the jiffy bag open.

Al was concentrating on what Beau was saying. 'It was *what?*' he said astounded. Then, '*Marla!*' he yelled, launching himself at her.

'*Jesus, Marla!*' he yelled again, and her mouth dropped into an astonished 'O' as he grabbed her, threw the half-open parcel across the room and her onto the floor beneath his desk with him on top.

And then she was screaming, loudly into the ear that was closest to her, but it didn't seem to matter because the whole room was one big roar as it erupted into diamond trilliants of shattered glass and heavy dark beams and dust and orange tongues of flame, and she was sobbing and shivering under him.

'*What is it? What happened?*' she stuttered as he pulled her to her feet, checked her rapidly for injuries, then led her through the burning debris out onto the stairway. Already the wail of sirens sounded along the Strip and he knew help was to hand.

'It means, Marla, that "Bonnie Harmon hereinafter called Laurie Martin" is alive and well and back in business,' he said grimly.

Chapter Forty-eight

Homicide Detective Lionel Bulworth perched his bulk uncomfortably on the edge of the small chair in the bar of the Sea Breeze Inn, Pensacola, Florida, surrounded by potted palms and a squadron of ceramic geese flying into infinity along one turquoise wall. Pow! Powers was sitting opposite him, and Pow! in civilian garb was a sight to behold in a k. d. lang-ish black suit, a white shirt and instead of a tie, a yellow bandanna knotted at her neck. The finishing touch was a pair of large tooled leather boots.

Like a gosh-darn urban cowboy, Bulworth thought amazed. But Powers was pulling her – not inconsiderable – weight all right. She had been out doing the legwork while he manned the phones. Now, they were comparing notes over a thankfully cold beer in the small lobby overlooking a glassy expanse of ocean. Or was it the gulf? He was never sure in Florida.

'I have here copies of Jimmy's wedding certificate, plus the death certificate issued by the doctor who saw him after the accident. Plus copies of the newspaper accounts of the accident. And with pictures of the wife, Bonnie.' Powers handed them over to Bulworth with a pleased grin.

He looked them over, staring hard at the picture of Bonnie. 'No one we know,' he said dismissively. 'And it says here she did a heroic job trying to pull him out of the burning trailer.'

'Except it wasn't Jimmy, it was someone else,' Powers pointed out.

'Right. And I've been onto the local PD about anyone who went missing around that time.'

'And?' She took a goodly slurp of the beer and picked up a fistful of pretzels.

'And a Gil Fearing was reported missing a couple of days after the accident in the trailer. A forty-year-old male Caucasian, around the same build and age as Jimmy Victor, lived in a downmarket apartment complex on the outskirts of town, worked occasionally on construction. When he wasn't drinking and chasing women that is. He and Jimmy Victor both. Our Jim turned out to be quite the boy. From what I've heard, any wife would have been glad to get rid of him.'

'Is that right?' Powers' brows raised as she popped another pretzel into her mouth. 'You think she killed him?'

'You betcha I do. Only trouble is nobody knows where she went from there. She just took off and nobody ever saw her again.'

'I don't get it, she kills the husband who turns out not to be the husband in the trailer fire, and then years later the husband turns up dead in a California canyon. Are we missing something or what?'

'You put it so succinctly, Powers,' Bulworth said with a sigh. 'We know nothing about Bonnie Hoyt/Victor except that she is alive and probably killed Jimmy in that canyon. Though what it has to do with Laurie Martin beats me.'

'Wonder what happened to *her?*' Powers said, brushing crumbs off her black suit and ordering up a second Bud light.

She was just taking the first sip when Bulworth's phone beeped. He fished it from his pocket. 'Bulworth here', he said.

An amazed look spread over his face. 'You're not bullshitting me?' he said sternly. 'OK, OK, so you're not – it has been known. Gosh darn it, man, of course I'm listening. OK, OK, Giraud, start from the beginning.'

Signalling to Powers for a pad and pen, he listened intently, occasionally interjecting a question, scribbling notes in his large flowing script that had won him first prize at the Headford Road Elementary School in Newark, New Jersey many moons ago.

'I'll be there, Giraud,' he concluded. You sure you're both OK?' Great, good, fine. I'm on my way. And why the hell didn't you tell me all this earlier, you bastard? None of my business huh? Don't give me that client-confidentiality-privilege-bullshit, this was police business and you know it. We might have been onto her by now ... No, I'm not blaming you for Loretta Harmon's death. If anybody could have found Laurie Martin it would have been you, I'll give you that Giraud. Yeah. I'll see you there.'

Powers was on the edge of her seat as he clicked off the phone. '*What?*' she demanded so loudly in her deep boom-box of a voice that people turned to look.

Bulworth felt the hot colour staining his cheeks. Damn it he had never grown out of that childhood habit and he could see by Powers' grin she knew she had embarrassed him.

'Too loud for you, am I, boss? Sorry about that, it's just my outgoing nature,' she said loudly again, causing more heads to turn.

Bulworth got to his feet, drained his beer in one long gulp and said, 'Get packed, Powers, we're off to the airport right now.'

'But I thought we had an investigation under way here ... where are we going?'

'Texas.' He was already half way across the room and in case anybody wondered what he did for a living, there was no mistaking it. Somehow Bulworth looked the picture-perfect cop.

'*Texas?*'

'That's right Powers, the place where your gosh-darn boots come from. You'll be right at home there.'

Chapter Forty-nine

Giraud and Bulworth, along with Pow! Powers were dining with Beau Harmon at Benboy's Steak House in Falcon City, Texas. The same place where Bonnie Victor had, as Beau put it, 'picked up my father and made a complete ass of him'.

Looking at the current crop of hefty middle-aged waitresses, sausaged into their black dresses like the best of Jimmy Dean's, personally Al wasn't surprised that cute redheaded Bonnie had caught the old man's fancy.

They had already gone through the formalities of sympathy about Beau's wife and were staying over to attend the funeral which was being held tomorrow. Bulworth was of the opinion that killers were drawn to their victim's funerals because in some weird way they wanted to see the results of their actions. The local police department would have detectives there, too, in plain clothes keeping watch for strangers or anything untoward and the graveside service would be videotaped and later each face checked.

'Of course Loretta being a Larson,' Beau said, tucking into his Texas-size Porterhouse with, Giraud thought, an appetite quite unseemly in the recently bereaved, 'Loretta being a Larson is a big deal around here. Larson Oil, y'know?'

Bulworth nodded, shooting a sidelong glance at Giraud. 'Sure, we all know Larson Oil,' he said.

Giraud knew what that glance meant. Did Beau or did he not now stand to inherit a large chunk of Larson Oil money?

And therefore did Beau have more to do with Loretta's death than anybody round here seemed to suspect?

'It's gonna be a big Texas funeral,' Beau added between mouthfuls of steak. 'Everybody who's anybody in the Lone Star State's gonna be there.'

Al caught Bulworth's eye again and shook his head. Beau Harmon didn't have enough brains to come up with the double letter-bomb plot that killed his wife and almost killed Marla and himself, just to implicate Bonnie. And he figured that whatever was coming to him from Loretta's estate, the poor sap had probably earned it – the hard way.

'What d'ya plan to do now, Beau?' he asked, tucking into the fried onion rings, which were maybe the best he had ever tasted.

'Well now, once the dust has settled I'm planning on putting the big house on the market. Think maybe I'll move on from San Antone – get away from things, y'know what I mean? Think I'll give Dallas a try, it's a lively enough town and I reckon I'll need a little diverting – away from the bad memories, y'know what I mean?'

Giraud guessed he knew what he meant. Loretta had left a bad enough stain on his own memory and heaven only knew what Beau's was like.

'So tell us about Bonnie Harmon,' Powers said suddenly. 'She must have been quite a woman to hook your Pa.'

'She sure was. Nice lookin' too, y'know what I mean?'

They nodded – they figured by now they knew what Beau meant without him asking every other sentence.

'Tall, slender, but she had good . . .' Beau glanced at Powers then shaped a buxom figure in the air.'

'Tits,' Powers said helpfully and Bulworth almost choked on his chili fries.

'Another Coors for my friend,' Giraud called to the passing waitress. He thought, exasperated, they were wasting their time. This trip to interrogate Beau Harmon was getting them exactly nowhere.

'Yeah,' Beau said, grinning lecherously. 'And she liked to

show 'em. Caught every eye in the place, she did. And there were plenty of guys in here younger than Boss, and better lookin' too. But *Bonnie knew* Boss had the money and *I knew* that was what she was after, first time I ever set eyes on her.'

'You ever come on to Bonnie yourself, then, Beau?' Giraud asked the question matter-of-factly and caught Beau off-guard.

'Well, you know, he said, grinning some more and practically strutting like John Travolta in *Saturday Night Fever*, if you could do that sitting down. 'She kinda gave me the look, y'know what I mean?'

'That come-to-bed look,' Powers said knowledgeably, taking a couple of chilli fries from Bulworth's plate. She had already finished her own. But Bulworth's astonished glare was for her comment not for the stolen fries.

'Oh, Bonnie knew how to do that, all right. Yessiree, she was one babe. And my old man fell for it, darned old fool that he was. Then he went and left her most of his money. But I soon put a stop to that.'

Beau went on to detail exactly how Loretta's important attorneys had rousted Bonnie Harmon and practically seen her out of town. With of course, two hundred thousand in cash in her purse.

Powers whistled, astonished. 'That's a lot of money.'

'Yeah, but not nearly as much as she stood to inherit if Boss's will had been enforced. And that's why I think it was Bonnie sent that letter bomb. Only I think she intended it for me.'

Beau took another mammoth mouthful of Porterhouse, chewing contemplatively. 'That, and one other reason,' he added after he'd swallowed. 'I killed her dog.'

Giraud's ears pricked up. 'You killed Clyde?'

'Ran over the little bastard right there in the driveway. Boy, I wanna tell ya, that Bonnie came racing over to my place fit to kill me right there and then. I swear to God I've never seen nothin' like the look she gave me. Evil, it was, and I knew I was right and that she had killed Boss. No doubt about it. And now she intended to kill me too. In return for Clyde.'

'An eye for an eye,' Powers said solemnly, finishing off

Bulworth's fries. He gave up and pushed his plate over to her.

Giraud's phone rang and he excused himself from the table and went out into the hallway to answer it.

'Help, I've been kidnapped. I'm a prisoner in my old home, being threatened with a visit from the thirty-six-year-old unmarried orthodontist.' Of course it was Marla, whom he had left in the hospital again, being treated for shock.

'Mom says if I even so much as *mention* seeing you again, she will personally kill you. I told her murder was no solution to this ongoing problem but she ignored me. Tell me, Giraud what am I to do?'

'Pacify her,' Giraud said. 'I'll send her a dozen roses.'

'Three dozen. And make them Oseanas, she likes pink.'

'Three dozen it is,' he agreed with a sigh.

'You must admit I seem to end up rather regularly in hospital after a date with you.'

'True, but that's the way love is Marla baby. Y'takes the rough with the smooth.'

'Isn't it about time for my smooth?' she demanded plaintively. 'I'm getting to be a regular at Cedars Emergency. When do I get a break, Giraud?'

'Soon as we've cleared up this case, honey, I promise. But you can't say I didn't warn you, this is a hazardous profession.'

'Yup,' she said. 'But I like my men hazardous.'

'Make that "man" and I'll be home tomorrow night, first flight out of San Antonio after the funeral.'

'Whoopeee. I'll try and extricate myself from Mom and the orthodontist. Meet me at my place?'

'I'll be there, honey, with roses for you this time.'

'Love you, Giraud,' she said longingly.

He was smiling as he said love you too baby and clicked off the phone.

Beau had not been wrong about the funeral, it seemed to Giraud that half of Texas turned out to bid goodbye to Loretta Larson

Harmon, as well as the entire San Antonio police department. The Police Chief was there, alongside the Governor of the State, and various civic bigwigs, as well as about a hundred ladies who lunch in their very best black with cartwheel hats and expensive stilettos that to their chagrin sank into the soft grass around the grave site, forcing them into a peculiar tottering walk which made them look like a bunch of drunken crows.

Beau looked dignified in a black Brioni suit and a white Stetson, accepting condolences stoically, surrounded by Loretta's lawyers in lieu of any living family.

The casket was ebony with plenty of the curlicued gold fittings which Loretta had so enjoyed in life and Beau had seen to it that it was lined in her favourite Colefax and Fowler lavender and peach chintz.

'She would have liked it that way,' he said humbly, to those who had passed by the open casket beforehand. Of course, Loretta's arms that no longer had any hands were well hidden under the silk-lined chintz quilt but the funeral make-up artist had decked her out with lavender eyeshadow and pink lipstick until she looked almost human.

Giraud smiled into the video camera when it turned his way, then he and Bulworth and Powers beat a hasty retreat. 'Heading out,' as Beau phrased it, 'for the airport.'

And back to LA to continue their search for Bonnie hereinafter known as Laurie Martin.

Chapter Fifty

'Think she's going to try it again, Al?'

Marla was reclining on her taupe chenille chaise, her feet resting on pillows, her head in Giraud's lap. She wore no make-up and her comfy old white terry robe and ancient bunny slippers, and her blonde hair was dragged back in an elastic band. She looked, Giraud thought, about fifteen. And she also looked scared.

'Nah, she wouldn't dare,' he said more confidently than he felt. 'Not now she knows we're on the alert, and the police are investigating. She can't afford to draw attention to herself. She has to lie low.'

He had calmed Marla's fears, but he was worried, no doubt about it. Laurie Martin was striking close to home, close to his heart. If anything had happened to Marla ... but he couldn't even finish the thought. It had been so close ...

'You know what, hon,' he said thoughtfully after a long silence, 'did you ever think maybe your mom is right? You know, about not being an assistant PI? About just getting on with your life. You're bright, educated, have a great job as a legal eagle ...'

She scowled at him, her eyes slitted. 'You mean I might be the perfect bride for Mr Right.'

'He doesn't have to be an orthodontist,' he said in what he considered was a reasonable tone, yelling loudly as she gave him a backward punch in the stomach.

'Jesus, Marla, I thought you were a convalescent. You have a punch like a prize fighter.'

'Fuck you, Giraud,' she said coldly. 'And don't you go fobbing me off on any Mr Rights, OK? And remember this, I'm not a quitter. And I'm certainly not afraid of Miss Evil Bitch hereinafter called Laurie Martin. So tell me, what's our next move?'

For once Giraud did not have an answer. 'We need a break,' he said wistfully. 'Just one tiny break. I only hope we get it before she has a chance to do any more damage.'

Marla swung her bunny feet to the floor and sat up abruptly. 'You know what? I need to see Vickie.' Her eyes were wide with sudden panic. 'I need to know she's all right.'

'I'll call the hospital, check on her with the nurse on duty.' He was already picking up the phone but she stopped him.

'No. You don't understand. I need to *see* her. I just have this feeling about her ...'

'It's late, Marla,' he objected checking his watch, 'visiting hours are over. Besides, you shouldn't be going out yet, you're not well enough.'

'Dammit, Giraud,' she stamped her slippered foot until the bunny ears flopped up and down like Dumbo's in the wind. 'You don't understand. *It's important* ... I just have this image of her in my mind, with her eyes wide open but not seeing and the tears sliding down her cheeks. Oh, Giraud, I feel that she needs me ... *someone* ... right now.'

He nodded, giving in. 'I'll call the hospital, see if they'll let us in,' and she kissed him as she dashed into the bedroom to throw on some clothes.

'They'll let us in,' she called over her shoulder. 'You can always work miracles, Giraud.'

He only wished it were true.

The drive to the hospital was unusually silent. Marla seemed lost in her own thoughts, huddled into the saddle-leather bucket seat of the Corvette, tense as an unsprung mousetrap. She smelled delicious, of the Hermes 24 Faubourg he had bought her on a romantic flying weekend visit to Paris the previous year. Was it only the previous year? Now it felt like a decade ago.

They were turning into the hospital forecourt when she said, 'You never told me what happened to Steve.'

'He's out of jail. There was no way Bulworth could keep him in there now. They don't want it known, though. Not yet. Not until they catch up with Laurie Martin. He's in a safe house, under guard. They're afraid once she hears he's free and no longer a suspect, she might go after him too.'

'*Kill* him you mean?' Marla's voice was subdued.

'Right. She can't afford to have him around, telling what he knows about her, not now they've found Jimmy Victor. In fact, our Laurie should be getting a little nervous by now, since her letter bombs failed and Jimmy was found.'

'You never know what she might try to do,' Marla added as they got out of the car and walked up the familiar steps into the hospital.

Vickie thought it was so lonely, being lost like this. She had never felt so alone, as though nobody cared ... But now there was something different, something new ... She could feel it ... no, she could *smell* it. The scent of a summer garden overlaying the everlasting clinical smell she had come to hate.

The air was heavy with perfume, it reminded her of her childhood holidays, of summer breezes and grass and dusky evenings filled with jasmine and nicotiana and roses. It was wonderful ... it made her remember that she was a woman ... that she was alive ... somewhere inside her head, surely she was still alive ...

She tossed restlessly on the pillows, eyes shut tight, trying to visualise those summer vacations on the eastern seaboard with her uncles and aunts and cousins, and how they had all played together, running along the beach until they were exhausted, yelling and screaming and fighting and wrestling each other ... *Oh my God, my babies, my little girls, who will take them on vacations like that now that I'm not there ...?* But she *was* there, she was alive ... she had to be, she could smell perfume couldn't she ... ?

A cool hand was on hers, smooth, soft. A woman's hand. She was talking to her, saying things ... Vickie struggled to organise those loose connections so she could listen, take it in ... it wasn't just another nurse, another doctor, this woman meant something to her though she had no idea who she was ...

'Vickie, sweetheart,' Marla bent over and spoke softly into her ear, which is why Vickie could smell her perfume so distinctly. 'It's Marla. Remember me? I was with you that night and I know what you went through.

'Vickie, I just felt the need to be near you tonight, I thought perhaps you needed me. And you do need me to tell you again that Steve is innocent Vickie, Steve is free now because they know who the guilty person is. They haven't caught her yet, but they will. Oh, *they will* Vickie, I promise you that. And when they do, Steve will be right here by your side, telling you all the things I am telling you now. Only he'll also be telling you how much he loves you, Vickie, and your little girls. I know that for a fact.'

Al propped his sinewy frame against the hospital-green wall, arms folded over his chest, watching, listening. He didn't understand why Marla had needed to come to the hospital right now, but he'd gone along with her woman's intuition and besides, whatever he could do for Vickie he would. He had an obligation to her, as well as pity for her.

Vickie thrashed her head from side to side on the pillows and Marla jumped back, alarmed. 'It's OK, Vickie,' she said, casting an anxious glance at the monitors ticking away Vickie's life, every heartbeat, every throb of her pulse, every leap or fall in her blood pressure. Life reduced to machines was not a happy thing.

She sat quietly, holding Vickie's hand for a long time, then with a sigh she looked up at Al. 'I guess I was wrong,' she said wistfully, 'it's just that I had this thing ... this gut feeling ... that Vickie wanted me here ... I can't explain it.'

'You don't have to.' He took her hand in his and pulled her

to her feet. 'Come on, honey, it's late. Say goodnight to Vickie. You've done all you can, for now.'

Marla sighed as she looked down at the pitifully pale face which was so transparent it looked drained of all blood. 'Goodnight, Vickie.' She stroked her fingers gently across Vickie's brow.

As she did so, Vickie's eyes opened. And this time Marla could swear they were looking directly into hers.

She grasped Vickie's cold hand, urgently. 'Vickie, sweetheart, if you hear me, if you understand me, squeeze my fingers. *Just squeeze my hand, honey, please . . .'*

Vickie's eyes stared expressionlessly into hers for the long moment, then the answering squeeze came, soft as a sable paintbrush, a mere flutter of pressure. But it was enough for Marla to know that she had been right to trust her gut instinct. She had broken through that invisible barrier which kept Vickie away from the land of the living.

Her tears fell onto Vickie's clasped hand as Al hurried to summon the doctors.

'It'll be all right now, Vickie,' she promised. 'Everything will be all right now.'

Chapter Fifty-one

Steve Mallard was pacing his nondescript room in a small non-descript hostelry optimistically named the Country Cabin Hotel, located between the noisy 101 freeway and the everlasting traffic on Ventura Boulevard in the San Fernando Valley, wondering how soon he could get out of here.

He'd been in this 'safe house' for a week now and already it seemed like a year. The drab hotel-style rectangle was filled with brown slightly worn furniture and a multi-coloured bedspread that was, he guessed, meant to bring a welcoming touch of colour to the room, but it only served to make the room look drabber.

His 'minder', a plain-clothes detective by the name of Chavez, was lying on the bed in the adjoining room watching Dateline on TV. The door was propped open between them, as it always was, though both outer bedroom doors were locked and bolted, and only Chavez or the current cop on duty – they rotated every eight hours – had the keys.

There was a knock at the door and Chavez leapt to his feet, sliding his Glock from the holster in a single smooth movement. Chavez was Mexican with the face of a prize-fighter and the tight physique of his namesake, the middle-weight Cesar Chavez.

Now Chavez peered through the peephole, checking that it really was the Dominos Pizza delivery he had ordered fifteen minutes ago.

'What ya got there, bro?' he demanded through the closed door.

'One pepperoni and onions, one double cheese, jalapeno and sausage.'

Chavez waved Steve back into his own room and motioned for him to close the door. He slid the gun back into the holster under his jacket and opened the door cautiously.

'Took you long enough,' the high school kid who was the delivery boy grumbled. 'What did you think I'd got? A time bomb or sump'n?'

'Here kid,' Chavez thrust the correct amount of money at him and added a tip. 'Next time watch your lip, though. It could getya into trouble.'

'Yeah, sure ... and who says?' the kid was still grumbling as Chavez locked and bolted the door behind him. 'Come and get it, bro,' he called to Steve, 'Enjoy it while it's still hot.'

Steve couldn't have cared less whether the pizza was hot or not. He didn't even want the cold beer Chavez offered him, though Chavez being on duty drank only a diet Coke.

'Gotta watch the calories, my wife says,' he said tucking into a dripping slice of sausage pizza lavished with tiny green nuggets of jalapeno chilis. 'So now I drink diet Coke instead of regular.'

'You might try cutting out the pizza as well.' Steve said with a tired sigh. Every night it was the same. Chavez showed up for his shift at six. At seven the pizza was delivered. Always the double cheese, jalapeno and sausage that Chavez devoured like a ravenous lion and from which he never gained an ounce. The routine was beginning to make him crazy. He couldn't even watch TV any more, couldn't concentrate on the movies the minders brought in to break up the routine, couldn't even read a newspaper or *Time* magazine.

All Steve wanted was to go see Vickie. To have her know the truth. To have life get back to normal again. He didn't give a damn about Laurie Martin and possible threats on his life. He wanted his wife and kids back. He wanted to live in his own home, sleep in his own bed with Vickie by his side, the way she had for ten years now.

But Vickie was still in the hospital and not responding to anyone. His girls were with her sister and though he heard about them regularly via Lister, they didn't even know he was out of jail and that their daddy was innocent of the terrible charges levelled at him. And his home was locked and shuttered and still the location of an investigation in progress, complete with yellow police tape and a cop outside.

The phone rang and Chavez put down the pizza and answered it. 'Yeah? Right, sir. Yes everything is OK here, Steve is doin' just fine, eatin' his pizza like a good boy.' He threw Steve a grin that was not reciprocated. 'Yes sir, Detective Bulworth. I'll be expecting you then, sir. In about ten minutes. You got it, sir. Better remember the password, though? You don't?' Chavez was laughing as he said, 'It's *de la Hoya*. See you later detective.'

'What's Bulworth want?' Steve moved away from the window where he'd been watching the traffic inching its way along a clogged Ventura Boulevard. He ignored the pizza waiting on the table and instead slumped into a chair in front of the TV. Dateline jumped before his eyes in bands of colour and sound. He had no idea what it was.

'Wants to see you. He and another guy, Al Giraud, the PI. They'll be here in ten minutes.'

Feeling like a condemned man, Steve wondered what was going to happen to him now. Whether they were going to re-arrest him and stick him in jail again, or — faint hope — let him go free. He waited out the ten minutes in silence until the rap on the door finally came.

'Who is it?' Chavez called, peering through the peephole again. Bulworth's big florid face magnified by the little circle of glass glared back at him.

'It's Detective Bulworth, Chavez, open up.'

'What about the password, sir?'

'Don't be an asshole, Chavez,' Bulworth hissed, you can see it's me, gosh darn it.'

'Not until you say the password, sir, that's the rules,' Chavez said grinning like a jackal as Bulworth pounded his fist against the door.

He opened suddenly and Bulworth staggered in, followed by Giraud who gave a broad wink in Chavez's direction on his way to shake hands with Steve.

It did not pass Steve's attention that the last time they had seen each other in the interview room at the Twin Towers jail, Giraud had deliberately not shaken his hand.

'Do I take this as a sign that all is forgiven?' he asked drily, as Bulworth too came over and clasped his hand.

'Not only that, Steve, but we have news for you.' Bulworth looked at Giraud, waiting for him to tell the story,

'It's about Vickie, Steve. She's responding to people, responding to touch and to instructions. She's coming out of it, fella, and the medico there says she's on the mend.'

Steve slumped into the chair, his head in his hands. 'Thank God. *Oh, thank God*,' he murmured as the tears threaded their way through his fingers.

'The thing is, the medicos think it would be good for her to see you, to know you are there. Maybe you can talk to her a little, not about what happened, but about your lives together, memories, the children, that sort of thing.'

'When do we go?' Steve was already on his feet, picking up his jacket.

Giraud grinned, 'Right now, buddy. Marla already told her to expect you.'

'Yeah, but then you come right back here again, into hiding,' Bulworth warned. 'This is risky enough and we can't take any chances.'

'Just let me see her,' Steve agreed humbly, 'that's all I ask.'

Chapter Fifty-two

San Francisco police officer Guido Minelli was at the wheel of a patrol car cruising the streets of Potrero Heights, when the call came through of a possible shooting a couple of blocks away. He switched his flashing lights on, put his foot down and weaving through dense traffic was in the area in minutes, easing down a narrow alley at the back of some warehouses.

It was dusk, a tricky time for seeing who was where and how many there were and who was holding a gun. His partner, Officer Luther Winesap, had his semi-automatic at the ready as they cruised slowly down the alley.

'Warehouse door's open on your right,' Winesap said tersely and Minelli stopped the car, unholstered his gun and got out.

'Don't see no bodies,' he whispered.

'Probably inside the warehouse. And if he's still around, so is the shooter.'

In the distance, Minelli heard the sound of approaching sirens. He figured they were at least five blocks away but it was good to know assistance was on its way, along with paramedics for the injured – or the dead. He motioned Winesap behind him and edged along the wall, alert for any sound. Then he heard it.

'Sounded like a groan, man,' Winesap said softly. 'There's somebody in there all right.'

'Let's go,' Minelli said, taking a quick cautious peek through the open door. The warehouse was in darkness, not even a glimmer of light and he felt the hair on the back of his neck prickle. Then he heard it again. A groan, louder this time.

'Help,' a male voice said. 'Help me, I'm shot. I'm dyin'.'

'Sounds to me he's too strong to be dyin',' Winesap commented.

'Police,' Minelli yelled, loud and clear. 'Come on out with your hands over your heads. Now! Out!'

'Yo, I bin shot, I cain't git up to come on out there. My leg's hurtin' like hell and the little fucker who did me's gotten away, left me to die ...'

Minelli sighed, he knew from experience you couldn't trust anybody. He flashed a light into the warehouse, saw a big old RV and a man lying on his back next to it. Even from here he caught the dull black gleam of blood on cement.

'Back me up,' he said, edging into the warehouse, his back to the wall, and Winesap crouched at the entrance, his weapon clasped in both hands, ready for whatever hell might break loose.

The sirens were closer now, no more than a couple of blocks, help was at hand should they need it. Suddenly a figure darted from the shadows, racing for the door. Winesap had him covered yelling at him to stop or he would shoot and the kid, for he was after all only a young boy, stopped and lifted his hands, defeated.

Minelli's eyes never wavered from the RV and the wounded man lying next to it. His bet was there were more of them inside that RV and he'd also bet that drugs were at the bottom of this shooting. It was usually drugs, or money or women that accounted for most crimes.

Winesap had the kid on his belly on the floor, hands behind his head as the reinforcements arrived and the scene was suddenly illuminated by the headlights of a couple of squad cars.

'You in there,' Minelli said, directing his weapon at the closed door of the old Winnebago. 'Put your hands over your head and come on out here. I give you thirty seconds ... and I'm counting ...'

He'd gotten to ten when the door swung open and another

kid stepped out, hands hovering in the air, eyes bulging with fear.

'He's one of 'em,' the wounded man said, 'but the one that shot me got away ... he's the one y'need bro, the little fucker's a killer ...'

'And I guess you're Mr Clean.' Minelli retrieved a couple of small cellophane packets from the floor. He recognised the crystals they contained as crack cocaine and he smiled grimly at the wounded man. 'Your blood's on these packets, man,' he said mildly, 'I guess they must belong to you.'

'What packets, I ain't niver seen no packets before ...'

'Cut the crap,' Minelli said wearily.

By now the two young suspects were already cuffed and in the squad car. The paramedics were on their knees examining the man, asking what had happened, where he hurt, was there more than one bullet wound, taking his carotid pulse, his blood pressure, stemming the blood flow.

'How bad is it?' Winesap asked, coming up to them, his automatic still at the ready.

'As they say in the movies, "it's only a flesh wound".' The young paramedic grinned.

'What's your name?' Minelli asked the wounded man as he was placed on a stretcher.

'Michael Jackson,' The guy met his eyes sullenly.

'Don't give me that crap.'

'It's the truth, man, I get this shit all the time about my name. Don't believe me, ask my Mom.'

'Your Mom's gonna be thrilled to know you'll be doin' jailtime again, Jackson. This RV belong to you?'

'Nope. The kids was livin' in it, hidin' out in the warehouse. Y'go inside there, the place stinks. Better'n axin' me 'bout them little packets, y'should be asking them little fuckers what they doing living in an RV and where they stole it from.'

'We're gonna be asking you a lot more questions once they get you fixed up at the hospital,' Minelli said. 'And don't worry, you're not dying, bro. Not this time anyways.'

*   *   *

The two young men – boys really, aged fifteen and sixteen, were booked as juveniles on charges of possessing an illegal substance. The third member was caught a few blocks away, hiding out at his grandmother's home and charged with possession of an illegal substance, illegal possession of a firearm, and assault with a deadly weapon. He had shot the drug dealer in a fight over payment. He was just eighteen and would do a considerable amount of time.

'So where'd'ya get the RV?' the detective in charge asked the kids.

'It was on the street man. Doors was open, keys was inside. We didn' steal it. Somebody jist left it, y'know what I mean. It was jist there for the takin'. We didn' have money for no more gas. We jist put it in the old, broke-down warehouse, kinda like a garage, and kinda lived in it, like it was home, y'know what I'm saying?'

The detective did know, and it didn't take much time or effort to check the Winnebago's registration on the computer.

Thanks to an old friend, Al knew that Jimmy Victor's Winnebago had been found in San Francisco at approximately the same moment Bulworth did, so when Bulworth called he already had the Corvette pointed north to San Francisco.

'Break number one – at last,' Bulworth said, sounding relieved. 'I have to tell ya, Giraud, I was up against a stone wall. This woman has done a disappearing act like I've never seen. So now at least we know she's in the San Francisco area.'

'Maybe,' Giraud said thoughtfuly. He knew Laurie Martin was too clever to leave the RV right around the corner from where she had taken up residence. 'Messin' on your own doorstep' was what that was called, and Laurie was not a woman to be that crude. 'She could have just dumped the Winnebago here and gotten a plane to Ohio for all we know,' he said to Bulworth.

It was the truth and they both knew it, but at least now

they also knew that the theory of how Laurie killed Jimmy at the house, then transported him to the canyon and made her own getaway in the RV was valid. Laurie was the killer not the killee. Now all they had to do was find her.

The shot man, Michael Jackson, had been right. The RV did stink. Of methamphetamine and stale beer and mouldy pizza, and three kids with a distinct lack of personal hygene. Giraud controlled his revulsion, watching the San Francisco homicide squad team doing their stuff, sifting through every grimy item in the ancient Winnebago, every scrap of paper, every soiled piece of clothing, every hair on the carpet and furnishings, every print there ever was and it seemed like there was a decade of prints because Jimmy Victor had been no great housekeeper either.

Nothing of great import seemed to be forthcoming, so Giraud took his leave of Bulworth and headed for the more civilised climate of Houlahan's, a dark chummy little saloon on North Beach that served great draught Guinness, chilled to perfection with four inches of creamy foam that took all of ten minutes to subside, as well as a nice line in Irish comfort food like corned beef and cabbage and Swedish meatballs, based, Matt Houlahan himself said, on the fact that there had been an influx of Scandinavian immigrants to Ireland in the early eighteenth century, a fact which Giraud took to be a typical piece of Irish blarney. Nevertheless the meatballs were the best.

'You got a *Yellow Pages*, Matt?' he asked his old chum.

'*Yellow Pages*? Is that how you ace detectives do your detecting these days? I'll bet you make a fortune, Giraud and all you do is look up some poor bastard in the *Yellow Pages*, then pass on the info to your client and Bingo, another hundred thou in the Swiss bank account.'

'Bullshit, Houlahan. You just wish you had thought of it is all, instead of being stuck behind a bar day and night.'

'You're right there, boyo. But a bar is an Irishman's destiny. It was written in Moses' commandments, along with thou shalt not covet thy neighbour's wife and thy detective's hundred thou.'

Giraud was grinning as he leafed through the *Yellow Pages* looking for churches but the grin turned to a frown as he scanned the long list. He thought that at this rate there must be more religious establishments in the San Francisco area than homes.

Finishing his Guinness, he waved goodbye to Houlahan, hailed a cab and checked in at the Holiday Inn on Eighth Street.

Up until now, Laurie had kept within the boundaries of her childhood upbringing and been strictly Baptist in her seach for eligible candidates to murder. Holed up in his room, he called every Baptist Church in the Yellow Pages, He called Sausalito and Mill Valley, Oakland, Napa, Sonoma, Mendocino, Monterey and Carmel. No one answering to the description of Laurie Martin, or Bonnie Hoyt/Victor/Harmon had been seen at any of them.

Wearily, he started again at the top of the list, this time checking every church whatever its denomination. The result was the same. Laurie had done another disappearing act. Either that or she was lying low, waiting until this whole thing had blown over.

Giraud wondered how she was managing financially. Her bank account with the twelve thousand in it was still untouched, she had not been near her condo and all her clothes were still there. Laurie had to have gotten some sort of job. She had to have gotten false identification. She had to have changed her appearance.

He sighed, as he picked up the phone again, this time to call Marla. It was going to be a long haul, but one thing he was sure of, Laurie wasn't going to get away with this. No sir, not and leave Steve Mallard with a permanent question mark hanging over his head.

Chapter Fifty-three

By a lucky coincidence, Marla was giving a lecture on criminal law at Berkeley that week so she was thrilled to be asked to assist the great Giraud in his church quest.

'Just like a proper PI,' she said, donning the appropriate outfit, a suitably Sunday church-going little number in beige with matching low-heeled pumps bought specially for the occasion. 'I'll submit my expenses later,' she told Giraud with a grin. 'You'll find most of them listed under Disguise.'

'I don't need any disguise, so why do you?'

'A woman's prerogative,' she said smartly. 'I'll bet Laurie has a disguise, so why shouldn't I? That way when we meet up neither of us will recognise the other.'

'Fat lot of good that will do.'

'Anyhow, Giraud, what are we doing in this Holiday Inn? You invite me up to San Francisco for an intimate little weekend – as well as for the private eye stuff, and expect me to find romance in the middle of an Elks convention?'

He grinned. 'I'll make it up to you.'

'How?' Her eyes gleamed with interest as she slid her arms around his neck, nuzzling the pulse at the base of his throat, feeling it speed up as she pressed closer.

'You want me to tell you right now?'

'Sure I do.' She nibbled his ear lobe tenderly and his hands slid down her back to her pneumatic behind. He held it firmly, pulling her even closer, if that were possible.

'Mmmm, you couldn't even get a knife between us at this point,' she sighed, her bones turning to jelly as she felt his hardness against her groin.

'Scuse me for reminding you ma'am,' he murmured in between long kisses, 'but we have work to do.'

She heaved a sigh, still clinging to his lips. 'Yeah, I know.'

'The Sunday church-going outfit.' he prompted her. 'Remember? Laurie Martin? Assistant private eye.'

Her sigh was even deeper as she moved relucantly away from him. 'Slave driver,' she grumbled, running her tongue over her bruised-with-love-looking lips. 'Anyhow, how are you going to make up for the Elks convention?'

'A night at Post Hill Ranch? he suggested. 'A cliff house perhaps, with the picture windows where we can watch whales migrating while we lie in a huge puffy bed, bathed in the glow of firelight . . .'

'After a long soak together in the slate Japanese tub with aromatherapy candles and the view of the moon hanging over the ocean and the firelight lending a warm rich glow to our nubile bodies . . .'

'*Your* nubile body,' he corrected her, kissing her again.

'My *nubile* body and your *slightly-worn* body,' she amended, still caught up in the dream. 'And after a long, long massage in our cosy room with Mozart on the CD player and some genius masseur from Esalan drawing the fatigue of the day out of our spines with his magic fingers . . .'

'*Her* magic fingers . . .' he interjected.'

'Don't keep interrupting my dream. And suit yourself, I'm having a him. I like my masseur strong.'

'And I like mine female.'

She ignored him. 'And then we'll linger over dinner in that wonderful minimilist dining room that hangs over the cliffside, and we'll eat only foods that are aphrodiisiacs . . .'

'I like that.'

'Then maybe we'll sit in the infinity pool for a while, pretend we're living on the edge . . .'

'The very edge of the cliff . . .'

'Yup, and hopefully we shall be all alone in there so I can practise the wonderful things I'm going to do to you later ...'

'In our cliff room with the grass and wildflowers growing on our earth roof, protecting us from the elements, or maybe you'd prefer a tree house, high up in the branches, or a butterfly house ...

'Don't interrupt,' she said again. 'And no, I want the cliff house with the ocean and the wild flowers blooming on our roof as we sleep ...'

'I wondered when we were gonna get back to that big soft downy bed. I figure after all this we'll be so worn out with all the soaking and massaging and food, we'll just fall right to sleep.'

'Don't bet on it,' she warned, kissing him again. 'And I accept your offer, thank you kindly Giraud.'

She fixed her lipstick and her hair, pulled down her skirt and picked up her bag, 'Don't wait up for me,' she said, heading for the door, 'I've got work to do.'

'Honey?'

She swung round at the door to look at him.

'You could have worn the little French maid number. The Reverend woulda thought you were a sinner opting for a little repentence.'

'I may just do that next time,' she said, flouncing out the door, though somehow a flounce in the matronly beige didn't have quite the same effect as a hot little Versace number.

Marla drove the Corvette at a sedate pace through the San Francisco traffic – Giraud would annihilate her if she got so much as a scratch on it – even though at the same time she was reading the list of churches he had given her, and the demographic breakdown of each area. Her list had only churches in wealthy neighbourhoods to visit – Giraud himself was checking out the ones in less salubrious areas.

All of hers were in Oakland and the surrounding areas and each was picture perfect in its white stucco Mediterannean style, or in white clapboard with sloping green lawns and a picket fence, or stern stone-walled edifices that looked as though anyone entering should prepare themselves for martyrdom.

There were campaniles and turrets, Victorian gingerbread and English gothic, and at none of them was there a member of the congregation who answered in any way to Laurie Martin's description.

By five in the afternoon, with the home-going traffic jamming every road and highway, Marla had had it. He beige was crumpled, she had a run in her stockings and the pumps hurt like hell. She kicked off her shoes and in the tight confines of the Corvette somehow wriggled out of her tights, which involved a brief spell with no hands on the wheel and a couple of astonished stares from passing motorists. She felt frowsty, hot, unattractive and fed up when she turned into the parking lot of the final church on her list. Actually it wasn't the final one, there were four more, but this was as far as she went.

It was simple, built of wood, white with a small cupola and a bell, and it was Episcopalian.

The Reverend Samuel Witty, a rotund man with a monk's tonsure fringe of silver hair and a paunch, looking like a modern-day Friar Tuck, greeted her warmly enough despite her lack of shoes and stockings, and asked how he could help her.

'You look as though you need aid, my child,' he said worriedly. 'There is no need for a young woman like you to walk shoeless on our streets. The Lord would not wish it this way.'

'Thanks Reverend,' Marla said breezily, 'but it's information I need not shoes. I've got some of those back there in the red Corvette.'

The Reverend seemed rather astonished that she was shoeless yet driving an expensive old car, but he asked no questions, letting her speak for herself.

Marla had already been through this a dozen times today. She showed the Reverend Witty the photograph of the more glamorous Laurie in her Californian-blonde, estate agent role, as well as the other dowdier church-going Laurie, in the photograph given her by John MacIver. None of the other pastors had recognised either woman and this one was no different.

'Sorry I couldn't help you, my dear,' the Reverend said, frowning with concern as she walked, barefooted, away. 'And you really should put on your shoes,' he added. 'There are no flower children in San Francisco any more.'

'How very sad Reverend,' Marla commented as she stepped into the Corvette, gunned the engine and swung into the exit lane. Just as a small blue car making a left into the lot came out of nowhere, almost clipping her wing.

'Silly bitch,' she snarled, glaring at the woman driver. Then suddenly it seemed the woman changed her mind. She backed dangerously out into the traffic amid a blast of horns and curses and drove away, fast.

Marla stomped on her brakes, staring after her. In the back window of the car she caught a glimpse of a small black dog. It was wearing a red bandanna.

Her heart bounced into her throat and she could hardly catch her breath, she was so excited. Her hands were trembling as she backed out of the exit lane almost hitting another poor woman who had just avoided serious injury by the driver of the blue car.

'Sorry,' Marla waved her hands helplessly, as the woman braked then sat with her head in her hands, looking shaken. 'Sorry,' she yelled again, sliding into a parking spot and trotting, shoeless back to the Reverend Witty's study.

'Scuse me, Reverend,' she said breathlessly, 'but does a member of your congregation drive a blue car and have a little black dog?'

She waited impatiently while he thought about it for a long minute. She could practically see the wheels clicking inside his silver-tonsured head.

'Why,' he said at long last, 'that'll be Maria Joseph.' He smiled, 'If ever a woman loved a dog, it's Maria. She rescued that little mutt from the pound, takes it everywhere with her.'

'Her address,' Marla said eagerly, stopping herself from jumping up and down with excitement with an effort. 'Where does Maria live?'

'Well now, I couldn't give out personal information like that, even if I knew it. Which I don't,' he added, looking surprised at Marla's loud, exasperated sigh.

'Well then, where does she work, you know, what does she do . . . ?'

I'm not sure I should be telling you this,' he said, suddenly suspicious, 'but Maria works as a waitress. And no I don't know where. And if I did I would not tell you. If you care to leave your name and phone number, then I'll make sure, of course, that she gets the message, next time I see her.

'Reverend,' Marla said, alrady on her way back to the Corvette, 'you will never see Maria Joseph again. I can guarantee that.'

'So Maria Joseph works as a waitress — somewhere in the city's ten thousand restaurants,' Giraud said sarcastically, when Marla told him. 'She'll never go back to that church, not now she knows we're onto her. Why didn't you get the car's make and number, Marla? What kind of detective are you anyway?'

Marla balled her fist and gave him a hard punch to the gut. 'Shut up, you jerk. I've just thought of something. That night when I went to meet Vickie at her house, there was a blue car. I remember noticing it because there were only two vehicles parked on the street. It was an old model pale blue Accura,' she said solemnly. 'And I'll bet it was Laurie's.'

Giraud was already on the phone to the Police Department. 'Marla, cancel the Post Hill Ranch,' he said over his shoulder, 'we've got work to do.'

'Ohhh . . . shoot,' she said crossly. 'I should never have told you!'

Chapter Fifty-four

The evening traffic was hell and Laurie fumed at the wheel of the old blue Accura, still raging at the near miss with Marla Cwitowitz. It had given her quite a jolt when she had seen that red Corvette. It was definitely not the kind of automobile the elderly members of the congregation of the Highlands Episcopal Church would drive, and it should have given her fair warning that Giraud was around, even before she had spotted who was driving it and made a quick getaway.

Had Marla seen her, she wondered, fingers tapping nervously on the steering wheel as she waited at yet another red light? And why was it when you hit one on red all the others were on red too, miles and fuckin' miles of them? Nerves strung out, she glanced at Clyde, curled up on the back seat. 'You OK, little honey?' she called to him and heard his tail thump on the seat in response.

'Well thank God *you* are, because *I* sure as hell am not.' Her fiery eyes met those of the man in the car next to her at the light and she scowled, causing him to jolt his eyes back on the road. He threw her another startled glance as the light changed and she beat him out, shooting away in the old clunker like she was at Le Mans.

Slow down, she warned herself, you don't want to be getting a traffic ticket . . . not now, baby . . . Just calm yourself down and think of what you need to do.

The failure of the letter bomb still rankled. She should at

least have got Giraud with that one, Marla would just have been the bonus, but somehow they had both escaped.

She frowned, concentrating on the traffic. And fuckin' Beau was still going strong. All she had done was give him an easy way out from Loretta. Plus he had inherited her money. She had done Beau a favour instead of killing him. Not that she wasn't glad Loretta was dead, sure she was, but Beau had been her main aim.

She glanced out of the corner of her eye again at Clyde curled into a tight ball, nose to tail, sleeping. She would have to try again with Beau, find out where he was, what he was doing. Take care of him once and for all. He was not going to get away with murdering her baby. No sir, the old Clyde would be avenged.

Meanwhile, she had a more urgent problem on her hands. Marla being at the church was too close for it to be mere coincidence. Giraud was on to her, though she didn't know how. And if Marla Cwitowitz was here, Giraud could not be far behind. She'd bet they were staying in some fancy San Francisco hotel, and she also knew it didn't take a genius to find out exactly which one.

First, though, she drove to a used car dealer and traded in the blue Accura for a second-hand black Ford pickup. The transaction took precious time, but she had to get rid of the Accura, just in case Marla had recognised her.

'Home' – such as it now was, loomed at the end of the busy street. The shabby apartment building seemed even more desolate and the pang of anger as she remembered her beautiful Laguna condo almost tore the guts out of her. She had sacrificed everything because of Jimmy Victor. But no more. She would get Giraud and Cwitowitz this time. Then she would be free again.

There was a little flicker of hope in her eyes as she parked the pickup beneath the building then stalked outside, letting Clyde run around and take care of his own affairs for a minute or two before she called to him and entered the dingy building which smelled of mildew and rotting carpet, bad drains and too many dirt-poor students who lived on cheap takeaways and beer. Her stomach roiled as she paced up the uncarpeted concrete stairs to her own domaine and she closed her door thankfully behind her, trying not to notice the shoddiness of it all.

All her life she had fought to better herself. Everything – with the exception of her schoolgirl friend Jennifer Vanderhoven – had been done to further her ambition for a beautiful home, expensive clothes, jewellery. To be a millionaire, that's all she had ever wanted. And what was so bad about that? Seemed like the normal kind of American dream to her.

She filled Clyde's water bowl, opened a can of Alpo, mixed it with some dry nuggets then stood watching him while he tucked in, tail wagging slowly from side to side. Clyde never forgot his manners, he always said thank you.

She slumped onto the sofa with the phone beside her, looked up the names of the best hotels in San Francisco, then systematically dialled each one and asked to speak to Mr Al Giraud. And at every hotel she was informed that no one of that name was registered there. 'Try Cwitowitz,' she demanded, starting all over again – but the Ritz said no Cwitowitz, and the Mandarin Oriental said no Cwitowitz, and the Fairmont and the St Francis and the Mark, and the Stanhope and all the other chic little boutique hotels it suddenly occurred to her that perhaps Marla might prefer.

She slumped even further into the hard sofa, longing for her white rugs, her soft pink velvet chaise in her pretty bedroom, the kind of girly room she had never had as a kid with the turquoise chenille throw and the immaculate white-canopied bed with its gilt Louis headboard . . .

She had to find them. If she did not, she would never have that kind of home again.

Picking up the phone she started again, with the Hilton, the Hyatt, the Ramada, the Holiday Inn . . .'

'Mr Giraud, please,' she demanded.

'Just one moment,' the clerk replied. And then the room phone was ringing.

She was smiling as she cut it off. And there was confidence

in her swagger now, as she went to the bedroom and changed into the nondescript black suit, picked up her purse and headed for the door.

'Bye, Clyde,' she called as the dog trotted hopefully after her. 'Be back soon. Don't wait up for me, boy.' And she was on her way in her new Ford pickup heading across the Bay Bridge into San Francisco.

As she walked into the lobby of the Holiday Inn, Laurie was confident that her new persona was perfect. She looked completely different with her black hair and heavy black-framed glasses, she even walked differently, held herself differently, like an older woman, clutching her handbag, peering round near-sightedly through the glasses. Her disguise was complete. Apart from the snake ring that she never took off.

She peered round now, checking the busy lobby, then took a seat near the door. Unfurling a copy of the *Chronicle*, she held it in front of her. She looked like any woman, waiting for a friend to show up.

Chapter Fifty-five

Giraud was on the phone with Bulworth, telling him about Marla's sighting of Clyde in his red bandanna, in the blue Accura that she also remembered seeing on the Mallards' street the night of the attempted murder.

'Whoever was driving – and my bet is it was Laurie – certainly recognised Marla, and the Corvette. She made one of the fastest about-turns in history, according to Marla. Almost side-swiped my Corvette in the process. Anyhow, my guess is now that we're onto the car, Laurie will dump it, and that means she'll have to sell it because our girl does not have much money.'

'I'll have the boys check out every used car dealership in the Bay area,' Bulworth promised. 'Just one thing, Giraud.'

'Yeah?' Giraud gazed absently out of the window. He was waiting for Marla to return from what she had said was a shopping expedition. Said she needed things for the Post Hill Ranch – though as far as he knew that was off. At least until they had tracked down Laurie Martin and he could concentrate again. On Marla, that is.

'Just don't go out there on your own after this woman, OK?' Bulworth begged. 'Work with us this time, Giraud. Any further info you get, I want to know. OK?'

'You got it, buddy,' Giraud grinned. Of course he wouldn't share – at least not immediately. He had a job to do and he intended to do it.

He was in the shower when Marla got back, laden down with expensive-looking shopping bags.

'What y'got there, hon,' he asked, wrapping himself in a towel and emerging to give her a welcoming kiss.

'Oh, just a little trousseau, you might call it,' she said with a sunny smile.

He eyed the bags doubtfully. 'You gettin' married then, hon?'

'You never know,' she said archly. 'Of course, I haven't asked the orthodontist yet, but Mom has him on hold.'

He was laughing as he embraced her and she didn't object even though he was still wet and drops of water spotted her pale green cashmere sweater that was so light it looked as though it was knitted from cobwebs.

'What d'you say we have a drink at the bar,' she suggested. 'I have a little proposition you might be interested in.'

'It's a deal. And I'll bring you up to date on what Bulworth said.'

He was dressed in less time than it took her to freshen her lipstick and comb her hair, which today hung straight and silky, curving gently upwards where it met her shoulders, the way it had the night he first met her at the Hollywood party. Al liked it that way.

They didn't even glance Laurie Martin's way as they walked, arm in arm through the lobby, heading for the bar. Didn't notice her get up and follow them at a discreet distance, hidden anyway by the milling crowd. Didn't look twice at the dark-haired older woman who brushed past them and took a seat at a nearby table, and who ordered a straight tequila then disappeared behind her *San Francisco Chronicle*.

'Tell me about Bulworth later,' Marla was saying as she sipped her vodka martini. 'I've decided it's time for *us*, Giraud.' She held up a warning hand at his *'But'*. 'And I don't want to hear any "buts". This is you and me, and less of the private eye. Tonight I'm going back to being plain old Marla Cwitowitz and you are going to be the guy I picked up at the party that night.'

'The same woman who figured she had to bed the boss to get the job, as I remember.'

'Bullshit. I would have bedded you anyway,' she said comfortably. 'Anyways, mister, I have made a reservation at the Post Hill Ranch for tonight. You and I are driving down there . . .'

'And you plan on making all my dreams come true.'

Her eyes linked with his. 'At least for tonight,' she whispered sweetly.

'Finish your drink, honey.' Giraud smiled back into those grey-green orbs that still sent shivers down his spine when she looked at him like that. 'You're on.'

'Of course I am,' she murmured even more sweetly. 'I already checked us out and asked the bellman to bring down our luggage. We're practically on our way.'

Laurie swallowed the tequila in one gulp, grabbed her purse, brushed hastily past the enamoured couple and paid the barman on her way out. Then she was in the black Ford pickup, heading out of San Francisco on Route I, barreling south to Carmel and Big Sur.

She was laughing as she gunned the engine. This time they had played right into her hands. This time she was beating them at their own game. It would be a breeze.

It was dusk and the fog was rolling in when she spotted Giraud's red Corvette driving through Carmel. Quickly she pulled out of the parking spot keeping a couple of cars behind, following at a discreet distance as they wound their way down the coast. It was late and she knew that soon the traffic would disappear and she would have them to herself.

Post Hill Ranch was built into a bluff near Big Sur where the coast road snaked edgily along the cliffs with a sheer drop to the ocean, hundreds of feet below. In daylight, and with good weather, it was an easy enough drive, but with the darkness and the fog, Giraud had slowed down and was taking the bends carefully.

Laurie hung back, driving carefully too, keeping out of sight.

Giraud's eyes darted between the dangerous road and the

rear-view mirror. He caught an occasional glimpse of a black pickup behind them and he was glad the driver was also being sensible and taking it easy. This road, especially tonight, was no picnic.

Marla turned to look at the shopping bags from the smart boutiques piled in the back and when she thought about their contents she smiled.

'That's a Cheshire Cat kinda grin,' Giraud commented. 'You got a secret I don't know about?'

'I'll tell you all about it later.' Her green eyes gleamed with mischief. 'All I'll say is I'm saving the best 'til last.'

Giraud frowned. In the rear-view mirror he could see the black pickup gaining on them. 'He's going too fast,' he said, alarmed.

They were on a tight curve as Laurie swept alongside, riding the double yellow, nudging them.

Giraud was yelling and Marla's terrified screams cut through the foggy night like a razor blade through silk, blending with the squeal of rubber as Giraud put his foot down, trying to beat the pickup and get away.

Laurie was laughing now, in her element as she slammed into the Corvette's rear left side, taking her foot off the pedal as the Corvette spun round and ended up, quivering like an aspen leaf, facing her.

She put her foot down again and screaming like a banshee, headlights blazing bore down on her enemies.

The Corvette spun out, she could see Giraud fighting to keep control. Laughing, she roared forwards, side-swiping them again, forcing them nearer and nearer the edge.

The Corvette swerved, swayed, then skidded.

And then they were sliding sideways through air.

Laurie waited until she heard the crash, then made a dangerous three-point turn, and with a triumphant look over her shoulder, sped back the way she had come.

She had finally removed the last link between her and the future.

Chapter Fifty-six

The Corvette bounced once, twice, three times, then, amid an explosion of shattered glass and grinding steel, landed foursquare on a jagged rock escarpment.

Those bounces rattled through Marla's every vertebra. Screaming, she threw up her hands to shield her face from the breaking glass though she didn't know why she bothered, her end had surely come.

'Are you all right?' Giraud's voice sounded unnaturally calm in the sudden silence.

'*All right?*' Marla stared horrified out of the shattered window at the surf rolling far below. 'Oh God, how can I be *all right?* I'm half way down a cliff, my butt is bruised and I'm bleeding.' She held up her arms to show him. 'And I'm driving with a madman whose old car has no airbags. It's lucky we're still alive.'

'Lucky for the moment,' Giraud said drily. 'Got any ideas about how we get out of this?'

She glanced out of the glassless window again at the sheer drop.

'Oh,' she said in a very small voice, suddenly losing all her bluster and with it the adrenaline rush generated by fear. One move and she might end up at the bottom of this cliff.

She sat perfectly still, hardly daring to breathe. 'It must have been Laurie,' she whispered, as though speaking normally might rock the car over the edge. 'The bitch tried to kill us.'

Giraud thought the bitch might still succeed but decided

not to tell Marla that. He felt as though his spine had been compacted and now he knew what people meant when they talked about him being a pain in the butt.

The Corvette was perched precariously on the edge of the rock. It swayed gently in the gusty wind and he knew it could fall at any moment.

He examined the area outside his window. They were about thirty feet down the cliff. A spiky-looking tree, a pine of some sort, clung to the rock face, as it must have through decades of storms and harsh weather. Now, it was his only hope.

'Tell you what, Marla,' he said, keeping his tone conversational so as not to panic her, 'why don't you ease over to my side. Slowly now.' He didn't want to upset the car's fragile equilibrium and he held his breath as Marla shifted her weight and he felt it tremble. '*Slowly*,' he reminded her ... '*slowly now, Marla.*'

She lifted her feet cautiously over the centre console, edging inch by inch his way. Finally, she was squashed next to him in the driver's seat and he could feel her heart thundering against his as he held her for a moment.

'Look, sweetheart,' he said, pointing through the gaping window, 'see that pine tree. It's one of the reasons the Corvette didn't just keep on sliding. If I lean out of the car, I think I can manage to grab it and haul myself out, but when I do I'm afraid the car will lose whatever stablity it has.'

'Don't do it,' she begged, panicked. 'Don't leave me here, it'll fall, I know it will.' Her eyes bugged alarmingly and her teeth were chattering with fear until she could hardly speak. The car swayed under them, groaning, and terrified, she clung to him.

'It's our only hope, honey,' he said gently. 'The car isn't going to last here much longer. Edge across the seat after me and grab tight hold of my hand, tight as you can, with both yours. Come Marla, now ... *now*, baby ... I'm gonna grab that tree and take you out with me ...'

She clung to his hand sliding across the seat, close as a good lover should be, as he hauled himself out of the broken window and reached for the tree ... God it was further away than he had thought . . . he felt the car spring beneath him, heard it groan as he shifted his weight then made a powerful thrust forward . . .

He had it. He gripped the branch with his left hand and Marla with his right, yelling at her to jump.

He turned to look, saw the car begin to slide, felt the unbearable pain in his right shoulder as Marla jumped and he hauled her, one-handed, upwards through the air. And they fell back onto the rock together.

They lay there, hands still clasped, staring up at the foggy night sky, listening to the terrible grinding noise of the Corvette in its death throes as it bounced down the cliff.

In the long silence that followed, Al cradled Marla to him. The pain in his right shoulder was excruciating. 'It's OK now, honey,' he murmured soothingly as she began to cry. 'Remember it ain't over until the fat angel sings. And I'm not hearing any fat angels singing for us yet.'

'Al,' Marla paused in her sobs as he took out his cellphone and began to dial 911. Then she said, doubtfully. 'Did you ever stop to think maybe my Mom was right?'

Chapter Fifty-seven

The fire rescue sirens were the most wonderful sound Marla had ever heard. And the sight of those brave men clambering down the rockface towards her, safely roped to their equipment at the top of the cliff, was surely a miracle. She shifted her grip from Al to her rescuer, crying loudly into his shoulder and apologising for doing so until he told her not to worry about it, just go ahead and have a good cry, he'd probably do the same thing in her circumstances.

So, a short while later bruised and battered, Marla sat still sobbing on the side of the stretcher in the paramedic ambulance taking them to the nearest hospital while Al, his dislocated shoulder with its torn ligaments temporarily immobilised, blood running from a dozen cuts and his spine feeling as though he had been on the old-fashioned torture rack, was as usual on the cellphone. This time to Bulworth, explaining what had happened and that he needed Bulworth to ask the local police not to issue any statement about their rescue.

'So Laurie will assume you're dead and gone,' Bulworth said and Al could tell he had a grin on his face.

'Yeah, that way she'll feel free to come out of the woodwork, act normal, get back to her old ways maybe.'

'And then we'll nab her.' Bulworth chortled. 'Meanwhile, we've got records checking all the used car dealers and so far haven't come up with anything.'

'You will,' Al said confidently.

'So listen, joking aside, are you and the legal-eagle OK?'

Al glanced at the still-sobbing Marla. 'Yeah, we're OK, except she's maybe figuring on marrying a regular nine-to-five orthodontist now.'

'Not a bad choice, buddy,' Bulworth was laughing as he put down the phone.

Laurie had treated herself to a bottle of expensive Patron tequila tonight and it tasted even better when she caught the eleven o'clock news report.

She took another slug from the bottle, pushing Clyde off her lap and leaning eagerly forward as the serious-faced newsreader told of a major accident on Route I near Big Sur.

They even had a camera there, pointing down the cliff at the wrecked Corvette perched upside down on the rocks below, and the fire rescue service trucks swarming with men in yellow slickers and helmets busy doing whatever they needed to do to get the vehicle up again.

'It's known that two people were in the vehicle at the time of the accident,' the newsreader concluded.

Smiling, Laurie beckoned Clyde to her. She picked him up and hugged him then walked with him into the ugly little kitchen.

Smiling, she fed him his nightly hamburger, watching as he wolfed it down in two gulps. Then she took him on her knee and brushed him until his fur gleamed and he nuzzled up to her, smiling doggy-style with pleasure.

'Well, baby, it's just you and me again now. Bonnie and Clyde. We're on our way,' she said triumphantly.

Chapter Fifty-eight

Steve Mallard was sitting at his wife's bedside, holding her hand and every now and then speaking to her in a light conversational tone, about their daughters and how much he loved them, recounting memories of their babyhood which Vickie and he had shared, the laughs and the traumas.

Like when Mellie fell into the pool when she was two and couldn't swim and he'd hauled her out by the scruff of her neck like a puppy. And how angry they had been that she had disobeyed them and somehow got into the backyard, until they realised it was all their fault and had stopped being angry and cried together because their precious baby was safe and alive and none the worse for wear.

And how Taylor was the star of the junior school soccer team and was doing well in class. 'Quite a little genius, our kid,' he said smiling fondly at the memory. 'Now I wonder who she gets that from?'

And every now and then, in between the memories of family vacations and Thanksgivings and High Holy Days, he stopped and kissed her gently on the lips and said, 'Vickie I love you, please come back to me. *Please*, Vickie, I need you. We all need you. Our lives are not the same without you. And I'm innocent Vickie. Now they know who did it and I'm a free man.'

Almost a free man, he added to himself because he was still holed up in a nondescript hotel room – a different one to be sure. They changed every week, sometimes every couple of days.

His life was in such chaos he had stopped even trying to think about how to sort it out any more and just got on with it. Waiting, waiting – forever waiting for the phone call that would reprieve him and give him his freedom again.

The only compensation was that they allowed him his daily visits to his wife. In fact, they were nightly visits, when there were fewer people around and it was deemed safer for him to be out. He was still a prisoner, though not an accused man, even though by now he would have been happy to take the chance of going free and letting Laurie Martin try to do her worst. He didn't give a damn about Laurie Martin any more.

He couldn't even begin to think about the future, though one thing he knew, he was not going back to his old job. No, sir. He was staying right here in the San Fernando Valley, in his own home, close to family and friends. If there were any friends left. And that was another thing to think about.

Whoever would have thought life would have become so complicated, when all he had been looking for, all he had wanted, was a nice house with an ocean view? Now, he knew that houses did not matter. Home was where your family was and that was good enough for him.

Vickie tossed her head restlessly and he placed his hand on her brow, lightly stroking her delicate eyelids, feeling them flutter under his fingertips.

He leaned over her, speaking into her ear, 'Wake up, Vickie, *wake up*, come back to us baby, we're waiting for you, right here. I'll never leave you, Vickie.'

Vickie stopped tossing her head, but she still did not open her eyes.

I want to wake up, she said to herself, *I want so bad to wake up and I can't, oh Steve I can't. Help me, please help me . . .*

He saw the gleam of tears on her cheeks and gently wiped them away. She was crying again. She cried quite a lot and the doctors assured him it was a good thing, that somewhere inside she was responding to some stimulus. And now, when he took her hand, she squeezed it, though the pressure was slight because, despite daily physiotherapy, her muscle strength was diminished.

He squeezed her hand in reply and said, 'I hear you, Vickie. I know you're trying to come back to us. I know it, baby. Just keep on trying and soon it will work. Keep on, sweetheart. We need you. Mellie and Taylor are waiting for you. We just want to take you home, darling, that's all.'

With an effort Vickie squeezed his hand again.

HOME, Vickie thought. *That magical word. It triggered memories of their first small apartment in Studio City, with just the two of them and somehow they were always in bed, couldn't get enough of each other. Then Taylor came and they moved into the little house with the big back yard in Tarzana, already thinking about schools and nervous as hell about handling the slippery little scrap of humanity that was their daughter. And then Mellie came along and a couple of years after that, her father helped them with the down payment on the new house, where they had chosen everything from the colour of the tiles to the style of the taps and the pattern of the berber carpeting. They had opened champagne that first night in their new house and family and friends had shown up to celebrate, bringing gifts of plants and ceramic cookie jars and baskets of fruit and everybody had had such a good time. Especially the two girls. They had run around, wild with excitement, showing everybody who was interested their rooms — 'My own room,' each girl had said proudly, since before this they had shared a room.*

HOME. That magical place of safety and security. That place of routine chores, of cooking meals and cleaning up, of making sure the girls got ready for school in time and driving them to school with lunch in their backpacks, and picking them up again in the afternoon.

HOME. The place of quiet nights alone with Steve, watching a video when the girls were in bed, of having friends over or leaving the girls with a babysitter whom she knew well and trusted, but still she got nervous. 'Like a mother chick,' Steve used to tease her. 'They'll be all right without you for a couple of hours, Vickie,' he would say. 'Let it go, just enjoy yourself.'

But she had always had that niggling little doubt in the back of her mind, no matter how good the dinner or the show. Were her babies all right?

HOME. With her girls and her husband. That's where she needed to be.

✵   ✵   ✵

Opening her eyes was like lifting a heavy weight but somehow she managed it.

Steve held his breath as he looked at her, not believing what he saw. 'Vickie,' he clasped her cold, thin hands in his, 'Vickie, I'm here, baby, look at me, I'm here with you. It's going to be all right, you're all right . . .'

Vickie's brown eyes looked even bigger now in her pale emaciated face.

She said only one word to him. '*Home,*' she whispered in a rough little voice that was almost a sigh.

But that word was enough.

Chapter Fifty-nine

Giraud's shoulder was strapped up. It would take a while for the torn ligaments to mend, and maybe even necessitate athroscopic surgery. But he had no time for that now. He was on a roll, and he was out to get Laurie Martin. He remembered with a grim smile how it had felt when his beloved Corvette had spun through the air and his beloved Marla had cried out that they were going to die.

He figured that Laurie had wanted rid of that old blue Accura so fast she had headed for the nearest dealership and traded it in for the black Ford pickup which had pushed them off the road and over the cliff. And now he was determined to find that dealer.

He was on the outskirts of Oakland in the area near the Reverend Witty's church, driving down what might be termed Motor Mall, past acres of car lots tricked out with jolly-coloured bunting and balloons and sharp-suited salesmen waiting to snare potential customers. Stickers promised bargains, no down payments, low interest rates, lease or purchase, and every new vehicle gleamed with the kind of polish it would never see again once it hit the real road of life. But Giraud was looking for used-car dealers.

Still, he slowed as he passed the Chevrolet showroom, his eye caught by the glittering display of brand-spanking-new Corvettes. His mouth fairly watered just looking at them. On an impulse, he stopped and took a look.

'Pretty snazzy automobile.' Your friendly salesman was at his shoulder quicker than you could blink.

'Yeah. I just lost mine,' Giraud said regretfully.

'Too bad.' The salesman's grin was wide, Giraud's loss meant his gain. 'Stolen was it, sir?'

'Nope. Totalled.'

The salesman's whistle was sympathetic. 'Like losing a member of the family, sir, if you don't mind me saying so. I've been driving one of these myself for ten years now. You can't get me away from it. I always say, once you've driven a Corvette you'll never drive anything else.' He held out his hand. 'Monty Portenski, sir.'

'Al Giraud.' He hadn't taken his eyes off the Corvette.

'What year was yours, Al?'

Giraud ran his palm over the glossy red hood, stroking the sleek curves as gently as touching a baby. 'Nineteen seventy,' he said with a sigh.

This time the saleman's whistle sounded impressed. 'A beauty, sir. You're not gonna find the likes of her again, but the new models are even better, I can promise you that. How about we take a test drive, feel the power under the hood, the response, not to mention the comfort? "Better than ever" is what the manufacturer claims and I can guarantee it.' He went on to mention the sensational 5.7 litre LSI V8 engine, the 345 hp at 5600 rpm, and the heated rear window that stored out of sight in the convertible model.

Giraud suddenly lost all will power. He had only meant to look but now he was in the driver's seat of a brand new red Corvette, slinking out of the lot and down the road, past the Toyota dealership, and the Nissan and Honda and Ford.

His eyes swivelled suddenly right and to the astonishment of the salesman he swung into the Ford lot and stopped in front of the glass-doored sales office.

'Al!' Monty Portenski protested. 'What're y'doin'? This is a road test not comparison shopping.'

But Giraud was already out of the car and heading across

to the corner of the lot where an old blue Accura sat looking as out of place as a dowager at a debutante ball.

A couple of the Ford salesmen came out to check why the brand new Corvette was being test driven in their lot and Portenski threw his hands up helplessly. 'Guy must be nuts,' he said doubtfully, watching Giraud walking round and round the blue clunker that looked about ready for the scrapyard. But now Giraud was striding back towards them, a pleased grin on his face.

'Either of you guys buy the old Accura from a lady some time this week?' He waved an impatient hand at Portenski and said, 'Be with you in a minute.'

The Ford guys looked at each other. 'Must have been a trade-in,' one of them said. 'But I don't know nothin' about it.'

'Me either,' the second guy shrugged.

By now Giraud was inside the glass-walled office, skirting the gleaming display cars, heading for the manager's office. Fortunately, it was a slow afternoon and he was not busy.

'How can I help you, sir?' the manager got to his feet and offered his firm handshake, just to let Giraud know that you could tell a man's character by his handshake and his was OK. Straight as a die, an honest car salesman.

Giraud took out his wallet, flashed his credentials and gave the Manager, a Mr Henry Jellicoe, his business card. 'I'm working with the San Francisco Police Department on this case,' he said, almost telling a lie. 'The old Accura out on the side lot? You know who brought it in and when?'

Jellicoe walked to the window and peered at the eyesore demeaning his spanking new car lot. 'That thing has been there for three days now,' he grumbled. 'One of our young salesman took it in trade, but he's been off for a while – his wife just had a baby. It should have been taken round the back into our pre-owned lot but I guess he didn't find time before the baby came. Anyhow, he's the only one who knows about it. And why d'you want to know anyways?'

'Homicide suspect,' Giraud said tersely, and saw Jellicoe's

jaw drop. 'And I know for a fact that both the San Diego PD and the San Francisco PD have been checking area dealerships for this car. So how come you weren't contacted. Or were you?'

Jellicoe shrugged. 'I don't recall any cop around here asking questions.'

'So meanwhile, what's the info on the Accura?' Giraud's fingers beat an impatient tattoo on Jellicoe's desk.

'As I told you, the salesman is off. I don't know anything about it.'

'Come on, Jellicoe. I wouldn't like to think you weren't co-operating with the police in their investigations. There has to be paperwork.'

Jellicoe heaved a sigh, glaring at the irate Corvette salesman hanging around outside the door, listening. 'Of course we would co-operate with the police, it's our civic duty. All I said was I have no personal knowledge of the matter. However, there should be some paperwork.'

He walked out of his office and Giraud followed him down the hall to another, smaller office with the name Mohammad Abid on a marker on the desk. An in-tray was brimming with papers and he watched as Jellicoe thumbed rapidly through them.

'Here it is,' he said at last, looking at the pink slip. 'Nineteen eighty-eight Accura registered in the name of Maria Joseph. She traded it in as a down payment on a second-hand '95 Ford 150 pickup, black. Jones gave her twenty-two hundred for it – too much, if you ask me, the car's a pile of junk.'

'Yeah, sure.' Giraud could barely control his excitement. He was this close to finding his prey. 'She take out a loan?'

Jellicoe frowned, reading the notes. 'She paid cash. Didn't give us her home address, said she was in the process of moving. But she left her workplace number and address. Seems Jones called them to confirm she actually did work there and got a glowing reference. She works at the Mansion Bar & Grill in Oakland.'

Chapter Sixty

The Mansion Bar & Grill was your old-fashioned roadside steakhouse with a dark interior and red-leatherette booths which had seen a couple of decades of wear from its customers' ample behinds. A few guys were belly-up to the long mahogany bar and the smell of whisky and draught beer permeated the room, along with the always enticing aroma of charcoal-broiled steaks.

Marla and Al slipped into a booth and looked around. There was nobody there who looked the least bit like Laurie Martin.

A young waiter with bleached platinum hair falling over his eyes like a Hollywood movie surfer, stopped by to ask if they wanted drinks and Marla ordered her usual vodka martini and Giraud a draught Bud.

'I'm not hungry,' Marla said, studying the menu.

'In case you had forgotten,' Giraud said, 'you are not here to eat.'

'Oh. Well in that case ... I had been thinking of maybe just a salad.'

'Marla!'

She shrugged one shoulder delicately. 'OK, OK, I can take a hint.'

'That was not a hint. That was a command.'

'Yes, sir,' she saluted smartly and turned her attention to the waiter, who had returned with their drinks.

'You ready to order?' he asked, pad and pen at the ready.

'Sure. Two burgers with the works, medium-well, no fries.' Giraud said briskly.

Marla glared at him. 'But you said . . .' His warning glance stopped her and she slumped back against the red leatherette.

'You wanna change that, maybe?' the waiter asked her, but she shook her head.

'Whatever he says,' she said, sounding martyred.

'Damn it, Marla, you're not gonna eat the thing anyway.' Giraud was on edge, eyes scanning the room. There were waitresses but none who in the least way resembled his prey and he wondered if he was too late and Laurie had already jumped ship, so to speak.

His right shoulder hurt like hell every time he moved and he got even madder just remembering what Laurie Martin had done to them.

Marla sipped the martini silently. He could tell she was fuming but this was no time for a blow up so he kept his mouth shut and concentrated on the clientele. It was after six now and the place was filling up. It was obviously a popular local hangout and nearly everyone seemed to be regulars, greeted with a friendly 'how're y'doing?', and 'how's things?'. And, with the busy witching hour, came additional staff.

Giraud's eyes narrowed as he focused on a tall, dark-haired woman clearing a table the far end of the narrow room. The lighting was dim, just little red-shaded table lamps and it was difficult to make her out exactly, but there was just something about the way she walked, kind of athletic, that contrasted with her frumpy ageing appearance . . . a below-the-knee skirt, heavy flat shoes, thick black stockings. Her white shirt was neatly pressed but it looked too big on her. She wore large black-framed eyeglasses and her dark hair was cut severely short in the back, almost like a man's, falling in a jagged fringe over her eyes. She looked thin, weighted down by the clumsy shoes.

Marla turned her head, following his glance. *She was looking at the woman she had almost bumped into on the steps of the LA City Hall. The one with the mad eyes. The one whom she had sensed was evil . . .*

306

'*That's her.*' Marla's voice was squeaky with excitement and nerves. '*I swear to God it's her.*'

The dark-haired waitress had finished clearing the table. She was coming down the aisle carrying a loaded tray. She was almost past them. And then Marla spotted the snake ring, coiled round her index finger . . .

'Oh, Laurie . . .' she said, her voice soft and friendly.

The tray slid from the waitress's hands and dirty dishes crashed to the floor, spattering steak bones and old fries and ketchup everywhere.

Laurie swung round. For a split second her burning eyes met Marla's, then she was swinging quickly through the crowd and into the kitchen.

Giraud was first on his feet, kicking his way through the debris, going after her. Marla ran the other way, out of the main door, followed by the platinum waiter yelling about their unpaid bill.

Outside, Marla scooted round the corner of the building, skidding on the rain-slicked blacktop, heading for the kitchen exit. Just in time to see Laurie, purse grasped in one hand, car keys in the other, running towards the black Ford pickup parked at the back.

'Laurie!' Marla's voice sounded thin in the wind and rain but Laurie heard all right. Marla saw her stiffen, lift her head like a hunted animal sniffing the wind for its pursuer.

Giraud was half way across the parking lot, his favourite old Smith & Wesson .38mm in his right hand. Only now he wasn't so fast with that right hand because of the shoulder injury. 'Stop right there, Laurie,' he yelled, crouching and taking aim.

Laurie turned to look. Eyes narrowed, she took in the two of them and the gun pointed at her. Rain plastered her black hair to her skull.

Later, Marla would swear she saw her eyes gleam red, like hot coals. It was as though the devil himself was looking at her. Shudders rippled coldly down her spine and she knew she was face-to-face with evil.

Then Laurie's head dropped, and her body seemed to sag

as the fight went out of her. She shrugged, stood head down, defeated.

Giraud walked toward her.

He should have known better, an ex-cop like him . . .

'Look out,' Marla screamed.

There was a flash of silver, the hot spark of a bullet. Giraud yelled, dropping his gun as blood spurted from his already injured shoulder. Then he was on the ground, rolling into the lee of a parked vehicle.

Laurie was in the pickup and Marla heard her gunning the engine. Swiftly, she darted out and grabbed the Smith & Wesson, took aim and fired.

The back off-side tire exploded like a clap of thunder as Laurie sped for the exit, and the pickup went into a spin.

Marla stood transfixed as the scene evolved in what seemed like slow motion in front of her. She could see Laurie's furious face, hear her screaming curses. Then the pickup hit the wall and flipped over twice.

The car's horn beeped into the sudden silence. Its wheels spun slowly and Laurie's bloody head rested against the shattered windshield. Marla could hear the little dog barking.

'Crime and Punishment,' she whispered, shocked by the result of her action.

'I'm hoping she hasn't gotten off that easy.' Giraud winced with pain as he struggled to his feet. 'I want her alive. I want her to face a jury of her peers. I want her inside where she can never harm anyone again.' But even as he said it he knew it was too late for that.

'Isn't it better this way?' Marla's eyes were brimming with tears. She was trembling as she turned to him.

People were running towards them now, diners from the restaurant, the chefs, waitresses. A crowd was forming. Somewhere in the background the wail of a police siren rapidly approaching could be heard.

'I keep thinking about Steve and Vickie. That poor family, what she put them through,' Marla murmured, choking up.

'There's no compensation for that kind of injury, though

now no doubt the tabloids will be after them to sell their story.'
Al stroked her rain-wet hair soothingly with his good hand.

'They could have lived without all this,' Marla said.

'And they will again. They will pick up their lives, get on
with things, the kids will be back in school. Steve Mallard will
be a hero now.'

'And Vickie?' Marla thought of the nice young woman
whose life had fallen into a black pit for so many long weeks.
'How can it ever be the same for her?'

Giraud leaned on her arm, watching the uniformed cops
approach them, guns drawn.

'Look at it this way, it'll be a new beginning.'

He grinned, that old sardonic cocky grin that made her
knees tremble. 'Better put your hands up, Marla, honey. We've
got company.'

Chapter Sixty-one

Al drove his new red Corvette up to the Ivory Tower. He waved hi to the doorman, who looked astonished, but then, finally recognising him in his Armani finery, waved him into the underground parking.

Marla had two slots. Giraud skirted the silver Mercedes parked in the first one and swung into the second. He stomped on the brakes, cursing loudly. He had almost hit the bike – a red Ducati Monster already parked there, all gleaming paintwork, sparkling chrome and unleashed power sitting prettily next to the Merc.

Grumbling, he backed out again and drove to the visitors' slots. He had expected Marla to be alone, after all this was to be their private celebration, not only for tracking down Laurie the Killer, but for surviving the chase. Tonight, Marla had said, they were celebrating just being alive.

So then who was visiting on the brand new Ducati? It surely couldn't be her mother – but it could be the thirty-six-year-old unmarried orthodontist. Mr Right had finally come calling. And on one of the fastest bikes on the planet. This guy was going to be competition after all, despite the teeth.

He checked his appearance in the elevator mirror as it zoomed silently up to the top floor. The Armani shirt Marla had bought him was a deep blue that she had said matched his eyes. He compared them anxiously, still thinking about the competition. He had taken the strapping off his shoulder because he figured it was tough for a guy to get romantic with his shoulder immobilised but, for love, he was prepared to suffer some pain. His Levis had benefited from a trip to the cleaners, though to his disgust they had put creases in them and he had spent ten minutes walking all over them to try to eliminate that uncool line. He was wearing brown suede J P Tod loafers which, he was discovering, were even more comfortable than his old Nikes. And that was it, apart from the usual Jockeys. No jacket, no socks, no tie. There was just so far a guy would go to please a woman.

The door to Marla's apartment stood open. He took in the firelight, the flowers, the scented candles, the Barry White and the small round table with a cream-tassled silk skirt set with silver and crystal, the champagne waiting in the ice bucket ... Marla, had gone for the works this time. It promised to be a good night.

He wandered in, called, 'Hi honey I'm home,' and took the weight off his feet. His shoulder hurt like hell and he still didn't have the mobility he would have wished for on a romantic occasion such as this, though he was glad that at least the bullet had exited on the other side without doing too much damage, and that the surgeon hadn't had to dig it out. 'A clean wound,' they had said and he thanked God for that. It could all have been much worse.

Meanwhile, where was the orthodontist with the Ducati? He glowered at Marla's closed bedroom door. Jesus, he couldn't be where he was thinking he might be. *Could he?*

Just then Marla poked her head around the door. 'Be right there, sweetheart. Make yourself at home,' she said smiling sweetly. And then she closed the door again.

Giraud drummed his fingers on the chenille sofa arm, frowning. But nah, she couldn't be in there with another guy. Not Marla. At least not when she was expecting him. Could she?

He got up, opened the champagne, poured himself a glass and took a sip. The bass on the speaker vibrated as Barry got deeper into the mood, singing about his sugar and hold me baby and do it to me honey ... the guy was sex on vinyl ...

'Be right there.' Marla peeked round the bedroom door again. 'Just one more minute. Oh, and pour me a glass too, would you, darling?'

Darling? Well, he guessed it made a change from sweetheart. Kinda upmarket for him, though. He was definitely not a darling man ... not when honey would do, or even as Barry put it, 'sugar ...' Yeah, he liked his women — *woman*, he corrected himself — sweet.

'*Badah!*' Marla posed in the doorway, one foot in front of the other, right knee slightly bent in the traditional Miss America pose. Except she didn't look like any Miss America Giraud had ever seen. She looked like the Stripper Bride.

She was wearing a strapless satin bustier that indented where it mattered and overflowed where it really counted. Between her breasts — which looked, he thought, even more satiny than the bustier but of an infinitely more sensual texture — nestled a long strand of pearls. There were more pearls woven into her upswept blond hair and embroidered down the length of the lavish tulle veil that flowed behind her like a train. Her eyes were dark with excitement, glowing greener than any emerald in the candlelight, and her pouty mouth was smiling oh so prettily at him.

That was the top half of her. The bride half.

Giraud's eyes travelled the supple length of her body, lingering on the tiny white lace thong, the garterbelt that left a lucious section of creamy thigh between the lacey-topped stockings, the long legs, the white stilletos ... Oh, and she was carrying a bouquet of what smelled like gardenias.

That was the bottom half. Marla.

'I think you forgot your skirt, honey,' he said with that grin that quirked the corner of his mouth and lifted his left eyebrow, making her heart flutter.

'This is what I bought in San Francisco,' she explained. 'They rescued it from the Corvette. I wanted to be a bride,' she said, still posing, still smiling. 'But I thought you might miss the other part of me.'

'You bet I would. They stood there, looking at each other. He guessed there was more to her plan than what immediately met the eye.

'You're wearing the shirt I bought you,' she said. 'I knew it would bring out the blue of your eyes.'

'And white becomes you, as do the pearls. Makes you look like a lady.'

'That's only one aspect of my character.'

He suddenly remembered. The orthodontist might still be lurking in Marla's bedroom . . . 'Whose is the red Ducati parked in your slot?' He tried his best to sound casual.

'All Ducatis are red, Giraud.'

'Yeah. So whose is it?'

She threw him a triumphant smile. 'I thought I needed the proper wheels for a PI. Something with a bit more pazazz than the legal-eagle Merc. Y'know what I'm sayin'?'

He was laughing as he walked towards her and took her in his arms. 'I know what you're saying, honey.' And then he was kissing her as though there were no tomorrow and they were molten with heat and love.

'Tell me something, Giraud,' she murmured, lying beneath him on the taupe chenille sectional, her veil askew and the scent of crushed gardenias almost overpowering them. Barry droned on in the backgrond and the firelight flickered becomingly on her creamy flesh. 'Tell me, if you were to ask me to marry you, exactly which aspect of my character would it be that you wanted?'

He looked up at her and that grin curved his mouth again. 'Marla,' he said, 'I want them all.'

And he did.